'You are...

With gentle [...] d curls
away from [...] across her skin,
exploring her features. Allegra closed her eyes, submitting
to his touch, revelling in it. The feel of his fingers on
her face felt as intimate as a kiss, his touch so gentle and
reverent it made her ache in an entirely new way. He slid
his hands lower, each touch a question, his fingers feeling
her collarbone and then his palm moulding to the curve of
her breast.

'A different kind of music,' he murmured, his mouth
following the trail of his hand, and she laughed, the sound
shaky and breathless.

Yes, this was new music, and he was teaching her its
breathtaking melody. She'd thought that in this moment
she might feel fear, or at least uncertainty, but she didn't.
She felt wonderful, and she wanted to keep feeling
wonderful—to come alive under someone's hands and
feel as close to another person as she could. For one night.
One moment. When would she ever get a chance like this
again?

Somehow Rafael had managed to slip her dress from her
shoulders, and now her upper half was bare to him. He
bent his head, nudging aside her bra with his tongue, and
she gasped aloud. The feel of him against her sensitised
flesh was a jolt to her whole body.

'Oh...' The single syllable held a world of newly gained
knowledge as pleasure pierced her with sweet arrows. Her
hands roved over his back, drawing him closer to her.

Desire was an insistent pulse inside her. Of their own
accord her hips rose, welcoming the knowing touch of his
hand. His fingers brushed her underwear and she bit off a
gasp.

She'd had no idea...

One Night With Consequences

When one night…leads to pregnancy!

When succumbing to a night of unbridled desire
it's impossible to think past the morning after!

But, with the sheets barely settled, that little blue line
appears on the pregnancy test and it doesn't take long
to realise that one night of white-hot passion
has turned into a lifetime of consequences!

Only one question remains:

How do you tell a man you've just met
that you're about to share more than just his bed?

Find out in:

Look for more **One Night With Consequences** stories
coming soon!

ENGAGED FOR HER ENEMY'S HEIR

BY
KATE HEWITT

First Published in Great Britain 2017
By Mills & Boon, an imprint of HarperCollins*Publishers*
1 London Bridge Street, London, SE1 9GF

© 2017 Kate Hewitt

ISBN: 978-0-263-92537-1

Printed and bound in Spain
by CPI, Barcelona

After spending three years as a die-hard New Yorker, **Kate Hewitt** now lives in a small village in the English Lake District with her husband, their five children and a golden retriever. In addition to writing intensely emotional stories she loves reading, baking, and playing chess with her son—she has yet to win against him, but she continues to try. Learn more about Kate at kate-hewitt.com.

Books by Kate Hewitt

Mills & Boon Modern Romance

Moretti's Marriage Command
Inherited by Ferranti

Seduced by a Sheikh

The Secret Heir of Alazar
The Forced Bride of Alazar

The Billionaire's Legacy

A Di Sione for the Greek's Pleasure

Secret Heirs of Billionaires

Demetriou Demands His Child

One Night With Consequences

Larenzo's Christmas Baby

The Marakaios Brides

The Marakaios Marriage
The Marakaios Baby

Rivals to the Crown of Kadar

Captured by the Sheikh
Commanded by the Sheikh

Visit the Author Profile page
at millsandboon.co.uk for more titles.

To my lovely editor, Victoria.
Thank you for all your help with this one!

CHAPTER ONE

IT SEEMED AS if a funeral was just a chance for people to get drunk. Not that Allegra Wells had personal experience of such a thing. She'd stuck to sparkling water all evening and now stood on the sidelines of the opulent hotel ballroom in Rome where her father's wake was being held and watched people booze it up. She could have felt bitter, or at least cynical, but all she could dredge up was a bone-aching, heart-deep weariness.

It shouldn't be this way.

Fifteen years ago it wouldn't have been.

She took a slug of water, half wishing it was alcohol that would burn its way down to her belly and make her finally feel something. Melt the ice she'd encased herself in for so long, so that numbness had become familiar, comforting. She didn't even notice it most of the time, content with her life back in New York, small as it was. It was only now, surrounded by strangers and with her father dead, that she felt painfully conscious of her isolation in the world she'd always viewed at a safe distance. The father who had turned his back on her without a thought.

Her father's second wife and stepdaughter Allegra knew, at least by sight. She'd never met them but she'd seen photos when, in moments of emotional weakness, she'd done an Internet search on her father. Alberto Mancini, CEO of Mancini Technologies. He was in the on-line tabloids often enough, because his second wife was young and socially ambitious—at least she seemed to be, from everything Allegra had seen and read online.

Her behaviour at the funeral, wearing black lace and dabbing her eyes with artful elegance, didn't make Allegra think otherwise. She hadn't spared Allegra so much as a glance, but then why would she? No one knew who Allegra was; she'd only known about the funeral because her father's lawyer had contacted her.

Around her people swirled and chatted, caught up in their own intricate dance of social niceties. Allegra wondered why she stayed. What she was hoping to find here? What did she think she could gain? Her father was dead, but he'd been dead to her for fifteen years, or at least she'd been dead to him. No messages, no letters or texts or calls in all that time. Nothing, and that was what she grieved for now, not the man himself.

The father she'd lost a long time ago, whose death now made her remember and ache for all she'd missed out on over the years. Was that why she'd come? To find some sort of closure? To make sense of all the pain?

Allegra's mother had been furious that she'd been at-tending, had seen it as a deep and personal betrayal. Just remembering Jennifer Wells's icy silence made Allegra's stomach cramp. Interactions with her mother were fraught at the best of times. Jennifer had never re-covered from the way her husband had cut both her and Allegra out of his life, as neatly and completely as if he'd been wielding scissors. Although it hadn't felt neat. It had felt bloody and agonising, thrust from a life of luxury and indulgence into one of deprivation and loneliness, trying to make sense of the sudden changes, her father's absence, her mother's tight-lipped explanations that had actually explained nothing.

'Your father decided our marriage was over. There's nothing I could do. He wants nothing to do with either of us any more. He won't give us a penny.'

Just like that? Allegra had barely been able to believe it. Her father loved her. He swooped her up in her arms, he tickled her, called her his little flower. For years she had waited for him to call, text, write, anything. All she'd got, on and on, was silence.

And now she was here, and what was the point? Her father was gone, and no one here even knew who she was, or what she'd once been to him.

From across the room Allegra saw a flash of amber eyes, a wing of ink-black hair. A man was standing on the sidelines just as she was, on the other side of the room. Like her he was watching the crowds, and the look of contained emotion on his face echoed through Allegra, ringing a true, clear note.

She didn't recognise him, had no idea what he'd been to her father or why he was there—yet something in him, the way he held himself apart, the guarded look in his eyes, resonated with her. Made her wonder. Of course, she wouldn't talk to him. She'd always been shy, and her parents' divorce had made it worse. Chatting up a stranger at the best of times verged on impossible.

Still she watched him, covertly, although she doubted he noticed her all the way across the room, a pale, drab young woman dressed in fusty black with too much curly red hair. He, she realised, was definitely noticeable, and many women in the room were, like her, shooting him covert—and covetous—looks. He was devastatingly attractive, almost inappropriately masculine, his tall, muscular form radiating energy and virility in a way that seemed wrong at a funeral, and yet was seductively compelling.

They were here to commemorate death, and he was all life, from the blaze of his tawny eyes to the restless energy she felt in his form, the loosely clenched fists, the way he shifted his weight, like a boxer readying for a fight. She was drawn not just to his beauty but to his vitality, feeling the lack of it in herself. She felt drained and empty, had for a long time, and as for him...?

Who was he? And why was he here?

Taking a deep breath, Allegra turned and headed for the bar. Maybe she would have that drink after all. And then she would go back to the *pensione* where she'd booked a small room, and then to the reading of her father's will tomorrow, although she hardly thought he'd leave her anything. Then home to New York, and she'd finally put this whole sorry mess behind her. Move on in a way she only now realised she hadn't been able to.

She ordered a glass of red wine and retreated to a private alcove off the main reception room, wanting to absent herself as much as she could without actually leaving.

She took a sip of wine, enjoying the velvety liquid and the way it slipped down her throat, coating all the jagged edges she felt inside.

'Are you hiding?'

The voice, low, melodious, masculine, had her tensing. She flicked her gaze up from the depths of her glass and her eyes widened in shock at the sight of the man in front of her. *Him.*

It was as if she'd magicked him from her mind, teleported him across the room to stand here like a handsome prince from a fairy-tale, except there was something a little too wicked about the glint in his eye, something too hard about the set of his mouth, for him to be the prince of a story.

Was he the villain?

Too stunned to form a coherent response, or one of any kind, Allegra simply stared. He really was amazingly good-looking—dark hair cut slightly, rakishly long, those glinting, amber eyes, and a strong jaw with a hint of sexy stubble. He was dressed in a dark grey suit with a darker shirt and a silver-grey tie, and he looked a little bit like Allegra imagined Mephistopheles would look, all dark, barely leashed power, the energy she'd felt from across the room even more forceful now, and twice as compelling.

'Well?' The lilt in his voice was playful, yet with a dark undercurrent that snaked its way inside Allegra like a river of chocolate, pure sensual indulgence. 'Are you?'

Was she what? She was gaping, that much was certain. Allegra snapped her mouth closed and forced her expression into something suitably composed. She hoped.

'As a matter of fact, I am. Hiding, that is. I don't know anyone here.' She took a sip of wine, needing the fortification as well as the second's respite.

'Do you make a habit of crashing funerals?' he asked lightly, and she tensed, not wanting to admit who she was…the rejected daughter, the cast-off child, coming back for scraps.

"Not unless there's an open bar," she joked, hefting her glass, and the man eyed her thoughtfully. Did he believe her? She couldn't tell. 'Did you know him?' she asked. 'Alberto Mancini?' The name stuck in her throat, and she saw a flash in the stranger's eyes, a single blaze of feeling that she couldn't identify but which still jolted her like lightning.

'Not directly. My father did business with him, a long time ago. I wanted to…pay my respects.'

'I see.' She tried to gather her scattered wits. The look of sleepy speculation in the man's eyes made her skin prickle. His gaze was like a caress, invisible fingertips trailing on her heated skin. She'd never reacted to someone so viscerally before, so immediately. Maybe it was simply because her emotions were raw, everything too near the surface. She certainly couldn't ever recall feeling this way before. 'That's very kind of you.' He smiled and said nothing. 'What did you say your name was?'

'I didn't.' His gaze swooped over her again, like a hawk looking for its prey. 'But it's Rafael.'

Rafael Vitali didn't know who this beguiling woman was, but he was captivated by her cloud of Titian curls, the wide, grey eyes that were as clear as mirrors, reflecting her emotions so he could read them from across the room. Weariness. Sorrow. *Grief.*

Who was she? And what was her relationship to Mancini? It didn't really matter, not now his business was done, justice finally satisfied, but he was still curious. A family friend—or something less innocuous? A lover? A mistress? She hadn't come just for the bar, of that he was certain. So what was she hiding?

Rafael took a sip of his drink, watching the emotions play across her face like ripples in water. Confusion, hope, sadness. A lover, he decided, although she was surely young enough to be his daughter. Mancini's wife and daughter were across the room, looking sulky and even bored. Rafael would have spared a second of sympathy for the man's widow if he hadn't known how she'd raced through his money. And tomorrow she would discover how little there was left...perfect justice, considering how Mancini had done the same to his mother, leaving her with nothing.

And as for his father…

He braced himself for the flash of pain, the memories he closed off as a matter of self-protection, of sanity. He never let himself think about his father, couldn't go to that dark, closed-off place, and yet for some reason Mancini's death had pried open that long-locked door, and now he was feeling flickers of the old pain, as raw as ever, like flashes of lightning inside him, a storm of emotion he needed to control.

'Take care of them for me, Rafael. You're the man of the house now. You must protect your mother and sister. No matter what…'

But, no. He needed to slam that door shut once more, and right now he knew the perfect way to do it…with this beguiling woman by his side.

'I hope the bar is worth enduring a wake for,' he said lightly, and she grimaced.

'I'm not really here for the bar.'

'I thought not.' He braced a shoulder against the wall so he was closer to her, inhaling her light, floral scent. A flyaway strand of coppery hair brushed his shoulder. She was utterly lovely, from her silver-grey eyes to her pert nose and lush mouth, her skin pale and creamy with a scattering of red-gold freckles. 'So how did you know him?' he asked.

She shrugged, her gaze sliding away. 'I knew him a long time ago. I'm not even sure he'd have remembered me, to be honest.' She let out a wavering laugh that sounded a little too sad, and Rafael resisted the tug of sympathy he felt for her. He didn't want to feel sorry for her, not now. Not when he'd already decided to sleep with her. Besides, she was no doubt been one of Mancini's cast-off mistresses, a gold-digger in it for the money and baubles. Why feel sorry for such a woman?

And yet he couldn't help but notice how fragile she looked, as if a breath might blow her away. There were violent smudges like bruises under her eyes, and her face was pale underneath the gold dust scattering of freckles. The figure underneath the rather shapeless black dress looked slender and willowy, with a hint of intriguing curves. 'I can't believe anyone would forget you,' he said, and was amused to see her cheeks turn pink, her pupils flare, as if she were an innocent unused to compliments.

'Well...you'd be surprised,' she returned with an uncertain laugh. 'What business did your father have with my—with him?'

'A new technology for mobile phones.' He didn't want to talk about the past. 'At least new at the time. The industry has moved on quite a bit since then.' But the technology would have made his father a lot of money, if Mancini hadn't cut him off. If he'd lived.

'I wouldn't know. I'm rather useless with technology. I can barely manage my own phone.' She took a sip of wine, golden-red lashes sweeping down onto her porcelain cheeks. Rafael had the desire, unsettlingly strong, to sweep his thumb along her cheek and see if her pale skin felt as creamily soft as it looked.

'What do you do, then?' he asked. 'For a living?' He reckoned she must be in her late twenties. Had she found a new sugar daddy?

'I work at a café, in Greenwich Village. It's a music café.'

'A music café? I've never heard of such a thing.'

'It's a shop for instruments and libretto,' Allegra explained. 'As well as a café. But it's so much more than that—it hosts concerts for aspiring musicians, and offers lessons to all sorts of people. It's a bit of a community hub, for music-lovers at least.'

'And you are one, I gather?'

'Yes.' Her voice was quiet and heartfelt, as well as a little bit sad. 'Yes, music is very important to me.'

Rafael watched her, disconcerted by this shy admission, by the genuineness of it, of her. He didn't want to confuse or complicate his feelings, had no intention of deepening what would be a shallow but satisfying sexual transaction.

'I suppose I should leave,' Allegra said slowly. 'I don't really have a reason to stay.' She sounded reluctant, and when she looked up at him her eyes were full of mute appeal, wanting him to stop her. And stop her he would.

'It's still early,' he said as he angled his body closer to her, his shoulder brushing hers, letting her feel both his heat and intent. Her eyes widened, and her tongue darted out to touch her lips. Primal need blazed through him. She was either artless or very, very experienced— he couldn't tell which, but either way she enflamed him. 'But we don't have to stay here. Tell me what your favourite piece of music is.'

'Oh...' She looked surprised, and then shyly pleased. 'I don't think you'd know it.'

'Try me.'

'All right.' She smiled, and it felt like a ray of sunlight on his soul, disconcertingly bright, reaching too many dark corners. It was just a *smile*. 'It's the third movement of the Cello Sonata by Shostakovich. Do you know it?'

'No, but I wish I did. I wish I could hear it.'

'He's not one of the most well-known composers, but his music is so emotional.' Her grey eyes developed a pearly sheen; she looked almost tearful. 'It moves me like nothing else does.'

'Now I really wish I could hear it.' The look of naked emotion on her face caught at him unexpectedly. He'd started the conversation about music as a way to invite her up to his suite, but now he found he genuinely wanted to hear the piece. 'I have a suite in this hotel,' he said. 'With an amazing sound system. Why don't you come upstairs and listen to the piece with me?'

Allegra's eyes widened with stunned comprehension. 'Oh, but…'

'We can have a proper drink at the same time. The bar up there is much better than the plonk they're serving down here.' He whisked her glass from her fingertips and deposited it on the tray of a hovering waiter. 'Come.' He held out his hand, willing her to agree. The evening couldn't end here, unsettled, unsated. He needed more. He craved the connection and satisfaction he knew he'd find with her, however brief.

Allegra stared at his outstretched hand, her eyes wide, her fingers knotted together. 'I'm not…' she began, and then trailed off, looking endearingly uncertain. Was it an act? Or was she really reluctant?

He didn't want her reluctant. 'I am,' he said, and reached for her hand, pulling her gently towards him. She came slowly, with hesitant steps, her wide-eyed gaze searching his face, looking for reassurance.

And he gave it as his fingers closed around hers, encasing the spark that had leapt between them at the first brush of skin. He drew her by the hand, away from the circulating crowds. A few people gave them curious looks, a veiled glance of envy that Rafael ignored, just as he'd ignored the subtle and not so subtle come-ons of the various women there. There was only one he wanted, and he was holding her hand.

They walked hand in hand out of the room, across the foyer, and then to the bank of gleaming lifts. Rafael's heart started to race in expectation. He was looking forward to this more than he'd looked forward to anything in a long time.

He pressed the button for the lift, holding his breath, not wanting to break the fragile spell that was weaving its way around both of them. Not wanting to let her entertain second thoughts.

The doors opened and they stepped inside, the lift thankfully empty. As the doors closed Rafael turned to her. 'You have the most enchanting smile.'

She looked completely surprised. 'Do I?' she asked, and he nodded, meaning it, because her smile *was* lovely, a shy, slow unfurling, like the petals of a flower. More and more he was thinking she was genuine, that her air of innocence and uncertainty wasn't an act. At least, not that much of an act. She must have had some experience, to be mourning Mancini, and yet she almost seemed untouched.

'You do. And I think it is a rare but precious thing.' He leaned back against the wall of the lift and tugged her gently towards him, close enough so their hips nudged each other's and heat flared, a spreading, honeyed warmth that left him craving more. 'I would like to see it more often.'

'We have been at a funeral,' Allegra murmured, her gaze sweeping downwards. 'There hasn't been much cause to smile.'

The doors pinged open before Rafael had to come up with a response to that thorny statement. He stepped out, directly into the penthouse suite he'd booked. Allegra looked around the soaring, open space, her eyes wide.

'This is amazing…'

Was she not used to such things? Rafael shrugged the question aside, drawing her deeper into the room. The doors to the lift closed. At last they were alone.

CHAPTER TWO

WHAT WAS SHE DOING? Allegra felt as if she'd stumbled into an alternate reality. What kind of woman followed a strange, sexy man up to his penthouse suite? What kind of woman fell headlong under his magnetic spell?

Certainly not her. She didn't do anything unexpected or impetuous. She lived a quiet life, working at the café, her closest friend its owner, an eighty-year-old man who treated her like a granddaughter. Her life was small and safe, which was how she wanted it. And yet from the moment Rafael's hand had touched hers she'd been lost, or perhaps found. She felt as she'd been wired into a circuit board she'd had no idea existed, nerves and sensations springing to life, making her entire body tingle.

She *felt*, and after the numbness she'd encased herself in that was both good and painful, a necessary jolt, waking her up, reminding her she was alive and someone, *someone* was looking at her with warmth and even desire, wanting her to be there. The knowledge was intoxicating, overwhelming.

Rafael was still holding her hand, his warm, amber eyes on hers, his smile as slow and sensual as a river of honey trickling through her.

It was dangerous, letting herself be looked at like that. Dangerous and far too easy to float down that river, see where its seductive current took her. They were here to listen to music, but Allegra wasn't so naïve and inexperienced not to realise what that meant. Why Rafael had really asked her up here.

Nervous and unsettled by her spiralling thoughts, Allegra tugged her hand from Rafael's and walked around the suite, taking in all the luxurious details, soaring ceilings and marble floors, ornate woodwork and silk and satin cushions on the many sofas scattered around the large living area.

'This place really is incredible,' she said. Her voice sounded high and thin. 'What a view.' Floor-to-ceiling windows framed a spectacular view of the city on three sides. 'Is that the Coloseum?' She pointed blindly, and then felt Rafael come to stand behind her, his body so close she could feel his heat. If she stepped backwards so much as an inch she'd be touching him, burned by him. She wanted it, and yet she was afraid. This was entirely new, and new meant unfamiliar. Strange. *Dangerous*.

Except…what, really, did she need to be afraid of? Rafael couldn't hurt her, not in the way she'd been hurt before, soul deep, heart shattered. She wouldn't let him. She was nervous, yes, because this was strange and new, but she didn't have to be *afraid*. She took a deep breath, the realisation calming her. She could be in control of this situation.

'Yes, it's the Coliseum.' His hands rested lightly on her shoulders, and a slight shudder went through her, which she knew he felt. Daring now to prolong the moment, to up the ante, she leaned back so she was resting lightly against him. The feel of his chest, hard and warm, against her back was a comforting, solid weight, grounding her in a way she hadn't expected. Making her want to stay there.

Rafael's hands tightened on her shoulders and they stood there for a moment, her back against his chest so they could feel each other's heartbeats. Allegra closed her eyes, savouring the moment, the connection. Because that's what she wanted, what she needed now...to feel connected to someone. To feel alive.

So much of her life had been lived alone, since she was too shy to make friends at school, too confused and hurt to reach out to her mother, too wounded and wary to seek love from the handful of dates she'd had over the years. But *this*...one single, blazing connection, to remind her she was alive and worth knowing...and then to walk away, unhurt, still safe.

'Shall we have champagne?' Rafael's voice was soft, melodious, and Allegra nodded. She wasn't much of a drinker, but she wanted to celebrate. Wanted to feel this was something worth celebrating.

'That sounds lovely.'

He moved away and she turned, wishing she could get hold of her galloping emotions, her racing pulse. Feeling this alive was both exquisite and painful. What was it about this man that made her want to take a step closer, instead of away? That made her want to risk after all this time?

The pop of a cork echoed through the room, making Allegra start. Rafael poured two glasses, careless of the bubbles that foamed onto the floor. *'Cin-cin,'* he murmured, a lazy look in his eyes, and he handed her a glass.

'Cin-cin,' Allegra returned. She hadn't spoken the informal Italian toast since she was twelve years old, and the memory was bitter-sweet. New Year's Eve at her family home, an estate in Abruzzi, snow-capped mountains ringing the property. Her father had given her her first taste of champagne, the crisp bubbles tart and surpris-

ing on her tongue. The sense of happiness, like a bubble inside her, at being with her family, safe, secure, loved.

Had it all been a mirage? A lie? It must have been. Or perhaps she was remembering the moment differently, rose-tinted with the innocence of childhood, the longing of grief. Perhaps her father hadn't been as doting as she remembered; perhaps he'd taken a call moments after the toast, left her alone. How could she ever know? She couldn't even trust her memories.

'Are you going to drink?' Rafael asked, and Allegra blinked, startled out of her thoughts.

'Yes, of course.' She took a sip, and the taste was as crisp and delicious as she remembered. She blinked rapidly, wanting to clear the cobwebs of memory from her already overloaded mind. She didn't want to get emotional in front of a near-stranger.

'Tell me about yourself,' she said when she trusted herself to sound normal. 'What do you do?'

'I run my own company.'

She raised her eyebrows. 'What kind of company?'

'Property. Mainly commercial property, hotels, resorts, that sort of thing.'

He was rich, then, probably very rich. She should have guessed, based simply on his presence, his confidence. Even his cologne, with the dark, sensual notes of saffron, smelled expensive. Privileged. She'd been privileged once too, before her parents' divorce. More privileged and even spoiled than she'd ever realised, until it had all been taken away.

Not that she'd been focused on her father's money. Although her mother complained bitterly that after the divorce she'd got nothing, that she'd had to scrounge and beg and pawn what jewellery she'd managed to keep, Allegra hadn't really cared about any of it. Yes, it had been a huge step down—from an enormous villa to a two-bedroom apartment too far uptown to be trendy, public school, no holidays, often living off the generosity of her mother's occasional boyfriends, a parade of suited men who came in and out of her mother's life, men Allegra had tried her best to avoid.

All of it had made her mother bitter and angry, but Allegra had missed her father's love more than any riches or luxuries. And at the same time she'd become determined never to rely on anyone for love or anything else ever again. People let you down, even, especially, the people closest to you. That was a lesson she didn't need to learn twice.

'And you enjoy what you do?' she asked Rafael. She felt the need to keep the conversation going, to avoid the look of blatant, sensual intent in his eyes. She wasn't ready to follow that look and see where it led, not yet, and Rafael seemed content to simply sip and watch her with a sleepy, heavy-lidded gaze.

'Very much so.' He put his half-full glass on a table and moved towards the complicated and expensive-looking sound system by the marble fireplace. 'Why don't we listen to your music? Shostakovich, you said, the third movement of the cello sonata?'

'Yes...' She was touched he'd remembered. 'But surely you don't have it on CD?'

He laughed softly. 'No, I'm afraid not. But the sound system is connected to the Internet.'

'Oh, right.' She laughed, embarrassed. 'Like I said, I'm not good with technology.'

'You can leave that to me. I can find it easily enough.' And he did, for within seconds the first melancholy strains of the music were floating through the room. Rafael turned to her, one hand outstretched, just as it had been before. 'Come.'

The music was already working its way into her soul, the soft strains winding around her, touching a place inside her no person ever accessed. Music was her friend, her father, her lover. She'd given it the place meant for people, for relationships, and she'd done that deliberately. Music didn't hurt you. It didn't walk away.

She took Rafael's hand, the sorrowful emotion of the cello resonating deep within her. Rafael drew her down onto the sumptuous leather sofa, wrapping one arm around her shoulders so she was leaning into him, breathing in his scent, her body nestled against his.

It was the closest she'd ever been to a man, and yet bizarrely the intimacy felt right, a natural extension of the music, the moment, both of them silent as the cello and piano built in sound and power.

Then Rafael drew her against him even more tightly, so her cheek was pressed against his chest, her body pressed against his, and Allegra closed her eyes, letting the music wash over her. She needed this. She closed her eyes, the music and Rafael and the champagne all combining to overwhelm her senses even as it made her want more, to let herself be swept away on this tide of emotion and see where it took her.

Underneath her cheek Rafael's chest rose and fell in steady, comforting breaths. His fingers stroked her arm and his breath feathered her hair. Everything about the moment felt incredibly intimate, more so than anything Allegra had ever experienced before. If only they could go on like this for ever, feeling each other's breaths, each beat of their hearts.

The music built to its desperate, haunting crescendo and then the strains fell away into silence. It had been, Allegra knew from having listened to the piece many times, just over eight minutes, and yet it felt like a lifetime. She felt both drained and intensely alive at the same time, and in the ensuing stillness neither of them moved or spoke.

'Do you know,' Allegra finally said softly, 'the cello is closest instrument to the human voice? I think that's why it affects me so much.' She let out a shaky laugh, conscious of the tears on her cheeks, the rawness of the moment. The music had affected her more now than it ever had before.

'It is a stunning piece of music,' Rafael said quietly. His thumb found her tear and gently swept it away, stealing her breath, making her ache. 'It causes me to both yearn and mourn.'

'Yes...' The sensitive, sincerely spoken observation pi018rced her to her core. *This* was the connection she craved, and unthinkingly she twisted in his arms, smiling through her tears, her face tilted up to his. Then she caught the blazing look in his eyes, felt its answer in the sudden, desperate thrill that rippled through her body. And this connection, even sweeter and more powerful than the last...

He dipped his head and she held her breath, the whole world suspended, expectant—and then his mouth was covering hers in a kiss that felt like both a question and an answer, a need both sating and sparking to life. It was enough, and yet it made her want so much more.

Allegra's hands clenched on the crisp cotton of his shirt as his mouth moved with thorough and expert persuasion on hers, gentle and yet so sure. She'd never known a kiss could be like this, touching her to her very core, piercing her right through, *knowing* her. And right now she wanted to be known.

And then it became wonderfully, thrillingly more. In

one easy movement Rafael swept her up and across the room and she found herself lying down on the soft leather cushions, his face flushed and his eyes jewel-bright as he looked down at her.

'You are so beautiful. So lovely.' With gentle hands he pushed her disordered curls away from her face, his fingers skimming across her skin, exploring her features. Allegra closed her eyes, submitting to his touch, revelling in it. The feel of his fingers on her face felt as intimate as the kiss, his touch so gentle and reverent it made her ache in an entirely new way.

He slid his hands lower, each touch a question, his fingers feeling her collarbone and then his palm moulding to the curve of her breast.

'A different kind of music,' he murmured, his mouth following the trail of his hand, and she laughed, the sound shaky and breathless. Yes, this was new music, and he was teaching her its breathtaking melody. She'd thought, in this moment, that she might feel fear, or at least uncertainty, but she didn't.

She felt wonderful, and she wanted to keep feeling wonderful, to come alive under someone's hands, feel as close to another person as she could. For one night. One moment. When would she ever get a chance like this again?

Somehow Rafael had managed to slip her dress from her shoulders, and now her upper half was bare to him. He bent his head, nudging aside her bra with his tongue, and she gasped aloud, the feel of him against her sensitised flesh a jolt to her whole body.

'Oh...' The single syllable held a world of newly gained knowledge as pleasure pierced her with sweet arrows. Her hands roved over his back, drawing him closer to her, desire an insistent pulse inside her.

Of their own accord her hips rose, welcoming the knowing touch of his hand. His fingers brushed her underwear and she bit off a gasp. *She'd had no idea...*

Rafael lifted his head, his gaze glittering as he looked down at her, his breathing as ragged as her own. The obvious fact that he wanted her as much as he wanted him solidified her certainty that this was what she wanted. What she needed. A connection, pure and true.

'Will you come into the bedroom with me?'

She nodded wordlessly, knowing there was only one answer her aching body and heart could give.

'Yes.'

In one fluid movement Rafael rose from the sofa and drew her towards the bedroom. Allegra followed, barely conscious of her rucked-up dress, her tangled hair.

The bedroom was as elegant and luxurious as the living area, and Allegra glanced at the massive king-sized bed, standing on its own dais and covered in a navy satin duvet. Rafael turned her to face him, framing her face with his hands as he kissed her again, even more deeply, and she responded, his kiss drawing a deep, pure note from her soul.

Rafael tugged the zip down the back of her dress so the black silk fell away, leaving her in nothing but her bra and pants, both simple and black, hardly sexy, and yet his gaze gleamed with approval as he looked at her, and her heart swelled. She had never realised how wonderful it felt, to have a man look at her like that. Want her like that. He drew her towards him, her breasts brushing against his chest, her hips nudging his so she could feel the hard length of his arousal against her stomach.

'Cold?' he whispered, and she shook her head.

No, she was not cold. It was a balmy spring evening,

and the hotel suite was warm. The shiver was because of him, and he knew it, and she didn't care.

He kissed her again, working his way down her jaw and collar bone to press his lips against the V between her breasts. She threaded her fingers through his hair, anchoring herself to him. She felt adrift in sensation, and his touch was the only thing that tethered her to earth.

Then he was moving his mouth lower, peeling away her bra and pants with his hands, sinking down onto his knees in front of her so Allegra swayed, shocked and overwhelmed by the feel of his hands on her hips, his *mouth…*

'Oh…' Her breath came out in shattered gasps. It was so unbearably intimate, to have him looking at the very essence of her, revering her in an act so selfless and giving and… *'Oh.'*

Rafael's dark chuckle reverberated through her bones as her body trembled on the precipice of an orgasm that felt like an explosion. He rose again and drew her to the bed, leaving her trembling and aching and wanting more.

She watched, dazed, as he shucked off his clothes, revealing a bronzed torso, the muscles of his abdomen scored into hard, perfect ridges. His legs were long and powerful, and as for the most male part of him…

He was a work of beauty.

'You may look,' Rafael said as he covered her body with his. 'And you may also touch.' And then he was kissing her again, his arousal pressing into her with thrilling insistence, and that restless ache became an overwhelming clamour in her body, drowning out all thought, all doubt.

She gasped out loud as his fingers touched her in her most intimate and feminine places, teasing, toying, exploring, knowing. Her fingernails dug into the satiny skin of his shoulders as her body strained for the glittering apex she felt, just out of her reach, a pinnacle she needed to find, that she wanted them to ascend together.

And then, finally, he was sliding inside her, his breathing harsh and ragged as he filled her up, the momentary twinge of pain lost in the utter rightness of the sensation, the union complete and total.

He stopped, swearing under his breath, and, lost in a haze of need, Allegra stilled underneath him.

'Rafael…?'

'You are *vergine*?' he demanded, and she gulped.

'Yes…'

He swore again, his forehead pressed to hers. 'I had no idea…'

'Why would you?' she managed, and he let out a shudder, his eyes clenched closed.

'You should have told me.'

'Rafael…' She arched her hips upwards, letting her body plead in a way her words could not. She couldn't let him stop now, not when everything in her was aching and demanding. With a groan he kept moving, the delicious slide of his body in hers making Allegra forget that tense moment as she gave herself up to the sensations cascading through her, building in a beautiful crescendo, and then the glittering apex burst into crystalline shards of pleasure around her as she let out a cry that rent the still air and then fell away like the most sacred note of music she'd ever heard.

Rafael rolled off Allegra, managing to suppress the curse that sprang to his lips once more. She'd been a *virgin*. He hadn't expected that, not even when he'd decided she was artless and genuine, and guilt soured like acid in his stomach. He'd stolen someone's innocence. He'd used someone who should have been protected, cared for. He'd done something he'd sworn he would never do again. Break a sacred trust.

He'd assumed she was a woman of some experience, even if she'd seemed a little shy. He never would have brought her upstairs otherwise. He never would have gone ahead with his seduction.

And yet…the music, the mood, the way Allegra had looked at him with hungry hope…all of it had made him yearn in a way that now left him feeling deeply uneasy. Sex was a transaction, nothing more, pleasurable and easy as it was. He didn't ever let it mean anything, and he hoped like hell Allegra wasn't imbuing it with some kind of emotion he would never let himself feel.

And yet it had been the innocent purity of her response that had been his undoing. *He hadn't even used birth control.* The realisation crystallised like ice inside him. He'd meant to reach for a condom, but in the moment he'd completely forgotten. He'd lost his head. He'd certainly lost control of his body.

Next to him Allegra was still, a rosy flush covering her pale, porcelain body, the perfect foil for the creaminess of her skin. Her hair was spread across the pillow in a tangle of red-gold curls, making him want to thread his fingers through them even now, and pull her towards him for an open-mouthed kiss. Even now, with his climax still thudding through him, knowing how innocent she'd been, he wanted her. He'd never wanted a woman so quickly, or so much.

Allegra rolled on her side, curling into him, her arms wrapped around his chest. Rafael froze, confusion colliding with alarm, irritation with guilt. He didn't do pillow talk. Ever. All of his bed partners knew what he expected in bed, and what he definitely didn't want. He made it very clear from the beginning that emotional attachments were a no-go zone, except Allegra, of course, hadn't received that memo. And as a virgin she would no doubt expect some intimacy now, some soft talk that he knew he was utterly incapable of. He didn't let people get close. People he could hurt. People he could fail.

As he'd already hurt Allegra, deflowering her in what amounted to a tawdry one-night stand.

Her leg found its way between his, her damp cheek pressed to his chest. She let out a shuddering sigh.

'I miss him,' she whispered, her voice sounding broken. 'I miss him so much.'

Shock had Rafael stilling. *What the hell...?* 'Miss him?' he repeated tonelessly.

'I know I shouldn't, there's nothing to miss,' she continued softly. 'I hadn't even seen him in fifteen years. But I do miss him. I miss what we once had, what I thought we had. That's why I came tonight, I think. Because I was looking for something, some kind of closure...'

She was talking about Mancini. But *fifteen years...* She couldn't have been his mistress. She was in her late twenties at most.

'Allegra,' Rafael asked hoarsely, turning to stare down into her pale, lovely face. 'Who are you?'

She looked up at him with tear-drenched eyes. 'I'm his daughter,' she said simply, and Rafael bit down on the curse that sprang to his lips.

Allegra was Alberto Mancini's *daughter*. The daughter of his enemy, his nemesis, was lying in his arms, seeking his comfort, because her dear father, the man who had as good as murdered his own, was dead.

His stomach heaved. He felt a thousand different emotions—fury and guilt, disgust and alarm, regret and sorrow. He was sickened by his own part in this unexpected drama, taking a woman's innocence, a woman who he should, by rights, have nothing to do with. He'd hated the Mancinis for so long, had wanted only justice…but what was this? What was *he*? Allegra was looking for comfort and he had none to give.

He rolled away from her and out of bed, grabbing his boxers and slipping them on in one jerky movement. From behind him he heard Allegra shift in bed, and then her voice, trembling, uncertain.

'Rafael?'

'You should go.' His voice was brusque; he didn't think he could have gentled it if he'd tried. Anger was coursing through him now, a pure, clean rage. Mancini's *daughter*. Did she know what her father had done? Did she realise the blood he had on his hands? Reasonably he knew she couldn't; she must have been a child when his own father had died.

And yet…she was a Mancini. She missed her father, a man he'd hated. She'd been innocent, and he'd abused it. His feelings were a confused tangle of guilt and anger, shame and frustration. It was all too much to deal with. He needed her out of his life. Immediately.

'You…you want me to go?' Her voice was a trembling breath of uncertainty.

'I'll call you a cab.' He reached for his trousers and pulled them on. Then, because she still wasn't moving, he grabbed her dress and tossed it to her. It fell on her lap; she didn't even reach for it.

She looked gorgeous and shocked, sitting in his bed, the navy sheet drawn up to her breasts, her hair tumbling about her shoulders, her eyes heartbreakingly wide.

'But… I don't understand.'

'What is there to understand?' Each word was bitten off with impatience. Innocent she might might have been, but surely she could figure out what was going on. 'We had a one-night stand. It's over.' He paused. 'If I'd known you were a virgin, I would have done things a bit differently. But as it was…' He shrugged. 'You seemed happy enough with how things happened.'

She blinked as if she'd been slapped, and then she lifted his chin, showing a sweet courage that made his emotions go into even more of a tailspin.

'I *was*,' she agreed with emphasis. 'I may be innocent, but even I can tell when an exit strategy needs some work. And yours sucks.'

'Thanks for the tip, but the sentiment remains the same.' Rafael folded his arms, a muscle pulsing in his jaw. Too many emotions had been accessed tonight, too many raw nerves twanging painfully. He couldn't take any more. She had to *go*.

Allegra took a deep breath, lifting her chin, blinking back tears. 'Will you give me a moment of privacy to dress?' she asked with stiff dignity, and although he could have retorted that he'd already seen her naked, Rafael didn't have it in him to be that cruel. Her fragile courage touched him in a way he didn't like, and he gave a terse nod before stalking from the room.

He needed a drink, something far stronger than champagne. This didn't feel at all like he'd expected it to, needed it to. He'd been looking for satisfaction, and instead he felt more restless than ever. Restless and remembering.

'All you have is your honour, Rafael. That's all that's ever left. Your honour and your responsibilities as a man.'

But he had neither now.

The door to the bedroom opened just as Rafael poured himself a generous measure of whisky. He forced himself not to turn as he heard Allegra's heels click across the marble floor of the living area. Remained with his back to her as she pressed the button for the lift and the doors pinged open.

'Goodbye,' she said, her voice soft and sad and proud all at once, and then she was gone.

Alone in his penthouse suite, Rafael raised the glass of whisky to his lips. He stared out at the unending night and then, instead of drinking, he threw the tumbler against the wall, where it shattered.

CHAPTER THREE

ALLEGRA SAT DOWN in the lawyer's office, her stomach seething with bitter memory as well as nerves. It was the day after her father's funeral, and also of the biggest mistake of her life. She'd left Rafael's hotel suite with her chin held high but her self-esteem, her whole self in tatters, everything in her reeling from his treatment of her.

He'd been so tender, and she'd felt so treasured. Had it all been a lie? *Again?* It seemed she did have to learn that lesson twice. People weren't what they seemed. They said and did what they liked to get what they wanted and then they walked away.

And she was the one left, alone and hurting.

Except, she'd told herself last night, staring gritty-eyed at the ceiling of her bedroom in the modest *pensione*, she didn't have to be hurt by this. Before it had begun she'd told herself she wouldn't be. What they'd done together might have seemed meaningful at the time, but he was still a stranger. A sexy, selfish, unfeeling stranger. It wasn't as if she'd loved him. She hadn't even known him.

She'd made a mistake, she told herself as she rose from bed that morning, body and heart aching with fatigue. A sad, sorry mistake, because she'd given a part of herself to someone who hadn't deserved it. She'd searched for comfort and affection from someone who had neither wanted nor offered neither. She'd survive, though. She had before.

She'd lost her father when she'd felt most vulnerable, had watched him walk away from her without a backward glance. She'd seen her mother withdraw into bitterness and desperation, and she'd fended for herself since she was eighteen. Over the years she'd lost plenty of dreams, and this didn't have to hurt nearly as much. She wouldn't let it.

Signor Fratelli had been insistent that she attend the meeting, although Allegra didn't know why. She doubted her father had left her or her mother anything; if he hadn't given her anything in life, why would he in death? She wasn't looking forward to the meeting, to sitting in a stuffy room with her father's second wife and stepdaughter, the family he'd chosen. Still, it would be a few minutes of discomfort and tension, and then she could return to New York. Act as if none of this had ever happened.

'Signorina Mancini.' The lawyer greeted her with a tense smile as Allegra was ushered into the stately room with its wood-panelled walls and leather club chairs. 'Thank you for coming.'

'It's Signorina Wells, actually,' Allegra said quietly. Her mother had reverted to her maiden name, as had Allegra, after the divorce. She glanced at Caterina Mancini, whose icy hauteur didn't thaw in the least as her arctic-blue eyes narrowed. Her gaze flicked away from Allegra and she didn't offer a greeting.

Next to her, her daughter Amalia, around the same age as Allegra, shifted uncomfortably, giving Allegra a quick, unhappy smile before looking away. Allegra felt too tired and on edge to return it. The other woman had her mother's cool blonde looks without the icy demeanour. In different circumstances, another life, Allegra might have considered getting to know her. Now she could barely summon the emotional energy to sit next to the two women who had taken her and her mother's places in her father's life.

Signor Fratelli began making some introductory remarks; through a haze of tiredness Allegra tried to focus on what he was saying.

'I am afraid, in recent weeks, there has been some change to Signor Mancini's financial situation.'

Caterina's gaze swung to pin the lawyer. 'What kind of change?' she demanded.

'Another corporation now has controlling shares in Mancini Technologies.'

Caterina gasped, but the words meant little to Allegra. She still didn't know why the lawyer had insisted she be there for such news.

'What do you mean, controlling shares?' Caterina asked, her voice high and shrill.

'Signor Vitali of V Property has secured controlling shares,' the lawyer explained. 'Only recently, but he is now essentially the CEO of Signor Mancini's company. And he will be here shortly to explain his intentions regarding its future.'

Allegra sat back and closed her eyes as Caterina's ranting went on. What did she care that some stranger now owned her father's company? None of this was relevant to her. She shouldn't have come. Not to the lawyer's, and not even to Italy.

'Ah, here he is,' Signor Fratelli said, and then the door to his office opened and Rafael appeared like a dark angel from her worst dreams.

Allegra stared at him in shock, too stunned to react other than to gape. He looked remote and professional and very intimidating in a navy blue suit, his eyes narrowed, his mouth a hard line. His cool gaze flicked to Allegra and then away again without revealing any emotion at all. Allegra shrank back into her chair, her mind spinning, her body already remembering the sweet feel of his hands... *What was he doing here?*

Signor Fratelli stood. 'Welcome, Signor Vitali.'

Maybe because she was so tired and overwhelmed, it took Allegra a few stunned seconds to realise what it all meant. Rafael was Signor Vitali of V Property. *He* owned her father's company. Had he known who she was last night? Was it some awful coincidence, or had *she* been part of his takeover? She pressed her hand to her mouth and took several deep, steadying breaths. The last thing she wanted to do was throw up all over Rafael Vitali's highly polished shoes.

She was so busy trying to keep down her breakfast that she missed the flurry of conversation that swirled around her. Distantly she registered Caterina's outraged exclamations, Rafael's bored look. Signor Fratelli was looking increasingly unhappy.

Allegra straightened in her chair, her hands gripping the armrests as she struggled to keep up with what was being said.

'You can't do this,' Caterina protested, her face pale with blotches of angry colour visible on each over-sculpted cheekbone.

'I can and I have,' Rafael returned in a drawl. 'Mancini Technologies will be dissolved immediately.'

Allegra stayed silent as Rafael outlined his plan to strip her father's company of its apparently meagre assets. Then Signor Fratelli chimed in with more devastating news—nearly all of her father's assets, including the estate in Abruzzi, had been tied up with the company.

The result, Allegra realised, was that her father had died virtually bankrupt.

'You killed him,' Caterina spat at Rafael. 'Do you know that? He died of a heart attack. It must have been the shock. *You killed him.*'

Rafael's expression did not change as he answered coldly, 'Then I am not the only one with blood on my hands.'

'What is that supposed to mean?' Caterina demanded, and Rafael didn't answer.

Numb and still reeling from it all, Allegra turned to Signor Fratelli. 'May I go?' She didn't think she could stand to be in the same room as Rafael much longer. He'd used her. More and more she was sure he'd known who she was, and had planned it. Had it amused him, to have the daughter of the man he'd ruined fall into his hands, melt like butter?

'There is something for you, *Signorina*,' the lawyer told her with a sad smile. 'Signor Mancini had a specific bequest for you.'

'He did?' Surprise rippled through her along with a fragile, bruised happiness, even in the midst of her shock and grief. Signor Fratelli withdrew a velvet pouch from his desk drawer and handed it to Allegra.

Caterina craned her neck and Rafael and Amalia both looked on as Allegra clasped the pouch. She didn't want to open it in front of them all, but it was clear everyone expected it. Caterina was bristling with outrage, seeming as if she wanted to snatch the precious bag from Allegra's hands.

Taking a deep breath, she opened the pouch and withdrew a stunning necklace of pearls, with a heart-shaped diamond-encrusted sapphire at its centre. She knew the piece; it had belonged to her father's mother, and her mother had loved to wear it. Tears pricked her eyes and she blinked them back. The value of the piece was not in its jewels but in the sheer, overwhelming fact that her father had remembered her. She clenched the necklace in her fist, gulping down the emotion, before she managed to give Signor Fratelli a quick nod.

'*Grazie,*' she whispered, the Italian springing naturally to her lips.

'There is a letter as well,' Signor Fratelli said.

'A letter?' Allegra took the envelope from the lawyer with burgeoning hope. Perhaps now she would finally understand her father's actions. His abandonment. 'Thank you.' The letter she refused to open here. She rose from her seat, making for the door.

As she brushed past Rafael she inhaled the saffron scent of his cologne and her stomach cramped as memories assailed her.

His hands touching her so tenderly. His body moving inside hers in what had been an act more intimate than anything Allegra had ever experienced or imagined. She'd understood all along that it had been a one-night stand; she'd known that they weren't building a relationship. And yet the reality had been both harsher and more intense than she'd ever expected—both the import of what she'd shared with Rafael and the cruelty of him kicking her out the door.

Now, on shaking legs, with her head held high, she walked past him and out the door. She'd just started down the steps when the door opened behind her and Rafael called her name.

Allegra hesitated for no more than a second before she kept walking.

'Allegra.' He strode easily to catch her, touching her lightly on the arm. Even the brush of his fingers on her wrist had her whole body tensing and yearning. Remembering. She shook him off.

'We have nothing to say to each other.'

'Actually, we do.' His voice was low and authoritative, commanding her to stop. She paused, half turning towards him, wanting to ignore how devastatingly attractive he looked even now.

'What,' she demanded in a shaking voice, 'could you possibly have to say to me now? You got your revenge.'

'Revenge?' His mouth firmed into a hard line. 'You mean justice.'

'Did you know I was his daughter last night?' Allegra demanded shakily. 'Did it…did it *amuse* you, having me fall all over you when you knew you were ruining him?'

'I didn't know you were Mancini's daughter, and if I had, I wouldn't have touched you. I want nothing to do with any Mancini, ever.' He spoke with a cold flatness that made Allegra recoil.

'Why? What had my father ever done to you?'

'That is irrelevant now.'

'Fine.' She wouldn't let herself care. She intended to forget Rafael Vitali ever existed from this moment on. 'Then we have nothing to say to each other.'

'On the contrary.' Once more Rafael stayed her with his hand. 'We didn't use birth control.'

Five simple words that had her stilling in frozen shock, dawning horror. She licked her lips, her mind spinning. She was so innocent, had felt so overwhelmed, that the fact they hadn't used birth control hadn't even crossed her mind. She was ashamed by her own obvious naiveté.

'If you are pregnant,' Rafael continued in a low, steady voice, 'then you will have to tell me.' His tone brooked no argument, no protest.

'Why?' Allegra demanded. 'You wanted to have nothing to do with me last night. Why would you want to deal with my child?'

'Our child,' Rafael corrected her swiftly. He handed her a business card, which Allegra took with numb fingers. 'Naturally I hope this will come to nothing. But if it does not, I am a man of honour.' Cold steel entered his voice, making Allegra flinch. 'I take care of what is mine.'

Come to nothing.

An appropriate term for the evening they'd shared, and any possibility emerging from it. Allegra longed to rip his business card into shreds, but the gesture seemed childish. She crumpled it in her fist instead.

'Suffice it to say,' she bit out, 'I have no desire ever to speak to you again, about anything.'

'I'm serious, Allegra.'

'So am I,' she choked, and then hurried down the stairs.

Back at the *pensione*, still trembling from her encounter with Rafael, Allegra finally opened the letter from her father.

Dear Allegra,
Forgive an old man the mistakes he made out of sorrow and fear. I cared more for my reputation than for your love, and for that I will always be sorry.

Your mother loved this necklace, but it belongs to you. Please keep it for yourself, and do not show it to her.

I don't expect you to understand, much less forgive me.
Your Papa.

Tears streaked silently down her face as she read the letter again and again, trying to make sense of it. He'd loved his reputation more than her? What did that even mean? The letter hadn't answered anything, only stirred up more questions.

And yet…he was sorry. He *had* loved her. But if that was the case, why had he been able to let her go?

Rafael sat in the lawyer's office, the acid of regret churning in his stomach. In his mind he could see Allegra's huge, silvery, tear-filled eyes, and another pang of guilt assailed him. He'd handled last night badly. He knew that, yet he also knew he couldn't have changed his reaction. Alberto Mancini had killed his father. What he'd done in exchange to Allegra—treating her harshly after a single night together—was negligible in comparison.

As for a possible pregnancy…he would provide for any child of his, absolutely. There was no question about that at all. But he hoped to heaven and back that Allegra was not carrying his baby. And he wished he'd been able to temper his actions last night, at least a little. Or, even better, that the whole night had never happened.

Yet even as the thought flitted through his mind he knew he was a liar. Last night had been incredible, explosive, the most intense sexual encounter of his life. He hadn't used birth control because he'd been so overcome with desire, with basic, blatant need. He'd wanted her last night and seeing her this morning, looking so pale and proud, he'd wanted her all over again, to his own shame.

'Signor Vitali? Is there anything left to say?'

Rafael blinked the lawyer back into focus, along with Mancini's widow and stepdaughter. He'd thought he'd enjoy seeing Caterina Mancini brought low but, despite the obvious fact that she was a gold-digger, he felt sorry for her. She'd had nothing to do with his father's downfall, and right now his eye-for-an-eye justice tasted bitter.

And if she was right, and Mancini had died of a heart attack, of shock at having his business bought out from under him...

Then he'd killed Mancini just as Mancini had killed his father.

Uncertainty and guilt cramped his stomach. He didn't like either emotion, would not entertain them for a moment. If his actions had brought about Mancini's death, then so be it. Justice had finally, fully been served. He had to believe that.

Allegra travelled back to New York in a daze, sleeping nearly the entire flight, wanting only escape from the grief and memory and pain.

The world felt as if it had righted itself a little bit when she was back in her studio apartment in the East Village, enjoying the quiet, peaceful solitude of her own space, the sound of muted traffic barely audible from the sixth floor. She'd said hello to Anton, her boss and landlord, and then retreated upstairs. All she needed now was some music to help to soothe and restore her.

Allegra automatically reached for her favourite Shostakovich before her hand stilled, her stomach souring. Had Rafael ruined her favourite music for her for ever? Maybe. She chose some Elgar instead, and then curled up on her sofa, hugging a pillow to her chest, trying not to give in to tears.

A few minutes later her mobile rang, and Allegra's heart sank a little to see it was her mother.

'Well?' Jennifer demanded before Allegra had said so much as hello. 'Did you get anything? Did I?'

'It was a lovely funeral service,' Allegra said quietly,

and Jennifer merely snorted. Her mother held no love, or even any sentiment, for Alberto Mancini. 'We didn't get anything,' she said after a tiny pause. Although she didn't understand it, she would heed her father's advice not to tell her mother about the sapphire necklace. 'He didn't even have much to give.' She explained about Rafael Vitali and his takeover of Mancini Technologies, striving to keep her voice toneless, betraying none of the emotion still coursing through her at the memory of that one earth-shattering night. She'd forget it. She'd start forgetting it right then. She had to.

'Vitali?' Jennifer said sharply. 'He bought the company?'

'Yes.'

'Not that it has anything to do with us.'

'No,' Allegra agreed dourly. 'Although Caterina Mancini accused him of practically killing...' Even now she could not say Papa. He might have signed the letter as her *papa*, but he hadn't acted or felt like one since she'd been a child. 'Him. Because the heart attack might have been brought on by shock.' The thought that Rafael might have actually killed her father was like a stone inside her.

And she'd given herself to this man.

Jennifer was silent for a moment. 'It's over,' she said at last, and that knowledge rested in Allegra's stomach like lead. Yes, it was over. It was all over.

Over the next month Allegra did her best to move on with her life. She worked at the café, she chatted with customers, she walked in the park and tried to enjoy the small pleasures of her life, but after that one earth-shattering night with Rafael, everything felt dull and colourless.

It was foolish to miss him when he'd treated her so brutally, and yet Allegra felt like Sleeping Beauty who had been woken up. She couldn't go back to sleep again. Retreat was not an option, and yet it was the only one she'd ever known.

So she tried to forget about that evening entirely, but a month after she returned from Italy she threw up her breakfast. She passed it off as having had a dodgy takeaway the night before, but when she threw up the next morning, realisation crept in, cold and unwelcome. The third morning she bought a pregnancy test.

She stared down at the two pink lines in shock, realisation coursing through her in an icy wave. It seemed too unfair that on top of having the misfortune to have slept with Rafael Vitali and then been brutally rejected by him, she now was carrying his baby. One night—and now this?

Her baby. Her child, living inside her, like a flower, waiting to unfurl. The maternal instinct was so strong it took her breath away. She hadn't expected it, had never even thought about having children, not seriously. After all, she was perennially single, with no one in the picture or even on the horizon.

And yet…*a baby.* Someone to love, someone to make a family with, a proper family. She would never abandon her baby the way her father had abandoned her. She'd never take out her frustration and bitterness on her child the way her mother had on her. She'd be the best mother she knew how to be, already loving this scrap of humanity with a fierceness that surprised and humbled her.

A baby. A new start, a second chance at love, at life, at happiness. Allegra placed one protective hand across her middle and closed her eyes.

CHAPTER FOUR

'CARO?'

The teasing, lilting voice of the woman Rafael had picked up in a bar only irritated him. He glanced across at her, noting the ruthlessly toned limbs, the well-endowed chest, the pouting mouth. None of it appealed to him. He couldn't even remember her name.

'You can go.'

Her lipsticked mouth dropped open in outrage and Rafael turned away, bored and disgusted. He hadn't even touched her, and he didn't want to. His libido had barely stirred once since Allegra had left his bed. He hadn't slept with anyone, had lost interest.

'Rafael…' She reached out her arms, her pout deepening, and impatience bit at him.

'Seriously. Go.' He gestured to the door of his penthouse suite. He was in Paris on business, and as the blonde beauty stalked towards the door, it occurred to Rafael that he was behaving just as he had before, throwing a woman out of his room.

Seemed he didn't have a great track record.

But, damn it, he'd expected her to call. A courtesy call, at least, to tell him she wasn't pregnant. Although why he should expect courtesy from her when he'd shown her so little he didn't know.

So she hadn't called. Obviously she wasn't pregnant, and he could move on with his life. He could forget Allegra Wells and the sweet purity of her smile, the tears that had streaked down her porcelain cheeks when she'd listened to that music, the way her body had yielded and curled into his, accepting him wholly in a way he'd never felt before. Complete. *Right.*

Idiot.

It had been a casual sexual encounter, one of many, nothing more. Allegra Wells was out of his life…for good. Which was just how he wanted it, because he was done with the Mancinis. He'd taken the man's business, dismantled the industry that had been built on his father's grave.

Justice had been served, and yet there was no one to share his victory. His mother and father were dead, and he didn't even know where Angelica was. The family he'd sworn to protect and provide for was scattered, destroyed. And Rafael still felt restless, vaguely guilty and unfulfilled, as if he was missing something…or someone.

'This might be a little cold.'

Allegra winced slightly at the feel of the cold gel on her tummy and then the insistent prodding of the ultrasound wand. It was her eighteen-week scan, and she couldn't wait to see her baby. She craned her neck to gaze in anxious curiosity at the black and white screen and the fuzzy image that suddenly appeared, along with the whooshing, galloping noise of her baby's heart.

Excitement leaped inside her as the figure gained definition and clarity—head, arms, legs, beating heart. Everything tucked up like a present waiting for her. Allegra let out a choked cry, smiling through her tears.

It hadn't been an easy pregnancy. It was over three

months since she'd made the decision to keep this baby, three months of debilitating morning sickness, throwing up nearly every morning and twice having to go to hospital to be treated for dehydration. She'd lost weight, struggled to work, and wondered how on earth she was going to manage as a single mother.

Because she intended to do this alone. She couldn't face telling Rafael about their baby. She couldn't face her child having a father like she'd had, one who would walk away when he felt like it. She still didn't understand what her father's note had meant, and she hadn't dared yet to ask her mother about it, but she'd experienced enough of Rafael Vitali to know she couldn't trust him to stick around.

Still she didn't know how she was going to manage, in a studio apartment with a low-paying job. She hadn't figured it out yet, but she would. Eventually. Now, however, her all of her fears fell away at the beautiful sight of her baby. *Her baby.*

The technician frowned and poked harder with the wand. Allegra winced. Then, more alarmingly, the technician put the instrument down and rose from her seat by the examining table where Allegra was lying.

'I'll be right back,' she murmured, and then left the room.

Allegra lay there, shivering from the cold gel, her gently rounded belly damp and exposed. Unease crept icy fingers along her spine. Technicians weren't supposed to leave in the middle of an appointment like that, surely?

She found out moments later when an important-looking doctor in a white lab coat followed the technician back into the room, frowning as she looked at the screen with the beautiful, fuzzy image of Allegra's child.

'What's going on?' Allegra asked, her voice high and strained with anxiety.

'Just a moment please, Miss... Wells.' The doctor glanced briefly at her file before turning her narrowed gaze back on the screen. Something was wrong. Allegra could feel it in her bones, in her frightened, hard-beating heart. Something had gone wrong with this pregnancy. With her baby.

She lay there, everything in her frozen and fearful, as the doctor took the wand and began to prod her belly once more, murmuring to the technician who murmured back, none of it audible to Allegra.

'Please,' she begged. 'Please, tell me what's going on.'

The technician gave her a smile of such sorrowful sympathy that Allegra wished she hadn't asked. Then she handed her a paper towel to wipe off the gel while the doctor continued to study the image on the screen— the image of her baby.

'Dr Stein will speak with you shortly,' the technician murmured.

Moments later Allegra had all the answers she didn't want. The words reverberated emptily through her, making horrible sense and sounding unintelligible, impossible, at the same time. Congenital heart defect were the three words that hurt the most.

'But what does that mean exactly?' she demanded, her voice shaking. She knew there were heart defects that were operable. There were even some that were asymptomatic, hardly worth mentioning. But looking at Dr Stein's compassionate face, she feared her baby didn't have one of those.

'The particular defect we're discussing is life-threatening,' Dr Stein said quietly. 'The baby wouldn't live past a few months of age, if that.' Allegra gaped and she continued, 'We'll order an amniocentesis as soon as possible, to know for sure what we'll dealing with. This may take up to three weeks, I'm afraid. Based on the ultrasound, it could be one of several heart defects, of varying seriousness.'

'But you think it's a more serious one?' Allegra whispered, and Dr Stein gave her an unhappy look.

'I'm afraid that, yes, it's looking like that, but we won't know until we get the results of the amniocentesis. It's difficult to diagnose this kind of condition from only a scan.'

Allegra walked home in a fog, barely aware of the steps that took her up to her sixth-floor studio. Anton poked his head out of his apartment to ask how she was, and Allegra didn't even know what she said. The world felt muted, as if everything was taking place far away, to other people. Nothing mattered. Nothing at all mattered any more.

She lay on her bed, one hand pressed against her middle. Already, she'd barely been coping, stumbling through each day, trying to survive the awful morning sickness that had exhausted her so utterly. She hadn't let herself think too much about the future, and now it looked like there might not be one. How was she going to wait three long weeks to find out?

And through the haze of her grief and fear, one fact kept coming back to torment her. *She should have told Rafael.* No matter how he had treated her, he should know she was pregnant with his child. He should be aware of what was happening.

Still she resisted. She didn't want to give him a chance to reject her all over again, along with their baby. She didn't want to face his accusations and anger, as he no doubt would be furious that she hadn't told him she was pregnant. She especially didn't want to open herself up to hurt.

Since Rome, she'd done her best to push all thoughts of Rafael out of her mind. She'd told herself there was still time to tell him about the baby, if she ended up deciding that was the best thing to do, which she wasn't at all sure it was. She just needed to feel better first, to find her feet. When she felt stronger, she could think about whether she wanted Rafael involved, even if everything in her had shied away from it.

But now? Now everything had sped up and become urgent. She had to make hard decisions, agonising choices. And Rafael deserved to be a part of that process, even if she dreaded talking to him again.

Allegra battled the possibilities in her mind as the date of her amniocentesis came closer. Finally, two days before the scheduled procedure, she took out the crisp white business card Rafael had handed her outside the lawyer's office. With trembling fingers she dialled the mobile number printed starkly on the card.

He answered after two rings. 'Yes?'

'It's Allegra.' Her voice was a thready whisper, and she straightened, determined to be strong. The silence on the end of the line stretched on for several seconds.

'Yes?' Rafael finally said again, his voice tense, guarded.

Allegra took a deep breath. 'I'm calling because something has happened.' Rafael didn't say anything and she forced herself to continue. 'I'm pregnant and—'

'You're pregnant?' His breath hissed sharply between his teeth. 'By *me*?'

'Yes, of course by you—'

'Then why are you telling me now? You must be halfway through your pregnancy.'

'Almost,' Allegra agreed.

'Then why—?'

'Rafael, please, just listen. I'm pregnant and I had an ultrasound and it looks like there is something wrong with the baby. Something serious.' Her voice caught and she dashed at her eyes with her hand. She couldn't break down now. She had to stay strong. The last person to look for comfort from was Rafael.

Rafael remained silent for a few taut seconds. 'What kind of thing are you talking about?' he finally asked.

'A congenital heart defect.' Allegra drew a ragged breath. 'I'm having an amniocentesis in two days' time to determine—'

'In New York?'

'Yes.'

'I'll be there.'

Shock had her mouth dropping open. '*Be* there? But—'

'Of course I'll be there,' Rafael said roughly. 'This is my child. Isn't it?'

'Of course it is.'

'Then I'll be there. I'll call again tomorrow to confirm the details.'

Allegra wasn't sure what she'd been expecting Rafael's response to be, but that wasn't it. As she hung up the phone she battled between trepidation at seeing him again and a treacherous relief that someone was going to walk through this with her. She was used to being alone, preferred it, but she didn't want to be alone in this.

And yet Rafael? She was, Allegra knew, going to have to be careful. With her baby, and with her heart.

Rafael drummed his fingers against the armrest as the limo cut smoothly through Manhattan's midtown traffic, heading towards Allegra's flat in the East Village. The shock and fury he'd felt that she'd hidden her pregnancy from him for so long had been replaced by a far greater fear for the health of their unborn child. He was going to have a *child*. Someone to protect and provide for, cherish and guard with his life. A life he would treasure, if he ever got the chance.

Rafael had never believed in the idea of atonement, and yet he thought of it now. Perhaps the sins of the past could be righted by this future…his child's future. Perhaps he would finally find the peace and satisfaction he craved, through the life of this innocent.

He'd deal with Allegra's wilful deception later; right now they needed to get through the current crisis…whatever happened. He'd let down those who'd depended on him before and he wouldn't do it again. He would not fail his child.

The limo pulled up in front of a tall brick building. Rafael's mouth thinned as he stepped out of the limo and scanned the names by the buzzers. His eyes narrowed as he saw that Allegra was on the sixth floor, and the building had no lift. She was walking up and down six flights of stairs every day? Surely that could not be good for her or their child.

He pressed the buzzer and her voice, sounding tired and wavering, came through the intercom.

'I'll be right down.'

Tense with anxiety, he shoved his hands in the pockets of his trousers and scanned the building again. It looked run-down and dangerous, a drift of takeaway menus littering the front step, the bins outside overflowing. This was no place for the mother of his child to live.

Moments later Allegra appeared in the doorway. As she opened the door, Rafael tried to hide his shock. She looked terrible—her face was pasty and pale, her hair lifeless and dull, and she'd lost far too much weight. The

T-shirt and light trousers she wore for a humid summer's day in the city hung on her like rags on a scarecrow.

Rafael stepped forward to take her arm. She recoiled slightly at his touch, but he held her arm anyway. 'You look as if a breath of wind might blow you away.'

'I've been ill.'

'You should have called me earlier.' He could not keep the recrimination from his voice.

'Please, let's not argue. It's taking all my strength to get through this day already.'

Rafael nodded tersely, knowing she was right. Every instinct in him clamoured to demand why she'd hidden the pregnancy from him when he'd been as clear as he could be that he'd wanted to know. But now was not the time. Still, he determined grimly, the time would come. He'd make sure of it.

He helped Allegra into the car, noting the way she sank into the seat with a relieved sigh, resting her head against the leather cushions.

'What did you mean, you've been ill?' he asked as the limo pulled away from the kerb.

'Morning sickness,' she murmured. 'I've had it terribly. I've hardly been able to keep anything down.'

You should have told me. He bit back the words. 'Isn't there anything the doctors can do? Medication…?'

'I was prescribed something, but it didn't really help. It's started to get a little bit better recently, thank goodness, and my doctors think it might go away soon if…' She bit her lip, her eyes bright with tears.

Rafael could finish that awful sentence. If she continued with this pregnancy, if their baby was healthy. 'We need more information,' he said gruffly, 'before any decisions are made.' But already he'd made a decision. He wasn't leaving her, and she wasn't staying in a walk-up flat in a run-down neighbourhood. Her place, no matter what happened, was with him. He would protect her and their baby. He thought back to that terrible day, outside his father's study door. He'd failed in protecting those he loved that day. He'd been too weak, too slow to act, too naïve. But he would not fail again. The need to protect his ill-gotten family burned within him, brighter and fiercer than anything he'd ever felt before.

Allegra could feel the tension emanating from Rafael, but she didn't have the energy to wonder or worry about it. All her strength was taken up with preparing for what lay ahead.

She'd barely slept last night, too worried by both the procedure and its possible results. She hadn't even had time to think about Rafael and seeing him again.

And yet now that he was here...she inhaled the saffron scent of his aftershave, felt the coiled, restless power of him, just as she had before. It made her ache. It made her remember. Even now she felt a treacherous dart of desire. How stupid, considering their situation, and the way he'd treated her.

They didn't speak all the way to the hospital, but that was okay. Allegra didn't think she could manage chit-chat, and talking about what mattered felt too hard. The limo pulled up to the front of the hospital, and Rafael leapt out before Allegra could so much as reach for the handle.

He opened her door and with one arm around her shepherded her into the building. She wasn't that fragile, but she craved his protectiveness now. It felt strange, when she'd taught herself not to rely on anyone. Now she wanted to. She needed to.

Before long they were in a treatment room, with Al

legra lying down on the examining table and Rafael sitting tensely on a chair next to her. A technician prepared her for the ultrasound, and the now-familiar whooshing sound of her baby's heart filled Allegra with both relief and joy.

She glanced across at Rafael, shocked and then touched by the look of tender wonder softening his face. His surprised gaze met hers and he gave her a smile that seemed almost tremulous. Another point of connection, as sweet as any they'd ever shared, and yet… Could she trust it? Dared she think about what happened next, or in the long term?

'Now this won't take long,' the doctor assured her. 'And it shouldn't hurt too much. I've given you a local anaesthetic to numb the area, but you might experience some minor discomfort and cramping.'

Allegra took in the size of the needle and instinctively reached for Rafael's hand. He encased her hand in his larger one, and she squeezed it hard as the needle went in. It didn't hurt, but it still scared her. Everything about this scared her.

In a few moments it was over, and the technician was wiping the gel off Allegra's stomach.

'Are you all right?' Rafael asked in a low voice, and Allegra nodded.

'Yes. I think so.' She felt shaky and a bit tearful, and she had some mild cramps, but nothing she couldn't deal with. She tried to shake his hand off, wanting to be strong, but he kept holding hers.

'You need to rest.'

'You should take the rest of the day off,' the doctor advised. 'Normal activity can be resumed tomorrow.'

Rafael frowned at that, but said nothing. Together they left the treatment room, and it wasn't until they were in the limo and Rafael was telling the address to the driver that Allegra realised he wasn't taking her home.

'Wait—where are we going?' she asked.

'To my hotel near Central Park.' Rafael sat back.

'But I want to go home,' Allegra said. She wanted her bed and her music and the comforts of the familiar.

Rafael glanced at her, his expression unreadable. 'That apartment is completely inappropriate for a woman in your condition.'

'You mean pregnant?' Allegra stared at him, surprised by his high-handedness even as she wondered why she should be. Rafael had been completely in control of every situation she'd seen him in.

'Climbing six sets of stairs to get to your home cannot be good for our baby,' Rafael stated.

'Plenty of women do that and more—'

'Yet you are the one I care about,' Rafael cut her off. 'And frankly you look terrible—tired, pale, drawn. You need proper rest.'

'Thanks very much,' Allegra snapped. Her feminine pride was hurt by his blunt assessment, even though she knew she didn't look good, and hadn't for a while.

'The reason I look tired, Rafael, is because I've had extreme morning sickness, not because I climb some stairs.'

'It can't help.'

'So what are you suggesting? That I move house?'

'Precisely,' Rafael answered in a clipped voice. 'You will live with me in my hotel suite until the results from the amniocentesis return.'

She stared at him in disbelief. She'd wanted someone to lean on, yes, for a little bit. But not someone to take over her life. Yet should she have expected anything else from this man? 'I can't live with you,' she protested. 'I don't want to live with you. I have a job—'

'Managing a café, on your feet all day? Take sick leave.'

'I can't—'

'Then I shall arrange it.'

Allegra simply stared, too shocked by his autocratic statements to frame a suitable reply. She should have expected this, but she'd been so tired and shaky and fearful, she'd just been glad to have someone to lean on for a little while. Now she was starting to wish she'd never called Rafael at all. 'This is ridiculous.'

'Even so.' Rafael was as unmovable as a brick wall, his expression obdurate. And meanwhile they were speeding towards Central Park, away from her flat, her job, her life.

'You can't just waltz into my life and make all these changes and demands,' Allegra persisted. 'I won't let you.'

Rafael raked a hand through his hair, taking a deep breath and letting it out slowly. Allegra had the strange sense that he was battling a deeper emotion than she understood. 'I realise you do not want me to tell you what to do,' he said evenly. 'But when you put your emotional reaction to that aside, you will surely realise that I am right.'

Allegra let out a huff of disbelieving laughter. 'What I *didn't* realise is how unbelievably arrogant you are.'

Rafael's mouth firmed. 'This isn't about arrogance. I'm not issuing orders simply to show who's in control.'

'Really?'

'I am considering your health, Allegra, as well as that of our child.'

'And if I refuse?' Allegra asked. 'What will you do?'

'Why would you refuse? You want what is best for our baby, do you not? As do I.'

A lump formed in her throat and her eyes burned. He dared to suggest she didn't care for their child? 'Of course I do.'

'Then surely rest and relaxation in a comfortable place is it? Why overtax and strain yourself when you don't have to? Why climb six sets of stairs when you don't have to?' He held up a hand to stem any protests she might have made. 'I understand that climbing the stairs might have no negative effect on your pregnancy. But what if there is the smallest chance that it did?' He leaned forward, his eyes burning bright. 'If you could turn back time, do things differently...' For a second his voice choked, and Allegra had the distinct feeling he was talking about something else.

'What would you change, Rafael?' she asked quietly. 'What would you do differently?'

He shook his head, the movement abrupt and dismissive. 'It is now that matters. Now you have the chance to make the best choice for your—our—baby.'

Allegra stared at him, both transfixed and uncertain. 'You can't keep me in some bubble. Pregnant women are able to live normally.'

'Two weeks is all I'm asking. Two weeks until we know what we're dealing with, and then we can reassess. Discuss.'

Discuss what was likely to be a life-threatening condition. The unshed tears that burned behind her lids threatened to fall. Suddenly it felt like too much; her resistance had been feeble but it was all she had. She couldn't fight any more, couldn't stay strong and remote as she always tried to.

'Fine.' She sagged against the seat as the limo pulled

up in front of one of the city's most luxurious hotels. 'You win.' Relief and triumph flashed in Rafael's amber eyes, and in that moment she wondered just how much she was conceding.

CHAPTER FIVE

ALLEGRA BLINKED SLEEPILY in the early evening gloom of the hotel suite's master bedroom. She'd fallen into a deep, dreamless sleep almost as soon as her head had touched the soft, feather down pillow, and judging by the twilight settling softly over the city sky she'd been asleep for several hours.

She stretched and then snuggled under the soft duvet, tempted to stay there for ever. When they'd arrived at the hotel suite, Rafael had been graciousness itself, insisting she take the master bedroom, ringing for some juice when she said she was thirsty, and telling her to sleep for as long as she'd liked.

When she'd crawled into the king-sized bed Allegra had realised just how exhausted she really was, and her last thought before she drifted off was that she was, in the end, glad Rafael had insisted she come here. Not that she intended on admitting as much to him.

Now, as she struggled to a sitting position with a wide yawn, she wondered what exactly she was supposed to do here. What *they* were supposed to do. An afternoon was one thing, but did Rafael really expect her to stay here for two weeks, kicking her heels, until the amnio results came back? And what was he going to do while she waited? How were they supposed to get along? Battling deeper unease, Allegra rose from the bed.

She treated herself to a long, lovely soak in the sunken marble tub and then dressed in her summery trousers and top before heading into the main living area of the suite in search of Rafael.

He was sitting at a desk in a study alcove off the sumptuous living room, frowning down at his laptop, but he looked up quickly as she stepped from the doorway of the bedroom.

His gaze scanned her searchingly from her damp hair curling about her face to her bare feet. 'You slept well?'

'Yes, very well. It's been ages.' It was, she'd seen as she'd dressed, nearly seven o'clock at night.

'Are you hungry?' Rafael rose from the desk. 'I ordered a variety of dishes from room service. I hoped something might appeal to you.'

'That's very kind of you.' After months of barely managing a mouthful, she knew she needed to eat more.

'Come into the dining room.'

Allegra followed him into the dining room that adjoined the kitchen, which was just as elegant as every other room in the suite. The place was twenty times the size of her studio, decorated with silks and satins, antiques and exquisite paintings. She felt almost as if she were in a museum—a very comfortable, luxurious museum.

'Wow,' Allegra managed, surprised and touched by the spread of food left in warming dishes on the table. She saw clear broths and simple pasta dishes, fresh fruit and half a dozen different salads. Amazingly, despite the constant nausea she'd been battling for the last few months, she felt a little hungry. 'This looks amazing.'

'Take whatever you like. We can eat out on the terrace.'

'Thank you.' He was being so kind, and yet she was afraid to trust it. Reluctant to start depending on his charity and consideration, when it all could change so suddenly…just as it had before.

Rafael handed her a plate and Allegra took it and began to serve herself from some of the dishes. 'How were you able to book the penthouse suite of this place?' she asked. 'I've heard it's booked months in advance.'

Rafael shrugged one powerful shoulder. 'Considering I own this hotel, it was not a problem.'

He *owned* this hotel? It was one of the city's best. Allegra had known Rafael was wealthy and powerful, but it was brought home to her yet again in that moment— along with the realisation of how he could wield that power, if he so chose. How he already had, taking over her father's business. This was man who was ruthless, brutal in his determination to get what he wanted…whatever that was. She needed to remember that.

Allegra finished filling her plate and then took it outside to the terrace overlooking Central Park. The air was a balmy caress, and the terrace was decorated with potted plants and fairy-lights, making it feel like a little bit of the park had been brought thirty floors up.

'This is lovely,' she said as she sat on a chaise and picked at a few mouthfuls of pasta salad. 'Thank you.'

Rafael sat across from her, his plate balanced on his lap. He was wearing the dark trousers and crisp white shirt he'd worn earlier, the shirt now opened at the collar, revealing the strong column of his throat. Stubble glinted on his jaw and the whiteness of the shirt was a perfect foil for his burnished, olive skin. He looked, Allegra acknowledged with a pang, as devastatingly attractive as he had that night in Rome. As irresistibly desirable…except, of course, she would resist him. She had to, because the situation was fraught enough, dangerous enough. She couldn't let herself depend on him any more than she already was. She certainly couldn't start to care for him.

'I've arranged for you to take the next two weeks off work,' Rafael stated as he forked a mouthful of pasta.

'What? How?'

'I spoke to your employer and landlord, Anton. He understands.'

Allegra's head was spinning. 'But you… Two weeks?' She blinked at him. 'But—'

'You have exhausted yourself, whether you realise it or not. You need a proper rest, both for your own health and our child's.'

Allegra couldn't deny that, but she still chafed against his commands. She was used to being independent. She needed to feel strong. 'That was not your call to make. This is my life, Rafael.'

'And as I said before, I know you want what is best for the baby.'

It was a trump card he could play every time, and there was nothing she could do about it, because he was right. She enjoyed her job, but it had been exhausting and she knew she couldn't keep it up for ever. A rest, even one that was enforced, had some merit, as reluctant as she was to admit it to him.

But a rest here with Rafael? Allegra still couldn't imagine spending the next two weeks with him. There was so much they hadn't discussed…his heartless dismissal of her after their night together, her hiding her pregnancy, even the business his father had had with hers. Her father's death. There was so much tension and latent anger and uncertainty—and now they were meant to get along?

And beyond that, she didn't even *know* Rafael. She'd intentionally tried not to think of him since they'd parted, wanting to forget about him completely. She's resisted doing Internet searches, even though she'd been tempted to know more about him.

And now here they were, sitting across from each other, their baby nestled inside her. Allegra didn't know what to think of any of it, how to respond, how to feel. Part of her was clamouring for retreat, while another part recognised that that was no longer an option, not with a child to think of. A child to love.

In any case, now certainly wasn't the time to tackle any of those difficult issues. They just needed to get through the next two weeks and see what the results of the amniocentesis were.

They spent the evening, incongruously, sitting next to each other on the sumptuous silk-covered sofa, watching TV on a huge flat screen that had been hidden behind an oil painting. After the first few tense minutes Allegra started to relax, enjoying being able to turn off her brain and watch reality TV fluff. And she enjoyed the feel of Rafael's strong body next to her, his thigh touching hers, his arm stretched along the back of the sofa. She could almost imagine this was normal, that she was normal, with a baby and a husband and a life like so many women wanted and had.

Which was a *very* dangerous way to think.

The next morning Rafael suggested they go to her flat to pick up her things, and they rode in silence down Park Avenue to her little studio. It felt strange to have Rafael in her personal space, his inscrutable gaze flicking over her belongings—her framed concert posters, her few personal photos—even the shelf of well-thumbed cookbooks in the tiny alcove kitchen felt revealing of her somehow.

'I didn't realise you actually played.' He nodded towards the cello on its stand in the corner.

'I don't, not really.' She looked away, not wanting to talk about her cello playing, or lack of it. She hadn't played since she was eighteen years old.

'Do you wish to bring it to the hotel?'

'No,' she said after a moment, her tone reluctant but firm. 'I won't play it.'

'Are you sure?'

'Yes.'

He stared at her for a moment, his gaze narrowed, as if he was trying to figure out what was going on in her head. Allegra looked away. She couldn't explain her complicated relationship to music, how much it meant to her, how it had provided something she knew instinctively people were meant to provide. She certainly didn't want to go into the reason why she'd stopped playing the cello, the dismal failure she'd been. Thankfully Rafael let the subject drop.

After gathering her clothes, books, and a few personal items, they headed back to the hotel. Allegra knew she couldn't put off something she'd been dreading—calling her mother.

Although they lived in the same city, she and Jennifer rarely saw each other. Her mother had her own life on the Upper East Side, tightly enfolded in a clique of aging socialites and impoverished divorcées, trying to live in the manner she preferred with the help of boyfriends and benefactors, and an endless diatribe of high-strung negativity.

Allegra understood the reason for it, knew her mother had never recovered from her father's divorce and abandonment, his decision to end their marriage so abruptly and cut them off with barely a cent, but it didn't make it any easier to deal with her.

Jennifer hadn't been much interested in Allegra's pregnancy so far, except to remind her repeatedly that single motherhood was no picnic, thereby launching down an endless memory lane trip of her own struggles and regrets until Allegra had tuned her mother out. But the mention of a wealthy father to her grandchild was sure to prick Jennifer's ears up and have her asking all sorts of questions. Questions Allegra didn't feel much up to answering right now.

After she'd unpacked in her room, and with Rafael installed in the study on his laptop, Allegra made the call.

'You're what?' Jennifer asked sharply when Allegra had explained she was staying at the hotel.

'Just for a little while.' Allegra took a deep breath. 'Rafael Vitali is…he's the father of my baby. We…we got together when I was in Italy.'

'Rafael Vitali? This is the son of Marco Vitali?'

Startled, Allegra said, 'I… I suppose so. I don't know. Why? Do you know his father?'

'Your father did business with him a long time ago,' Jennifer said after a pause. 'It didn't work out.'

Unease prickled along Allegra's spine. She thought of Rafael's cold remark. *I am not the only one with blood on my hands.'*

'What do you mean, it didn't work out?'

'It doesn't matter,' Jennifer dismissed. 'It's in the past. But be careful,' she added in an unusual display of motherly concern. 'Your father didn't trust his, and I… I wouldn't trust him either.'

She didn't trust him. Didn't want to trust him. And

yet... 'I trust Rafael to care for his child,' Allegra said, because that, at least, was true.

Out in the living area Rafael looked up from his laptop when she emerged from the bedroom.

'You called your mother?'

'Yes.' Allegra paused, wondering how much she wanted to probe the past. 'She mentioned that your father did business with mine, and that it didn't work out.'

A lightning flash of emotion sliced across Rafael's face, too quickly for her to discern what it was, and then he carefully closed his laptop. 'Yes, that is true. They worked together on a mobile phone technology that would now be considered laughably obsolete, and they fell out over it.'

'Fell out?' Allegra regarded him uneasily, sensing something dark flowing beneath his calm surface, and nervous to dip a toe into it. 'Is that why you decided to take over my father's company? Some kind of revenge for what happened before?'

'Justice,' Rafael corrected swiftly. His face remained bland, but Allegra saw that his eyes were watchful and hard.

'What do you mean, justice? What are you not telling me? And why... why did you make that comment about blood on your hands?'

Rafael's jaw tightened, his eyes like chips of amber. 'Now is not the time to delve into the past.'

'But it's obviously important—'

'What is important is your health and well-being.' He rose from the desk. 'I have booked some spa treatments for you this afternoon to help you relax. They are aimed specifically at pregnant women.'

'Oh...' Allegra blinked, startled all over again. 'Thank you.' She felt as if her head was spinning. One moment

Rafael seemed as hard and unyielding as granite, and the next he was all softness and solicitude. Which was the real man? Who did she dare trust...if either?

Rafael paced the living room of the hotel suite, waiting for Allegra to return from her afternoon of spa treatments. He felt anxious, and he didn't even know why. At least, not *exactly* why. Since Allegra had catapulted back into his life he'd been struggling with a tidal wave of fury that she'd attempted to hide her pregnancy from him, and a stronger surge of both protectiveness and fear to keep both her and their child safe.

The memory of when he'd failed his family, his fists beating on his father's study door, his useless words. And then the aftermath. His mother's wan face, his sister's desperate defiance...their whole family falling to pieces, disintegrating before his eyes. It tormented him, when he allowed himself to think of it. The thought of failing Allegra and their child in a similar way or even at all was appalling. Unacceptable. And he wouldn't let it happen. He would do everything in his power to keep Allegra and their baby safe and well. *Everything*...for her well-being as well as his own.

He knew Allegra had questions about his father. His past. The deception and death that still haunted his nightmares and could ruin things between them. She still loved her father—that much was obvious—even though the man had abandoned her. He couldn't tell her the truth about him, not without jeopardising their own situation and Allegra's barely-there trust in him. The past, he determined, would have to stay buried.

The door to the suite opened and Allegra stepped inside, and the clear purity of her smile, the ivory blush of her skin made something twist hard inside Rafael's gut. He suddenly felt breathless, which was entirely a new feeling and made him feel poleaxed, reeling from the strength of his own reaction. He forced a smile.

'How was it?'

'Wonderful. I feel more relaxed than I have…well, ever.' She let out a little laugh, her grey eyes sparkling like silver. 'I've never even had a massage before. And look at my nails!' She held out her hands to him, her nails painted pale pink, and as a matter of course Rafael caught them up in his, drew her to him.

Allegra came easily, caught up in the moment, and he wasn't even thinking as he bent his head to kiss her, already anticipating the sweet, soft taste of her. Her lips parted soundlessly, her eyes fluttering closed, her golden-red lashes fanning onto her porcelain cheeks.

His lips brushed hers and Allegra let out a little sigh. Rafael pulled her closer and then he felt her stiffen in his arms. Her eyes flew open, filled with confusion. She shook her head and then drew away.

'No, I'm sorry…we can't…'

Of course they couldn't. The last thing they needed was this kind of complication…except he wanted it so badly. Rafael raked a hand through his hair, desire surging through his body. He was shocked by his instantaneous and overwhelming response, his heart thudding.

Allegra was still looking at him in dazed confusion, her pupils dilated with desire even as her mouth twisted with uncertainty.

The time would come, Rafael decided. Maybe not yet, not when everything was so uncertain, when their child's future hung in the balance. But the time would come. It had to.

CHAPTER SIX

'I HAVE A surprise for you.'

Allegra looked up from the book she was reading with a cautious smile. Rafael stood in the living-room doorway, the slight curve of his mouth softening his harsh features.

It had been a strange and unsettling ten days, living in the hotel with Rafael, finding a new and tentative normalcy. It had taken a little while, but eventually she'd been able to relax into a routine. Rafael had spent most of his time working in the hotel's business centre so Allegra hadn't seen him nearly as much as she'd expected to, which was, to her irritation, both a disappointment and a relief. He was often out in the evenings, although they'd shared a few rather tense meals together, neither of them completely comfortable co-existing in this weird limbo.

Rafael seemed as closed off as ever, his inscrutable manner giving nothing away, although towards her he was all solicitous concern, arranging for private museum tours, taxis and, recalling her shelf of cookbooks in her apartment, baking.

Rafael had insisted she order whatever ingredient or implement she wanted, and with a fully stocked, gourmet kitchen at her disposal Allegra was soon enjoying experimenting with new recipes. Her morning sickness was easing and she was actually starting to enjoy food again.

And then, of course, there was the almost-kiss they'd shared. She'd come back from the spa both buzzing and relaxed, and for a moment, with Rafael's warm gaze on her, it had felt so natural, so easy to fall into his arms. To tilt her head and wait for his kiss, that connection.

The shock she'd felt when his lips had barely brushed hers, the deep desire that had blazed a streak of lightning need straight through her, had thankfully made her take a step back. Getting involved with Rafael that way was far too dangerous. She was already well out of her comfort zone, simply being here with him, seeing him in passing in the hotel suite. She couldn't stand an even deeper intimacy, as much as her body craved it.

'A surprise,' she repeated now, her eyebrows raised. 'What kind of surprise?'

Rafael drew two tickets from the inside pocket of his suit jacket. 'Box seats to the New York Philharmonic playing Bach's cello suites at the Lincoln Center.'

'Oh!' She stared at him in unabashed delight—those were the kind of tickets that were usually well out of her price range, and she was touched that Rafael had thought to buy them. 'That's wonderful. When?'

'Tomorrow night.'

Allegra's smile faded as she admitted, 'But I don't have anything to wear...' Her maternity clothes consisted of a couple of pairs of loose cotton tops and shorts, and soon her burgeoning belly was going to require more.

'Problem solved. I've arranged for one of the top maternity designers to come here with a selection of evening gowns. You can take your pick.'

'Oh. Wow.' Not for the first time, Allegra was both touched and unsettled by Rafael's thoughtfulness and generosity. At times he seemed a million miles from the cold, hard stranger who had booted her out of his bed. But then at other times...

'Thank you,' she said now. 'For all of it. You're very kind.'

Rafael shrugged. 'I thought it might be nice to have a distraction. And when I saw it was a concert for the cello...'

'You're very thoughtful. And a distraction would be wonderful,' she said, smiling shyly. Rafael nodded and gave her the tiniest of smiles back.

The next morning a glamorous woman dressed all in black arrived with a couple of assistants carrying several plastic-swathed hangers each. While Allegra relaxed with herbal tea and croissants, the assistants laid out all the different evenings gowns—silks and satins, above-the-knee and full-length, in every colour of the rainbow. Allegra had never felt so spoilt for choice, or simply spoiled. She felt positively indulged as she stroked the dresses' soft fabrics and fingered exquisite lace.

'I don't know which to pick,' she admitted, and Amanda, the fashion designer, swooped in.

'With your colouring I'd advise the ice-blue. It will make your eyes pop and do wonderful things for your complexion.'

'Will it?' Allegra asked, bemused that a simple dress could do so much. Of course, the gown in question was far from simple, with its diamanté-encrusted halter-neck top and daring backless design. 'I don't know.' She nibbled her lip. 'It looks a bit...sexy.'

'Why can't a pregnant woman be sexy?' Amanda countered with a little smile. 'You're blooming and gorgeous. Let people know it.'

Allegra laughed. 'I haven't felt either all pregnancy. I've felt as worn and wrung-out as an old dishrag.'

'You don't look it now,' Amanda said firmly. 'And you won't look it in that dress.'

Persuaded, Allegra tried on the ice-blue gown and was amazed at how different she looked. The dress clung to her fuller breasts and slight swell of her bump before flaring out from her thighs to swirl about her feet. The backless design left the entire creamy expanse of her back bare, right to the swell of her bottom. She blushed to imagine Rafael seeing her in something like this. What if he thought she was trying to impress him? *Was* she? Suddenly her feelings were in a ferment.

'I don't know...' Already she was reaching for the diamanté ties, doubtful as to whether she could carry off something like this. Amanda stayed her hand.

'Trust me, no man could resist you in this dress, and certainly not the father of your child.' Her small, knowing smile made Allegra blush.

Did she want to be irresistible to Rafael? Sex was out of the question, and even kisses would complicate their already ambiguous relationship. The last thing she wanted was to be hurt...again. And yet...she'd felt worn out and ugly for months. The thought of looking good, *really* good, and having Rafael's eyes widen with surprise and then flare with desire...

She was tempted. She was seriously tempted.

That evening, as Allegra got ready for their night out, she started to doubt the wisdom of picking such a blatantly sexy dress. What if Rafael was put off by it? What if he thought she was throwing herself at him? What if she *was*?

And, really, the whole ensemble, from the diamond chandelier earrings Amanda had insisted she wear to match her father's sapphire necklace to the four-inch silver stiletto heels encasing her feet, felt a little much. Some people wore jeans to the Philharmonic. She didn't need to be quite so OTT.

And yet it was nice to feel beautiful. The silky material slithered over her skin and the diamonds winked at her ears. The heart-shaped sapphire nestled in the hollow of her throat, winking and glinting. Amanda had arranged for a make-up artist and hairstylist to finish her look, her hair held up by diamond-tipped pins, with a few curls cascading down to rest on her shoulders. She'd never, Allegra knew, looked so good.

Even so, she was still battling doubt as she left the safety of the bedroom. Outside the Manhattan skyline glittered, the entire city spread out before them. Rafael turned, his eyes narrowing as he took in the sight of her.

Allegra tried to smile but she felt so nervous and exposed that she wasn't sure she managed it. Rafael looked almost unbearably sexy in a midnight-black tuxedo, the snowy white shirt offsetting his olive skin, his hair brushed back from his forehead, his eyes glittering like polished bronze, everything about him radiating that restless energy that had drawn her to him nearly five months ago.

'Is it too much?' she asked with an uncertain laugh. 'The dress, I mean?' Her hands fluttered at her sides and she lifted her chin, trying for pride. She'd chosen this dress. She'd wear it no matter what Rafael thought... and yet she wished he'd smile or say something. He was practically *scowling*.

'You look...' Rafael stopped, his voice hoarse. Allegra waited, her heart fluttering like a trapped bird in her chest. 'Magnificent.'

A smile unfurled like a flower across her face, and

then she was beaming. She couldn't help it. A distant voice in her head was telling her not to be so obvious, not to let Rafael affect her. Why should she care what he thought? Why should she want to please or impress him? She shouldn't. She most certainly shouldn't.

And yet as Rafael grinned back that voice was silenced. Tonight she was a beautiful woman, and he was a handsome man, and they were going to hear the most wonderful music together. Allegra wanted to let herself enjoy it without trying to stay safe or sensible. She wanted to forget that she didn't trust him, wasn't even sure she liked him, and that the future was entirely uncertain. Tonight she wanted to leave all that behind and enter into the magic. And so she would.

Rafael had never seen Allegra look so beautiful. She was more than merely beautiful—she was incandescent, breathtaking. The ice-blue of her gown flowed like cool water over her perfect curves, the faint bump of her belly making a deep, protective urge rise within Rafael like a primal howl of possession. She was *his*. No matter what the results of the amniocentesis were, no matter what the future held. His to protect, to provide for, to possess. *His*.

Then he saw the sapphire pendant at her throat and it slammed into him yet again who her father was, who his was, and all the hard history that lay between them… dark, difficult history Allegra didn't know about, but which marked every moment of Rafael's life. History that reminded him that letting someone into your life, even just a little, was a terrifying responsibility as well as a formidable risk.

A faint frown marred Allegra's brow and Rafael banished the memory, the realisation, the fear. Those were not for tonight, when all he wanted to do was enjoy the evening...and Allegra. He stretched out his hand and she took it, slender fingers sliding between his. She squeezed his hand, and it felt like a promise, an agreement. Tonight was for them, for magic.

Wordlessly he led her downstairs to the waiting limo.

The evening felt expectant, although for what Rafael couldn't say. Despite their near-kiss over a week ago, he didn't actually expect anything physical to happen between them. He didn't want it, not if he forced himself to think rationally. If he let his libido lead the way, he'd peel that slippery dress from her creamy skin and have her in the back of this limo.

Yet far more unsettling than his desire for her was his desire to please her. He'd found himself arranging small treats and pleasures for her all week, simply to see her reaction. He told himself it was part of his duty, his responsibility to take care of her. The feeling inside him, as if his heart was a balloon floating higher and higher, was just a fringe benefit.

In any case, he wasn't going to start *feeling* things for Allegra Wells. After losing everyone he cared about, he was hardly going to let someone else get under his skin. Into his heart. No matter what happened with their child.

The Lincoln Center was glowing with lights as the limo pulled in front of the concert hall where the Philharmonic was playing. Rafael saw more than one man steal a speculative or even lascivious look at Allegra as she moved through the crowd, a stunning goddess with her red-gold curls tumbling artfully onto her bare, creamy shoulders.

She turned to glance back at him, grey eyes sparkling like silver stars. 'This is amazing, Rafael. Thank you.'

Every time she said his name he felt an arrow of satisfaction pierce him sweetly. He told himself it didn't matter.

They took their seats, Allegra excitedly perusing her programme like a child on her first trip to the circus.

Her enthusiasm made Rafael smile as he leaned forward to ask her, 'Haven't you been to concerts before?'

She wrinkled her nose. 'Oh, dear. Is my newbie status showing?'

'It's charming,' Rafael replied, 'but I would have thought, as a seasoned New Yorker, as well as a music-lover, this would be old hat to you.'

She shook her head, curls bouncing. 'No, not really. Not at all. I've been to concerts, but they've been free ones in churches and things like that. I've never heard the Philharmonic play live.'

'Never?' He was surprised.

She gave him a laughing look. 'Not everyone's a millionaire.'

Billionaire, actually, but he wasn't going to debate the point. He sat back in his seat, legs stretched out in front of him. 'Your father had plenty of money.' Not that he remotely wanted to talk about her father.

'My father did,' Allegra agreed quietly, some of the sparkle gone from her eyes, 'but we didn't. My mother didn't get anything from the divorce.'

Rafael frowned. 'She must have had some financial settlement.'

'Nope, not a penny.' Allegra shrugged. 'I don't know why.'

'She didn't sue for alimony?' It didn't make any sense.

'I was only twelve, I didn't ask. And I haven't asked since then because, to be honest, it just gets her going. She's always been bitter about it. All I know is my father managed to arrange things so we were left with nothing.'

Rafael supposed he shouldn't be shocked; he knew how heartless Mancini had been. But he was surprised, on Allegra's behalf. Why did she still care about him when he'd treated her so badly? 'So how did you survive?'

'My mother sold some jewellery to start, and she also had various boyfriends who helped.' Allegra made a face. 'That sounds awful, doesn't it? But my mother was used to living in a certain style, and it still makes her furious that she can't.'

'And what about you? Does it make you furious?'

Allegra shrugged, her gaze sliding away as her fingers touched the sapphire nestled at her throat as if it was a talisman. 'I don't care so much about things. And I've supported myself since I was eighteen.'

'Eighteen.' Another surprise. 'Did you go to university?' He realised that, despite having spent the last week and a half in her company, he didn't know that much about her or her life. Not that he'd actually spent much time with her. He'd intentionally stayed away, not wanting to complicate matters. Not wanting to get close. Now, however, he realised he wanted to know more about her... even if it unwise.

'No, I didn't.' Allegra pursed her lips, her gaze shadowed. 'I decided it wasn't for me.'

Rafael felt sure there was something she wasn't saying, but he had no idea what it was. 'What about you?' she asked. 'Did you go to university?'

'No, I went to work when I was sixteen.' He felt his chest go tight, his jaw hard, just because of the memories. His fist bunched on his thigh and he forced himself to relax. 'We needed the money.'

'Then we have something in common.' Allegra gazed at him in sorrowful compassion, and Rafael knew she was keeping herself from asking about their fathers on purpose. Neither of them wanted to prise open that Pandora's box right now.

'Yes, I suppose we do,' he said, and smiled. She smiled back and he felt the tension in him ease.

Then the lights dimmed, and they both settled back in their seats as the music began. Rafael wasn't that much of a connoisseur of music, but he loved seeing the look of rapt attention on Allegra's face. She was utterly arrested, a pearly sheen in her eyes, her hands clasped to her chest. He'd never seen someone look so thoroughly enthralled, and it touched a place deep inside him, a place he hadn't accessed in a long time. It made him yearn and mourn, just as he had when they'd listened to Shostakovich. Watching Allegra, he wanted to feel as much as she did. He wanted to let himself.

The concert came to an end, the last notes of music fading away into an aching stillness, and Allegra rose from her seat, dashing the tears from her face with an embarrassed laugh. 'Sorry, music always affects me like that.'

In the space of a second he was catapulted back to that night in Rome when she'd said the same thing. When he'd felt as powerfully as he did now, wanting this woman with an intensity that both thrilled and terrified him.

He'd wiped away her tears then, and she'd let him, and then they'd made love. It had been the most incredible sexual experience of his life, and he could remember every exquisite detail of that evening, of Allegra's response, of the way she'd felt under his hands and mouth.

He watched a rosy blush sweep across Allegra's skin and knew she remembered it all too. They stared at each other for a prolonged moment, eyes wide, hearts beating hard, the moment spinning on and growing in strength.

The desire was still there, and more powerful than ever. More dangerous too. Would they act on it as they had before?

Neither of them spoke in the limo on the way back to the hotel. Rafael couldn't keep from imagining himself reaching out one hand to tangle in Allegra's hair, drawing the diamond-tipped pins out one by one and then anchoring his lips to hers. He pictured sliding his hands under her gown, hauling her onto his lap so she was straddling him. With a suppressed groan he shifted on his seat, trying to ease the now persistent ache in his groin. He was torturing himself with these kinds of thoughts.

Allegra was quiet, her face pale, her expression thoughtful as she gazed out at the traffic streaming by in a bright blur of light. He thought she was feeling what he was, but even now he couldn't be sure. She'd drawn away from him once already. Even if she desired him, he knew that she didn't want to.

It was a pertinent reminder that, no matter what, sex would be complicated between them. Fraught and maybe emotional. And he didn't need or want to feel more for this woman than he already did. Then his leg brushed hers and an electric current zinged through his body. He couldn't help but feel.

They rode up the lift in silence, and then he was swiping the key card and they were in their suite, the rooms dim and hushed, as if everything was waiting for this moment.

It would be so easy to take her into his arms. To plunder her mouth. To peel the dress away from her body. All the things he'd been imagining, wanting...

Everything, anything, felt possible. He heard Allegra draw a shuddering breath and knew she felt it, just as he did. Just as much.

'Allegra…' His voice was an ache in the darkness, and he reached out one hand, fingertips brushing her shoulder. Her skin was as soft and silky as he remembered. She shuddered again, a ripple of longing that went through her whole body, and he knew, he *knew* she would yield. And he wanted her to, desperately. So desperately.

Then Allegra's phone pinged with an incoming message and in a split second the mood shattered. She slipped away from him, taking her phone out of her clutch and then frowning as she looked down at the screen. A new, different kind of expectation tightened Rafael's gut.

'What is it?'

She swallowed audibly. 'It's a voicemail from the doctor.'

'He called in the evening? While we were out?' His voice was sharp and tense.

'No, this afternoon. I missed the phone call and the voicemail just came in now.' She slid him a quick, worried glance. 'My phone's old. The messages don't always come in right away. I should have checked…' He heard the recrimination in her voice, along with the fear.

'What does he say?'

Allegra swiped a few buttons and then listened to the call. Rafael watched her face, noticing the way her lips pursed and her eyes clouded, pale red-gold brows drawing together.

'Allegra…?' he prompted when she ended the call. Everything in him felt coiled tight, ready to snap.

'No real news.' She let out a shuddering breath. 'Just that the results from the amnio are in and he wants to discuss them with us tomorrow morning at ten o'clock.'

'All right.' They stared at each other, the weight of the information pressing down making it hard to breathe. The insistent desire Rafael had been feeling had vanished, leaving only cold trepidation in its wake. 'At least then we'll know.' And then what? What would happen to their child, to *them*?

'Yes.' Allegra tossed her phone and clutch on a chair and wrapped her arms around herself. With her tumbled, fiery curls and her ice-blue gown she looked like a slender, burning flame, and Rafael wanted to wrap her in his arms, not out of desire now but to offer her comfort. The compulsion was so strong it felt like a pain, breaking open a scar deep inside him, a barely healed wound from when he hadn't been able to help. To save anyone.

'I should go to bed,' Allegra said softly. 'It's late.'

'Allegra…' He wanted to say something of what he felt, desperately needed to offer her some comfort—and yet what comfort could he give? Tomorrow would bring whatever news it did, and there was absolutely nothing he could do about it.

A shudder racked her body and it felt like a wound to his heart. He hated seeing her suffer, knowing she was afraid, just as he was. Then she lifted her head, regarding Rafael with tear-damp, pain-filled eyes. 'Goodnight, Rafael,' she whispered, and walked out of the room.

CHAPTER SEVEN

ALLEGRA COULDN'T GET to sleep. She lay on her bed, staring gritty-eyed at the ceiling, everything leaden inside her. It had been such a magical evening, going to the concert with Rafael. All night excitement had been fizzing like champagne through her blood, bubbles popping inside her head. The music. The mood. The moment when Rafael had looked so sexy and intent…and then the realisation, cold and hard, that this was all ephemeral and tomorrow reality would return with a dreadful thud.

She pressed one hand against the soft swell of her bump. *Oh, baby. Stay strong. Be safe.* Yet she knew it wasn't in her baby's power to be healthy. It wasn't in hers either.

Around two in the morning she finally rose from bed, knowing sleep wasn't going to come. She was planning to make herself a cup of herbal tea and then sit out on the terrace, watching the city settle down to sleep, but she stopped on the threshold of her bedroom door, for Rafael was sitting in the living room, dressed only in a pair of loose, drawstring pyjama bottoms, a tumbler of whisky cradled in his hands.

He looked up at her quick intake of breath, giving her a smile that was both sad and wry. 'You couldn't sleep either?'

'No.' She shook her head. 'I was going to make some tea. I'd ask if you wanted some, but I see you've got something stronger.'

'I need it.' Rafael's voice was hoarse, and pain flashed like lightning across his face.

It surprised her, because although Rafael was doing what he saw as his duty by her, Allegra had assumed, rightly or wrongly, that he didn't really want this child. He'd said as much back in Rome, and he'd refused to talk about the *what if?* scenarios until they knew more. She realised she'd assumed he hadn't really cared, not the way she did, and yet now, looking at the set of his jaw, the slump of his shoulders, she wondered if he shared her fear, her agony. If he longed for their child to live and be strong and healthy as much as she did.

In the kitchen she brewed a cup of chamomile tea and then brought it to the living room, curling up on the opposite side of the sofa from Rafael. He looked unbelievably sexy, stubble shadowing his strong jaw and the perfect, sculpted muscles of his chest on glorious display, a sprinkling of dark hair forming a V down to the low waistband of his pyjamas.

But Allegra wasn't thinking about how handsome he looked. She was realising how sad he seemed, and it made her ache.

'I've felt the baby kick,' she said quietly. Rafael turned to look at her, his mouth dropping open in surprise.

'You have?'

'Just in the last few days. I didn't know what it was at first. It feels like bubbles popping inside me. Little flutters.' She took a deep breath. 'But they've become a bit stronger in the last day or two, almost…almost as if the baby knows. As if he or she is telling me…' She broke off, her chest tight with the force of her feeling, the strength of her emotion.

Rafael leaned closer, his expression intent. 'Telling you what?'

'Telling me that he—or she—wants to live.' She scanned his face, looking for clues to how he felt, what this could mean—for both of them. 'That this baby wants to live, no matter what.'

His expression was both intense and unreadable as he stared at her. 'What exactly do you mean?' he asked in a low voice.

Allegra let out a shuddering breath. 'I mean that no matter what the results are tomorrow, even if we know this baby's life is going to be short and hard, I want to keep him. I want to know this baby, I want to hold him, I want to love him. Or her.' She let out a trembling laugh and brushed at her eyes. 'I seem to be rather emotional lately. It must be the pregnancy hormones.'

'I feel emotional,' Rafael said, his voice hoarse. 'This is hard, Allegra, and it might only get harder, for both of us...if you mean what you say.'

'I do, and I know.' But did she, really? The words were easy to say—sort of—but the actions that might test them in later months would be far harder. *Was* she strong enough? There was only one way to find out. 'What about you?' she asked quietly. 'Do you...do you feel differently? Because I won't hold you to anything, Rafael. You didn't ask for this. You didn't even want a baby...'

'I didn't want you to be pregnant,' Rafael corrected. 'And I imagine you didn't either. We were strangers, Allegra.'

'We still are,' she said softly.

'But this child is real and growing and I want it as much as you do.' He took a deep breath, meeting her gaze directly. 'Do you honestly think I would leave you to cope with this alone?' She was silent for a second, and he drew back, deep hurt scoring his face. 'Is that the kind of man you think I am?'

'I don't know what kind of man you are,' Allegra confessed. She knew she was hurting him with her words but she had to be honest for both of their sakes. 'You left me once before, Rafael. You pushed me away, dismissed me out of hand. I'm scared...' *That you'll do it again.* She couldn't say the words, admit so much.

Rafael's mouth twisted. 'We had a one-night stand, Allegra. I admit my exit lines could have used some work, but you can't judge me by a single conversation.'

'Or lack of conversation.'

'If you are going to carry this baby to term,' Rafael stated, 'then I am staying with you. No matter what.' His tone was flat and determined, unyielding as stone. Allegra didn't know whether she should be heartened or alarmed by the strength of his conviction. Was this simply a matter of responsibility and duty, or the heart?

And what was this going to mean for both of them? For their future? She'd intended on going this alone, because that's how she did everything. She didn't want to invite someone into her life, someone who had the power to hurt her, who had already hurt her once before. And yet she couldn't kick Rafael out either. He was this baby's father. He had a say, a right, just as much as she did.

Allegra stared down into the fragrant depths of her tea, her emotions a tangled web of confusion, of opposite desires to stay strong, safe and alone—and to run straight into Rafael's arms. To seek a comfort there that she didn't even know if he could give.

Inside her their baby kicked, and with a tremulous

laugh of surprise she pressed one hand against her belly.
Rafael drew a quick breath. 'Did you feel…?'

'Yes.' She looked up, a new shyness coming over her.
'Do you want to…?'

'Yes.' His tone was heartfelt, emboldening her to reach
over and take his hand, pressing it over her bump, their
fingers interlaced. His palm was warm and strong and
she liked the feel of it there. 'Wait,' she whispered, and
they both remained still, holding their breaths, *hoping*…

And then it happened. A light kick, right into his palm.
Rafael laughed, a sound of total joy. Allegra smiled, feel-
ing tearful again. Everything about this was so *much*…
Rafael, their baby, *them*.

Rafael kept his palm on her belly and their baby kicked
again, stronger this time. He looked up at her, his smile
now one of fierce pride. 'He's a fighter.'

'It might be a girl.'

'Then she is. I don't care either way, boy or girl. I just
want the baby to be…' He trailed off, a confused torment
creasing his features, and Allegra squeezed his hand.

'Healthy,' she finished softly. 'I know.' Wasn't that
what all parents said? *I just want the baby to be healthy.*
The words sounded trite when you felt assured of the outcome. In this moment of terrible uncertainty they were
painfully earnest, and yet it was the not knowing that
drew them together, that made Allegra feel as connected
to this man, or even more so than she had during that
terrible, wonderful night in Rome.

They remained on the sofa, hands interlaced on Allegra's bump, as minutes ticked past. Their baby kicked a
few more times and then settled down, and after a while
Allegra fell into a doze, only to wake when she felt Rafael scoop her into his arms.

'Sorry,' she mumbled. 'I didn't realise I'd fallen asleep…'

'You're tired.' His voice was gruff, a thrum in his chest as Allegra pressed her cheek against the steady and comforting thud of his heart. She felt so treasured and small in his arms, in a way she hadn't felt in years, if ever.

Rafael carried her into her bedroom, depositing her gently down on the bed. Allegra looked up at him, still half-asleep, missing the feel of his strength and warmth all around her, barely aware of what she was doing and yet knowing she needed him now more than ever. And maybe, just maybe, he needed her as well.

'Rafael,' she whispered. 'Stay with me. Please.'

A look of surprise flashed across his face and then Rafael slid into bed next to her. He pulled her into his arms, drawing her back against the solid wall of his chest so their bodies were like spoons in a drawer, fitting perfectly. With a sigh of contentment Allegra settled against him and drifted back to sleep. She didn't know what tomorrow would bring, but tonight she felt safe and happy and hopeful.

Rafael sat in the doctor's office, Allegra looking pale and tired next to him, both of them incredibly tense. Now was the moment of reckoning.

Last night had been one of the most intimate and intense experiences of his life—first feeling their baby kick and then holding Allegra in his arms all night long. The ache of desire at feeling her body so tantalisingly close to his had been overwhelmed by the fierce need to comfort and protect her. She needed him, and he wanted to be needed. Wanted to provide for her what only he could.

But this moment, he acknowledged with painful certainty, was outside his control.

The doctor came into the room, her bland expression giving nothing away. 'Miss Wells, Mr Vitali.' She smiled at them both before sitting down at her desk. 'I have the results of the amniocentesis, and there is good news and bad news.'

Allegra's hand snaked out, searching for his. Her skin was icy cold as Rafael clasped her fingers between his own, trying to imbue her with his warmth, his strength. 'Yes?' he asked, wanting to hear the worst and get it over with. Once they knew they could figure out how to move forward. What to do, even how to feel.

'Your baby does have a heart defect,' the doctor explained gently, her smile seeming kind. 'But it is not as serious as it first looked. We'll need to do some tests, but I believe the condition is operable and there is every chance your child will live a full and healthy life.'

Rafael stared at her in shock, barely taking in the words. He'd been bracing himself for the absolute worst news and now he felt blindsided by this wonderful surprise. Next to him Allegra let out a small, soft sob and brushed at her eyes, clearly overcome.

'What kind of heart defect?' Rafael asked. 'What kind of operation?'

Rafael and Allegra both listened as the doctor explained the situation. Allegra would need to have some tests done in the next week, but if all went well then her pregnancy could continue normally to term. She would be scheduled for a C-section to avoid the traumatic effects of labour and delivery on their baby, and then a few days after birth an operation would be performed to fix their baby's heart. The recovery would take several months but then their baby would, God willing, be healthy and whole.

'Besides the heart defect,' the doctor continued, smiling, 'your baby is perfectly healthy, and everything looks normal. Do you want to know the sex?'

Rafael glanced at Allegra, saw a shy hope lighting her features, making her look radiant. She nodded.

'It's a boy,' the doctor said. 'A healthy baby boy.'

A boy. Rafael's mind was reeling with the news.

Instead of the baby most likely doomed to die that they'd both been expecting, the awful outcome that Rafael had been bracing himself for, they could hope to have a healthy child. A baby boy whose condition could be healed, who was going to live and grow and know him. A *son*. He was filled with an incredible, overwhelming joy, almost too great to contain, and then realisation slammed through him, leaving him breathless.

This changed everything.

Allegra walked from the doctor's office in a daze of hope and incredulous relief.

'I can hardly believe it,' she said as they climbed into Rafael's waiting limo. 'Our baby is going to be *healthy...*' Again she was both laughing and blinking back tears, overcome by it all as she had been in the doctor's office.

It had been such an intense twenty-four hours, with the concert last night and then learning they would discover the amnio results today. And then those wonderful moments when Rafael had put his hand on her belly and felt their baby kick. Everything in Allegra had ached at the look on his face, and when he'd held her for the rest of the night she'd felt so safe and secure. She'd never wanted that feeling to end.

Since then she hadn't let herself think about any of it or what it meant, because the doctor's appointment had taken precedence. Now she glanced at Rafael and saw the frown that settled between his brows, noted the hard line of his mouth, and unease rippled through her.

She'd opened a part of herself to Rafael last night, had let him in, let him affect her, let him *matter*. All the things she'd promised herself she wouldn't do. It had felt so right, but now she feared she was going to pay the price for her trust and need. And so she scrambled to erect some barrier, find that much-needed distance. And yet how could she, when their baby was healthy? When every emotion she had was scraped raw?

'Rafael?' she asked cautiously. 'You...you are pleased, aren't you? About the baby?'

'Yes, of course. Pleased and relieved.' He paused, swinging his hard, amber gaze towards her and pinning her with it. 'But you realise, Allegra, how this changes things.'

It was more statement than question, and it made her blood freeze. The look on his face was hard and unrelenting. He looked as he had when he'd ordered her out of his hotel room, and she felt the way she had then, uncertain, vulnerable, confused. 'What...what do you mean?'

Rafael's gaze remained unyielding as he answered. 'Before this news the situation appeared temporary. It had an ending point, sadly.' His gaze flicked away from her to the window where traffic streamed by in a blur of colour and sound. His jaw hardened, his profile reminding her of a Roman statue, perfect and cold. 'Now the situation is ongoing and permanent, and that changes things between us, naturally.'

Allegra swallowed hard. Yes, she understood that. Now they would have a healthy child together, a child who would, God willing, live to adulthood. A child they would somehow have to raise together, because it was obvious Rafael wanted to be involved. And Allegra wanted him to be involved. She knew the searing loss of a father. She wouldn't subject her child, her son, to it, if she didn't have to.

And yet…how was this going to work? What was Rafael saying?

And what if he walked away from her and her son, just as he had before?

'Of course,' she said stiffly, 'we'll have to come to some arrangement.' Surely they could, although right now she could not imagine what kind of custody arrangement would actually work. She was in New York and Rafael lived in Sicily. They could hardly pass a baby between continents like some parcel, and she wouldn't want that anyway. Anything else, however, was unthinkable.

'Arrangement?' Rafael swung back to subject her to a cold stare. 'I am not interested in *arrangements.*'

His eyes resembled shards of glittering amber as he kept his gaze on hers. 'I… I don't understand,' Allegra said, although she was afraid she was beginning to. Here was the ruthless man who got what he wanted, who took over a failing company, who kicked a woman to the door. Here was the father of her child.

'I'm not going to be fobbed off with some custody agreement,' Rafael stated. 'I would not wish such a thing on any child, and certainly not mine. I'm not going to be satisfied with weekends or holidays, an evening here or there.'

'I think you're being extreme,' Allegra protested. 'Plenty of children have divorced parents and they grow up well adjusted and happy. We can find a way forward that suits us both…'

Rafael arched an eyebrow. 'Was that your experience?'

She bit her lip, caught by the admission. 'That was different.'

'How?'

'Because we wouldn't be getting divorced. Our child wouldn't know one thing and then have to learn another. There wouldn't be a sense of loss, because it would be how it always was, our son's normal.'

His lip curled. 'My lack of involvement would be normal?'

Allegra looked away. 'Why does it have to be your lack of involvement? Surely we can work something out.'

'How? You live in New York and I live in Sicily. A baby's place is with his mother, I recognise that. So what happens? I get our son when he's two or three? Four? Five?'

'No.' The word was torn from her, trembling and indignant.

Rafael gave a nod of cold satisfaction.

'You wouldn't want that either. You don't want to share our child, and neither do I.'

Realisation crept coldly through her, a seeping mist obscuring rational thought. She understood what he was saying, and yet… 'Then what are you suggesting?' she forced herself to ask.

'I want to be involved in our son's life, Allegra,' Rafael stated. 'Completely involved. You cannot deny me that. You will not.'

Allegra stiffened, hearing an implied threat in the words. 'And if I do?' she dared to ask.

'Do not even think of it.' Rafael's voice was a low thrum of grim intent. 'You do not want to experience the full force of my anger and power.'

'Wow.' She let out a shaky laugh, amazed and horrified at how they'd got to this place. Last night he'd held her so tenderly, she'd been halfway to caring about him. Trusting him. Today he was the merciless stranger who had kicked her out of his bed. There was a lesson to be learned here. She'd thought she'd learned it already, but it seemed she hadn't taken it in, not fully. 'You're bringing out the big guns, aren't you? And I thought I'd felt your *anger and power* once before.'

'Not even close,' Rafael answered coolly. 'Trust me.'

Never. The limo had pulled up to the hotel. Allegra gazed at the elegant building overlooking Central Park, and felt as if she were about to enter a prison, one to which Rafael held the keys. She couldn't go inside, not willingly.

'We can discuss the necessary arrangements,' she told Rafael in as dignified a tone as she could manage. 'Of course I want to accommodate you as best as I can. I want our baby to have an involved father as much as you do. A completely involved father. We can work something out, Rafael. I know we can.' A bellboy came forward to open her door. 'But I also want to return to my life,' Allegra said as firmly as she could. 'My apartment, my job. Now that we know things are okay there's no need for me to stay here.' And she could use some distance from Rafael and his autocratic commands, his unsettling presence. She moved to get out of the car and Rafael stayed her with one powerful hand encircling her wrist, the proprietary touch shocking her.

'You don't understand, Allegra,' he informed her in a lethal tone. 'You're not going back to your apartment or your job or even your life. As soon as possible you're coming to Sicily to live with me...as my wife.'

CHAPTER EIGHT

ALLEGRA STOOD IN the centre of their hotel suite, her whole body trembling. *As his wife?* The words he'd spoken moments ago in the limo reverberated through her. With no choice but to get out of the car and deal with this head on, she'd stalked up to their suite and then turned to face him, every atom of her being radiating outrage. Shock. *Fear.* Rafael, on the other hand, looked cool, calm and completely in control.

It was impossible. *He* was impossible. How could he issue such an outrageous command without batting an eyelid? Even now Rafael was shrugging off his jacket and heading for his laptop, as if it were a normal business day. As if their whole world hadn't shifted on its axis.

'Rafael.' Her voice trembled along with her body. 'You can... *I* can't...'

He didn't even look at her as he answered, 'You can and you will.'

'Just like that?' Her voice rang out. 'You want me to leave everything and marry you? That was your *proposal*?'

Irritation flickered across his face as he turned to her. 'Don't be melodramatic.'

'Don't be *insane*,' she snapped, well and truly angry now. Anger felt better and stronger than the fear that surged right beneath it. Because even now she was afraid Rafael would win. He was richer, stronger, more powerful. And so far he'd achieved everything he'd wanted. Nothing stood in his way, and yet Allegra clung to her ground. She had to, because the alternative… 'I'm not marrying you.'

Rafael regarded her levelly for a long, tense moment. Then he shrugged and went to sit down on one of the plush sofas. 'Fine, let's talk about it. What are your alternatives, do you suppose?'

On shaky legs Allegra moved over to the sofa opposite him and sat down. 'To stay in New York and live my life.'

He arched an eyebrow. 'Working in a café for most likely little over minimum wage, and living in a studio flat in an insalubrious neighbourhood?'

'It is not insalubrious,' Allegra snapped. 'For heaven's sake, talk about being melodramatic.'

'I am not having my child raised in a near-slum.'

All right, maybe her street wasn't the fanciest in Manhattan, but it was hardly a slum. 'You're being ridiculous.' In all sorts of ways.

'And I think you're being ridiculous,' Rafael countered coolly. 'What about your job, Allegra? How do you propose to continue working with a newborn baby, one that will have particular and crucial needs at the start, and maybe after that as well?'

'I'll take time off, naturally.' She lifted her chin, determined to remain strong. Defiant. She'd meet every challenge he threw at her.

'And do you get maternity benefits with your job? Proper healthcare coverage?' He sat back against the sofa cushions, the twist of his mouth belying the dangerous emotion she saw sparking in his eyes. Despite his level tone, his reasonable demeanour, she had the feeling that he was angry. Very angry.

He was also right. Her job provided healthcare, but it wasn't the best coverage and she wouldn't get much time off after their son was born, plus she couldn't afford the kind of childcare she knew she'd need. All things she hadn't yet had time to think about, much less sort out. She looked away, silently fuming, saying nothing.

'You clearly haven't thought this through, Allegra. Unless you intended to rely on your mother's scant generosity?'

'No.' The word was squeezed out of her throat. She hadn't thought through all these details, at least not enough, mainly because she'd just been trying to struggle through her pregnancy.

And now, thanks to Rafael, she had to think about them immediately. Allegra took a deep breath, trying to steady her jangling nerves. 'I'll admit there are some difficulties,' she said as calmly as she could. 'But that doesn't mean the only other option is living in Sicily as... as your wife.' A blush swept over her entire body at that thought. *Marriage.* In all the possible scenarios she'd envisioned, that one had never even crossed her mind. Yet Rafael now seemed to think it was a foregone conclusion.

'Then name one option that would be acceptable to us both,' Rafael stated.

'I can't,' Allegra retorted, 'because you're being so unreasonable.'

'*I'm* being unreasonable?' Rafael leaned forward, his tawny eyes glittering. 'What if you are the one who is being unreasonable, Allegra? You seem to think it is your right not to have to make any changes or adjustments to your life circumstances for the sake of your child. Is that reasonable?'

'I didn't say—'

'You want to stay in your tiny apartment, walking up and down six flights every day?'

'Plenty of women—'

'Where would you even keep a stroller? Or a cot? That place is minuscule. There isn't room for a baby, and you know it.'

Her lips trembled and she pressed them together. 'I could get a bigger apartment, then.'

'Can you afford it? Or are you expecting me to pay for it—to fund your freewheeling lifestyle while I take whatever scraps I can? What do you think is going to happen?' Rafael demanded, his voice like the lash of a whip. 'I fly over to New York for occasional visits? I don't get to know my son until he's school age? Impossible. I refuse.' He glared at her, his whole body radiating both determination and rage. 'That is not how I intend to be a father.'

Allegra glared back at him, caught between misery and fury. All right, yes, she saw there were problems with her unthought-out plan. Of course she did. But she hated being railroaded into a huge decision, with Rafael expecting her to acquiesce instantly. *Marriage*...she'd never considered it. Never wanted to be that close to a person, that vulnerable—and why would Rafael?

But of course that wasn't the kind of marriage he was talking about. Even so Allegra couldn't countenance it. Couldn't let Rafael have that much power over her. Because, she knew, it would be power. Already he affected her too much. Made her want too much.

'You're not being fair,' she said quietly. 'I'm only four and a half months pregnant, and I've barely been able to keep a mouthful of food down until this last week. I'm sorry if I haven't worked out every last detail of my plan yet. And anyway,' she added, her voice rising, 'I didn't even know you were going to be involved at all until a few weeks ago.'

'Which begs the question why didn't you tell me,' Rafael returned, clearly unmoved by her words. 'I asked you specifically to tell me if you were pregnant. I told you I wanted to be involved in my child's life. And you chose to ignore me.'

'You also booted me out of your bed,' Allegra returned. 'Is that the kind of man I want in my child's life?'

'Now you have no choice.' Angry colour appeared in slashes on Rafael's high cheekbones. 'And no matter how I treated you on that night, Allegra, you had no right to deny me my child. There is a world of difference between ending a one-night stand rather abruptly and refusing me access to my son.' His jaw was bunched, his mouth a hard line. 'Even you should acknowledge that.'

Allegra stared at him, chilled to the very bone by the dangerous glitter in his eyes, the harsh, implacable certainty in the set of his features. The man who had treated her so tenderly, who had cradled her last night was gone. Vanished, as if he'd never been, and perhaps he hadn't. Perhaps that Rafael had been no more than an expedient mirage. She knew what it was like for people to change. To show their true colours.

'And yet you want me to marry you,' she stated shakily. She felt sick and dizzy, her skin clammy and cold. All the relief at their son's good health had drained away, leaving a dark-edged terror in its wake. The future loomed, menacing and more and more certain. Rafael would not be dissuaded.

'Marrying me is the sensible option,' Rafael answered. 'The only option. I want to be involved in my son's life, Allegra. Completely involved. He's my heir—'

'Your *heir*? It's not as if you're some king,' she interjected. Rafael's gaze narrowed.

'I am CEO of a multi-billion-euro empire. I intend to pass that on to my son, raise him to follow me into what would become a family business. He is my heir, and he is going to be raised in Sicily by both his parents.'

Staring at him, seeing how utterly implacable he looked, Allegra realised how trapped she really was. Rafael had all the power, all the money. If he wanted to—and at this point she wouldn't put it past him—he could use the force of his influence to take complete custody of their child. She could resist all she wanted or dared, but she'd still lose in the end. Maybe even lose her own child.

She pressed her hands to her temples, a crashing headache beginning its aching pulse. 'I need to think,' she muttered. 'And I need to lie down. I'm tired, and not everything is certain, Rafael. The doctor said I'd have to undergo some tests later this week.'

She rose from the sofa, stumbling slightly, and in one quick, fluid movement, Rafael rose to grasp her arm and steady her.

'Rest is a good idea,' he murmured. 'I'll make you some herbal tea to help settle you. Chamomile is what you like, isn't it?'

She glanced up at him in confused disbelief. Who was this man? 'Don't do this,' she whispered. 'Don't be horrible one moment and kind the next. I don't understand it. I can't take it.' *Not again.* With what felt like superhuman effort she shook off his arm and walked alone to her bedroom, closing the door behind her.

Rafael stared at the closed door and swore under his breath. That had not gone as he'd hoped or wanted. Yet what else could he have done? He wasn't going to negotiate, not about something as important as this. He certainly wasn't going to settle for some custody arrangement. And trying to woo Allegra with false words and oozing sentiment had felt like a waste of time and, well, *wrong*.

When he'd learned their child would be healthy all his protective instincts had risen to a clamour inside him. He needed Allegra and their son with him. He needed to be in control. He needed to make sure nothing went wrong. Things would be different this time. He would be different. But first he had to get her to agree.

Impatient and yet resolute, Rafael stalked to the kitchen and switched on the electric kettle. He'd make her the promised cup of tea, at least, to show he wasn't a complete boor.

But when he tapped on Allegra's door and the quietly opened it, he found she was already fast asleep, her Titian hair spread across the pillow, one hand tucked under her cheek, golden-red lashes feathering her pale cheeks. She looks so vulnerable and lovely it made something in him twist and tighten, and he promised right then that he'd make it up to her, to *them*. They could make this work. They would.

Several hours later Allegra opened the door to her bedroom and appeared, yawning and sleepy. Rafael turned from where he'd been trying to do work on his laptop and mostly failing.

Now he tried for a neutral expression as he watched her stretch, the thin T-shirt pulling across her breasts. 'Did you sleep well?'

'Yes, surprisingly. I didn't realise quite how tired I was.' She went to the kitchen and returned with a glass of water, her hair tumbling about her face in corkscrew curls, her face now set in serious lines. 'You asked me what my life would look like if I stayed in New York,' she said as she curled up on the sofa opposite him and took a sip of water. 'So now I want to ask you the same thing. What would my—our—life look like if I come with you to Sicily?'

Relief and hope expanded in his chest, made his head light. *She was going to agree.* He kept his expression steady, his voice mild as he answered. 'We would live on my estate in the mountains above Palermo. It is spacious and comfortable, with every luxury to hand. A large garden, a pool, every amusement for a growing little boy.'

Allegra nodded slowly, looking less impressed than Rafael had expected or wanted her to be. 'And what about schooling?' she asked. 'When the time comes? And friends?'

'Of course those as well,' he answered. 'There are plenty of good schools in the area and if we could not find one that was to our satisfaction, I would be willing to consider other options.'

She arched a delicate eyebrow. 'Such as?'

Rafael shrugged, his mind racing. He felt that Allegra was looking for something from him and he didn't know what it was. 'We could relocate, within reason. To Rome or Milan, perhaps. I have offices in both cities.'

'Or New York?'

He hesitated, sensing a test. 'The majority of my business is in Europe,' he said finally. 'A relocation to New York is not out of the question for some time in the future, but not now.'

She nodded, her lips pursed, and Rafael waited. 'What about me?' she finally asked. 'What would my life look like in Sicily, Rafael?'

He hesitated, wanting to say the right thing—but what

was it? 'You will need for nothing,' he said with a shrug. 'Clothes, jewels, whatever you like. They're yours.' Her mouth twisted and he realised he'd said the wrong thing. Allegra had not been particularly impressed or even interested in clothes or jewels, as far as he could see. *So what did she want?*

The women he'd dallied with in the past had been only interested in material possessions, a diamond bangle, a funded shopping spree in a designer boutique, but he knew Allegra was different. 'And of course you can make the house your own. Decorate it as you wish. Garden...' What else might she want to do? 'Music,' Rafael said at last. 'You can have your own music room. Play as much as you want. Host concerts, even.' He was practically babbling, and was irritated with himself for being so pathetically *eager*. She regarded him quietly, saying nothing, offering no encouragement.

'Why don't you tell me what you want?' Rafael bit out. 'Instead of looking disappointed because I can't read your mind?'

She flinched at his tone and he silently cursed himself. What did she want from him? He could give her everything. Everything but love. Rafael stiffened, appalled at the thought. Was that what Allegra was holding out for? Some ridiculous, romantic fairy-tale? Surely not.

'I don't know what I want, Rafael,' Allegra said quietly. 'This is all so unexpected. I haven't had time to process any of it properly. I'm still reeling from the news about the amnio results.' She let out a weary sigh. 'I know you don't want to, but please give me a little time to catch up.'

'Fine.' He bit the word out, still tense. 'But I do need to return to Palermo as soon as possible.'

'Then maybe you should return and I'll come later,'

Allegra countered. 'Why must we rush things? We could at least get to know one another first...'

'With me in Palermo and you here? No.' Rafael shook his head, resolute. She would just find an excuse to stay in New York. The thought, stupidly, hurt. 'I want you where I can see you, Allegra. Where I can protect you and take care of you and our son.' His voice thickened, much to his shame. 'That is important to me.'

Her expression softened as her silvery gaze swept over him. 'You have far more of a protective streak than I ever realised.'

'I do. I don't want to let you or our child down.'

'And you're afraid you will?'

'No.' He rose from his desk, determined to end this conversation. It had all got stupidly emotional, and he hated that. He didn't do emotion. It was for the weak. He'd learned that to his eternal cost with his father, when he'd goaded him with his childish complaints. When he hadn't been able to stop what had happened next. *Enough.* There was nothing to be gained by thinking of that now. 'I will never let that happen, Allegra. At least in that, you can trust me.'

Allegra sat down across from her mother, her expression resigned and set.

'You're *what*?' Jennifer Wells screeched.

'I'm going to Sicily,' Allegra answered. 'With the father of my child.'

'But you don't even know him.'

'I know he'll take care of me and our son.' That was at least one aspect of Rafael's character that she was sure of. It had been three days since Rafael had issued his ultimatum, and Allegra had spent those days thinking long and hard about her future. *Their* future. When the further tests with a neonatal cardiologist had revealed the extent of their son's heart defect, which wasn't as simple as they'd hoped but still within the realm of good news, her choice felt even more limited.

She couldn't do this alone. She'd lived most of her life in determined independence, chosen isolation, *loneliness*, but she couldn't do this by herself, and she didn't even want to. But even more importantly she didn't want Rafael or her son to miss out. She'd been denied her father's presence in her life from the time she was twelve. Could she wilfully deny her son the chance to know his father, and Rafael the chance to know his son?

It would be the height of selfish cruelty to choose self-preservation over her family. Because it *was* a matter of self-preservation. Rafael held a power over her, one she didn't fully understand. She was attracted to him physically, of course, but she'd felt stirrings of something even deeper. When he held her...when he'd felt the baby kick... if she let herself, she could start to care for him, and that would be a disaster. Because there was every chance Rafael would walk away from her as her father had. But he wouldn't, she prayed, walk away from their son.

And so she'd told Rafael she would go to Sicily, but she wouldn't marry him—not yet, anyway. They needed to get to know one another before she made actual vows, agreed to that level of commitment. To her surprise, Rafael had acquiesced. Tersely, but still. She'd been half expecting him to frog-march her down the aisle.

Then yesterday she'd gone to her apartment and packed up what she'd wanted to take, which had been surprisingly little. Looking around the tiny space, she wondered at how she had ever thought she could have managed there with a baby. And yet how she was going to manage in this strange new life in Sicily? So much was unknown.

'I can't believe you're doing this, Allegra.' Jennifer's voice rang out in censure. 'This stranger…running away with him? Have you thought this through at all?'

'Yes, and it makes sense,' Allegra answered. 'Considering the alternatives.' She felt weary right down to her toes, and tomorrow evening they were leaving for Palermo. She'd already handed in her notice for her job, said goodbye to Anton, who had been her friend and boss for nearly ten years. He'd kissed her on both cheeks with tears in his eyes.

'Is Vitali being…difficult?' Jennifer asked after a moment. She looked on edge.

'Pragmatic,' Allegra said, even as she wondered why she was being loyal to Rafael. Perhaps because, in his own hard way, he was being loyal to her. And whether she liked it or not, they were a family now. 'As am I.'

'You remember what I told you about his father?' Jennifer said, and now she sounded diffident.

'He did business with my father and it didn't work out, you said.' But it was more than that. Blood on his hands. What had happened? How much did it matter? She couldn't ask Rafael now; things between them were tense enough.

'Yes, and your father didn't trust him.' Jennifer expelled a breath. 'I don't know the details, of course, but there has to be a reason for that. I got the sense that there might have been something…' She paused, pursing her lips. 'Criminal involved.'

'Criminal?' Allegra stared at her, appalled by this new revelation. 'What do you mean exactly?'

Jennifer shrugged, her gaze siding away. 'I don't really know, but soon after they did business Vitali went broke. He lost everything, and narrowly avoided prison. That's…that's all I know. Perhaps it's better buried in the past.'

It was more than Allegra had ever known, and underscored how little she knew Rafael or his history. How little he'd told her. She'd have to ask sometime, and while she didn't look forward to that conversation, she needed to know what she was getting into. What their child was getting into. She needed to trust Rafael…yet how could she, when she didn't know him? When she didn't like to trust anyone?

'That might be so,' Allegra told her mother, 'but Rafael has his own business and I really don't think it involves any criminal activities.' At least she hoped not.

'But you can't be sure.'

'No.' She couldn't, Allegra knew with a pang of true fear, be sure about anything.

CHAPTER NINE

ALLEGRA GAZED OUT the window of the passenger jet at the hard blue sky, not a cloud in sight, and tried to bolster her courage as well as calm her seething nerves. They were due to land in Palermo in less than an hour, and after a sleepless night in the first-class cabin she felt exhausted and overwhelmed.

'Do you need anything?' Rafael asked as he looked up from his tablet where he'd been scanning the morning news. 'Herbal tea? A hot compress?'

'I'm fine.' He'd been all solicitousness for the flight, but it was a formal, distant concern that set Allegra's nerves on edge. She felt like his patient, or perhaps his possession. Maybe both. And she was conscious, more than ever, of how much she'd left behind. Her job. Her life. Freedom and independence.

'How far is your villa from the airport?' she asked, and Rafael put his tablet aside.

'About an hour. A limo will pick us up.'

She nodded, gripping the armrests, wishing she felt more at ease. More confident that she was doing the right thing. She'd be living in the lap of luxury after all. Rafael had promised her just about anything she wanted. And yet…he could be such a hard man. Even when he was being kind there was a distance to him, a remoteness that made her uneasy. And she knew no one in Sicily other than him. Their baby wasn't due for over four months. What would she do all day? Could she be happy?

'Please don't worry,' Rafael murmured, resting one long, lean hand on top of hers. 'It will all be fine.'

Allegra nodded again. Rafael squeezed her hand, and the simple touch had the power to affect her, reminded her that despite all their differences they did have chemistry. Chemistry Rafael no doubt expected them to act on…but when? She couldn't even begin to think about *that*. Sex seemed like an impossibility, although the doctor had, with a smile and a wink, given them the all-clear.

'There's no reason,' he'd said, looking at them both, 'why you can't have a normal pregnancy from now until your delivery…and a normal sex life.'

Allegra had blushed and stared down at her lap. Rafael had said nothing. She had no idea what to expect from him, from anything, and it made her feel uncertain. Vulnerable. Which was a feeling she hated.

'Please prepare for landing.'

Allegra put her seat up as the steward went through the cabin and the plane began its descent. Below she could see Sicily spread out in a living map: dusty, rocky hills and towns with red-roofed buildings that looked as if they were clinging to the mountainside. It was unfamiliar and yet it struck a chord, reminded her suddenly and sweetly of her childhood in Italy. A soft sigh escaped her and Rafael gave her a sharp look.

'Are you all right?'

'Yes, I was just thinking about when I lived here. That is, in Italy.' She gave him a small smile. 'It feels like a lifetime ago.'

'You lived in Rome?'

'I lived in Rome during the school year,' she answered,

'and spent summers at our estate in Abruzzi. I loved it there.' The land had been harsh and rugged and unrelentingly beautiful, snow-capped mountains piercing a brilliantly blue sky. She'd loved the quiet, the sense of solitude and stillness and peace. It had spoken to her shy, solitary spirit.

'You missed it?' Rafael asked after a moment.

'Yes, especially because my first year in New York was so awful.' She shook her head at the memory, her mouth twisting.

'What was so awful about it?'

'Everything. My English was terrible, and the school was big and rough—I felt lost. I was teased too, but it helped when I kept myself to myself. Then I was just invisible.'

Rafael frowned. 'That doesn't sound like much fun.'

'No, but I've always liked my own company.' She paused. 'It's easier, isn't it, not to depend on anyone? Not to care.'

Rafael didn't respond, merely frowned and looked out the window. Allegra wondered what he was thinking and decided not to ask. Better not to share any more feelings than she already had.

The plane touched down with a bump, and for the next hour they were kept busy clearing Immigration and collecting their luggage.

By the time Allegra slid into the limo she felt exhausted, and although she'd meant to take in the scenery on the drive to Rafael's estate, she ended up falling asleep as the limo climbed narrow, twisting roads, making the steep ascent into the mountains.

When Rafael nudged her gently awake she discovered she was lying on the seat, her head in his lap, her cheek resting on his powerful thigh. Rafael's hand rested lightly on her hair. It felt wonderful and alarming at the same time, and she scrambled up to a sitting position as quickly as she could. 'Sorry,' she mumbled as she pushed tangled hair away from her eyes. She felt thick-headed, her body clock completely out of synch, and she had a feeling she looked like a disaster. 'I didn't even realise I'd fallen asleep.'

'You were tired. We're here now, and after the doctor checks you out you can have a proper rest.'

Allegra looked at him in confusion. 'The doctor?'

'I've put a doctor on retainer for the duration of your pregnancy. He's living in one of the estate's cottages. It seemed sensible, considering the remoteness of our location. Of course, Palermo's emergency medical facilities are less than an hour away, and I have a helicopter on the estate.'

She stared at him in surprise. 'But the doctor in New York said my pregnancy was normal, Rafael. This seems a bit excessive.' Which was massive understatement. She didn't need a doctor on call, surely. And yet Rafael looked obdurate.

Rafael flicked a glance at her. 'There is no harm in taking precautions. You want what's best for our son, don't you?'

Once again he was playing that trump card. Allegra decided not to argue. She was too tired, and she supposed there was no reason to mind having a doctor around.

Rafael opened the door to the limo and ushered her out, one hand resting on her elbow as he guided her towards the villa. Allegra paused on the portico, breathing in the warm, fir-scented air as she took in the curving drive that snaked through dense trees, the rolling, rocky hills visible beyond.

She turned to the house, a sprawling and imposing

villa of weathered stone, its double doors of ancient, scarred wood now flung open. A smiling, red-cheeked woman, her greying hair piled on top of her head in a round bun, gave them both a wide smile while next to her a tall, lanky man nodded and bowed.

'This is Maria and Salvatore, my housekeeper and groundsman,' Rafael explained to Allegra. He spoke in Italian, which he hadn't done with her all the time they'd been in New York, and even though it was her native language, after so many years in America it took Allegra a moment to make the adjustment.

Maria came forward, exclaiming about her bump, and then kissed her soundly on both cheeks. Salvatore bowed again. The exchange heartened Allegra, and made her feel a little less alone.

'Now is not the time for a tour,' Rafael said. 'Since you are tired. I'll show you your room and then summon the doctor.'

'I'm fine...' Allegra protested, because now that she was here she wanted to explore. From the soaring foyer she could see a comfortable-looking lounge with huge sofas in cream linen and French doors overlooking a terrace. On the other side she saw the cheerful yellow walls of a large kitchen, and another set of French doors leading to what looked like a large vegetable garden. All of it made her want to see and know more. She felt the stirrings of excitement, which was a welcome change from all the apprehension.

'You need to rest,' Rafael said, clearly brooking no argument, and with his hand on her elbow he guided her up the curving stairs to a large bedroom. While he went to fetch the doctor, Allegra explored the room—it was every bit as luxurious as the one she'd enjoyed in the hotel back in New York.

There was a huge king-sized bed on its own dais, a massive fireplace that would make the room cosy in winter, and wide windows whose shutters were open to the tumbling gardens below. She rested her elbows on the stone sill as she took in the infinity pool sparkling under the sunlight, and the tangle of bougainvillea and hibiscus that covered the steep hillsides. The air was warm and dusty, scented with rosemary and pine. She felt as if she'd stumbled into paradise.

'The doctor will examine you now.'

Allegra turned to see a stern-looking, white-haired man with an old-fashioned black bag standing in the doorway, and her heart sank. Determined to be as accommodating as possible, she submitted to a battery of routine checks while Rafael watched.

'I really am fine,' she said as the doctor tucked his stethoscope away. 'Everything's fine.'

'Well?' Rafael turned to the doctor for his verdict, and Allegra gritted her teeth. Since when had she become incapable of speaking for herself?

'She's a little dehydrated,' the man said. 'And she needs some rest.'

Rafael nodded. 'Thank you.' He turned to Allegra once the man had thankfully left. 'I'll have Maria bring up some water. You should drink at least two glasses.'

Allegra folded her arms. 'I'm capable of making my own decisions, Rafael.'

His mouth thinned as he arched one dark eyebrow. 'You are fighting me on this small matter?'

'Yes, because you're treating me like an idiot. I don't need to be fussed over by a doctor every moment.'

'I simply wanted you to be checked out after our travel. What is the problem?'

She stared at him, frustrated, because he made it

sound so reasonable. It was his attitude she didn't like, the high-handed way he dealt with everything. With her.

'The problem is you're being aggravatingly bossy.'

'I am caring for our child.'

'Which is very important to you, I know. I get that, trust me. But you can't…you can't be in control of everything.'

Rafael bit back a response and then looked away. 'This is important to me, Allegra,' he said after a moment. 'I don't want to fail in my duty as a father. Please…indulge me.'

A bleak look had come into his eyes, and it made her wonder what hidden hurts Rafael was keeping from her. Or was she just being fanciful, and he was simply an arrogant, autocratic, domineering man? From the obdurate look on his face Allegra knew she'd get nowhere pressing the point now.

'Fine, I'll indulge you,' she said wearily. 'At least in this.'

Several hours later she woke from a deep sleep and stretched languorously. Long, golden rays of late afternoon sunshine slid across the floor. She'd been asleep for hours, so clearly she'd needed the rest.

Allegra got out of bed and went to explore the huge en suite bathroom, enjoying the enormous marble walk-in shower. Dressed in a strappy sundress, her hair damp and curling about her shoulders, she headed downstairs in search of Rafael.

She didn't find him, but she did see Maria in the kitchen, and the housekeeper bustled around to have Allegra sit at the round kitchen table and then plied her with iced tea and fig cookies.

'Something smells delicious,' Allegra said.

'Ah, it is a welcome feast for Signor Vitali and his lovely lady,' Maria said with a smile. 'It has been a long time since I have been able to cook so much!'

'Is it?' Allegra nibbled a cookie, wondering how much she could press the housekeeper for information. 'Has Rafael not had…guests here before?'

Maria gave her a shrewdly knowing look. 'Signor Vitali has never had anyone here before. He has always been a very solitary man. Salvatore and I have served him for more than ten years.' She smiled fondly. 'He worked so hard, he had little time for anything else.' She nodded meaningfully towards Allegra's bump. 'Perhaps now that will change.'

'Perhaps.' Although Rafael had certainly immersed himself in work since he'd come back into her life. Despite his insistence that he wanted to be an involved father, Allegra wondered if he simply wanted to be in control.

Replete with cookies and tea, she wandered out of the kitchen to explore the villa—and find Rafael. She discovered the lounge she'd seen earlier and a media room with a huge flat-screen TV and a state-of-the-art sound system. A dining room with a table that easily seated twelve was empty, as was a smaller room with a cosy table for four. She slipped through the French windows onto the terrace that overlooked the infinity pool, breathing in the scents of bougainvillea and rosemary. The sun was setting, painting the sky with livid violet streaks, and she heard birds chirping in the tall, stately firs that surrounded the villa on most sides, the mountains towering above them.

But where was Rafael—and why did she want to find him so badly? Perhaps he intended for them to live separate lives here in Sicily, a prospect that filled her with a treacherous disappointment. She wanted to know what their future was going to look like...and, she realised, she wanted to know Rafael. It had been all right to maintain a holding pattern while they'd waited for the amnio results, but now they were meant to have some kind of life together. Rafael was insisting they marry, and while that prospect still filled her with fear, it also made her want to get to know the man she might be spending the rest of her life with, at least a little. So where was he?

Maria had started to serve dinner in the smaller dining room, several fragrant dishes that made Allegra's mouth water. Then she noticed the place setting for one.

'Is Rafael not eating?' she asked, hating how small her voice sounded.

Maria made a face. 'Signor Vitali said he needed to work tonight.'

So the feast was for her alone. Allegra sat at the table and nibbled course after delicious course, feeling sorry both for herself and for Maria, who had gone to so much effort for her employer. Why had Rafael refused to come down for dinner? Surely his work couldn't be that important. Was he avoiding her on purpose, setting the pattern for their married lives?

Loneliness swamped her at the thought. Already she was losing that sense of independence she'd maintained for so long. She wanted Rafael with her, needed his presence in a way that made her feel unsettled. She wasn't used to needing people. Depending on them. Perhaps it was better this way...except it didn't *feel* better.

At the end of the meal she took her decaf coffee out onto the terrace, curling up on a lounger as she watched the stars appear in the sky, like diamond pinpricks in a bolt of black velvet. He was avoiding her, she acknowledged with leaden certainty. He had to be. To absent himself all afternoon and then through the evening… He was telling her how he intended things to be, and Allegra didn't like it. If he was going to leave her alone, she might as well have stayed in New York.

She liked it even less when she woke up the next morning to an empty-feeling house. Maria was in town at the market and Salvatore was outside, working in the garden. Rafael was nowhere to be found.

She decided to go for a walk—only to be told, regretfully, by Salvatore that Signor Vitali had forbidden her from leaving the formal gardens, as the mountainside was steep and dangerous. Allegra looked at the high stone walls, the whole world shimmering out of reach, and realised she was truly trapped.

She stalked inside the villa, fury rising in her like a tidal wave. So she'd been brought to this beautiful estate to be kept as a prisoner. She didn't know what hurt most—Rafael's controlling attitude or his deliberate absence. She stewed for most of the morning while Rafael kept his distance, and then finally she'd had enough. She'd find him, and, by heaven, she'd tell him what was on her mind.

'Where is Signor Vitali?' she asked Salvatore, who looked shocked by her strident tone.

'He is working…'

'Where?'

'In his study, but he does not wish to be disturbed.'

'Perhaps he needs to be disturbed,' Allegra answered. 'Could you please tell me where his study is?'

'I don't think—'

'Tell her, Salvatore,' Maria said quietly, coming into the room behind Allegra. 'She is carrying his child. She deserves to talk to him. And Signor Vitali…he needs company too.'

With a shrug of his thin shoulders Salvatore pointed upstairs. 'The top floor. A room on its own.'

Allegra stalked upstairs, her anger giving her a boldness she hadn't known she'd possessed. A narrow, twisting staircase at the end of the corridor led to a single room on the villa's top floor, its heavy, oak door shut fast. She knocked on the door hard enough to bruise her knuckles.

After a pause she heard Rafael's gruff voice. 'Salvatore?'

'No. Allegra.' She turned the handle, gratified when it opened, and walked into the room.

Rafael's study was spacious, with wide windows on three sides offering stunning views of the mountains. A huge mahogany desk took up the centre of the room, and Rafael sat at it, his eyes narrowed, his mouth compressed.

Allegra planted her hands on her hips as she faced him. 'If I'd known you were going to imprison me here, I wouldn't have agreed to come.'

'Imprison?' Rafael arched one eyebrow. 'I'd hardly call this a prison.'

'I'm serious, Rafael. Since we've arrived you haven't shown your face once—'

'I have much work to catch up on.'

Allegra hesitated for a second, wondering if she was overreacting. Wondering why she wanted his company so much, why she felt so *hurt*. Then she took a deep breath and ploughed on. 'So why can't I even take a walk?'

Rafael's nostrils flared. 'These are simply measures to ensure your safety.'

'I'm not made of glass,' Allegra burst out. 'I'm not going to *break*.'

For a second Rafael's face contorted, and then he looked away. 'You don't know that,' he said quietly.

'Anything could happen, Allegra.' His voice went hoarse. 'Anything.'

Allegra stared at him in confusion, her heart twisting at the look of bleak despair on his face. 'Rafael…' she asked softly. 'What is it that you're so afraid of?'

'I'm not…' he let out a shuddering breath, wiping his hand over his face '…losing you. Losing our child.' He turned away, dropping his hand, the set of his shoulders resolute once more, that brief glimpse of raw vulnerability gone. 'We came close to losing this baby, Allegra, or at least thinking we were going to lose it. Him. I don't ever want to feel that again.'

She stared at him, wishing she understood more. Wishing she knew how to reach him. 'You can't control everything, you know,' she said quietly. 'You can't prevent accidents from happening, or just life. I need to live, Rafael—'

'You are living,' he cut her off dismissively. 'Enjoy the villa and all it has to offer. Lounge by the pool.'

'I don't want to spend every day *lounging*.'

His expression closed up. 'I really do not know what you are complaining about.' And with that he angled his body away from her, pulling a sheaf of papers towards him. So she was being dismissed, like some unruly servant. He wouldn't even look at her any more. This was how Rafael dealt with people. He wasn't overprotective, he was compulsively controlling. And it hurt to realise she was just a cog to him, something to move and manipulate accordingly. Stupidly it hurt, because she hadn't wanted to let herself care. Yet here she was, caring. Hurting.

She stood there for a moment, watching him work, seeing the way he'd completely blanked her out. It was as if she no longer existed. His gaze didn't flick to her once.

She felt the fury rise again, but with it something far worse. Despair. She couldn't fight this. Arguing with Rafael, just trying to have a reasonable discussion with him, was like battering her head—her heart—against a brick wall. Because now that she was here, now that she'd come into his life and brought him into hers, she wanted more than this. And she had no idea how to get it.

Without a word she turned on a heel and left his study, slamming the door behind her. The loud thwack as it crashed against the doorframe was satisfying even though she knew the gesture was pointless and childish.

She walked downstairs, fury still pounding through her, along with the despair. She wrenched open the French doors to the terraced gardens, causing Maria to bustle in from the kitchen, her expression alarmed.

'*Signorina*—'

'I'm just going for a walk.'

Maria frowned. 'Signor Vitali—'

'I don't care about Signor Vitali.' Allegra cut her off, wishing it were true, and she walked out of the house.

CHAPTER TEN

FROM THE WINDOW of his study Rafael watched Allegra stride through the gardens, her entire body rigid with affront. He fought the urge to run after her, insist she return to the villa. Keep her safe. He couldn't control everything, but he'd damned well try. The alternative was unthinkable.

His gaze narrowed as he saw Allegra make her way through the garden to the latticed gate in the high stone wall. He'd forbidden her from leaving the formal gardens, didn't want her to navigate the steep and rugged mountain terrain surrounding the estate. Cursing under his breath, he saw Allegra wrench open the gate and then stride through the forest, swallowed up by the trees and the dark.

He waited an hour before he went out looking for her, just to show how reasonable he could be. A tense, endless hour when his mind raced with worst-case scenarios and he did his best to stave off the panic he felt skirting the edges of his mind, blurring rational thought. Memories danced like shadows in his mind, of his mother, his sister, his father. Their faces, their words, closed doors, shattered hope.

With a muttered curse Rafael flung open the door to his study. He yanked on a pair of hiking boots and headed outside, the air hot and dusty and dry, the sun beating hard on his head. She shouldn't have been out in this heat. He didn't even know if she'd put on sunscreen. And what about a sunhat and proper walking shoes? What if she'd tripped or fallen? His stomach clenched hard and he tasted the metallic tang of fear as he followed her path through the gate, picking up her trail through the broken ferns and grasses along the mountainside. With each step his anxiety grew and his fists clenched at his sides. He felt deep in his gut that something was wrong, that something had happened on his watch. *Again.*

For a second he could see his mother's empty eyes, his sister's wasting body. His *father*…

Dammit, he couldn't keep opening the door to all that remembered pain. What was it about Allegra that brought it to the surface? He needed to lock that door tightly, so tightly, before the memories surged around him and he drowned.

He'd been walking for about fifteen minutes, calling Allegra's name, his voice starting to grow hoarse with panic, when he saw her. She was crumpled up at the bottom of a large boulder, one leg awkwardly angled beneath her, her head lolling back. Her eyes were closed but they fluttered open as Rafael ran towards her, cradling her head in his lap as he said her name over and over again, tears of grief and self-recrimination springing to his eyes.

Her eyes fluttered open and fastened on his. 'Next you're going to handcuff me to my bed,' she murmured. Her face was pale and waxy with a pearly sheen of perspiration but her tiny smile made Rafael's heart turn over. 'Just spare me the I-told-you-so, please.'

'Are you hurt?' Rafael demanded, his hands shaking as he ran them lightly over his body, looking for bruises or broken bones.

'My ankle,' Allegra answered on a shuddery sigh. 'It's not broken. At least, I don't think it is. But I tripped on that stupid rock and went sprawling.' She pressed one hand to her bump, her voice trembling and her face crumpling as she added, 'I think the baby's all right.'

Rafael's insides felt icy as he bundled her in his arms. She felt light and precious, a treasure he wanted to cling to for ever. *The mother of his child.* 'Let's get you home,' he said, and, scooping her up, he started back towards the villa.

The trip back to the villa was a blur; Allegra curled into Rafael, resting her cheek against the hard wall of his chest, taking comfort from the steady thud of his heart. The last hour she'd spent trapped in the woods, the trees dark and menacing all around her, her ankle throbbing, had been truly awful. She'd been afraid for their baby, afraid for herself, and she'd cringed to think of what Rafael's reaction would be. Yet it wasn't her freedom or lack of it she was worried about, she realised—it was Rafael. Something was driving him to act in so domineering a manner, something dark and desperate, and she feared in her impetuous folly she'd made it much worse.

To his credit, Rafael didn't lambast her then. He treated her tenderly, carrying her through the woods, and then calling to Maria to bring cool cloths and compresses and tea as soon as they arrived back at the villa.

The doctor came and looked her over, pronouncing the baby well, the steady thud of his heart on the Doppler wonderfully reassuring. Her ankle was sprained and the doctor bound it up and then gave her strict instructions not to put any weight on it for at least a week, which would undoubtedly please Rafael.

After the doctor had gone Allegra fell asleep, grateful

to retreat into oblivion for a little while. When she woke up Rafael was sitting by her bed, his head in his hands, his long fingers driven through his dark, unruly hair. The sight of him looking so exhausted, so unguarded made her heart squeeze in a way she wasn't used to. A shaft of yearning pierced her sweetly, although what she wanted she couldn't say. To comfort him, perhaps—but would Rafael even accept her comfort? What was between them now? What *could* be between them?

'Hey.' Her voice sounded scratchy and she licked her dry lips. She must have become a bit dehydrated out in the hot sun.

Rafael looked up, his bloodshot eyes widening at the sight of her. 'You're awake. Here.' He reached for a pitcher of iced water and poured her a glass, holding it to her lips.

'Thank you,' Allegra murmured, and drank. She scooted up in bed, pushing her tangled hair out of her face as she noted the haggard lines of his face, the bleak set of his mouth. 'I'm okay, Rafael,' she said quietly, and to her shock his face crumpled almost as if he might weep. 'Rafael...' she whispered, reaching out one hand, and even more to her shock he took it, his fingers interlacing with hers.

'But you could have so easily not been.' His voice was a ragged whisper as he clung to her hand.

'I behaved foolishly,' she said. 'I'm so sorry.'

Rafael shook his head, the emotion reined in now but still visible in the lines of strain on his face. 'I am the foolish one. You wouldn't have gone off like that if I hadn't driven you to it. If I had been more reasonable.'

'You shouldn't blame yourself...'

'But who else am I to blame?' Rafael returned starkly. 'I am responsible for you, Allegra, and for our child, whether you like it or not. I cannot shirk or ignore that responsibility. I did once before and I will never do so again.'

'When…?' The word was a breath of sound. She realised she wanted, needed to know what drove Rafael. What made him the man he was. She wanted to know so she could understand him, but also so she could comfort him. So she could help. The strength of her own feeling surprised her, but she didn't back away from it. This was too important. *They* were too important. At least she hoped they were.

'My mother,' he said after a moment. 'My sister, in a different way.' He pressed his lips together. 'I lost them both, when it was my sacred responsibility to care for them. I failed them, failed my entire family.' He looked away, blinking fast. 'If I seem too controlling, it's because I can't contemplate the alternative.'

Allegra felt tears sting her eyes at the pain she saw in Rafael's face, heard in his voice. She didn't understand everything but she knew he was hurting. 'I'm sorry,' she whispered, reaching up to brush her hand against his cheek. 'For all you've suffered.'

Rafael closed his eyes, leaning into her brief caress, and then he pulled away. Opened his eyes and didn't look at her. 'In any case,' he said, a stiffness entering his voice, 'I will relax some of the measures I put in place.'

'That still makes me sound like a prisoner.'

'You're not a prisoner.' Now his tone was touched with impatience. Their moment of bonding was well and truly over. 'You're living in the very lap of luxury. I hardly see any reason to complain.'

Allegra tried to tamp down on the frustration she felt rising again. 'Don't *do* that,' she pleaded.

Rafael looked startled. 'Do what?'

'*Change*. One minute you're all solicitude and tenderness and the next you're acting as if you can't spare two minutes to talk to me. It makes my head spin. And it reminds me—' She broke off, biting her lip, and Rafael's eyes narrowed.

'Reminds you of what?'

'My father,' she said after a moment. She leaned her head back against the pillow and closed her eyes. If he'd shared something of his past heartache, then so could she. 'My father because…because after he divorced my mother I never saw him again, as you know.' Her throat thickened and she swallowed hard. 'And before the divorce…he loved me. He acted like he loved me, anyway. He called me his little flower. He tickled me, he tossed me in his arms, he gave me presents and tucked me in at night…' She gave a trembling laugh and brushed at her eyes. 'To have his love, to feel so important, and then to be cut off completely…it was awful, Rafael. The worst thing that ever happened to me.'

'The loss of a father is a very hard thing,' Rafael said after a moment.

'How did you lose yours?'

'He… An accident.' He looked away. 'A terrible accident.'

Allegra wanted to ask more, ask about the history between their fathers, but in that moment she didn't dare.

'Your father left you that necklace in his will,' Rafael said after a moment. 'He must have cared, at least a little.'

'Yes, but I don't even know why he gave it to me.' Allegra smiled sadly. 'There was a note…he asked for my forgiveness, saying he'd cared more for his reputation than for me. But I don't understand that at all.'

'Who can say?' Rafael answered. His voice was

guarded, his jaw bunched. Allegra wondered what he knew and wasn't telling. Or was she being paranoid?

'I keep telling myself he really did love me. He must have loved me, but something happened…something that made him act the way he did, cutting us off. But I can't imagine what it was.'

'And I remind you of him.' Rafael sounded cautious and diffident, and realisation scorched through Allegra.

'Only because you keep changing,' she said quickly. 'It's not as if— You don't need to worry, Rafael, I'm not going to fall in love with you or something like that.' She felt herself blush hotly as Rafael jerked back, almost as if she'd slapped him. Clearly the prospect of her falling in love with him was horrifying. Allegra rushed to fill the ensuing taut silence. 'I'm not looking for love,' she hastened to explain. 'I'm not interested… I mean, any… relationship between us wouldn't have to have that. I wouldn't want it to have that. I want us to get along, of course, but… I'm not looking for love, not from you, not from anyone.'

She finally, thankfully, managed to make herself stop speaking. Rafael had sat back in his seat, his expression terrifyingly inscrutable.

'Why not?'

'Because love hurts,' Allegra said simply. 'Doesn't it? To let someone matter that much to you. To let them hold your heart…because hearts can break.' She let out a shaky laugh. 'I sound fanciful, I know, but the truth is I don't believe that old adage about it being better to have loved and lost than never to have loved at all.'

'So you've never been in love? Romantic love?'

'No.' She drew a quick breath. 'Surely you realised that, considering…considering I was a virgin.'

'There's a difference between sex and love.'

'Yes.' Although for her she wasn't sure there was. Her one experience with sex had been far too intense and emotional.

Rafael fastened his resolute gaze on her. 'In any case, we will have a proper marriage.'

A flush swept over her at the thought of what a proper marriage would look like. Feel like. Could she keep herself from loving Rafael, loving the tender, caring man he could be when he wanted to, if she gave her body to him again and again? 'I haven't actually agreed to marry you,' Allegra reminded him.

'Yes, but it's only a matter of time. For our son's sake, Allegra.'

He was so aggravatingly arrogant. Allegra closed her eyes, overwhelmed by it all. 'I asked you to give me time to get to know you,' she said. 'And for you to get to know me. But we can hardly do that when you hide away in your study all the time.'

'I'm not *hiding*,' Rafael snapped.

Allegra opened her eyes. 'Rafael, as soon as you'd brought me here you disappeared. I don't care how busy you are, that's just rude. And cowardly.' His eyes flashed fire and Allegra wondered if she'd gone too far. 'Let's just spend some time together.' Surely there was no real danger in that.

Rafael was starting to look seriously uncomfortable. 'What exactly are you suggesting?'

'An hour or two every day,' Allegra returned. That felt safe. 'Meals spent together. Evenings...some conversation. We had a little bit of that in New York, didn't we?' A very little. 'But you need to stop avoiding me.'

'I'm not avoiding you. I am a busy man.'

'Well?' Allegra pressed, not to be dissuaded. As nervous as she was, she knew she wanted this. 'That's all I want, I promise.'

He leaned forward, his eyes glittering. 'That's all? Are you sure?'

Allegra's breath caught because she recognised the look of ferocious intent in his eyes. Of course she did. She also recognised the hot swirl of longing she felt unfurl inside herself, a languorous warmth that was lazy and urgent at the same time, wrapping her up and making her want. *Him*.

She licked her lips, her throat and mouth turning dry. 'I'm… I'm not ready for that yet, Rafael.'

'The doctor said it was safe.' His gaze roved over her, assessing, probing, demanding.

'That's not what I meant.'

'I know.' He leaned back in his seat, the heat in his eyes turning to a slow simmer. 'But think about it, Allegra. It could be very enjoyable for us both. It *will* be.'

'I… I know.' She had no doubts on that score. How could she, when the memory of their one night together still had the power to scorch her? And yet…the memory of the awful afterwards had the power to scorch as well, in an entirely different and unwelcome way. Things had changed between them since then, but Allegra still didn't trust Rafael—not in that kind of situation anyway. And, she acknowledged, she didn't trust herself.

Rafael's mouth curled in a lazy smile as his gaze raked over her once more. 'Let me know when you are ready. It will be soon, I think.'

She looked away, unable to stand the heat of his gaze. 'I will,' she answered shakily, and then wondered just what she had promised.

CHAPTER ELEVEN

RAFAEL STARED UNSEEINGLY at the screen of his laptop as Allegra's words ricocheted around his head, as they had been for the last three days, since she'd said them. *You don't need to worry, Rafael, I'm not going to fall in love with you.*

Words that should have filled him with sweet relief—and they did. Of course they did. But they'd surprised him too, because he hadn't expected such cold, clear pragmatism from her. Allegra was sensitive, emotional, romantic—whether she realised it or not. And yet she'd stated very clearly, with great certainty, that she would never love him. That she *couldn't.* What the hell did that mean anyway? Was that because of her—or him? Because he wasn't worth loving?

It was a question he hated asking, much less answering. It was a foolish, romantic question not worthy of his time. He should be thankful that his wife-to-be was so sensible. So like-minded. Moodily Rafael shut his laptop and gazed out the window of his study instead.

It was a day of lemon sunshine and blue skies, and he was tired of spending it inside. Tired of mulling over everything Allegra had said.

In the three days since their conversation he'd made an effort to spend more time with her. It wasn't always easy, and their conversations were sometimes stilted and jarring, but he had to admit to himself he actually liked being with her. Enjoyed hearing her clear, crystalline laugh, seeing her infectious smile. She'd had much sorrow in her life, but she was made for joy. Joy he wanted to give her, whether it was a gift or a touch...or more. But did she want to receive it? Receive him?

Why was he thinking like this?

The sound of crunching gravel had Rafael rising from his seat. A delivery van was approaching the front of the villa, and he knew what it held. A smile touching his lips, he headed downstairs.

'What is all this?' Allegra asked as the delivery man began bringing in boxes.

'Your things,' Rafael said simply. 'I had everything shipped from your apartment.'

'You did?' She looked flummoxed.

'Did you think we would leave it behind?'

'I don't know. I suppose I did. I knew you were terminating the lease on my apartment.'

'But I thought you'd want your things around you.'

'I do. Of course I do.' She shook her head slowly, smiling at him with a pure radiance that felt like a spotlight on his soul. 'You can be so thoughtful sometimes, Rafael. Thank you.'

'Only sometimes?' he teased. Their banter felt new and fragile, but kind of wonderful too. Allegra's smile deepened.

'Definitely only sometimes,' she teased back. 'But your rate is improving.'

He laughed, and with all of the boxes brought in Allegra began to open them, exclaiming over everything like a child at Christmas. 'My books...my cheese plant!' She looked up at him with laughing eyes, making something in Rafael's chest expand. 'I've had this thing for years, you know.'

'It looks like it needs a little water,' Rafael said, and took it from her. 'It's been in a box for days.'

'Everything came so quickly.'

'Expedited shipping.'

'That must have cost a fortune!' she exclaimed, and he shrugged.

'I can afford it.'

He took the cheese plant to the kitchen and when he went back to the lounge, Allegra was sitting on the sofa, her cello case in front of her, a thoughtful look on her face. She almost seemed sad.

Rafael propped his shoulder against the doorframe, watching the way her face softened as she opened the case and stroked the buttery-soft wood of the instrument.

'How long have you had that cello?' he asked quietly, and she looked up, blushing at being caught out.

'Since I was nine. My father bought it for me.'

'Did he?' Rafael said quietly.

'Yes…he loved to hear me play.' She let out a soft sigh. 'Even when I wasn't very good, sawing away at it. He'd always clap and say "Bravo."'

'Perhaps you'll play for me sometime,' Rafael said, and saw her eyes flare in surprise. Then she shook her head with sorrowful but firm decision.

'No, I can't.'

Rafael tried to hide the expression of affront and even hurt he feared was on his face. 'I see,' he said, unable to keep his tone from turning cool.

'I haven't played in almost ten years,' Allegra explained. She rested her hand on the cello. 'Not since I was eighteen.'

Intrigued, Rafael straightened. 'Why not?'

She shook her head, her eyes downcast, and he didn't think she was going to answer. 'Because when I was eighteen I auditioned for Juilliard,' she finally admitted on a little sigh. 'Or I should say I tried to audition.' She kept looking downwards as she continued, 'I'd sent an audition tape, and I was invited in for a live audition, which felt huge. It was my dream, to play music. I've taken lessons since I was a small child.' She bit her lip, and Rafael held his breath, waiting.

'It was a big step for me, to send the tape in. I know it might not seem like much, but I was so shy, especially after…well, after my parents' divorce. Music was a personal, even sacred thing to me. It still is.'

'So what happened?' Rafael asked. He felt anxious on her behalf, wanting to hear a happy ending to the story, even though he knew there wasn't one.

'I froze.' She let out a shaky laugh. 'I got there and I couldn't play. It was as if I was paralysed. I literally couldn't do it. The examiners were kind at first, but then they were impatient, and then I was dismissed. And that was that.'

'But why haven't you played since then?'

'I just couldn't. It's as if… I don't know. I just lost it. The desire as well as the ability. If I played now you'd probably cover your ears.'

'I wouldn't,' Rafael said, meaning it utterly.

Allegra stroked the cello again and then closed the case. 'Anyway, silly as it seems, I still like having my cello, so thank you.'

'You're welcome.' Rafael was silent, trying to sift through his emotions—the sorrow he felt for the shy, vulnerable young woman Allegra had been. Empathy, because her father had turned on her just as he'd turned on Rafael's father, his father, and just as with his father, his family, that rejection had had consequences. Protectiveness, too—because he never wanted her to feel that kind of anxiety again. And lastly, stronger than either of those two, desire, different and deeper than any he'd known before. He wanted her to play again. He wanted her to play for him.

But what on earth made him think he deserved such a privilege?

The next week passed in a lovely haze. Allegra felt herself relaxing into everything, especially the time she spent with Rafael. While he still spent a fair amount of time in his study, or going to Palermo on business, he made an effort to make time for her.

One afternoon when Allegra's ankle was feeling better they walked into the nearby hill town to shop at the market. Allegra enjoyed the simple pleasure of inspecting fat, red tomatoes and juicy melons while Rafael followed behind her, a wicker basket looped over one arm.

The ancient, cobbled streets were charming, and the view of the twisted olive trees and dusty valleys below truly magnificent.

Rafael suggested they have a picnic, and so they bought salami and bread, cheese and olives and grapes, and took it all to a stretch of grass overlooking the valley.

'This is wonderful,' Allegra said as she stretched out on the grass and Rafael fed her bread and cheese.

'As long as you don't get sunburned.'

'Don't fuss,' she chided gently, because she knew Rafael was trying, and it tugged at his heart. At moments like this, with everything relaxed between them and the sun shining benevolently above, she felt a marriage between them could work. Maybe it could even be wonderful.

Was she falling in love with him?

The question reverberated through her. When Rafael was kind and gentle and tender, she felt it would be easy to fall in love with him. Easy and amazing. But what if he changed? He had before, and she didn't know whether she could trust him yet. More and more she realised there were reasons Rafael acted the way he did—reasons he hadn't shared with her yet. Although they'd talked about many innocuous things, he hadn't spoken again of his family, and she hadn't asked.

Now, lying on the grass, feeling sleepy and secure, she decided to broach the topic. 'Rafael…what happened between your father and mine?'

Rafael tensed, his gaze turning guarded. 'Why are you asking that now?'

'Because it seems important. And because the more time we spend with each other, the more I want to have no secrets, no hidden things.'

Rafael was silent for a long moment. 'And if you don't like the answer?' he finally said, his voice toneless, his gaze shuttered.

Allegra felt the first stirrings of unease. 'Why wouldn't I?'

'Because your father treated mine unfairly. Very unfairly.'

Already she was prickling. 'How do you know—?'

'I know.' His gaze was opaque as he turned to look at her. 'But even that much is hard for you to hear.'

'Yes…but that doesn't mean I don't want to hear it.' Allegra took a deep breath. 'I know he wasn't perfect. Of course I know that. Look how he treated me.'

'Yet you're still protective of him.'

'I never wanted to hate him.' She looked away. 'Maybe because I always hoped he'd come back. But he won't now, and I want you to tell me. Please, Rafael.' She held her breath, waiting, and finally Rafael spoke.

'Twenty years ago our fathers were in business together.'

'The mobile technology you mentioned.'

'Yes. Your father provided the science, my father provided the parts. They were partners, friends.' He paused, his expression still shuttered, although Allegra heard the emotion in his voice. Felt the tension in his body next to hers.

'And what happened?'

'Someone embezzled a great deal of money from the company account. Your father blamed mine.'

She searched his face, looking for clues. 'But you don't think it was him?'

'I know it wasn't,' Rafael returned swiftly. 'I know. But your father insisted he had it on good authority, and he let it be known my father was a cheat, even though he couldn't prove it. No one would do business with him any longer. Within months he was ruined, and we were destitute.'

Shock sliced through her, and for a moment she struggled with what to say. How to respond. 'That's why you bought out the company.'

Rafael's mouth firmed. 'Justice was served.'

She sat up, hugging her knees, her mind still spinning. 'Why didn't you tell me this sooner?'

'I didn't know if you would believe me. And,' Rafael admitted, 'I didn't want to hurt you. I knew you loved your father, even if that love was misplaced. Things didn't feel strong enough between us…' He paused, searching her face. 'Do you believe me?'

'Yes,' Allegra said after a moment. 'I do.' And she ached for all Rafael and his family had endured. 'But I also believe that my father must have genuinely thought your father was in the wrong. I don't think he would have acted in such a manner without good cause.'

Rafael made a sound of disgust. 'And do you still think he abandoned you with good cause, Allegra? Why can't you see the man for what he is? *Was?*'

She recoiled, shocked by the vitriol in his voice. 'What does it matter to you if I choose to believe he was a good man?' she demanded stiffly. She felt hurt, and she wasn't even sure why. 'Why can't you let me love him still?'

'Because in my mind he is a demon,' Rafael returned flatly. 'And I will never forgive him.'

They didn't talk all the way back to the villa. The last few days had been so lovely, so promising, and now it all felt flat and strained. Over the last few days she'd actually been starting to care about Rafael. She *still* cared, which was why their argument hurt so much. And, Allegra acknowledged that evening as she lay in bed unable to sleep, it hurt because she know there was truth in Rafael's words. Why did she have to believe her father loved her, when everything pointed to the opposite? Why did she cling to that frail, pointless hope?

Sighing now, Allegra shifted restlessly in bed. The baby kicked, and she placed one hand on her bump, taking comfort from those fluttery movements. Tomorrow they were going to Palermo for a scan, and she was looking forward to the reassurance of an ultrasound, that lovely whoosh of their son's heartbeat filling the air.

But tonight she wasn't thinking about their baby. She was thinking about *them*.

The sudden, soft strains of music floating from downstairs made Allegra still in her restless movements. It almost sounded like...

Holding her breath, she rose from her bed and slipped

on the silky wrap that passed for a dressing gown in this hot weather. Even at two in the morning the air inside the villa held a remnant of the day's heat, although the tiles were cool under Allegra's bare feet as she made her way downstairs, following the haunting strains of the cello she heard.

Downstairs all was dark save for a single lamp burning in the lounge. Allegra hesitated on the threshold of the room; she saw Rafael sprawled in a chair, his long legs stretched out in front of him, his button-down shirt several more buttons open than usual. His hair was rumpled and a tumbler of whisky dangled from his fingertips.

'It's Shostakovich,' Allegra said softly, and he glanced up, his eyes bloodshot and bleary. He was, she realised, a little drunk.

'The third movement of the cello sonata,' he agreed. 'It reminds me of you.'

It was the piece they'd listened to before they'd made love. Allegra was jolted to the core by the fact that he was listening to it now—that he'd remembered, that he cared. 'Why do you need reminding?' she asked softly. 'I'm right here.'

'Are you?' The question hung in the air between them, hovered like a ghost. Rafael gave her a long look before he glanced away, taking a large swallow of his drink.

'Is this about this afternoon?' Allegra asked after a moment. 'Our argument?'

'What do you mean, this?'

'You're sitting downstairs, listening to sad music and drinking whisky.'

Rafael looked away. 'I couldn't sleep.'

'I couldn't either.' She paused, then decided to up the ante, even if part of her shied away from being so vulnerable. Admitting so much. 'The truth is, I think you're right, at least partly. I want to believe my father still loved me because the alternative...' She stopped, catching her breath, her heart starting to thud. Confessions like this were *hard*. 'The alternative is he didn't love me, and that means... I'm unlovable.'

Rafael lifted his head to skewer her with a burning stare. 'You are not unlovable, Allegra.'

'My own father?' She tried to keep her voice light but it trembled. 'Come on. Parents love their children. That's a given.'

'Maybe your father was incapable of love.'

'You really think he was a monster,' Allegra said slowly. Rafael didn't answer. She stared at him, trying to divine something from the resolute, almost resigned set of his features. 'I don't want this to come between us, Rafael. Whatever happened...it's in the past. Let's leave it there.'

'You were the one who wanted to know.'

'And now I do.' She drew a quick breath. 'Is there anything more? To know?'

A pause, infinite, endless. 'No,' Rafael said finally. 'Nothing important.'

Allegra supposed she should feel relieved but she didn't. She felt anxious and also sad because, whatever Rafael had just said, she sensed that there was still something he was holding back. She could see it in his face, the set of his shoulders. He was carrying a world of sorrow, and she didn't understand it. She didn't know how to comfort him. But she wanted to.

'Our son is kicking,' she said softly. She pressed both her hands against her bump, laughing a little as their baby kicked against her palm. 'He's a fighter for sure. He's kicking me right now.' She looked up at him, a tremulous smile curving her lips. 'Do you want to feel him?'

He hadn't felt their baby kick since that night after the opera. They'd barely touched at all since then. It felt like a lifetime ago.

'Yes.' The single word was certain and utterly heartfelt. Rafael tossed his empty glass onto the table before rising from his chair and coming across the room to kneel in front of her. The warm wash of light caught the bronze strands in his dark hair, the glint of stubble on his jaw. Allegra held her breath, conscious of his closeness, his heat, the yearning inside her to reach him, comfort him. She touched his hair, threading her fingers through its softness, drawing him closer to her.

Slowly Rafael slid his hands along her bump, the warmth of his palms seeping through the thin silk of her nightgown and dressing gown. 'You're bigger,' he said softly. 'Even in just a few weeks.'

'He is growing,' Allegra answered with a little laugh. 'And I'm eating better.'

'You're beautiful,' Rafael answered, his tone almost fierce. 'I've never seen anything so beautiful as you—as this.' His palms curved around her belly, cradling their unborn child. Allegra's heart bumped unsteadily as desire and something deeper flooded through her.

And then their baby kicked, a sharp flutter, almost making her wince. Rafael laughed aloud. 'That was him.'

'Yes.'

'It feels so strong. Stronger than before.'

'Yes, he's quite a kicker.'

'He needs to be strong. He needs to be a fighter, with what's ahead of him.' Allegra thought of the planned surgery, the frightening uncertainty amidst the longed-for news—and the knowledge, sweet and sure, that Rafael would be by her side for all of it. Dependence—trust—could be a wonderful thing.

'Yes. We all have to be strong,' she whispered.

'It will be all right, Allegra.' Rafael's hands continued to cup her belly as he looked up at her, his gaze burning and intent. 'I'll make sure it will be all right.'

Tenderness flooded through her at his fierce expression. She knew he meant every word, and while the future held no promises or guarantees, she believed him. She believed *in* him, in his sincerity, and that faith compelled her to touch her hand to his cheek, her fingers smoothing across the gentle abrasion of his stubbled jaw. 'I know you will, Rafael.'

A brighter light blazed in his eyes and he turned his face so his lips brushed her palm. A shudder went through Allegra; her body shook with the force of it, and her breath came out in a ragged gasp. To be touched again, and so sweetly, so tenderly…

'Rafael…' His name slipped from her lips, and then he opened his mouth and sucked on the tip of her thumb, and her whole body twanged like a bow that had been beautifully plucked. Around them the music swelled, a crescendo of sound to complement the one of sensation Allegra could feel inside her, building, *building*…

Rafael let go of her thumb to turn back to her, and Allegra didn't know who moved first. With his hands on her belly and their baby between them their bodies bumped together, mouths clashing, hands tangling. The kiss went on and on, desperate, urgent and hungry, a symphony whose notes played their sweet music through her body.

Rafael's hands went from bump to her hair and then to her shoulders and breasts, touching her everywhere, and yet it wasn't enough. She needed him, needed now more than ever to feel the closeness, the connection she'd felt once before. And she thought he needed it too.

Then he pulled away, just a little, but it was enough to make her cry out with the loss of it, of him.

In the shadowy light from the lamp she saw his face, his expression resolute, ready, eyes like fire, a silent question waiting for her yes.

She placed one trembling hand against his chest, felt the steady, comforting thud of his heart. Pressed. Rafael glanced down at her hand, fingers spread out, seeking. He covered it with his own. They remained like that for a suspended second, everything about to tumble into free fall.

And then he bent his head, his lips a whisper away from hers, still waiting for her response. Her yes. And she gave it, leaning forward to kiss him deeply, her hands tangling in his hair, the action a promise, a vow.

He tensed under her hands and mouth, his body like a bow while she was the strings. And then the music began, a glorious symphony, as his hands came up to grip her shoulders hard and his mouth opened under hers, turning her whisper of a kiss into a shout, a plea, a demand—she answered all of them with her mouth, her body, her heart. An offering of everything she had.

His mouth moved on hers as he propelled her across the room and then up the stairs; she stumbled on a step and with a muffled groan against her mouth Rafael scooped her up into his arms, drawing her against his chest. Allegra nestled there, feeling both precious and small, as Rafael carried her easily up the stairs and then down the hall to the master bedroom.

He put her down gently, steadying her as she swayed against him. The room was dark, moonlight spilling through the latticed shutters over the window, and they stood there for a moment, silent, breathing, his hands on her arms.

Allegra couldn't see the expression on his face but she

felt the emotion thrum through him as he tightened his grip on her shoulders.

'Are you sure?'

Everything so far had been a resounding and over-whelming yes, and yet still he asked. Allegra placed one hand on his cheek, her thumb smoothing the line of his jaw, learning him, letting him know how sure she was. 'Yes,' she said simply. *'Yes.'*

He didn't ask again. He simply pulled her towards him, his smile gleaming whitely in the dark, and then her clothes fell away; she kicked off her pyjama shorts as Rafael slid her T-shirt over her head.

His breath hissed between his teeth as he looked at her, and Allegra didn't feel self-conscious or big with her belly on display. She didn't feel vulnerable or exposed. Under the heat of his gaze she felt only beautiful.

His hands followed his hot gaze, smoothing over her dips and curves, learning the feel of her with slow, thorough deliberation. She shivered under his touch, his fingers sending sparks along her skin, and then she grew bold enough to touch him, hands flat upon his chest, fingers spreading and seeking the sculpted ridges of his muscles.

'I like that,' Rafael whispered. He remained still under her questing fingers, and with shaking hands she slipped the first shirt button from its hole, and then another and another, until his chest was bare and she was pushing his shirt off his bronzed shoulders, revelling in his body, satiny skin over hard muscle. She hadn't touched him very much that first night. She'd been too overwhelmed by it all, both the pleasure and the grief. Now she revelled in the hot, silky feel of him, running her hand across his chest, down to his abdomen, fingertips brushing the waistband of his trousers.

Rafael let out a groan and Allegra laughed softly,

amazed at how she was able to affect him. Now she felt powerful as well as beautiful.

'You were beautiful before,' he murmured as he reached for her, hands cupping her breasts, thumbs sliding across their aching peaks. 'And you are even more beautiful now, carrying my child.'

'You make me feel beautiful,' Allegra whispered, and then he was bending his head and Allegra slid her fingers through his hair as his lips sought and found her, causing a lightning bolt of pleasure to blaze deep down inside.

He scooped her up again—she felt boneless, weightless—and carried her to the bed. Deposited her on top of the duvet, the silk cover slithering and sliding underneath her. He shucked off his trousers and boxers, leaving her breathless. She'd seen him naked before but the sight still overwhelmed and undid her. He lay next to her and drew her into his arms, their bodies bumping and touching in all sorts of places, making her shudder. It felt so much. She'd known it would; it was why she'd resisted this before, because the intensity felt exquisite and painful at the same time, and she had to brace herself for the tidal wave, to keep herself from falling, drowning.

She'd been telling herself he wouldn't feel the same way, that sex wasn't as important or sacred for him, but in that moment as his fingers touched her face and his body arced into hers she believed it was. He couldn't touch her like this, give of himself like this, without it meaning something. She felt it in his kiss, in his gentle hands, in the love he lavished on her body, finding and plundering all of her secret places.

And then—yes, finally—he was inside her, so big and right she gasped out loud and he lifted his head, his gaze blazing down into hers. 'Are you all right? I didn't hurt you?'

She clasped her legs around him, pulling him deeper

into herself, accepting him fully, feeling complete. 'I'm all right,' she said. 'I'm...' But she had no words, because the feelings were coming faster and stronger now, wave after wave as Rafael began to move and Allegra matched his rhythm, reaching, *reaching...*

And finding. Finally, gloriously finding, her body shuddering with the force of her climax, Rafael's face buried in her neck as he murmured words of endearment and promise, their bodies intertwined in every way possible. How could you be this close to another human being, Allegra wondered, and *not* fall in love?

She tensed, though, as their heart rates slowed and Rafael, who had been bracing himself above her so as not to press against her bump, rolled onto his back. The sudden whoosh of cool air on her heated skin felt like an unwelcome wake-up call.

What now?

She waited, barely daring to breathe, afraid of this moment and what had it had meant before. Would he dismiss her from his bed? Leave her here alone? Then Rafael reached out one arm and hooked it around her shoulders, drawing her against him so her bump was pressed against his side, her knees snugging into the backs of his thighs. Allegra expelled a silent sigh of relief. It was going to be okay. More than okay.

Gently Rafael caressed her bump, his palm curving around the taut roundness of her belly. He laughed softly as their baby kicked.

'I guess something woke him up.' A smile in his voice, in her heart.

'I guess something did,' she answered, and wrapped her arm around his chest.

CHAPTER TWELVE

HE COULD SMELL THE BLOOD. Sharp, metallic. He didn't recognise it, though, didn't understand as he pushed the now broken splintered door open with his fingertips and took a step inside the room.

'Papa?'

His voice was soft, scared, the voice of a child even though he was sixteen years old.

'Papa...'

He saw his father's hands first, slack, hanging down, fingers dangling. Then the drops of blood on the desk, a delicate spray, making him think ink had spilled. As if anyone used ink any more, let alone a bottle of bright red. And then his gaze moved upwards and he saw his father's shattered face. Heard a scream rip from his throat— except it wasn't his scream, it was his mother's; she stood behind him, hands raised to her blood-drained face, and the awful unholy sound went on and on.

'Rafael... Rafael!'

The hand shaking his shoulder woke him up; he came out of the dream like a bullet from a gun, the screaming still echoing in his ears. Next to him Allegra's face was as pale as his mother's had been, pale and frightened.

'Rafael...' she whispered, and he shook off her hand, roughly, and saw her flinch. Hated himself, but he couldn't keep from doing it, from turning away. He swung his legs out of his bed and strode to the bathroom, slamming the door behind him.

In the mirror his face was pale, his forehead beaded with icy sweat. Bile churned in his stomach and he thought he might be sick. Thankfully he swallowed it down, bracing his hands on the pedestal sink as he lowered his head and took several steadying breaths.

He hadn't had that dream in years. A decade, even. He hadn't let himself, had closed that part of his mind right off. *Don't think of it*, because if you did you'd be lost, lost for ever, no coming back. He knew that. Knew if he remembered how he'd begged, begged his father... You couldn't go back from that. You couldn't recover, and so he refused to think of it.

Except, he acknowledged as he looked at his pale reflection in the mirror, he thought of it all the time. Not consciously, but it remained, a canker inside him, destroying everything good. Allegra had asked how her father could leave her, if he'd loved her. Rafael knew the answer to that in his own case times a thousand.

Because he didn't love me. Because I couldn't keep him from destroying himself. Because it's all my fault.

He'd seen how his mother had gone, and his sister too. They'd been swallowed up by their nightmares, their memories, until there had been nothing left but a pale husk of a self, and then nothing at all. He couldn't let it happen to him. But why the dream, why now?

Slowly he lifted his head and stared at his reflection. The answer was right there in his dazed face, the acidic churn in his belly. *Allegra.* Their lovemaking had been both sweet and powerful, and it had woken up long-dead parts of him, parts of him that remembered and felt and feared. Parts of him that he'd iced over with thoughts of justice, kept frozen with cold, cold fury. Now everything was waking up, a spring of the soul, and this was the result. Dreams he couldn't bear to have. Memories he didn't dare think about. *Weakness.*

He turned the taps on full blast and washed his face, scrubbed hard as if it would make a difference, and then turned them off again. He stared in the mirror, his eyes opaque, hard, and then he nodded once and left the bathroom.

Allegra was curled up on her side, her back to him, one hand cupping her bump. Thankfully she'd fallen asleep, but even in sleep her face looked sad, her mouth puckered, a frown feathering her brow. Rafael reached out to smooth a red-gold curl away from her cheek and then stopped. No need for that.

Tonight had been intense, and now he needed to get things back the way they had been, comfortable, enjoyable, but not threatening. No danger of scars being reopened, him bleeding again, bleeding right out. Take a step back, make it safe. That was what he needed to do... and preferably without hurting Allegra too much. But hurting Allegra couldn't be his main concern any more. Keeping those memories locked tight away was.

Allegra woke slowly the next morning, blinking in the sunlight streaming from the windows, her body aching in delicious places. For a wonderful moment all she remembered was the pleasure, intense and overpowering, of being with Rafael. The way he'd held her, moved inside her...

Then another memory slammed into the first, leaving her breathless. The nightmare he'd had, the way he'd shut her out. She turned and saw that his side of the bed was empty, the duvet pulled tight across, as if he'd never been there. Had he even come back to bed?

Slowly she got out of bed, sorting through possibilities. What should she do now? How should she act? Despite what they'd shared together last night, she didn't yet know how to handle this moment. Whether to press or pull away. She pulled on the thick terrycloth robe hanging from a hook in the bathroom and then gathered her clothes up, tiptoeing back to her room. Downstairs she could Maria humming in the kitchen, Salvatore's tuneless whistle. Nothing from Rafael.

Back in her bedroom she showered and dressed; her mind sifting through memories, options. What to do? How to feel? Taking a deep breath, she went in search of the father of her child.

She found him in his study, forehead furrowed as he gazed at his laptop, his headphone set dangling from his neck. Allegra stood in the doorway for a moment, an ache in her heart, in her soul. She wanted to walk easily into the room and plop herself into his lap; she wanted to smooth away the furrows on his forehead and kiss that lovely, hard, mobile mouth. She wanted it to feel natural, right, and yet she simply stood there, wondering and waiting.

'Did you have a conference call?' she finally asked, her voice high and nervous as she nodded towards the headset.

Rafael's gaze flicked towards her and then away, revealing nothing. Giving nothing. 'Yes.'

'Are you able to manage most of your business from here?' He'd only gone into Palermo a few times over the last weeks.

'I'll need to start going into Palermo more often.' He

turned back to his laptop in a way that felt like a dismissal. 'As well as Rome and Milan.'

'I could come.' She kept her voice light. 'I'd like to come.' Rafael didn't answer, and Allegra took a deep breath. 'Rafael…about last night…'

His mouth tightened, his gaze still on the screen. 'Let's not do a post-mortem.'

'Post-mortem?' Hurt flashed through her. 'Really, that's what you'd call it?'

'You know what I mean.'

'I'm not sure I do.'

Finally Rafael lifted his gaze from his laptop, but then Allegra wished he hadn't. His eyes were opaque, fathomless, hard. 'Last night was pleasurable, Allegra, for both of us. That's all that matters. Let's leave it at that.'

'Rafael…' She took a deep breath, dared. 'What about everything we talked about? What about the dream you had?' As soon as she said the words she wished she hadn't. An emotion flashed across his face like quicksilver, gone before she could decipher it, but she knew it hadn't been good.

'Forget about that,' Rafael said flatly, and as he turned back to his screen Allegra knew she'd truly been dismissed. Still she wouldn't give up that easily.

'I have a doctor's appointment this afternoon in Palermo,' she said. 'An ultrasound. Will you come with me?'

He hesitated, and for that heart-stopping second she thought he wouldn't. That he was turning away from her and their child completely, for a reason she could not understand. 'Yes,' Rafael said at last. 'Of course I will.'

Rafael sat tensely by Allegra as the technician squirted cold, clear gel onto her stomach. They'd barely spoken on the drive into Palermo, which should have suited Rafael perfectly but instead made him feel restless and irritable.

He didn't know what he wanted. The remnants of his old dream still clung to him, ghost fragments he couldn't shake. They made him want to keep a little distance between him and Allegra, but another part of him howled in protest. Hated hurting her…and hurting himself.

'Everything looks good,' the doctor said as he prodded the ultrasound wand on Allegra's burgeoning bump. 'Baby is the right size…a growing boy.'

The fuzzy black and white shape on the ultrasound screen looked like a proper baby. Head, body, hands, feet, even fingers and toes. He was sucking his thumb and kicking his legs and the sight of him made a pressure build inside Rafael, a pressure he couldn't even begin to understand. His hands curled into fists at his sides and he had to fight to keep his breathing even.

What was happening to him?

He felt too much. Happy. Thankful. Afraid. All of it combined inside him, making it hard even to speak. He focused on practicalities instead, helping Allegra up from the table, listening and nodding as the doctor asked them to book another appointment in four weeks' time.

'What shall we do now?' Allegra asked as they left the doctor's office for one of the city's sweeping boulevards.

'Do?' Rafael looked at her cautiously. 'What do you mean?'

'I'm sick of being stuck at the villa,' Allegra said. 'It's lovely, of course, but I've never been to Palermo and I'd like to see it properly. Can we look around a bit?'

Rafael looked at the tremulous hope on Allegra's lovely face and knew he'd have to be a monster to refuse. 'Yes,' he said, the single word drawn from him with reluctance. 'I suppose.'

For the next few hours they strolled down boulevards to squares with sparkling fountains, explored narrow alleys with charming shops and market stalls, and ended up at a café facing the lovely Piazza Pretoria, with its iconic fountain.

Allegra had kept up a steady stream of innocuous conversation the whole time, and Rafael hadn't done much more than offer monosyllabic replies. He was trying to maintain that little bit of distance but it was hard…and becoming harder with every moment.

As they left the café Allegra bent over to reach her bag under the table and the sound of fabric splitting rent the air.

'Oh, no.' She straightened, her face fiery, one hand clapped to her back. 'I've split my skirt,' she whispered, looking mortified, and Rafael looked down at her clothes, realised she'd been wearing the same few loose tops and summer skirts since he'd seen her back in New York.

'I think you need some new maternity clothes,' he said, wishing he'd thought of it sooner.

'I definitely need a new skirt,' Allegra answered, laughing a little. 'I'm not decent!'

'I'll ring a boutique right now.' He draped his jacket over her as he shepherded her from the café into the waiting limo. Moments later they were stepping into one of Palermo's best boutiques on the Via Liberta, several assistants already waiting to serve them.

Allegra was whisked away to a dressing room while Rafael sat on a white velvet settee, sipping champagne and scrolling through messages on his phone. This was more like it; he could take care of Allegra in the manner he wished to—and that she deserved—without actually having to engage her. She wasn't even in the room.

'What do you think?' Allegra's voice was soft and hesitant and Rafael looked up from his phone, his brain instantly going blank.

Allegra stared at the nonplussed look on Rafael's face and wondered if she'd made a mistake. All afternoon she'd been trying to reach him, keeping up a cheerful one-sided conversation, determined to stay positive.

They'd shared a connection last night. She had to believe that, had to believe it had been real…and that they could have it again.

In the boutique's dressing room she'd tried on several outfits, and then paused when the assistant had given her a sexy, slinky cocktail dress in soft black jersey. This one, she decided, she would show Rafael. See if she finally got some kind of reaction out of him. And now she was standing here, feeling faintly ridiculous, and Rafael was looking blank.

'Well?' She managed a laugh, and then she did a little twirl. 'What do you think?'

'I think…' Rafael cleared his throat. 'I think you look…' He stopped, shaking his head as if to clear it. Allegra smiled. As far as reactions went, she'd take it.

She went back into the dressing room to change while the assistant took her clothes to the shop's till. She was just pulling off the dress when the door opened.

'I think I might need help with the zip,' she said, and then to her shock Rafael answered.

'I think I can do that.'

'What are you doing…?' Allegra began, her breath coming out in a soft sigh as Rafael gently tugged on the zip and then pressed his lips to the nape of her neck.

A shudder went through her and she swayed on her

feet, flinging one hand out to brace herself as Rafael's mouth moved down her back.

'Someone will see...' she murmured as he slid the dress further down so it pooled about her hips. She could feel the hard, hot strength of his body behind hers and she leaned back, sagging against him as he kissed the curve of her shoulder.

'No one will see.'

'They'll know.'

'I don't care. I can't see you in that dress and not touch you.'

Touch her but not talk to her. She'd spent all afternoon trying to reach him but it seemed he didn't want conversation. He wanted this.

And so did she.

Rafael pressed against her and Allegra's eyes fluttered closed. *This* was rather wonderful.

'Signor Vitali? We just need your card...' The musical voice of the assistant floated towards them and they both tensed. With what felt like superhuman effort Allegra moved away. She stepped out of the dress and reached for her clothes as Rafael left in search of the assistant.

They didn't speak on the way home, twilight cloaking the mountains in soft violet. Rafael had withdrawn into himself again, his expression shuttered and distant as Allegra curled up in a corner of the limo and dozed.

Back at the villa he disappeared into his office and with a sigh she went to put away her new clothes, sifting through the day's events in her mind. Was she crazy to try to break through the wall Rafael seemed determined on putting up? Foolish to try for more when for her whole life she'd settled for so much less?

Allegra sank onto her bed, her unseeing gaze resting on the moonlit hills outside the window. She'd come to

Sicily because she'd believed it was best for her child. It had felt like a sacrifice, one she had been ready and willing to make.

But now? Now, when she'd felt so much pleasure and happiness and connection with Rafael? When she sensed his overprotective, controlling nature disguised a man who could be tender and loving?

Now she didn't want to come to some *arrangement* where they married and raised their child together, but lived as virtual strangers. Now she wanted a proper husband…and not just in bed.

But how to go about getting it? Was she strong enough to reach Rafael, to keep trying even when he pulled away? To face failure and rejection and keep holding on? She wanted to be. She wanted to make this work.

The click of the door opening had her turning, her surprised gaze arrowing in on Rafael.

'Is everything all right?' she asked uncertainly, because he looked intent and serious and a little sad.

'Now it is,' he said, and relief rushed through her, along with desire, as Rafael came towards her and took her in his arms.

CHAPTER THIRTEEN

ALLEGRA GAZED AROUND the nursery with a smile of satisfaction. She'd made decorating the room her project over the last week, and she was proud of what she'd accomplished. Pale blue walls with stencilled white elephants cavorting across them, and a cot bed in blond oak with fresh blue sheets ready and waiting, although she didn't actually know when their son would sleep in this room.

The doctors had said he'd be in the hospital for several weeks at least, and then she planned to keep him in a bassinet next to the bed for easy feeding in the night. Still, she was excited about the room, could picture herself in the oak rocker by the window, her son cradled against her chest, sunlight streaming through the window, the perfect picture of familial happiness. Almost.

A sigh escaping her, Allegra moved to the window and looked out at the dusty hills. It hadn't rained in weeks and the air felt stuffy. Now in her sixth month of pregnancy, she felt huge and awkward and more than a little grumpy. She rested one hand on her belly, trying yet again to banish the fears that skirted her mind, threatened to swamp her heart.

For the last few weeks she and Rafael had reached a holding pattern of spending their nights together—and what wonderful nights they were—and the days mostly apart. While she couldn't fault Rafael for his solicitude and kind concern, the remoteness she sensed in him, the careful emotional distance he always kept between them, made her want to scream.

She wanted more. She tried for more, but at every turn Rafael foiled her obvious conversational gambits, her clumsy attempts to increase their intimacy. Was this what love was? Because she thought—she feared—that she loved him. Or at least that she could let him, if he'd let her. If he opened up.

But since that first incredible night he'd stayed remote. He didn't even spend the whole night with her when they made love. He held her for a little while afterwards, but he never slept with her and every morning Allegra woke to an empty bed and an aching heart.

She wanted more than this. She needed more than this. After a lifetime of trying to avoid intimacy and love, here she was, desperate for it. The very situation she'd been wary of had happened, and it felt as if there was nothing she could do about it.

'I have to go to Naples.'

Allegra started in surprise at the sight of Rafael in the doorway of the nursery. She couldn't tell anything from his usual, closed-off expression, but even so she felt a ripple of alarm. 'Naples? Why? Is it business?' He'd gone to Palermo several times a week, and Milan and Rome once each.

There was a slight, taut pause. 'No.'

Allegra frowned. 'No? Then…what? I mean, why?'

Rafael didn't answer for a long moment. Allegra thought he wouldn't. 'My sister,' he said finally, shocking her.

'Your sister…but…' She trailed off, unsure what to say. She'd thought he'd lost his sister, that she'd died. He'd spoken about her as if she was gone, and so Allegra had assumed the worst.

'She's not well,' Rafael said abruptly. 'I need to…go to her.'

Allegra stared at him, sensing the dark undercurrent of anxiety under his terse tone, and she ached to help. Wanted to comfort him, but knew he wouldn't let her. And yet…if he kept her apart in this, what hope was there? How could she ever get closer to him?

'Let me come with you,' she said, part entreaty, part demand, and Rafael's face shuttered.

'No.'

'Why not?' Allegra challenged. 'Please don't keep shutting me out, Rafael, and pushing me away. If we're going to have a child together, if we're going to marry…'

'You are being melodramatic. I haven't pushed you away.'

'Not at night,' Allegra agreed, lifting her chin. 'Not in bed. But in every other way you have. You know you have. I keep trying to reach you, and you keep refusing me. Please, Rafael, don't refuse me in this. I want to support you…'

Rafael stared at her for a long moment, his expression both hard and bleak, and then he finally gave one quick, terse nod. 'Fine,' he said. 'But I need to leave within the hour.'

He shouldn't have let her come. A deep unease settled into Rafael's gut as he climbed into the helicopter after Allegra. He hadn't intended to let her come, of course he hadn't. The last thing he wanted was for Allegra to see Angelica, see his shame.

But, he thought with a resolve tinged with despair, perhaps it was better this way. Perhaps, instead of having to maintain that careful distance, it would yawn between them, gape wide, because finally Allegra would see just what he was and how he'd failed.

The call had come that morning, from a doctor in Naples who had found his sister's ID in her bag, as well as his name and phone number. She'd been discovered in an alley, unconscious, unresponsive. The last time the doctor had warned that another overdose could kill her. Angelica didn't seem to care, and Rafael feared that was because she wanted to die. His father's death had been quick, a single shot; his mother a slow, deliberate wasting away. Angelica was choosing self-destruction. And it was all his fault.

'Is your sister ill?' Allegra asked, shouting over the sound of the helicopter that would take them to Palermo for the short flight to Naples.

'In a manner of speaking.' Rafael turned to look out the window to avoid answering any more of Allegra's questions. She would see soon enough what Angelica was like. What he was like.

And then? The unease he'd been feeling deepened into dark regret. Then things would be changed between them for ever.

They didn't talk much on the flight to Naples; Allegra seemed to sense his mood and kept quiet, while Rafael kept his head down, his eyes on his tablet, dealing with work issues.

A car was waiting for them when they emerged from the airport, blinking in the afternoon sunlight, the muted roar of the city's traffic, the raucous honking of horns and exclamations of passers-by hitting Rafael like a smack in the face. He didn't like the busy, dirty streets of Naples. He'd offered a dozen times or more to pay for Angelica to move somewhere more congenial, but she'd always refused.

He gave the address of the hospital to the driver and then leaned back in the seat. Allegra looked at him in concern.

'Won't you tell me what's going on?' she asked quietly.

'What is there to tell?' Rafael shrugged, dismissing the question with a lift of his eyebrows. 'My sister is in hospital.' He paused, pressing his lips together. 'A drug overdose.'

He could tell he'd shocked her with that one. And that was just the beginning.

'What...?' Allegra's face crumpled with sympathy. 'Oh, Rafael...'

'Don't.' He shrugged away her compassion. 'It happens often enough. And there's nothing I've been able to do about it.'

Allegra lapsed into silence and Rafael looked away. He really shouldn't have brought her, but perhaps it would, painfully, be for the best.

Allegra's mouth was dry, her heart pinging in her chest, as she followed Rafael into the hospital lift. He pressed a button and then folded his arms over his chest, biceps bulging, face like an iron mask.

She'd been surprised and gratified when he'd agreed to let her come, but since he'd made that decision he'd seemed only to regret it, and he'd been colder and more remote that ever. She wondered if asking to come had been a mistake, and if Rafael would simply use this as a way to push her even further away.

The doors of the lift opened and Rafael strode out, while Allegra hurried to keep up. Then he was tapping perfunctorily on the door of a room before opening it and slipping inside. Allegra followed him.

The woman in the bed was asleep, dark lashes sweeping gaunt cheeks. Allegra stifled a gasp at the heart-wrenching sight of her—scars on each wrist and bruises and needle puncture marks scoring her arms in dozens of places. Her hair was dirty and tangled, her limbs scrawny, tendons sticking out like ropes. Rafael let out a shuddering breath. The woman's eyes fluttered opened and then focused on Rafael.

'You shouldn't have come,' she rasped out, her eyes burning like coals as she glared at him.

'Of course I came.' Rafael gazed at her for a moment, his expression closed and yet his eyes full of pain. 'Why, Angelica?'

Angelica shook her head, her eyes closed again. 'I don't want to talk to you.'

'Let me help you,' Rafael said, his voice taking on a strident edge. 'Please. There is a room waiting at the best clinic in Europe, in Switzerland. It's luxurious, Angelica, and discreet. You'd want for nothing.'

Angelica shook her head again, without opening her eyes. Allegra's heart started to splinter. She hated seeing Rafael like this, knowing how helpless, how hopeless, he must feel.

Rafael pressed his lips together, staring at his sister in a heart-breaking mix of grief and fury. 'I've only wanted to help you, Angelica. That's all I've ever wanted.'

Angelica opened her eyes, and Allegra stifled a gasp at the hatred and anger she saw in their depths. 'Help me? When have you ever *helped* me?' she demanded in a raw and ragged voice. Rafael flinched but didn't reply. Didn't defend himself. 'Do you know what he did?' Angelica demanded, turning to Allegra. She stared, speechless, unsure how to respond, how to feel. 'Do you?' Angelica's voice rung out. Allegra licked her lips.

'I… I don't…'

'He killed our father,' Angelica spat. 'He *killed* him. My brother only ever thought of himself. He didn't… he couldn't…' She turned away, sobs tearing her chest.

Allegra had no idea what to say. She didn't believe Angelica, the words of a vindictive and desperate drug addict, and yet…

Why wasn't Rafael saying anything?

'You can't deny it, can you?' Angelica said, her voice still coming in ragged gasps.

'No,' Rafael said after a moment. 'I can't.'

Shock rippled through Allegra. Rafael shot her a cold, hard glance. 'Now you know,' he said, but Allegra didn't feel she knew anything.

'Leave me,' Angelica demanded in a low voice. She seemed drained, lifeless. 'Leave me, I beg of you.'

Rafael gazed at his sister for a full minute while Allegra watched, her heart thudding in her chest. Then he turned and walked out of the room.

Allegra followed, her heart aching now, everything aching. 'Rafael…' she began when they'd entered a small waiting room, but he shook his head.

'Don't. I shouldn't have brought you here.'

'I asked to be brought here,' Allegra answered. 'I want to share your sorrows along with your joys. Please, Rafael…'

Rafael just shook his head again, pacing the small waiting room like a panther in a cage.

'How long has she been like this?' Allegra asked quietly.

Rafael didn't still his stride. 'Since she was fifteen. A year after my father died.'

'How…how did he die?'

He lifted his tormented gaze to hers, his mouth twisting. 'You heard her.'

'I don't believe her.'

'Don't you?'

'No,' Allegra said, but her voice wavered. She didn't believe Angelica, not really, but she knew something had happened, something that tormented Rafael, that made him the way he was, dark and distant, and she was afraid to find out what it was.

'Well, you should,' Rafael said, and turned away.

'Why don't you tell me your version?' Allegra asked quietly. 'What really happened?'

'What really happened?' He stopped, raking his hands through his hair and then dropping them in one abrupt movement. 'My father killed himself. I was the last to see him.'

Uncertainty mingled with sorrowful relief rushed through her. 'Then you didn't kill him…'

'I drove him to his suicide. And then I wasn't able to stop him from pulling the trigger.'

'Oh, Rafael…'

'And my mother and my sister blamed me. They blamed me, and they should have blamed me, because… because I couldn't…'

'But it wasn't—'

'You know what I was saying to him before he killed himself?' Rafael didn't wait for her to reply, not that she had any idea what to say. 'I was complaining about having to leave my private school, because there was no more money. My father had lost everything, everything, and I was whinging about school.' He shook his head slowly.

'Rafael, you were a boy…'

'A stupid, selfish boy. And it broke my father. He left

the room and locked himself in his study…' He stopped, shaking his head again. 'But there's no need to talk of it. Angelica won't see me again. You might as well return to the villa. I never should have brought you in your condition.'

'I'm not an invalid.' Her heart was aching, aching for this man she loved. And yet Rafael's expression was stony, and when she reached out a hand he jerked away from her.

'I'll arrange your flight.'

'What…what about you?'

Rafael shook his head. 'I won't come with you. I have business to see to.'

Allegra stared at him helplessly, knowing that Rafael was taking another step away from her, and this one far worse than any before. Yet what could she do?

'Please don't do this, Rafael,' she whispered, but he was already getting out his phone.

It was better this way. Rafael continued to tell himself that as he arranged Allegra's flight and saw her onto it. She looked at him with a face full of hurt and desperation, but he steeled himself against it.

She might want to make explanations, excuses, but he couldn't. And he wasn't about to open either of them to more pain. What it meant for their future, he didn't know. But now he knew he needed distance. Space.

He stayed in Naples for another two days, trying to reason with Angelica, but she wouldn't even talk to him. He called Allegra, and was reassured she had returned safely to the villa.

'When are you coming back?' she asked, her voice soft and sad.

'I don't know,' Rafael answered tersely. 'I have business in Milan and Rome.'

'I miss you,' Allegra said quietly, and he didn't answer. But after the call he spent several long minutes staring out the window at the dark night.

'I miss you too,' he said into the empty silence of his hotel room.

CHAPTER FOURTEEN

THE NEXT WEEK WAS ENDLESS. Allegra drifted around the villa, wishing she could make things better and feeling utterly powerless. She went over her conversation with Rafael again and again, considering all that he had and hadn't said.

Did he really blame himself for his father's suicide? If anyone, she thought with a bitter pang, he should blame her father, for ruining his. No wonder Rafael had been so driven to see justice served. His family had been utterly destroyed.

But *they* didn't have to be destroyed. She couldn't let this ruin them, and yet Rafael seemed hell bent on letting the past destroy any chance of their future.

She thought she understood now why he'd been so distant these last few weeks. Not because he didn't care but because he cared too much…at least, that's what she hoped. She hoped that it was fear of getting hurt that was keeping him away rather than brutal indifference.

Because that's how she'd felt for so long. Loving someone was risky. Loving *hurt*, because people left you. People hurt you. And Rafael didn't want to be hurt.

She hadn't either. She'd lived her life for safety's sake, never letting anyone get close, missing out because it was easier. Safer. But she didn't want to do that now. Now she wanted to risk. Now she was willing to risk everything, because she knew she loved Rafael. And love risked. Love fought. Love, she hoped and prayed, won. But first Rafael had to come back.

Rafael unlocked the front door, every muscle aching with weariness. He'd spent the last week working as hard as he could, in a desperate and fruitless effort to forget. To erase the memory of Allegra, the sweetness of her, so he'd be strong enough to come back here and maintain his distance. Stay separate.

It was late and the villa was swathed in darkness, everyone hopefully in bed. Rafael intended to creep quietly to his bedroom and avoid Allegra altogether. He'd barely taken a step before he heard a creak on the stair and then he turned to see Allegra standing there.

Her hair was tumbled about her shoulders and she wore a silky white slip of a nightgown that left frustratingly little to the imagination. Already desire was surging through him, and he wondered if he could make this simple. If he could make it about sex.

Then she took a step forward, one pale, slender hand held out in appeal. 'Rafael,' she said softly, and he tensed because there was no supplication in her voice. No accusation. There was just warmth. Acceptance. He turned away.

'I thought you'd be asleep.'

'I've been waiting for you.'

'You didn't even know I was coming back tonight.'

'I know.' She let out a soft, sad laugh. 'I've been waiting since you left, Rafael. A whole week.'

His chest felt tight and he tried to shake the feeling off. 'You shouldn't have.'

'Why not? Why are you pushing me away?'

'Why aren't you pushing me away?' The words burst out of him, revealing, and yet he couldn't keep himself from it. He turned to her, his voice ragged, his gaze burning. 'Why are you still here?'

She looked hurt, shocked. 'Do you want me to leave?'

'No.' He scrubbed his eyes with the heels of his hands. Something felt broken deep inside him and he couldn't articulate what it was, even to himself. 'I'm getting a drink.'

He stalked into the lounge, and after a taut moment Allegra followed him. Rafael poured himself a large measure of whisky from the crystal decanter and drank it down in one healthy swallow. He could feel Allegra's presence behind him. He could feel her confusion and hurt. 'You should go back to bed.'

He heard a sound, something he couldn't quite identify. She was moving or opening something, and he didn't know what it was. He stayed with his back to her, willing her to leave him alone even as a deeper part of him ached for her to stay.

Then he heard the first sorrowful note hover in the room, steal into his soul, and shocked blazed through him. She was playing the cello.

He turned slowly, his glass dangling from his slack fingertips as he took in the sight of Allegra, her hair tumbling about her shoulders in a fiery halo, her expression serious and intent as she drew the bow across the strings of the cello and another sonorous note flowed through the room.

'But…' His voice was hoarse, breaking the stillness. 'You said you didn't play. Hadn't played for ten years.'

Her gaze lifted and something deep in him trembled at the expression in her eyes, silvery and huge, clear and full of sadness. Full of *love*.

'I haven't. But I want to play for you, Rafael. Music…'

She paused, her voice choking. 'Music has been the greatest comfort to me. And I don't know of any other way to comfort you.'

She bent her head again and began to play once more, the notes sure and true and piercingly beautiful.

Rafael's throat thickened with emotion and he sank into the sofa as the music washed over him, note after perfect note, the music haunting and powerful, *breaking* him. He was broken inside, nothing but jagged pieces, his heart a handful of splinters. He let out a sound, a choking cry that would have shamed him if he hadn't felt so overwhelmed.

Allegra kept playing, each note touching his soul, undoing him. He let out another choked sound, and then Allegra was kneeling there in front of him, her arms around him, her face pressed against his chest as she whispered words that felt like sweet, sweet arrows, piercing the armour he'd surrounded himself with for so long.

'I love you, Rafael. I *love* you. Nothing matters to me but that. But you. Please believe me. *Please.*'

He let out a groan, defenceless against the onslaught of her heartfelt words. 'How can you love me…?' The words spilled from him, heedless.

'How can I not?' She pressed her lips against her jaw. 'I fell in love with you the night of my father's funeral.'

'I was only trying to seduce you…'

'And I wanted to be seduced. I saw glimpses then of the man you really are, the man you want to be. Don't turn away from me now, simply because you're afraid.' She laid her hand against his jaw, her skin silky and cool. 'Because that is why you've been keeping your distance, isn't it, these last few weeks, and even more so since we went to Naples? Because you're afraid of being hurt.'

He closed his eyes, not wanting to admit it, knowing it was true. He'd tried to separate his body from his heart but it hadn't worked. Allegra affected him in every way, right down to his core. And yet still he found himself saying, 'I didn't think anyone would love me. That anyone could love me…after my father…' He shook his head, his eyes closed, and Allegra kissed him again, her lips soft against his jaw. 'How could he do that? How could he walk away from me and kill himself? I begged him, Allegra. Pleaded with him with everything I had, pounded on the door, and still he did it, knowing the cost of it on me, on my mother and sister. How could he do that?'

The question rang out, the cry of a hurt child. It had festered inside him for twenty years, until his heart was nothing but scar tissue, barely healed over the old, old wound. And Allegra, and her love, had broken it all—him—open.

'I asked you something similar,' she whispered, her lips moving against his cheek. 'Do you remember? And you told me it wasn't my fault. Now I say the same thing to you, only even more so. Your father was a desperate man, Rafael, driven to terrible things because—because of my father. It wasn't your fault, just as my father leaving wasn't mine. Let's leave the past behind us and make our own future, for the sake of our child and for the sake of us.'

'But it was my fault,' Rafael groaned, his voice breaking on the word. 'Not his death, perhaps, but my mother… my sister…the choices they made, the fact that they felt compelled to make them. That they didn't trust me to provide for them, to see us through the darkness and the mess. *That* was my fault. I was the man of the family, I was in charge, and I failed utterly. I can't forgive myself for that. How can anyone else?'

* * *

Allegra squeezed Rafael's hands, holding on tight, wanting to imbue him with her strength, her love, because she felt as if everything teetered on this moment. Whether he would pull away for good or if the walls would finally come down for ever.

She recognised the core of honour and compassion that he'd kept hidden for so long, realised now that his withdrawal from her had not been from indifference but because he'd cared too much.

She knew that he now suffered from both guilt and hurt—just as she did, with her father's abandonment. Because when you were hurting, you assumed it was something in you that drove a person away. Something bad or wrong. And she would give anything now to show Rafael that there wasn't.

Slowly she leaned forward, still holding his hands, her bump pressing against him as she brushed her lips across his in a kiss of acceptance and healing. A kiss where she offered her whole self, there for the taking.

His body was still, his lips slack under hers, and her heart trembled at the terrible thought of his rejection, but then he opened his mouth and made the kiss his own, one hand coming to rest on the back of her head, and he took what she offered and gave even more back.

Moments later they broke apart and with a shuddering breath Rafael leaned his forehead against hers. 'When my father died,' he murmured, his breath fanning her face, 'I felt like my world had shattered...not just because we lost everything but because I'd lost him. Because he'd been driven to such despair, and I couldn't stop it. Couldn't stop him.'

'I'm so sorry, Rafael...'

'I felt powerless and out of control. And I never wanted

to feel like that again. But then I cruelly inflicted that pain on another family. I killed your father too, Allegra.'

'What are you talking about?'

'If what Caterina said was true…then your father died of a heart attack when he heard the news about me taking over the company. I killed him—'

'No, you didn't,' Allegra said quietly. 'You can't know exactly what happened, and in any case you can't blame yourself for my father's death along with everyone in your family.'

His eyebrows rose in disbelief. 'You absolve me?'

'I'm not the one to do that, Rafael. You don't need my forgiveness.'

'Whose then?' The question was genuine, yearning.

'Your own,' Allegra said softly. 'Rid yourself of these ghosts and demons. Your father chose to kill himself—there was nothing you could have done. Despair leads people to feel there's no way out, no hope. That was not your fault.' He opened his mouth to protest but she continued, her voice rising in strength and conviction. 'And your mother—that was her choice too. Perhaps she didn't want to live without her husband. It's not a reflection on you—'

'It is—'

'*No*. Maybe she should have wanted to live for her children, but some people are not strong enough. Don't blame her, Rafael, but don't blame yourself either. For your mother's death or your sister's addiction.'

'And your father?' Rafael asked after an endless moment of silence. 'Don't you…aren't you angry for what I did?'

Was she? 'I understand why you wanted to take over his business,' she said slowly. 'And I wish I understood more fully what happened back then. Did my father blame yours on purpose, knowing he was innocent? Who else could have embezzled the money?'

Rafael stiffened. 'It wasn't my father.'

'I know,' Allegra soothed. 'And maybe we'll never know who was truly responsible. But let's put it behind us, Rafael. For ever.'

He stared at her, and Allegra held her breath, waiting, everything in her aching. She'd given him everything. Her love, her heart, her body, her soul, her music. Everything. And she still didn't know what he was going to do with it.

'I want to try,' Rafael said at last, and Allegra nodded as she blinked back tears.

'Yes,' she said. 'Let's try.'

CHAPTER FIFTEEN

THE REALISATION WAS like a thunderclap, startling her awake. Allegra stiffened in bed, her heartbeat coming in thuds. Next to her Rafael slept on. They'd gone to bed together, holding hands, silent and accepting. It felt like a new start, fresh and fragile. Allegra hoped it would endure. That they would.

And then, in the midst of sleep, she'd had that sudden thought slam into her, leaving her breathless and reeling. *Her mother.* Her mother had embezzled that money. It made such horrible sense. Someone close to her father had taken the money; that same person had pointed the finger at Rafael's father. And it made her parents' sudden divorce understandable too, along with the lack of alimony, her father's concern for his own reputation. But where had the money gone?

Although Jennifer had always claimed poverty, after the divorce they hadn't been exactly destitute. It wasn't as if they'd been out on the streets. Looking at the situation now, a grown woman, Allegra doubted that a few pieces of jewellery could have really kept them afloat. Even the embezzled money wouldn't have lasted long in Jennifer's hands—the woman was a spending machine—but it would have tided them over for a while…until she'd found another man to fund her lifestyle. It seemed, all of a sudden, entirely, horribly possible.

If it was true…what would it mean for her mother—but far more importantly, for her and Rafael?

Allegra slipped from the bed, throwing on a dressing gown before reaching for her laptop. She typed in the Internet search box and within seconds she had the dates of both Marco Vitali's suicide and her parents' divorce. Weeks apart. *Weeks.*

Allegra pushed the laptop away as she stared unseeingly into the distance, her mind racing. If her mother had taken the money…if her father had discovered it… if he'd divorced her so abruptly because of that, wanting to separate himself from his wife but unwilling for his reputation to suffer…

There was only one way to find out. One way to truly know. She needed to talk to her mother. Allegra toyed with the idea of a phone call but she knew she wouldn't be able to get the truth over a telephone line. She needed to see her mother face to face, and see the truth, or lack of it, in her eyes. She needed to know. Because perhaps then she and Rafael could finally put the past to rest and move on as a family. Perhaps then he could find the closure he so desperately needed.

She glanced back at him, his face relaxed in sleep, his dark lashes feathering his olive-toned cheeks. He looked beautiful, like something out of a Renaissance painting, and he made her heart ache with love. But would he countenance a trip to America? What would his reaction to the possibility of her mother's crime be?

As if he could sense her thoughts Rafael opened her eyes. He blinked away the dazed confusion of sleep, his amber gaze arrowing in on her. 'Allegra? Is something wrong?'

She licked dry lips, her heart starting to pound. What if he was angry? What if he blamed her somehow? Despite everything they'd said and shared, she still didn't know if Rafael actually loved her. He hadn't said the words. He'd fought against the feeling, even last night, everything in him resisting, but she'd pressed and pushed and tried so hard...

'Allegra?' Rafael said again, his tone sharpening.

'I think I know who embezzled the money. Back then.'

'What?' Rafael sat up in bed, his eyes narrowed as he raked a hand through his hair. 'How could you possibly know that?' He almost sounded suspicious. Of *her*.

Allegra took a deep breath. She felt nervous, even afraid. Why was she risking this—*them*—so soon? Before she even knew the truth or strength of Rafael's feelings? And yet, with this new truth lodged inside her like a stone, how could she not?

'It came to me last night.' She gulped, Rafael's stare still hard and unrelenting. 'I think... I think it was my mother.'

'Your *mother*?'

'It makes sense, in an awful way. She had some money, but she didn't get it from my father. And the divorce was so sudden, so abrupt...'

Rafael swung his legs out of bed, sitting so his back was to her, his hands raked through his hair.

'This doesn't have to change anything between us,' Allegra said quietly. 'Does it?'

'There's no proof, is there?' Rafael's voice was flat, toneless. 'We could never prove it.'

'I... I don't know. I thought, perhaps, we could go to New York. Confront her. Maybe...maybe then you'd feel...' She trailed off, uncertain and miserable. Why had she begun this wretched conversation? Yet she couldn't have kept such an awful suspicion, a huge secret, to herself. She didn't want there to be secrets or lies between them, ever.

'You can't go to New York in your state.'

'Rafael, I'm barely into the third trimester. And I want to be there. Let's do this together. Even if there's no proof, it would be good to know, wouldn't it? Maybe then… maybe then you could finally let the past go.'

'While your mother walks free?'

Allegra blinked at the savage note in his voice. 'I'm sorry,' she whispered, because she was, even if none of it was her fault. Still everything felt complicated and messy, painful.

'I'll book the tickets,' Rafael said, and then he rose from the bed and walked out of the room.

It felt like too much, on top of everything that had happened last night. Allegra's *mother*. She'd as good as signed the death warrant on his family. He didn't blame Allegra, knew she had nothing to do with it, and yet…

It felt bitter, almost too much to bear.

Rafael got ready in taut silence, booking the tickets, packing clothes, telling himself he'd feel better when he knew.

Salvatore drove them to Palermo; Allegra looked tired and miserable, huddled on one side of the limo, one hand resting on her bump. Guilt flashed through him, an acidic rush. She'd given him so much last night. She'd told him she loved him. And he'd fought her every step of the way, couldn't bear the thought of being that vulnerable. That exposed.

And yet he'd shown her the worst of him and she still hadn't walked away. Even now, when he was practically ignoring him, Allegra was there, for the duration, determined to stay by his side, to see this through.

And maybe she needed this as much as he did. If her mother was guilty, it had affected Allegra's life as much as his. They'd both been ensnared by the past—and perhaps the truth could now set them *both* free.

The thought was radical, shifting truths inside him, tilting the world so his perspective was sharper, clearer.

Rafael reached over and took Allegra's hand; surprise flickered across her face as he laced his fingers through hers. He didn't speak; he didn't think he had the words. But he hoped she knew what he was trying to say.

The city was resplendent with autumn colour as they took a cab from the airport to Allegra's mother's apartment in the less fashionable end of Park Avenue, skirting Harlem. Allegra had slept for much of the flight, taking comfort from Rafael's silent support. He hadn't said much, but the mood had shifted between them, the tension focused outward rather than inside. Allegra rested her hand on his shoulder as she dozed and prayed that this would be what she wanted it too—closure. Peace.

Jennifer's expression was almost comical in its shock as she took in the sight of both of them standing in the doorway of her apartment. Her hand fluttered towards her throat and her face paled. 'Allegra...and you must be Vitali.'

'Rafael Vitali,' Rafael answered in a low, gravelly voice. 'Marco's son.'

'I never met him.' Jennifer's expression had cleared, hardened. She was, Allegra realised with a sinking feeling, going to put up a front.

'Mother, may we come in?'

'Of course. Have you…have you come all the way from Sicily?'

'This very afternoon,' Rafael answered. They followed Jennifer into her sitting room where she perched on a white leather sofa, eyebrows elegantly arced.

'What a lovely surprise.'

'Is it?' Allegra asked quietly, and Jennifer's eyes narrowed.

'What is that supposed to mean?'

Allegra took a deep breath. 'Mother, Marco Vitali was accused of embezzlement and lost his business as a result.'

'I told you that,' Jennifer answered with a dismissive flick of fingers. She shot Rafael a quick, wary glance. 'I'm sorry for it, of course, but it has nothing to do with me.'

'He killed himself as a result.'

Jennifer's expression didn't change. 'Again, I'm sorry.'

'There was never any proof it was him, though,' Allegra continued, determined to see this through. She and Rafael both needed to have this reckoning. 'The only so-called proof was that someone close to Papa told him it was Marco.'

Jennifer shrugged her bony shoulders. 'So?'

'So, who was that person? And who really did take the money? Because it was someone close to my father, someone he trusted.'

'You flew all the way to New York to talk about this?' Jennifer demanded, her lips twisting in a sneer. 'I suppose he put you up to it?' she added with a glare at Rafael.

'I did not,' Rafael returned, his voice a low thrum in his chest. 'In fact, I did not want her to make the trip in her condition. But I realised I did want to know. Not for my sake,' he emphasised, his voice lowering to a growl of menacing intent, 'but for Allegra's.'

'What...?' Allegra turned to him, her lips parting in wordless shock.

'If your mother is guilty,' Rafael said, 'then she affected your life as much as mine.' He turned to Jennifer, skewering her with a gaze full of knowledge and accusation. 'Because that's why her father stayed away, isn't it? You made him.'

Jennifer's mouth dropped open and for a few seconds she struggled to speak. 'I don't know what you're talking about,' she finally blustered.

'No,' Rafael answered, so firm, so sure. 'You do know. Because you tried to use Allegra as a bargaining chip.'

'What?' Allegra's mind raced. 'How do you know...?' she demanded of Rafael, the words torn from her.

'I don't. I'm guessing.' He nailed Jennifer with a look. 'And I'm right.'

Jennifer glared at him for a full minute, and then she rose from the sofa, flouncing over to the bar where she poured herself a stiff drink. Allegra watched her, her heart seeming to beat its way up her throat.

'Mother, is that true? Did you threaten Papa? Is that why—?'

'You always thought your father was a saint,' Jennifer said as she tossed back her drink in one swallow and then flung the glass on the table. 'Even when he walked away from you for good.' She turned around, her arms folded tightly against her chest. 'You can't prove anything. There's no paper trail, nothing. Trust me on that.'

'So you did do it,' Allegra cried, tears streaking down her face. 'How *could* you...?'

Jennifer pressed her lips together. 'Your father kept me on very short purse strings.'

'But why did Papa leave...?'

She looked away. 'I told him if he made me leave he'd

never see you again. He didn't want to go through the courts, didn't want the stain on his precious reputation. To have a criminal for a wife! He couldn't bear it. And I thought... I thought he'd change his mind, if he couldn't have you. I didn't know he'd be so bloody stubborn.'

Allegra leaned back against the sofa cushions, her whole body weak and trembling with shock.

'I never meant Vitali to be blamed the way he was,' Jennifer said defensively. 'I just suggested it once. I didn't expect Vitali's business to be ruined by it.'

'You destroyed the life of an entire family,' Allegra said, her voice shaking. '*You* have blood on your hands.'

'Is it my fault that he chose to do that?' Jennifer cried. 'He didn't have to.'

'No, he didn't,' Rafael interjected quietly. To Allegra's surprise he didn't look as angry as she expected him to. He looked sad and resolute, and the surest rock upon which she could depend. He put his arm around her, drawing her close to him. 'You are not to blame for his death,' he said to Jennifer. 'But you are a criminal all the same, and you know it.'

Jennifer's eyes shot sparks as she lifted her chin and said nothing. 'Tell me,' Rafael said quietly. 'Did Mancini ever try to contact Allegra?'

Jennifer looked as if she wasn't going to answer. 'There were letters,' she said finally, and looked away.

Allegra let out a gasp. '*Letters*... Did you keep them? Why didn't you show them to me?'

'I could hardly do that,' Jennifer dismissed. 'You would have started asking questions. But I'm not completely heartless, you know.' She pressed her lips together, and then she turned on her heel and walked out of the room.

Allegra pressed her cheek against Rafael's chest and

he put his arms around her. 'How did you know…?' she whispered.

'I guessed.'

'I never thought…never imagined…'

'Maybe now you'll find some answers.'

Allegra look up at him, her eyes wet with tears. 'I already have, Rafael. With you. In you.'

A brief, trembling smile touched his lips and he rested his forehead against hers. Allegra closed her eyes.

'I'm so sorry to interrupt this touching scene,' Jennifer said. She tossed a packet of letters on the table in front of them and Allegra took them up, scanning the faded envelopes. There had to be at least a dozen.

'We'll go now,' Rafael said, rising from the sofa.

'Wait.' Allegra touched his sleeve. 'Don't you have anything to say to Rafael?' she demanded of her mother. 'Do you know how much he has suffered? His family has suffered?'

Jennifer flinched a little but then pressed her lips together and said nothing. She wouldn't admit any more guilt than she had to.

'It doesn't matter, Allegra,' Rafael said quietly. 'This isn't about me.'

'But it is—'

'No.' He cut her off with gentle firmness. 'This was about you. You needed to hear this.' He gestured to the letters. 'You needed to see this.' He tugged her up to standing, his gaze intent and full of—dared she believe it?—love. 'And now we can truly move on.'

Moments later they were standing in front of her mother's building, blinking in the bright sunlight. Allegra pressed her father's letters to her chest as she shook her head in wonder.

'I never expected this…'

'I'm glad it has happened.'

'But what about you, Rafael? Does it…does it matter, knowing my own mother…?'

'Someone I love taught me that the sins of our parents do not have to affect or define us. The past doesn't have to destroy our future.'

A tremulous smile bloomed across her face, planted its roots deep in his heart. 'Do you mean that?'

'I love you, Allegra. I've loved you for a while, but I fought it because I am a blind, hard-headed fool. And I was afraid, just as you guessed and said. Afraid of being hurt. Of seeming weak. But you saw all my weakness and failure and you loved me even then. Even more.'

'I love you,' she said. '*All* of you.'

'And I love all of you.' He put his arms around her and drew her to him. 'Especially since you can forgive me when I act so foolishly, pulling away when I should have pushed closer.'

'I understood it was scary, Rafael. It was scary for me too.'

'But you wised up a lot faster than I did,' he said with a smile. He brushed his lips across hers. 'Now let's go home.'

EPILOGUE

Eighteen months later

'HE'S THE SMARTEST baby that ever was,' Allegra declared.

'Of course he is,' Rafael answered easily, as he joined her on the lawn, stretching his long legs out on the blanket. The sunshine bathed them in a golden glow, and above them the leaves rustled pleasantly. Their son, named Marco after Rafael's father, babbled excitedly as he attempted to heft his chubby self to his feet.

'He's trying to walk,' Allegra exclaimed. 'And the doctors said he wouldn't walk until he was at least two.'

'Yes, but what do they ever know?' Rafael teased.

It had been a long, hard year and a half in many ways. Little Marco had spent four months in the neonatal unit, first getting strong enough to handle heart surgery and then recovering from that surgery. There had been a few scary moments along the way—a bout of pneumonia that had tested his lungs, and an infection after his surgery. But he'd grown stronger and stronger and finally, when their son had been nearly five months old, they'd brought him back to the villa to begin their life together as a proper family.

Three months ago they'd got married, a small, intimate ceremony in the nearby town, with only a handful of guests. Allegra hadn't wanted a big do, and neither had Rafael.

They were happy as they were, living quietly, with Rafael commuting to Palermo for work. Allegra had started offering cello lessons to local children, and enjoyed playing more than she ever had. The local priest had asked her to play a concert in the church in the nearby town, and Allegra had agreed.

Love, she realised, made her bloom. Made her believe more in herself, because Rafael believed in her. And she saw the same unfurling in Rafael, the lightness and sheer joy in his face, his eyes. Love made you bloom and love also healed.

In recent months Rafael had taken new steps with Angelica, talking more honestly to her than he ever had before. Last week Angelica had moved into the clinic in Switzerland and was undergoing several months of rehab and therapy. So many miracles.

'Allegra, look!' His voice filled with amazement, Rafael pointed to their son who, with a look of both determination and terror on his face, was taking his first step.

'He's amazing,' Rafael declared, and, laughing, Allegra reached out to clasp Marco's hands.

'Just like his father, then,' she said, and, smiling, Rafael leaned down to kiss her.

* * * * *

A smile curved Andreas's mouth, rendering him starkly beautiful. "You and my father missed one small detail in your plan. If I had never discovered you were alive it wouldn't have mattered so much. But I did."

"What detail?" Ariana was shouting now, her voice lost in the gray bleakness around her.

Everything about those few days was still jumbled in her head. She'd been acting on pure animal instincts—fear the overriding one—and listening to King Theos had been the worst kind of mistake.

All she'd wanted was to escape Drakon before Andreas came back from his summit. Before she was caught in the web of her own love for him.

Her leaving him was a betrayal to a man who didn't break the rules for anyone—an unforgivable mistake to a man whose word meant everything.

She clasped his jaw, forcing him to look at her. "*What* detail, Andreas?"

He still didn't hold her. Didn't touch her in any way. Those eyes trapped her again, until even breathing was a chore. Those eyes betrayed all his emotions—fury, shock, and the cold enjoyment of her fate now.

"You are still my wife."

The Drakon Royals

Royalty never looked this scandalous!

To the outside world, the Drakon Royals have the world
at their feet. Yet beneath the surface black-hearted
Crown Prince Andreas, his daredevil younger brother
Prince Nikandros and their illegitimate sister Princess
Eleni hide the secrets of their family name…

Until one brush with desire, and then all the Drakons
find themselves at the heart of their very own scandal!

Crowned for the Drakon Legacy
April 2017

The Drakon Baby Bargain
June 2017

His Drakon Runaway Bride
September 2017

You won't want to miss this outrageously scandalous
new trilogy from Tara Pammi!

HIS DRAKON
RUNAWAY BRIDE

BY
TARA PAMMI

First Published in Great Britain 2017
By Mills & Boon, an imprint of HarperCollins*Publishers*
1 London Bridge Street, London, SE1 9GF

© 2017 Tara Pammi

ISBN: 978-0-263-92537-1

Printed and bound in Spain
by CPI, Barcelona

Tara Pammi can't remember a moment when she wasn't lost in a book—especially a romance, which was much more exciting than a mathematics textbook at school. Years later, Tara's wild imagination and love for the written word revealed what she really wanted to do. Now she pairs alpha males who think they know everything with strong women who knock that theory *and* them off their feet!

Books by Tara Pammi

Mills & Boon Modern Romance

The Sheikh's Pregnant Prisoner
The Man to Be Reckoned With
A Deal with Demakis

The Drakon Royals

Crowned for the Drakon Legacy
The Drakon Baby Bargain

Brides for Billionaires

Married for the Sheikh's Duty

The Legendary Conti Brothers

The Surprise Conti Child
The Unwanted Conti Bride

Greek Tycoons Tamed

Claimed for His Duty
Bought for Her Innocence

Society Weddings

The Sicilian's Surprise Wife

Visit the Author Profile page
at millsandboon.co.uk for more titles.

CHAPTER ONE

"Is this a coup to overthrow me?" Crown Prince Andreas Drakos of Drakon joked as he walked into his study to find his family staring at him with a spectrum of emotions— concern in his sister Eleni's eyes, stubborn resolve in Mia's, something he couldn't define in his brother Nikandros's and pure frost in Gabriel's.

"None of us want your job, your popularity rating or your life, Andreas," replied Nikandros, the financial genius who had set Drakon on its path of recovery after the mess their father had made in the last decade.

Nik was right. The state of his life currently—utter chaos with the Crown Council breathing down his neck for the announcement of his choice for the next Queen of Drakon, the questions the media was raising about his mental health, his frequent disappearances from Drakon in the last year, sometimes even his sexuality—would have usually had the effect of fire ants crawling all over his skin.

But he didn't have any mental energy left beyond the hunt he'd been on for two years now. He was getting close, he knew it in his blood.

He settled down next to Mia. The smell of baby powder drifting from her was strangely calming. "How are you, Mia?"

Mia took his hands in hers. He tried not to flinch. Physical contact made him twitchy and now Mia knew it. But somewhere in the last few months, his sister-in-law and he had become strangely close.

"You didn't come to see the twins, Andreas. After all the hullabaloo you raised about heirs for Drakon, I'm feeling neglected."

He smiled. "I have just this hour returned to Drakon."

"Which nicely segues to why we are all here. Andreas, what is going on?"

"You let her leave Tia and Alexio's side to ask me this question?" Nik glared at him in response. Dark shadows bruised Mia's eyes. "You look awful."

"Stop posturing, Nik. You know he's just trying to get a rise out of you." She smiled and her eyes lit up with that same incandescent joy he'd seen in Nik's of late. "I have two very good reasons for *my* ghoulish look, Your Highness," she said, her gaze tracing the angles of his face. "You however do not.

"You look like hell," she said with that forthrightness he'd come to expect from her, "and whether Nik and Gabriel will agree to put it like that or not, we're all...very worried about you."

He frowned, looked up and, with a strange knot in his gut, realized it was true. "It's not necessary."

"There's talk from the Crown Council about asking you to step down. Your popularity level is at its lowest," Nik said in a deceptively calm voice. "Some political pundits have dared say Father's madness has already begun to manifest in you. You leave Drakon for days, not one of your aides knows your schedule, you refuse to see even Ellie and me..."

"That's why you're all worried?" Andreas asked with a laugh. "That Theos gave me his madness in addition to everything else?"

Eleni spoke up. "Of course not. But we do think you've been acting strange. Andreas, the House of Tharius is waiting for your word to release news of your engagement. The coronation is in two months and you—"

His phone pinged and every nerve in him went on high alert. He knew even before he switched on his phone's screen what the news was going to be. His fingers shook when he swiped the screen.

Found the target. Sending location specs now.

His breath balled up in his chest, and he had to force himself to exhale.

Anticipation bubbled in his blood, coupled with savage satisfaction. "Let the House of Tharius know it's off."

The shock that spread through the huge room made the hairs on his neck rise. Nik and Eleni looked at him with such concern in their eyes that for the first time in months Andreas felt a little guilt. "I apologize for leaving you both in the lurch these past few months. I needed—"

"*Thee mou*, Andreas!" Nik burst out. "We don't care that for the first time in thirty-six years, you took a few months for yourself."

"Not the first time," he said automatically. "I took a free year just when your health improved. Almost ten years ago."

Nikandros frowned. "When Theos tried to make me his leashed dog?"

"A few months before that happened, yes." When Andreas had, in a fit of madness, threatened Theo that he would walk out on Drakon if he didn't give him some time off.

"Andreas." Eleni reached him, her voice wavering. "You can't be crowned King without a wife. That's one of the oldest Drakonite laws. No member of the Crown Council will let you defy it. Are you…are you giving up the crown?"

Nikandros cursed so filthily that he had to laugh.

Andreas patted his sister's hand awkwardly. "I'm not doing any such thing, Eleni. I will be crowned as scheduled."

"You need a wife for that." Nik again. Only Gabriel

stood silent, staring at him from those steel-grey eyes. Gabriel, his brother-in-law, who had figured out the truth.

"Whatever you're considering—" Eleni was close to tears now "—please tell us. Nik and I would never judge you for what—"

"I can't marry Maria Tharius because I already have a wife. For two years, I've been trying to locate her."

You are like me, Andreas, in every way. The same taste for power and control runs in your blood. Why do you think your little wife ran?

Those words had haunted him for two years now. But he didn't give a damn.

He would willingly be a monster if that meant she was back in his life.

"You're married? To whom? When? Why didn't you ever…" Eleni faintly shook with the force of her questions, until Gabriel put his hands on her shoulders and absorbed her petite form into his.

"She was Father's ward. I married her during that sabbatical year in a secret civil ceremony."

"Father had a ward?" Another curse from Nikandros, for he knew that meant another life his father would have played games with.

"Your pity is wasted on her, Nik," Andreas said stonily. "Turns out Father and she understood each other perfectly well."

"Ariana Sakis." Eleni pronounced the name that had become so much a part of his own makeup that Andreas couldn't remember a day before her life tangled with his. "She was shy of eighteen by a few months."

Utter shock was etched on their faces now.

He'd been twenty-six and he'd married a barely legal eighteen-year-old in a secret ceremony… He could have grown two horns and a tail and it would have been less shocking.

"Her parents…died in a car accident. There were rumors that they'd been arguing, that her mother had driven it into the tree on purpose," Eleni explained to Nik. "Her father… was a military general, a close friend of Father.

"There was a lot of talk about what an abusive husband he was and Father immediately severed the connection between the House of Drakos and him.

"Only a handful of people knew he had her custody and he sent her off to…no one knew where. I don't think she even set foot in the palace."

"To a fishing village off the coast," Andreas finished. "Having met Father a couple of times, she'd been more than willing to go."

"That's where you met her?" asked Nikandros.

Andreas nodded. "I… I demanded Father give me a year to do as I wanted, to research a book I wanted to write. He agreed, after a lot of ranting.

"Little did he know that I would end up at the same little village that summer."

Crisp mountain air, blue ponds surrounded by lush woods, a remote cabin, a single coffee shop…and a girl with copper-colored hair and a wide, impish smile.

Andreas swayed as the past reached into him with a clawed hand. Those months in that village with Ariana had been the most glorious of his life.

Too good to last, he realized now with a bitterness that choked him.

"If you married her, how come none of us met her? We didn't even know."

"Father and I decided to wait for a more opportune time to announce that I had wed. For the three months of our marriage, she stayed in an apartment ten miles from the palace."

"You've been looking for her…since Father's decline began." Eleni jerked her chin up. All the pieces were beginning to fall into place. "Where was she all these years, Andreas?"

"Father told me she died in a boating accident after I returned from that oil summit in the Middle East that year."

"Instead?" Nik asked the question, tension filling his shoulders.

"Instead, she took the ten million he offered, faked her death and disappeared under a new identity."

"That's...horrible." Eleni, always loyal to her brothers, had formed her opinion. "How could she make you think she was dead?"

Mia frowned. "You've found this woman now, haven't you?" Something almost like fear glittered in her tired gaze. "Andreas, what is it that you intend to do? Clearly, the woman has made her choice. All of Drakon's eyes will be on her."

It was an edict he'd heard since before he'd even hit puberty. All of the media's eyes would be on him and the woman he chose, Theos had whispered continuously.

She must bring either incomparable wealth—Gabriel's sister had met the first condition—or good breeding in her own blood—Maria Tharius had met both—or be a woman with powerful connections who would agree to become the perfectly ornamental Queen.

Ariana had been none of the above.

"You could divorce her." Gabriel spoke for the first time.

"Drakonite law mandates the couple wait for eighteen months after they file for divorce," Eleni supplied, frowning. "With the coronation in two months, he can't file for a divorce now."

Andreas smiled, uncaring what they all saw in his face. "Father, in his Machiavellian masterminding, assumed that her being officially dead was enough to terminate our marriage. But she's alive. So, even if I wanted, I could not marry Maria Tharius now.

"Ariana will be the next Queen of Drakon." The declaration fell from his mouth, resonated in the very air that filled the King's Palace.

He found he liked the sound of it. An additional bonus was that his father would be rolling in his grave.

Ariana stared at the white stone building of the small, beautiful church in downtown Fort Collins and shivered from head to toe. The frigid October wind that stole through her flimsy wedding dress had nothing to do with it.

The past would not leave her alone today. Didn't matter that it was over ten years since she had married Andreas Drakos, the Crown Prince of Drakon, in a little forgotten church in a backwater fishing village near the mountains.

Didn't matter that in a few hours she was to marry Magnus.

A vein of utter misery ran through her day and night.

She was Anna to her friends, to her colleagues at the legal aid agency where she worked, and to the little community she belonged to amidst the Rocky Mountains in Colorado.

Anna was not an impulsive, reckless woman that self-destructed in the name of love. Anna was not a woman who gave in to the dangerous passion for a man who didn't know how to love.

Instead Anna was supposed to be married this evening to a nice, understanding man. Her friends must be thinking she'd lost her mind. But she had needed to get away from the madness of it all. She'd barely eaten a morsel of food yesterday and nothing at the dinner their friends had arranged for her and Magnus.

Against every better instinct, she pulled her phone out of her coat jacket and compulsively opened a browser. The page was still open to the same article she'd been reading for the last month.

She perused it greedily, as if reading it for the hundredth time would somehow change the gist of it.

Crown Prince Andreas Drakos of Drakon was to announce his choice for his Queen, before his coronation as the King of Drakon, a tiny principality in the Mediterranean again making its mark in the financial world.

A woman who was regal and educated, a doyenne of charities, born to wealth and perfect bloodlines. A woman who would be soft and womanly, a perfect complement to his brooding, controlling masculinity.

She had known that Andreas would one day take another woman, a woman far more suitable than her, to be his wife, to be the Queen of Drakon. That he had waited this long at all, when she knew of his devotion to Drakon, was a shock in itself.

And yet, from the moment she'd seen the little article, her world had tilted on its axis.

Was Anna really any better than the impulsive hothead she had been then? Was there any other reason except that her heart had broken a little again when she'd seen news of Andreas's coronation and it had prompted her to accept Magnus's proposal?

Thee mou, was she willing to destroy Magnus's life, too?

Whatever sun had been shining this morning had receded under dark clouds, the weather resonating her own dark thoughts. She had to break it off. Before she hurt Magnus, before...

The smooth swish of a finely tuned engine broke her focus.

She looked up and froze, wishing with every cell inside of her that she could truly freeze, become invisible, blend into the gray, leaf-bare trees around her. Could become one of the statues that littered the lovely town.

The pounding of her heart in her ears said she was far too alive.

For she recognized the little black-and-gold flag fluttering in the harsh wind on the hood of the European luxury car idling not two steps away. She knew the symbol of the golden dragon with fires spewing out of its wide jaws. She knew the man inside and his body and he knew hers, better than she did her own.

Legs quaking under her, she stumbled away from the curving stone wall that led to the steps of the church. Wrapped her arm around a tall tree for support.

Every primal instinct she possessed screamed at her to run, to flee. And yet not a single cell obeyed. Not a single muscle moved even as she heard the click of the car door, even as she saw polished black shoes step out of the car, even as the tall angular form straightened.

He'd found her.

Dear God, after ten years, he'd caught up to her. Just as she had always known he would, in the deep dark of the night when she couldn't hold the memories at bay.

Crown Prince Andreas Drakos, soon to be King of Drakon, was here.

A long black coat fluttered around his ankles, wavy hair the color of a raven's wing carelessly combed away from a high forehead. Power stamped across those high cheekbones, the patrician nose, the thin-lipped mouth. Arrogant entitlement and self-confidence dripped from him with every movement of his body.

Jet-black eyes, hard and flinty like glittering opals, eyes that reflected nothing back, eyes that had sometimes felt as if there was nothing behind them, swept over her shivering body and came to rest on her face. "*Kalimera*, Ariana."

Their eyes collided and held, sending a tsunami of emotions racing through her body. God, those eyes...she had drowned in them once. She had reveled in making them glow with humor, in making them darken in passion, in trying to break through that opaque shield.

She pressed her bare hands against the rough bark of the tree, hoping to jerk some kind of self-preservation instinct into life, for some kind of rationality to master the sheer emotional assault she was under.

Hands tucked into the pockets of his trousers, clad in all black, he looked like a dark angel come to serve swift justice. "It does not seem like a good day to be getting married. Does it, *pethi mou*?"

So he knew.

Ariana licked her dry lips, swallowing away the knowledge that she'd been about to call it off. Her gut instinct had been right. "What…what are you doing here?"

"Here on this side of the pond, in Colorado, in this little wonderful town that you've been hiding in?" He didn't move, nor did a muscle flicker in his face. In that deep, gravelly voice of his, he could have been inquiring after the bitter weather.

They could have been a couple of friends discussing trivialities. No anger or emotion fractured his cool expression. Only a faint thread of sarcasm bled through.

"Or here in front of this beautiful little church on this bleary afternoon where you're waiting for the man you're supposed to marry in a few hours? Should I answer the general or the specific?"

Ariana closed her eyes. Didn't help one bit. His presence was a hum of power in the air, making something in her vibrate in tune. Dragging cold air deep into her lungs, she flicked her eyes open. Feeling was beginning to come back into her muscles. And along with it memories and an unholy amount of panic.

How had she forgotten that the smoother Andreas's voice got, the hotter his rage? The deeper the fracture in his self-control, the colder and calmer his actions? It was his shutdown mode, where neither reason nor begging would filter through. Fresh wind made her eyes water. It had to be the wind. "I don't have your magic with words, Andreas."

He inclined his head in a regal nod. "I am to be King soon. I thought now would be a wise time to take care of the little business between us. After all, you ran out on me without a word, and who knows when you will decide you want to come back to me?"

Shivers raced down her spine. "Go back to your precious Drakon." She couldn't help the bitterness in her voice, even as she cautioned herself against it. "You have nothing to worry about with me. You and I—" her voice caught, and still, nothing changed in his expression "—were an episode from a different life. The media will never catch hold of our little story, neither will I claim even an acquaintance.

"Ariana Sakis, for all intents and purposes, is dead."

She glanced up and her breath seized in her lungs.

Suddenly, he was there in front of her, blocking everything else from her vision. Blocking the entire world from her. Sandalwood, flared by his body's heat, taunted her nostrils. Filled her with sensations and memories. Such an interestingly warm scent for a man whose blood was decidedly cold. But then his passion had been just as contrasting to the ruthless lack of his heart.

"Ariana Drakos," he corrected with the faintest trace of warning. "Do not forget you belong to me."

Nothing so tacky as a raised voice or a teetering temper from the House of Drakos.

"You might be King of your bloody palace, Andreas—" panic rushed reckless words to her mouth "—but not of me. Magnus will be here any minute and I won't—"

"Your fiancé has been made aware of the situation and is not coming."

So polite even as he stood there, playing havoc with her life. So infuriatingly calm. Her hands itched to muss up that perfectly placid expression of his. The devil in her

burned to unsettle him as he did her. That urge was dangerous. Just being near Andreas was like throwing herself off
a cliff—exhilarating and terrifying. And she had stopped
doing that to herself a long time ago.

"What the hell did you tell Magnus?"

"That he should call it quits while his life is still under
his control."

"Is this what you have sunk to? Chasing away the man
in my life? Have you become as low and manipulative as
your father then, Andreas?"

His jaw tightened. "I didn't have to chase him, Ariana.
Like any sensible man, Magnus seemed uninclined toward
being the other party in bigamy. In fact, he sounded angry
at your deception."

"Bigamy?" She covered the distance between them without caring. Her heart seemed to slow down in her chest, a
dreadful cold filling her. "What do you mean, bigamy?"

His mouth relaxed, he stood waiting against the same
tree as if he had all the time in the world. As if there was
nothing that would give him more pleasure than to watch
the ground being pulled away from under her. As if he'd
planned and lived this moment a thousand times and he
couldn't let his enjoyment end.

She shook her grip on his coat but he didn't budge.
"What do you mean?"

A smile curved his mouth. Rendering him starkly beautiful. "My father and you missed one small detail in your
plan. If I had never discovered you were alive, it wouldn't
have mattered so much.

"But I did."

"What detail?" she was shouting now, her voice lost in
the gray bleakness around her. Everything about those few
days was still jumbled in her head. She'd been acting on
pure animal instincts—fear the overriding one—and listening to King Theos had been the worst kind of mistake.

All she'd wanted was to escape Drakon before Andreas came back from his summit. Before she was caught in the web of her own love for him.

She'd been so naive that she had played right into Theos's manipulative hands. But Andreas wouldn't believe her now.

Her leaving him had been a betrayal to a man who didn't break rules for anyone, an unforgivable mistake to a man whose word meant everything to him.

She clasped his jaw, forcing him to look at her. "What detail, Andreas?"

He still didn't hold her. Didn't touch her in any way. Those eyes trapped her again, until even breathing was a chore. Those eyes betrayed all his emotions—fury, shock and the cold enjoyment of her fate now. "The papers you signed for Theos, dissolving our marriage, he never presented them to me.

"Your supposed death bought him time and then... I don't know what he and you planned. I never saw those papers until a few months ago. The motion didn't even get filed in court.

"You are still my wife."

CHAPTER TWO

SHEER TERROR FILLED her eyes as she stared at him. "Your wife?" she repeated, as if she couldn't think past those two words.

Andreas studied her greedily, his skin prickling with that sensation only Ariana could arouse.

Her lips were dry, trembling. Her copper gold hair, her crowning glory, was tied into that messy knot she'd always put it in, complaining that it was too much. Her cheekbones were sharp and high, forever giving her that malnourished look. Her skin was still that golden shade though it looked alarmingly pale just then.

"You and I are still married, Ariana. Ten years and going strong. Except for the little problem of you wanting to marry another man."

Her fingers became lax around his coat, her body trembling with tension. "Ariana is dead," she kept repeating through pale lips.

Words that had haunted him for eight years.

He had imagined her death a hundred different ways, a million different times. He had hated himself for leaving her with his father. He had been through hell and back because he thought he hadn't protected her.

He fisted his hands by his sides, fighting the urge to wrap his hands around her. Fighting the overwhelming impulse to push her against the tree and crush her mouth with his.

Because to see Ariana was to want Ariana. He didn't remember a time he hadn't wanted to possess her with that raw longing.

And yet lust was only a pale shadow behind the need to

ensure that she was alive and not a figment of his imagination, a flimsy shadow from his feverish nightmares.

Outwardly, she hadn't changed at all.

Thin, angular body built with lean muscle. Wide, brown-ringed eyes too big for her gamine face. Sharp, bladelike nose followed by a mouth so lushly pillowy, so poutingly full, that no man could see it and not think dirty, lustful thoughts.

It was as if all the austerity that had been executed in her face had to be made up for in that mouth.

She looked just as common and nondescript as Theos had called her back then.

Only her eyes had changed.

That twinkle that had made them glow, as if she held the glorious flicker of life itself inside her, it was gone. Wariness filled them now. He wanted to shove her away from him, stop her from touching him like she used to do.

But the damage to his system was already done.

His body roared to life at the soft imprint she left with hers. Long, toned legs tangled with his, her body trembling faintly against his. The scent of her—just her skin and the lavender soap she apparently still used—invaded his bloodstream. Like Pavlov's dog, every cell inside him stood to attention. Memories and sensations of pleasure and something else, a sense of being utterly alive, poured into his skin, making him heated.

"This is your petty revenge on me," she finally whispered, her mouth only inches apart from his. A loud thrum began under his skin. "Your way of playing with my life while you announce your own marriage to the world. You will let me dangle at your fingertips, holding this ridiculous threat over my head.

"Because I had the temerity to walk away from the controlling, arrogant, ruthless man you are, Andreas."

He scowled. "You think it was my pride that was dented by your betrayal, by your lies?"

"Yes," she said defiantly. "For you're not capable of feeling anything else."

Andreas flinched, her words landing like barbed fists on his flesh. *Thee mou*, it seemed even now, when she was utterly in the wrong, she dared to challenge him, dared to call him out for her mistakes.

"You could have done this through your lawyers. You could have sent me the divorce papers through one of your lackeys. But no...you had to do it personally because you couldn't forego the pleasure of ruining my life before you go back to rule your bloody kingdom."

"You're mistaken again, Ariana. I did not come simply to ruin your engagement."

"Then why are you here?"

"For two years, since Father let it slip that you were alive, I've been waiting for this moment.

"I will be crowned King of Drakon soon and I need my wife by my side. I have come to take you home to Drakon."

Her gaze searched his, desperate. What little fight had been there seemed to deflate out of her. As if she was shrinking right in front of his eyes. "You've got to be kidding me."

He touched her then, tracing the delicate line of her jaw with the tip of his forefinger. Her skin was silky smooth to his touch, a faint tremor running through it. "But you already know I have no sense of humor."

"You...can't..." her breath came in little gasps "...do... this."

Her thin body going slack against him, his wife did what she'd always forced him to do. She fainted and forced him to catch her. Forced him to hold her fragile body in his, before he was ready for any such contact. Feeling fear, and panic and a hundred other emotions that he'd never had encountered otherwise.

Her gown's bodice was so tight that Andreas drew his pocket knife out of his coat and cut the front off. The blue tinge around her mouth began to recede, his own panic fading with it.

He easily lifted her slender form and made his way to the waiting car, icy anger thawing and giving way to shock.

She might not have changed outwardly but there was something different about her. Something fragile and fractured. Almost as if there was a piece missing.

He'd expected a radiant, carefree bride, ready to ride into another adventure with another man she'd sucked in with her effervescent personality, with her vivacity and wit. He'd expected her to be living it up in some party town with the money she'd taken from his father.

He hadn't expected this…this *waif*, with bruises under her eyes, working away all hours at a nonprofit legal agency. She made barely any money. She shared a one-bedroom apartment, the size of his closet, with another woman. He'd have never believed that silly, rebellious girl would have the interest to study law much less the grit to get a degree and practice.

Barely out of breath, he slowly lowered her into the seat and slid into place next to her.

Every savage promise he'd made himself that he'd make her suffer crumbled as he gathered her body into his.

Once again, all his plans turned to dust by the infuriating woman.

Just as she had been able to make him laugh, make him long for something he had never known back then. Make him lose his mind in the desperate need to possess her.

All through that summer, Ariana had wielded some kind of magic over him.

That laughing, reckless girl had shattered through to

his core, given him a taste of an unparalleled joy he'd never known.

And so he'd done the unthinkable and married her when it had been time to leave. Possessing Ariana had equaled holding that joy in the palm of his hand. It had meant being something more than the Crown Prince, something he hadn't even realized he'd needed to be until then.

He had forgotten who and what he was, he had clung desperately to that feeling, had thought it enough to have her in his life.

Except it hadn't been enough for her.

With that same recklessness that had lured him to her, she had destroyed their lives. It was that same girl he had expected to find today.

But she was right.

This was not the Ariana he had met that summer, the Ariana he had married.

And yet, letting her go was not an option.

Ariana came awake slowly, her throat parched, her mind blank. Air filled her in quick, choppy bursts.

"Drink this."

Ignoring the questions buzzing through her head, she took the bottle and drank the water. It was cold and crisp, what she desperately needed.

"Iedas Mountain Springs," the label on the water bottle said, with a small sketch of the majestic mountain range in Drakon... *Drakon!*

She jerked upright. Cream leather walls greeted her, understated luxury permeating the ambience. Soft lights from the ceiling cast a golden glow around the cabin.

Cabin... She was in the rear cabin of a private jet—a jet that belonged to the blasted House of Drakos.

The events of the afternoon came back in a fast reel.

Andreas had said they were still married.

Andreas had said he was going to take her back to Drakon.

Andreas had caught her when she'd fainted.

The panic felt like ants crawling all over her skin. She pushed her legs out and stood up. The cabin tilted but she had to get out of here.

The slither of her dress, her wedding dress, alerted her. She looked down, found the corset cut neatly down in the middle. The beaded bodice hung open through the center, gaping open to reveal her slip and the shadow of her breasts.

Ariana held it up with both hands and forced her Jell-O legs to move.

Before she took another step, he was before her.

A man as hard as the rock on which his palace sat. Yet, as she looked at him now, there were white lines around his mouth, and he was not so solid.

"Why am I here? What is that sound?"

"They're readying for takeoff."

"No!"

"Sit down, Ariana."

"Get out of my way."

"You're in no shape to go anywhere."

"I swear, Andreas, if you don't move out of my way—"

His fingers gripped her arms, exerting pressure backward. "Calm down before you faint again!"

"How dare you? You bastard!" Ariana let her hand fly.

The crack of her palm against his cheek was like a pop of thunder, leaving an utter silence behind. She clutched her wrist with her left hand, shock jarring it. Breathing hard, she looked up.

He hadn't even touched his jaw. Except for the tight clench of it, the little jerk of his head, he showed no reaction to what she'd done. He still supported her.

"Does that conclude this episode to your satisfaction, Ari?"

Her shortened name made her breath catch. "I will not apologize."

He shrugged.

That casual gesture was like fuel to her rage.

"You're kidnapping me. Really?" She fisted her hands and went at him, lost to all reason. "After all the propriety and decorum and a hundred other rules you demand of everyone, you're actually kidnapping me?"

Of course it was exactly what he had planned. And Ariana had so nicely played into his hands, by literally fainting at his feet.

Damn it, Ari.

"You will not like it if I subdue you on the bed, Ari. Or maybe you will, since we both know what will happen the moment I lie on top of you." The cold matter-of-factness of his threat made everything still in her.

Ariana turned and met his inscrutable gaze, wrapping her mind around this.

"Should we put my theory to the test or shall you calm down?"

"Let me go."

He did instantly. With an urgency that made her flush. Her legs simply gave out and Ariana slid into a graceless heap on the bed.

This had been coming, Ari, a nauseating voice whispered. *You just buried your head in the sand. You knew he was going to catch up with you one day.*

She didn't know how long they sat like that. She on the bed, trying to catch her breath, trying to quell the panic, and he sitting in the one armchair in the corner, watching her.

A lion crouching in silence, waiting for his prey to show weakness.

The long coat and jacket were gone. Replaced by a white designer dress shirt with a white undershirt—nothing so scandalous as going without one for the uptight Crown

Prince of Drakon—and black custom-made trousers for his six-four height. Dark olive skin at his throat beckoned to her. She followed the trail of the chain around his neck with her eyes.

His dog tags from his time in the Drakonite Army, where he'd trained from fifteen to eighteen, would be under that undershirt. Platinum cufflinks. A platinum-plated watch glinted on his left wrist. Black Italian handmade shoes gleamed where he'd folded one foot on top of his thigh.

The soft lightning of the cabin wreathed his face in shadows, showing the sharp planes and hollows of his face to perfection.

He was leaner than she remembered and it made him look even more distant and withdrawn. There were lines on his face now, especially around that thinly sculpted mouth. At twenty-six he'd been gorgeous in an uptight, starchy kind of way.

Ten years later now, he seemed even more comfortable in his skin. Even more arrogant and ruthless about his place in the world.

Every small thing she noticed brought back a memory thudding into her conscious, as physical as a blow to her solar plexus. Her throat dried promptly again, her heart forever in that lurching rhythm when he was near.

Slowly the impact of this, *of him*, hit her in its completion. She wasn't running away from this, not yet at least.

No, there was no running away at all from this, she corrected herself. Not unless she wanted him to give her chase for the rest of their lives.

Realizing she'd been gaping at him, she pulled her gaze up. Chin propped against his fist, he raised a brow. He didn't tease her for gawking at him like a teenager.

He didn't need the validation to his masculinity, to his ego.

Power was second skin to him, women flocked to him

like buzzing bees. Actresses and models, CEOs and princesses, women had been falling at his feet since puberty. If he'd been merely one more vacant, lazy royal out to have a good time, maybe he wouldn't have so much pull.

But no, Andreas Drakos was smart as a whip. A historian, an army veteran, a weaver of words. *Christos*, there wasn't anything he didn't excel at.

And yet he'd chosen her.

She frowned, the question had tormented her for years, struggled into a comfortable position and took stock of her body. A leaf fluttering in a harsh gale would have more strength than her at the moment.

Of all the stupid, moronic things to do in front of this man... She pressed a hand to her temple.

She felt the heat of his body instantly in the air around the bed. Whatever reprieve she'd gotten was over.

In silent scrutiny, he fluffed the pillows and propped them against the wall, and then pulled her into a sitting position. With economic movements, his fingers barely touching her, he arranged the duvet around her. Gave her another bottle of water that she emptied within seconds.

Hysteria began to bubble up through her throat and she laughed. Water spurted out of her nose and mouth inelegantly, and he promptly wiped her nose and mouth with a napkin. On and on went her near manic laughter until tears streamed out from her eyes. Until the ball of tension that had lodged in her chest since she'd seen him standing in front of the church slowly deflated.

He raised a brow again.

"How many women can claim Crown Prince Andreas Drakos waited on them like a lowly member of staff?" she quipped, perfectly understanding his question.

A sudden tightness gripped her chest. Wordless communication had been so their thing.

"So you still possess that ridiculous sense of humor."

She tensed as he sat down at the edge of the bed. Not near enough to touch, yet tantalizingly close. Her body couldn't take this much heightened awareness after what had been a drought of ten years. Not for long, not without combusting with need.

"What the hell was that?"

"Be glad I didn't scratch that perfect face. Or maybe I should have. A little imperfection would have at least made you look human."

A jagged sigh. An echo of all the times Ari had pushed his buttons. "I speak of your fainting."

"You showed up after ten years and I fainted." She sighed. *Regression much, Ari?*

"Continue like that and it will only confirm my belief that you're still that reckless, juvenile, rebellious brat I knew back then."

"What can I say? You bring out the worst in me, Your Highness."

Their eyes sought each other instantly.

Are you my watchdog, Your Highness?

Crack a smile, Your Highness.

It's called a vodka shot, Your Highness.

Had she been that naive, that foolish to have teased this man like that? Had he actually let her?

"Ariana, focus." It wasn't even a warning. Just a smidgen of his impatience leaking. "If I hadn't been there, you would have been on the grass, in the cold, for God knows how long. Is this your new thing now, fainting?"

"New thing?"

"Yes. Pot brownies, vodka shots, fasting for days to lose weight… *Christos*, do I need to go on? You were always ridiculously reckless about your well-being."

Ari massaged her temples with her fingers. He was right.

She had thrown herself into her sudden, boundless freedom, as naively as jumping off a cliff. Guilt over her parents' deaths had stolen reason from her. The need to experience life to the fullest after seventeen years of being trapped in a golden cage...it had consumed her.

He'd thought her ditzy, willful, reckless and any number of even less complimentary things. She had been all those and more. But not in the past ten years, not anymore.

Her hands settled on her belly, corrosive grief scratching her throat.

The freedom she'd finally got, the need to make something of her life, it had come at such a high price. But it had helped her find herself, helped her achieve control over those impulses that would destroy her.

Until this past month when his impending announcement had undone her again. And that made fear whisper through her bones. It was the same circle of self-abuse her mother had been stuck in with her father.

"Ariana?"

"I...had a salad for lunch yesterday and nothing since then. It has been a stressful week—the caseload at the firm is crazy right now and then a doubly stressful morning. I've never fainted before." Except that one time after she had left Drakon and him behind. Because in her recklessness, the same that he accused her of right now, it had taken a fainting spell to realize she'd been three months pregnant.

His instant control of the situation, his interrogation of her as if she were a child, grated like nothing else. But to be fair, that's what she had been then. "Because of the elevation above sea level of this town, I sometimes find it hard to breathe."

"Mountain air makes your asthma worse. I checked your little purse and you didn't have your inhaler on you."

She looked up then and swallowed. She'd thought he would delete anything related to their time together from his life, from his mind. At least after learning of the biggest lie she'd ever told.

Apparently, like her, Andreas had forgotten nothing of their time together. Of their short-lived marriage. Of how they made each other burn up in flames when they touched, and ruined each other when they didn't.

"It does flare it up from time to time. But it makes up with everything else."

A little frown appeared between his brows. "Makes up?"

"The fact that it flares my asthma is a little inconvenience to what I have found here. I...found a community here, Andreas. My life has meaning here. There are women who count on me." She held his gaze, air ballooning up in her chest, smothering her lungs. Time to face the facts. "You can't really mean what you said earlier."

"Have you ever known me to say anything I didn't mean?"

No. He'd never once said that he loved her, even in the throes of passion, even when he'd let his control slip. And it was something to watch the iron-control-clad, emotionless, uptight Crown Prince lose it in the sheets.

She swung her legs out of the bed and stood up slowly. When he neared her to offer assistance with clear reluctance—because of course every touch and look had to be calculated in that steel trap that was his mind—she held him off with her hand.

The cut corset of her wedding dress hung limply around her waist but Ariana didn't care. She didn't care one bit what her sheer slip showed.

She didn't care that his gaze traveled all over her, noted her defiant pose, and yet didn't betray anything.

He had unraveled her life all over again and she was not going to hide and feel shame about it. She had to face Andreas and whatever came now, if she ever wanted to move forward in her life.

"Think about what you're proposing, Andreas. Your father was right in one thing—I hardly possess the bloodlines. I was never brought up to be the next Queen of Drakon.

"You...completely agreed with him." It took no small amount of effort to put this forward rationally. "You... The moment we left the village..."

"What about it, Ariana?"

He had regretted what he'd done, she knew. But the past was done, useless. "Do you think I would be any more malleable this time around?" She lifted her chin. "The last ten years have only made me realize how right I was. We would have destroyed each other if I'd stayed."

He reached her then. Breath serrated her throat as he lifted his hand and softly clasped her jaw. For one sheer, indefinable moment, a wealth of emotion danced in his jet-black gaze. Pure rage and something else. A bleakness?

"Silly Ari. Do you think I give a damn about what you want or need right now?

"Your death tormented me for eight years.

"The little slip from Theos's mouth that you were not only alive, but that you took money from him to disappear—" tight lines emerged around his mouth, a small fracture in his control "—that news has tortured me for the last two years."

Ariana stared, stunned. A dent to his ego, she'd expected. But for Andreas to admit that losing her had tormented him...it was akin to the sun revolving around the earth. The pithy declaration raged through her, kindling feelings she couldn't handle.

Had he truly felt something for her then?

"This is exactly what your father wanted you to become."

"Theos is dead, *agapita*," he said softly, a wicked gleam in his eyes. "It has been years since his will, his word, has had the power to move me. The power to persuade me. The power to control me.

"I have become my own man, Ari. Isn't that what you wanted long ago?"

She'd have given anything to hear that ten years ago. But not anymore. "The moment we land in Drakon, I'll yell what you've done through the rooftops. Your image can't survive a scandal."

He bared his teeth in a feral smile. "So you have kept tabs on me."

The sound that fell from her mouth was half growl, half screech. "I know my place even in the illustrious world that you're the unrivaled lord of. One word from me will plunge the House of Drakos into a horrible scandal."

"Do you really want to threaten me?"

Panic bloomed, making her voice rise. "My entire life is here. Even more importantly, my clients are here."

"Your fiancé fell over himself in his haste to accept my conditions. He gets to keep the legal agency running and keeps quiet about your secret identity for the rest of his life."

"I built that agency with my blood and tears." The one good thing that had come out of the loss she'd suffered.

"You built it with the dirty payoff you took from my father. Even your education was paid for by the House of Drakos. And since we're still married—"

"Half of everything I own is yours," she finished. Her mind whirled. "And you need Magnus to keep quiet about where I've been and what I've been doing."

His jaw clenched and Ariana exhaled roughly. Finally, there was one point she could negotiate with. But he didn't give her even that chance.

"Your clients, what do you think will happen if the media gets hold of who you truly are? That you've been living a lie for ten years."

"It's not a lie. I busted my ass to earn my law degree. I opened that nonprofit legal aid agency because I wanted to help those women."

"And when the world finds out that you're not Anna Harris but Ariana Drakos, wife of the King of Drakon—"

"My clients will be dragged into the limelight along with me." She exhaled roughly. "Those are women who have already been abused by men they trusted. Which will keep me quiet. Am I getting close, Andreas?"

He smiled then—a jagged mockery that made her chest ache. "You know what I find truly hard to believe in this new, peachy life you've made for yourself?"

"What?" She snarled the question at him.

"Am I to believe that you have found your true, deep purpose in your scattered life finally? That you truly devote yourself tirelessly to those women and their plight?"

If there was a moment that Ariana truly wanted to sink her nails into that perfect, arrogant, condescending face and scratch it, it was then. Ten years of striving to make something of herself, to give meaning to what she'd lost, to make a meaningful path for herself, and his careless disdain crushed it all.

And he knew it. He was all but challenging her to launch herself at him again, to go back to that lowest denominator of herself she'd once thrived on.

She would attack him and he would subdue her…and it would lead to only one conclusion. The knowledge suffused the very air around them with a dense heat.

Every time they had fought in those horrible three months of their marriage, they'd ended up in bed. Or against the wall. Or on the chaise longue with the Crown Prince on his knees, with his arrogant head between her thighs.

The memory shimmered like a bright glitter in his coal-black eyes.

With the sheer will that had helped her survive through the darkest night of her life, Ari looked away. Air rushed into her lungs, clearing the haze.

Her biggest defense against Andreas was to show leaving him hadn't been a whim. That she wasn't a car crash in the making anymore. That she had come into her own strength these last ten years. That she'd proactively made something of her life.

"I care about my clients, about their privacy, about not turning everything Magnus and I worked for into a lie. So, yes, you win my silence. But nothing else."

"How refreshing that you're capable of loyalty, even if it's toward another man, *pethi mou*. I told him, soon enough you'd have found a reason to run out on him. That your precious freedom would have come calling.

"Is it not your pattern?"

Ariana flinched, the softly delivered statement even more painful for she'd been about to do exactly the same thing to Magnus. Not for some kind of femme fatale reason but because she'd realized Magnus deserved much better than her.

"I didn't think you of all people would be crass enough to typecast me as some kind of vacant-headed, freewheeling slut. If for no other reason than that it would taint your own pristine image, your own association with me."

"What does that mean?"

"I was eighteen, Andreas. I… I was bowled over by you. I threw myself at you. I was…messed up after my parents' deaths, and you were a high unlike anything I'd ever known.

"You were—you *are* unlike any other man I've ever known.

"Jesus, did you know what your attention, your reluctant interest, meant to me? You…who didn't show interest in princesses, and models and CEOs.

"You looked at me. *Me*—messed-up, frightened, guilty Ariana.

"You married me knowing who and what I was. So, if

we have to call out someone for the…*twisted* mess that was our marriage, it's you."

"Was that the justification when you let me think you had died in a horrible drowning accident," he bit out and she flinched. "Maybe I will let you go, Ariana. Maybe one of these days I will find that little bit of decency within myself again. Maybe you can go back to being Anna Harris and the savior of those women in your little town again."

And in those statements of his, Ariana saw his shredded control for what it was. Saw his loathing that she was still an obsession with him. He despised himself, and her, because he couldn't give her up.

Any hopes she had of convincing him perished in that moment. After all, she did know him better than anyone.

"So this is about revenge?"

"Call it whatever the hell you want to." His gaze tracked her face and her torn clothes. He fisted his hand so tight by his side that the knuckles were white.

For the first time that day, Ariana realized how tremendous his self-control was.

"You need food and rest. Do not force me to manhandle you into that, too. We both know whether it will be pleasure or punishment."

Ariana fell onto the bed with a soft thud, the recrimination in his eyes burning through her like acid. Her skin still prickling, for the first time since she'd known him, she was grateful for his iron-clad self-control.

Because, even after all these years, she had none when it came to resisting the Crown Prince of Drakon.

CHAPTER THREE

"Mrs. Drakos? Your Highness?"

For the second time in a few hours, Ariana jerked upright so suddenly that her neck gave a painful twinge. She looked at the stewardess patiently waiting for her to wake up.

So the cat was out of the bag.

Instead of the panic she braced herself for, all she felt was a…quiet resignation. Not the give-up-and-become-his-wife kind. But the guilty-as-hell kind.

Whatever he had done to her, however much she had despised him at the end of their marriage, it was clear that she had miscalculated the effect of her supposed death on Andreas. On hearing of his swift engagement to a real estate mogul's sister, her own guilt had been alleviated.

She didn't belong in the Crown Prince's world and that he'd replaced her so fast had been proof enough.

Of course, that miscalculation had been aided by his father.

If Andreas had grieved her loss, who knew how Theos had twisted that to his advantage?

King Theos, she had realized within a week of meeting her guardian as her father-in-law, had possessed an unhealthy hold on his heir. He'd seen her as nothing but a weakness to eliminate from his son's life.

What had been painful was from the moment he had presented her to King Theos, even Andreas had begun to see her as that—a weakness to be hidden away.

The stewardess's eyes traveled over Ari's hair, which could rival the Amazon forest for its wildness right now, to the torn dress she had fallen asleep in.

Ari cringed. She stood up from the bed, and pushed the dress off her shoulders and hips.

Ill-concealed curiosity scampered across the woman's face. "I will take care of the dress, Your Highness. Have it mended. I'm sure you'd want to—"

"No, that's not necessary," Ari replied, pulling the slip off her shoulders. Her strapless bra stuck to the underside of her breasts uncomfortably, thanks to her habit of smothering herself under the covers. She stepped out of the slip seconds before the woman took it, almost dislodging Ari off her feet.

"Have it burned," a soft voice commanded from the entrance.

The need to cover herself was instinctive, self-preservation at its primal. Shaking, Ariana covered her midriff with her arms.

The stewardess had that look again, switching between her and Andreas, as if she could figure out the secret as to how this average-looking, falling-apart-at-the-seams waif had snared the most powerful, gorgeous man in Drakon.

It was a question the whole world was going to ask this time, not just King Theos, if Andreas had his way.

His gaze dipped past Ari's face this time—as if he'd given himself permission to look, to linger—moved to the pulse beating wildly at her neck, betraying the sudden tension that suffused her every cell, to the curves of her breasts rising and falling. A languorous ache settled low in her belly, her nipples hard against the flimsy bra.

"Checking up on me already?" Fear of how just one look from him turned her on destroyed the need for discretion in front of a member of the staff. "There's no way to escape, unless you're willing to provide me with a parachute. You can see me plummet to death, at least."

He closed his eyes, his chest barely lifted and fell with his exhale, and then leveled that black gaze at her again.

Military precision to every single breath. "I came in to see if you were awake. Petra needs your prescription for your inhaler. I will not have you fainting everywhere."

"Petra?"

"Yes, my secretary." He looked down at his phone, frowned, typed a message and looked up again.

Tall, blonde, with a voluptuous body, armed with a master's from a renowned university in Drakon, and hailing from a highly connected Drakonite family. Andreas's oldest friend and shadow. Theos's spy. If Ariana could give a form to all her self-doubts and insecurities back then, it would be Petra Cozakis. "I know Petra runs your life. And for the last time, it was the stress of the last week and that dress that did it today.

"Do not treat me as if I am still an imbecile, Andreas."

He raised a brow. Confirmation enough that that was exactly how she was acting. "Petra is on this flight. Let her know if you need anything."

"No," she said loudly.

His gaze pinned her. "Precisely what are you saying no to?"

"If you're dragging me to the King's Palace, it will be different this time. I will not be hidden away like some stain on the great House of Drakos. I will not let your uptight, snobbish staff run circles around me. I will not communicate through your minions, will not let you pawn me off on them as if I was a thing to be managed." Maybe what Andreas needed was a dose of reality. For his staff and his family and the world to realize who he had chosen and how unsuitable she was.

Lines formed between his brows. "Leave us," he said to the stewardess without moving his gaze from Ariana.

The woman froze in the process of folding the damned dress. She thought Ariana and Andreas had gotten married in that dress, Ariana realized.

"Burn. That. Dress," he repeated. The stewardess nodded and scurried out.

Arms still around her waist, Ariana turned, grabbed the duvet and pulled it around her like a shroud. However she tried, the choice was to either cover her chest or her midriff.

She covered her midriff. Her bra was enough for her meager breasts. It wasn't like he hadn't seen the little she had to offer before.

The small scar she bore above her pubic bone might not be visible in the soft light, but she couldn't take the chance. Closing her eyes, she willed the grief down. The situation with Andreas was explosive enough without adding her discovery *after* she had left him that she'd been pregnant.

That she had lost her precious little baby boy was an unbearable, ever-present weight on her soul. For Andreas, it would only mean more betrayal. Worse, the loss of a *potential heir*, a figurehead to represent the House of Drakos's future.

Ariana couldn't bear to hear his dismissal of that tiny life. The guilt of it, the grief of it was all her own.

At least, it served as a reminder that she couldn't chance a pregnancy again.

Because there was no point in denying that she was going to end up in his bed. The attraction between them, it seemed, had survived despite everything.

She took a Post-it note and pen from the small bedstead and scribbled the name and number of her GP. Shards of glass seemed to be stuck in her throat when she turned. "I also need the prescription for my birth control pills filled."

The memory of their last fight, the bitterest and dirtiest of them all, sculpted sharp grooves in his already gaunt cheeks. His hesitation was like handing her a live grenade. Bulky duvet and all, she reached him, her heart threatening to rip out of her chest. "Have something to say, Andreas?"

As if pulled from the past, he slowly looked down at her. "No. Even I'm not cruel enough to bring a child into this. At least not anymore."

"Does that mean you intend to let me go at some point?"

This time, his answer was more thoughtful than driven by fury. "No."

"But isn't my only duty as your wife to produce as many healthy heirs as soon as humanly possible? My purpose, to be your broodmare?"

Deep grooves etched on the sides of his mouth as he responded without inflection. "Nikandros's twins will be heirs."

"Of course," she said, swallowing away the ache. She had no idea why she was pushing him like this. Only that she wanted to hurt him as she was hurting. "How does the timeline look then? Do I have enough time to find a new GP in Drakon and get my pills without Petra and the entire palace knowing my business?"

His chin tilted down. "What?"

"The sex, Andreas? You and me and the humiliating sex that we're going to have, you have a timeline for that, right?

"Sex is your weapon in this revenge scheme, *ne*? The thing I could never refuse you, the thing that you threatened to hold against—" Her voice broke, and he...his features paled. "So, yeah, if your schedule allows me to wait, then you don't have to ask your secretary to fill your wife's birth control prescription."

When she'd have turned away from him, he gripped her arms so tightly that Ari knew she'd have bruises tomorrow. But the pain was worth the satisfaction that she had finally, finally ruffled him. "Humiliating sex? Punishment sex?" He turned her until she was facing him, her duvet forgotten, her stomach tying itself in knots. "Have you convinced yourself that with my power and prestige, I somehow forced you?

"Have you conveniently twisted the truth in that too, *agapita*? That you gave your innocence unwillingly?"

Laughter fell from her mouth, serrated and strange. "No, it was never that, whatever it was." Her nose rubbed against his biceps, her mouth curving into a smile against the fabric of his shirt. Faint tension emanated from him, making Ari throw caution to the wind. "Even in this we disagree, *ne*, Andreas?"

He looked at her as though he was afraid she was going mad. She was a little afraid of that herself. "How?"

"To this day, I'm convinced that I seduced you and you're convinced that you seduced me. Even in this, we have a power struggle."

He didn't outright laugh. The rigid, sculpted curve of his thin lips didn't even move. But his grip on her arms eased. Something softened in his black eyes. A flash of that dry humor she had seen back then. Only she.

He lifted a finger and touched the tip of her nose. Her breath suspended in her throat, for Ari had a feeling he had been about to touch her mouth and changed his mind at the last second.

He'd been tempted. And it filled her with a heady power she didn't want.

"It was not so much a power struggle as it was you defying me. Defying everything I stood for—Drakon, the Palace, the House of Drakos, my father and me." His tone became far off, as if he too was reliving those first heady months when they had met.

Memories permeated the very air around them.

The first day he'd arrived at the café, he'd introduced himself as simply Andreas. As if he could ever be just that. But, of course, she'd known who he was. Ariana had only laughed at his imperious command to let him or his team know if she needed anything. Until she realized he'd been in earnest. That he meant to keep an eye on his father's ward.

Keep an eye, he had.

He would come to the café where she had worked every night, two huge tomes, and newspaper cuttings and reams of paperwork spread out on his table. Not a word, not a greeting after that first one. No chatting with any other customers. Just that dark gaze tracking her all over the café, until the early hours of morning, as if he found her endlessly fascinating. After the first day, he'd walked her home to the apartment, again with nary a word exchanged between them.

Ariana had never found herself so thoroughly captivated.

He had done that for a whole month before Ari had lost her patience and approached him.

Are you my very own watchdog, Your Highness?

She cringed, remembering how outrageous she'd been.

His reply: *You should not be drinking with strange men, Ms. Sakis.*

And then he'd followed her to the party where she'd proceeded to get drunk. Taken her home to her little apartment she'd shared with three other girls.

No more exchanges except her increasingly reckless taunts to break his self-assurance over the next month.

Until the afternoon the verdict had come out about her parents' deaths. There had been no doubt that her mother had deliberately caused the accident.

She'd taken her life and her husband's, a day after he'd struck Ariana.

She'd been mindless with grief, desperate to run away from her own life. Andreas hadn't asked her a single question that day, nor left her side. Like a shadow, he'd been at her back throughout the day and night as she'd flitted from the café to a party, from the party to a walk along the coast and then back to her apartment.

Finally, she had broken down into anguished sobs, finally, she had realized that she was now forever alone, a fate she'd wished for for so long. At her apartment, he had sat by her on the couch—not even their shadows touching, always so careful to not touch her even by accident—and he had started talking, uncaring of whether she was listening.

In that deep, gravelly voice of his that had been just a tether to hold on to at first.

He'd started with the reason for his stay in the little village, a question she'd asked of him countless times. Told her of how his trail had led him there.

It was the first time she'd heard of the story of the dragon and the warriors. For hours, he'd told her of his fascination with the history of Drakon and its centuries-old lore since he'd been a little boy. Of the painstaking years of research he'd put together in his free time, which was far too little and rare. Of his fierce determination to pin down the real truth behind the war the warriors had waged on the dragon.

And in the passion in his words that had been a revelation—when she'd relentlessly taunted him for being an uptight, dutiful, one-dimensional prince puffed up with his own privilege and power—Ariana had seen the man beneath the Crown Prince's mantle. A historian, a weaver of words, a dreamer; a man that struggled to survive within the constraints of his birth and his position of power without even knowing it. A man who liked her, her company, her laughter, yet wouldn't, or couldn't put it in a simple sentence.

A man who could have the world at his feet and yet saw something worthwhile in her.

The realization that somehow the Crown Prince of Drakon, powerful and gorgeous, needed her just as much as she needed him, had reverberated through her.

As dawn had painted the sky a myriad of purples and pinks, his voice had slowly guided Ariana back to the world, to the life waiting for her.

Through her death, her mother had given her a gift. She had given Ariana her own life back.

With a fiercely alive feeling coursing through her veins, she had done what she'd been dying, but had been terrified, to do, until then. She had wiped her tears away roughly, kneeled between his long legs and pressed her mouth to his.

Her first kiss, she had decided so full of herself, would be the Crown Prince's.

Of course, he hadn't kissed her back as she'd mashed her lips against his. Tenderly, he'd clasped her jaw and pushed her back while she'd been burning with humiliation and thwarted desire, had guided her to her room, tucked her in, waited until she fell into a dreamless sleep.

The next morning, she'd woken up, brimming with a renewed verve for life and determined to have him, in whatever form she could.

Thee mou, she'd been playing with fire. Was it any wonder she'd been burned?

He'd made her feel so secure that night—a feeling she'd never known. Like she could survive the bitterest grief if only she had his words, *him* by her side.

Except she hadn't foreseen that what had attracted him to her would be what he would despise in the end.

"Challenging everything I had ever believed in," Andreas said, pulling her back into the now, a strange glitter in those dark eyes, "about myself, about the world, about my place in the world.

"You were this skinny, reckless seventeen-year-old and the first person I had ever met in my life who…"

"Who what?" she whispered, desperate for more. Even knowing that this self-indulgence would only lead to pain.

"Who didn't care how powerful, educated, or accomplished I was. With you, I was…" she'd never seen him lost for words, yet right then, she was sure he was choosing them carefully "…just Andreas for the first time."

They were words Ariana had never heard him say before. Almost regretful. A little wistful. They gouged open a longing she'd shut away.

Tears filled her throat. She wanted to pound at him for never saying those things to her then, for never telling her... No. Ruthlessly, she pulled herself to the present. They would have never survived, she needed to hold on to that.

He slowly disentangled himself from her, pushed away a lock of hair that had fallen onto her jaw. Small touches. Calculated touches. Her skin prickled. "I will make you a promise, Ari."

She scowled, more angry with herself than with him. "It won't be without some hidden motive."

And this time, he really smiled. The flash of his even white teeth against his darkly olive skin was breathtaking.

Unlike him, patience had never been her strong suit. "What is it, your promise?"

"I will not touch you until you come to me. I will not take you, *agape mou*, until you beg me to take you. Until you crawl into my bed and ask me to be inside you.

"Taking you when you can't breathe for wanting me... it is unlike any high I've known."

Ariana jerked away from him, slumberous warmth pooling low in her belly. A throbbing between her legs. "Like I did the last time."

A flare of heat darkened those impossible black eyes. It was all there in them—the log cabin at the foot of the mountains, the storm that had been raging outside for a week, the huge king bed with soft-as-sin sheets and Andreas and she stuck inside, with their supplies dwindling every day and the fire between them raging higher with every moment.

The knowledge that she had turned eighteen four weeks earlier was explosive in that silent cabin; that they had both been ignoring King Theos's summons; the knowledge that her dare in trapping the Crown Prince, who seemed to be made of stone and rock like the mountains around them, far too dangerous when she'd seen the evidence of his attraction to her finally in those first few days in the cabin.

Until the day he had decided that he was going to give in.

Sparks filled her body at the memory of that decadent night. It was the night she had begun to understand the uptight, arrogant Crown Prince, to realize what she'd thrown herself into. But it had been too late.

She'd already fallen in love with him.

Her fingers shaking to hold the duvet, Ariana pushed out the breath lodged in her chest. Barely a few hours with him and she was on fire. She cleared her hoarse throat.

"Why?"

He shrugged. "To level the field a little."

"This is exactly what you wanted when you kidnapped me—me at your mercy."

"Yes, but having you at my mercy when you have no fight in you..." he made a bored sound "...that is not the Ariana I want. What fun is tormenting you when you have no say in it?

"This way, I will know that when I'm inside you this time, you have surrendered despite the little self-preservation it seems you have developed."

Thee mou, it was impossible. The man she had married would have never been open to a challenge like that, much less taunt her with it. He would have never given the reins of anything to her hands. Much less his revenge scheme. Or the simple matter of when they'd have sex.

Had he changed or was it just a game?

He leaned a hip against the wall, all lean masculinity and hungry eyes. "Since you've always blamed me for wanting to control everything, I will leave this in your hands. We will have sex only when you want it."

"Don't you get it? I'm not self-destructive anymore, Andreas. The last time burned me enough for an entire life-time."

Sudden stillness seemed to come over him. His gaze probed hers, as if he wanted to plumb the depths of her. "Did I burn you, Ariana?"

The question was not a taunt or even a rebuke. It rang with curiosity that made her stomach twist. Tears pricked behind her eyelids, making him a shimmery vision.

Say no, Ari. Let the guilt be your own.

"Yes," she whispered. "I still have scars from it."

He nodded, a thoughtful look shuttering away his thoughts. "Then I owe you this, *ne*? This little game of ours can proceed as you want it or it could end as soon as you desire."

She trusted this reasonable Andreas even less than the controlling one. "End?"

"You could get naked and invite me to join you in the bed right now." Their gazes flicked to the bed and back. The soft duvet seemed to burn her skin. "I could give you the wedding night you'd have had tonight with your adorable little fiancé." His eyes hardened to dark chips, his mouth edging into that cruelly ruthless curve. "The longer you hold me off, the longer this whole thing will take."

The bastard! He had nicely trapped her. She was damned to stay with him the longer she denied this thing between them, and she was damned if she gave in. Because it had been apparent within two minutes of seeing him again, within seconds of breathing that scent of him, that she was into the special brand of masculinity that was only Andreas Drakos.

"You will be waiting a long time, Andreas. And we both know being denied what you want is a foreign concept you, *ne*?

"Also, from what I remember, celibacy makes you extra cranky."

"True, but after dealing with your deceit, my tolerance for everything has changed, Ari. You have no idea what or who I've become anymore." He turned and left the room, closing the door behind him.

Ariana buried her face in her hands, panicking over the lack of panic. Did she believe him? Would he truly give her a choice now that he had her close? And even if she did somehow resist not falling into the old patterns, she scoffed at herself, what was the point if it meant being his wife again?

A groan erupted from her mouth.

He was right in one thing, though.

Just because he had her where he wanted didn't mean she was going to roll over and let him do as he pleased. The image that her overactive mind supplied at that made the rub of her thighs excruciating.

This time, she knew what came of playing with fire. What came of tangling with Andreas Drakos.

First things first, she needed to take a shower, wash off the grime and doubts from the day she'd had so far. Ari made a note to thank the stewardess for the new set of underwear and designer jeans with their tags still intact, all in several sizes. Several shirts and blouses, too.

Why Andreas's private jet had a supply of women's underwear and clothes was something she was not going to dwell on. Not her business.

Shedding her underwear with a grimace, she grabbed a towel and walked into the small, but luxuriously decadent shower.

The jet head of steaming hot water on her tense muscles was glorious. She scrunched her nose at the row of high-end perfumed shampoos and gels, and found a bar of soap with minimum ingredients.

Running away was not an option. Avoiding him was not an option. Staying married to a man who thrived on control like it was air—even without the history between them—was not an option.

Being the Queen of Drakon…a hysterical laugh hurtled past her throat, was not at all an option.

Her only option, she stilled with her hands in her hair, was the truth. Andreas would not let her go until he figured out why she'd deceived him, until he understood how any woman, much less Ari, could walk away from him.

But the truth was a jagged, thorny, twisted mass. Her hand moved to the scar on her lower belly.

There were other things she could make him see. She could convince him, for one thing, that it hadn't been a juvenile game to her. That she had been foolish, naive, not willfully destructive. That leaving him had been a point of survival.

She had to convince him that she could never be that Ari again. That she would never put him or his precious Drakon or his duties to the Crown before her life. That she would never love him, never put her obsession for him before her happiness.

That she had learned how destructive love could be.

CHAPTER FOUR

I STILL HAVE SCARS.

What had he done to hurt her so much?

Andreas had hated her for two years, had dreamed of ways he would ruin her when he got his hands on her.

And now that he had her…now that he had found her on the eve of her wedding to another man, the rage and betrayal simmered down, morphed into something much more insidious.

All his energy in the last hour had gone into burying the urge to stalk back into the rear cabin and demand what the hell she had meant by it.

The sight of her—the globes of her breasts falling up and down, the expanse of golden flesh, the pulse beating violently at her neck, the defiant tilt of her chin… No, right now, he wanted her more than he wanted answers. His fingers itched to run through the silky mass of her hair, to reach that sensitive spot above the nape of her neck and see if she'd respond with a moan.

He could have spanned that tiny waist with his hand, brought her up to him until those breasts crushed against his chest, could have kissed away the dare in her eyes. Within seconds, he could have had her panting for him.

Could have pressed her down onto that bed, torn out her underwear and buried himself inside her. The images his thoughts painted made him shift uncomfortably in his seat.

Thee mou, that's all he needed, to give his staff a view of his inconvenient arousal. But instead of satisfying his body's craving, he'd made that ridiculous promise desperate to banish those shadows from her eyes.

There had been something so fragile about her in that

moment. As if a single wrong word about the pills could forever shatter her.

Damn his arrogance for forgetting that anything that involved Ariana could never be simple.

"Your Highness? Andreas?" Petra repeated, a little impatience slipping into her tone.

He met her silent accusation and shrugged apologetically. He could hardly blame her. After all, he'd heard nothing of what she'd said in the past fifteen minutes. Tilting his head up, he found Ariana.

Tension filled his shoulders and neck.

A white dress shirt, custom made for him, hung loose on her slender frame and was tucked into a pair of tight jeans that seemed to have been poured onto her lithe body.

The denim hugged the long muscles of her thighs and the flare of her hips. A moment's relief filled him. She did not look as unhealthy as he'd assumed earlier. Her wavy hair, she had tied into a messy knot at the back of her head. A knot he had reveled in undoing, as many times as he'd wanted.

She wore no jewelry except for a thin gold chain.

Her gaze flicked to each member of his team, an array of expressions passing through her face. When she saw Petra, a little frown appeared between her brows. When she saw Thomas, one of his oldest security guards, she threw herself at him with a grin.

A grin that turned her from that wary, resentful woman he'd kidnapped to that smiling girl he'd known long ago. Not that it was news that Ariana had always found more in common with the staff than him.

And then her eyes found him. With a regal nod that would have made the starchiest of his royal ancestors proud, she took a seat on the opposite side of the cabin. When the steward inquired if she wanted to eat, she rattled off food enough for his entire team.

All vegetarian, he remembered. At least, his private chef was more equipped than Andreas himself had been to feed her.

Andreas continued to listen to his team's updates with one ear while he watched her polish off most of the food she'd ordered. A little color returned to her cheeks and her hair glittered like drying copper left out in the sun for too long as it began falling from her knot.

He went back to discussing the security arrangements for the upcoming coronation, the details of the new trade deal he would be signing with their neighbor courtesy of Nikandros and Gabriel. "Petra?" He was about to ask her to bring him the proposal the Crown Council wanted him to push to the cabinet when he saw Ariana standing before him.

"Do you intend to work the entire flight?"

He lowered his head back to his work. "Yes. My coronation is in two months and I have let my duties slide in the last few months. Nikandros has been carrying the brunt of them."

She sat down in front of him, and raised her brows when he silently stared at her. Her skin had that freshly scrubbed look. Her body, lithe and toned, he fought the urge to give in.

"You...ditched work? Had hell frozen over?"

He frowned, remembering the number of times after they had returned to Drakon that she had pled with him to take the day off. Or to spend the evening with her. Or at the least, to eat dinner with her every day.

And he remembered his answers very well, too.

No.

He'd always said no, pushed her every request off as juvenile or attention-seeking. He'd been far too busy trying to prove to his father that his lapse in judgment was limited to marrying her. That he was still capable of representing

Drakon at the oil summit that year. That he could shoulder the tremendous task of digging Drakon out of the financial pit it had fallen into.

And then one day, she...had stopped asking.

How hadn't he noticed that until now?

"I had other things on my mind."

She flicked her gaze to his face and then back to her hands on the table. "I'm sure losing your father must have been very hard."

He laughed. Maybe he could tell her how terrified Theos had been that Andreas would kill him with his bare hands. That would discourage the sympathy in her eyes. "I was obsessed with finding you."

"Oh."

Petra stood silently by them. Waiting for him to dismiss Ariana, he slowly realized. It was not an incorrect presumption. Nor out of place.

Andreas did not let work slide for anyone. Even when he'd been searching for Ariana the last year, Petra had accompanied him most of the time. He'd done as much as he could to stop Nik from drowning under the weight of Drakon. Petra had been with him since he'd returned from the navy at eighteen and his father had chosen her to be his secretary. She knew him, knew his priorities. Maybe even came closest to a friend, though the simple art of making friends had never been allowed to him.

Petra knew him enough to come to the conclusion that whatever he was doing with Ariana, which bordered on the insane, would not affect his other functions.

The words to dismiss Ariana hovered over his lips when he noticed the edge in her smile, the whiteness of her knuckles gripping the table.

"Petra, we will continue later."

Petra hovered, her shock clear in the air. Andreas frowned and let her see it. *Christos*, his entire team had been with him for too long if Petra was questioning his orders.

Ariana crossed her legs in a casual gesture but the tension didn't leave her mouth. The flash of vulnerability reminded him again of how young she'd been then.

The cabin was now mostly empty for his look had dispersed his team. He let the silence build.

She had come with an agenda.

He waited patiently. And with a thrum of anticipation. She had always been full of crazy schemes. Like when she'd suggested they run away to the States for a couple of years and leave Drakon behind. When he had looked astonished at that, she'd modified it to say she'd wanted to backpack through Europe for a couple of months while he sorted out Drakon and its myriad problems, since their marriage hadn't been publicized.

The thought of reckless Ariana wandering through the hostels in Europe while he stayed back in Drakon…he had shot her down quite harshly.

Only now, however, he began to see the pattern. Crazy or not, he had denied her everything she had asked for. He'd given her over to his father, returning to the apartment when he'd needed sex. When he couldn't go without touching her for another minute. When he'd made some headway through the myriad of issues on his desk and she was his reward for it.

As if he'd ration his quota of her.

And every time he'd gone to see her, he'd found her to be increasingly restless, coming up with crazier plans.

He had given her the most coveted role in his life, in all of Drakon and it had been utterly lost on Ariana.

How had he forgotten those months of their marriage? It had been hell, the direct contrast of the months they'd spent in the village.

"Did you ever sleep with her?"

His head jerked up at her soft whisper.

The filthy curse that had been about to fly from his mouth arrested when he saw that her question was in earnest. The wariness in her expression, as if she were bracing for the answer, the way she seemed to retreat into herself... It galled him that even when she was in the wrong, Ariana made the most primal, possessive, protective urges come out in him.

"You lost the right to ask me that." But her question rankled. "Are you asking me if I cheated on you when we were together?"

"No." Her immediate denial seemed to surprise her just as much as it did him. "I don't think so."

He leaned back and wrapped his arm around the seat. Wanting to touch her became secondary to the questions building up in his head. "I'm beginning to realize you did not think much of me when we were together."

"No. I thought the world of you, actually," she replied in that honest way she used to have. So where had it all gone wrong? "I knew..." Her gaze was serious when she met his. "I know that you wouldn't have cheated on me.

"I meant before...before we met. Or maybe after." She sighed. "But like you said, I've no right to ask that question."

Just as easily as she provoked his ire, she mollified it. "Petra is my employee. A woman who depends on me for her livelihood. You're aware that my sister, Eleni, was born of an affair between Theos and my nanny. Do you think anything could provoke me into repeating his scandalous, abusive behavior?"

Ariana looked away. There could be a hundred women ready to fall at his feet among his employees like Petra, a hundred more who adored the very ground their Crown Prince walked on. He didn't notice the women as anything but staff members.

Petra was no more than his three aides, who were thankfully all men, no more than his security guard Thomas, no more than his tailor, or his fitness instructor or his chef.

Another cog in the complex machinery that made his life run smoothly.

And yet… "You worshipped your father."

From the moment they had returned to the capital city, Ariana had seen the frightening truth. The man she had married was really no different from the cold, ruthless King Theos who had looked at her just as her father had done—as if she were a failure. A stain that had to be hidden far away from the gilded brightness of his palace.

"There were days when you were frighteningly similar to him." As if the world and the people in it were accessories to his own life. They were present only to provide his life with certain value.

Even Ariana had been another cog, just a pleasurable one.

His self-imposed isolation at the village, she'd made the mistake of thinking that was his life. Instead it had been a stolen pocket of time.

He laid his head back now and rubbed his jaw with the base of his palm. A bristly stubble had come in since this afternoon. Coupled with the dark shadows under his eyes, he looked a mess. Tired and almost imperfect.

A twinge of ache settled in Ari's chest. It was that same ferocious protectiveness for a man who owned the world, who didn't need it that had led her into following him into fire. Had she gained no sense in ten years?

"Because at the height of his regime my father had been a magnificent statesman. Nik had a better measure of him far before I did. He hated that Theos alienated him from me." The regret in his words stunned Ariana. "All I saw in Theos was the man who equipped me to rule Drakon. A man who'd worked tirelessly for years to make me perfect. A man who only wanted me to have the world and rule it.

"Only later did I realize that in his personal life, Theos was a manipulative monster."

Ariana bit her lip. She didn't have much time. Not if she wanted to stop him from parading her next to him come coronation day in front of all of Drakon. "I would have given anything for you to see that side of King Theos back then, Andreas."

"It must be so tempting to put this all on him, but he only aided you, Ariana."

She caught his hands on the table and laced her fingers through his. To anchor him to her, to not lose him to the memory of a cruel old man. "That's not true. He knew everything that was going on between us. Every fight, every disagreement. Petra relayed everything to him."

"He was a ruthless bastard, yes, but do not put your faults on him."

When he jerked his hand away, she held fast. For a man who spent hours at his desk signing treaties, he'd always had such rough hands.

"Andreas, it was never my idea to fake… I never agreed to pretend that I was dead. I only signed the papers dissolving our marriage. I took the money your father offered, yes, but I…"

He pulled his hand away from her as if she was poison.

Ariana stood up and blocked him. "If you're determined to make us walk through this hell again, at least listen to my side."

His hands fisted. "How did you realize what he had done if you didn't even look back?"

"I received all the paperwork through a lawyer. God, I didn't even completely understand the ramifications for a month. I panicked and called Giannis who told me what Theos had done behind my back."

Such bleak rage emanated in his black eyes that Ariana stepped back. "Of course, you kept in touch with your little security guard friend."

The insinuation in his tone cut bone deep. "Giannis was my friend. He understood what I was going through. He…"

"What happened when Giannis told you of Theos's convoluted lies? Why didn't you call me then?"

"It was too late."

"Too late to tell me that you were alive?"

"Your engagement had been announced. I was not in a good—"

"What, Ari?" His voice caught, his words clipped like hard gravel. "You thought I deserved to continue believing that my young wife was dead. Probably at my own father's hands or because of my own negligence, of which you'd been complaining for months."

"You thought he killed me?"

"Yes." The haunted look she'd thought she'd imagined was back in his eyes. The pain there…it was a knife in her chest. "He didn't hide his satisfaction that you were out of my life for good. After all his rages for weeks because I had ruined our legacy—because I had…" He ran a hand through his hair roughly. "It was the first time I saw Theos for what he could be.

"But it was only a suspicion. I threw myself into my work, I alienated Nik, I hurt Eleni. I thought I was going mad, suspecting my own father of a terrible thing.

"Theos hated the thought of you as my wife. It was as much a shock to him as it was to me that I…married you. That I could make such an unprecedented, uncharacteristic decision with my life."

"Then why did you, Andreas?" The question burst from her lips. A question she should have asked instead of running away. "You could have had me for as long as you wanted and walked away. I wouldn't have made a peep."

"I told you. You were a virgin that night and I didn't use protection."

"We could have waited to see if there were any consequences."

"I seduced you!"

"You took me to bed after I threw myself at you for months. Repeatedly."

"Still, you were eighteen, my father's neglected ward. You had no one in the world to look after your interests. What I did was—"

"Don't you dare take that away from me. I wanted you, God, I needed you just as much you needed me that night.

"But after, you...could have walked away. You could have paid me off. You could have... Why marry the shallow, ditzy, reckless failure that I was? Why marry me when you knew what your real life was like, when you knew how wrong I was for you?"

His breath was rough, his eyes blazing with an unholy light. "Because I got used to it."

Her heart thumped so hard against her rib cage, Ari could hardly breathe. "Used to what?"

"Used to being adored by you. Used to being loved by you." Shoulders tense, he rubbed his nape. For a man who exuded arrogant self-confidence out of every pore, the gesture was disconcertingly hesitant. "I was the center of your universe and it made me lose sight of who I was and who you were.

"Thanks to Theos, I had tasted every kind of power that was to be had in the world. But you, Ariana...your adoration for me even as you mocked everything I was in this world, it was a drug I couldn't give up on.

"I thought I could keep that, keep you for myself. One selfish indulgence that I would allow myself.

"It was the biggest mistake of my life. In that, Theos was right."

Ariana wound her arms around her trembling body, something deflating out of her. Hope, after all this time. Hope that he would admit that he'd married her because he'd loved her, too. That he had been shattered at the loss of her not because he felt responsible or guilty but something else.

"Then put a stop to that mistake. Don't continue the farce of our marriage."

"What do you suggest? That I marry another woman, make her my Queen and keep you on the side?

"Should I give you the place you're so determined to prove is yours, Ari? Should I visit you in the dark as if you were a paid whore, a kept mistress my father encouraged me to make of you?

"Would you have me become the monster Theos and you made me out to be? Because nothing has changed, *pethi mou*. I still want you with that same madness.

"You're still a weakness—the only one that I can't overcome."

Her hands boldly reached for his face, the scent of her skin a familiar twining in his blood.

With his fingers on her wrist, he stayed her movements. He could not bear to be touched by her. Not yet, and not like this. Not when he felt like a cauldron of volatile emotions, not when all he wanted was to push her into the bed, and bury himself in her.

"I shouldn't have run away like that, not with his help. But…but it was not a bid for freedom because I got bored with you or because I was shallow enough to fall in love with another man who was nothing but my friend. It was not a fickle game."

"No?"

"No. I…loved you. You. But loving you… I realized, slowly began to kill me and in the end, I chose survival."

Her words pinged through his mind like a bullet ricocheting through a closed room. Puncturing and tearing, scraping and scorching the walls of his mind.

He wanted to hate her as he had done for two years. He'd opened the Pandora's box of their relationship willingly and it seemed there was no end to the things that could come crawling out.

Things Andreas wasn't sure he wanted to face. "How was I killing you?"

Utter helplessness filled her face. And it was seeing that in her eyes, when Ariana never stopped fighting, that made him believe everything she'd said.

"It doesn't matter anymore," she whispered.

The pilot broke the tense silence with an update that they were landing soon.

Between mourning her death for eight years and the discovery of her treachery, he had forgotten that he was at the root of this.

The enormity of his marrying Ariana had only sunk through when his father had confronted him. Had shown him the hopeless state of the treasury of Drakon, the mounting national debt. The alliance that Theos had carefully cultivated with Gabriel Marquez, to make his sister the Queen of Drakon, crumbling to dust.

So he'd immediately tried to right his world.

He'd been prepared to do anything for Drakon but not give her up. She was only a small part of his life, he'd told his father. After all, the Queen's role was only titular in Drakon.

For the first month, it had worked. She became his escape from the weight of his nation's problems. From his father's spiraling moods and sudden rages. Then slowly, things had changed.

It was as if he'd lived in two different realities, one as

the Crown Prince and one as the man obsessed with his young wife.

As long as they didn't merge, he'd convinced himself his world would be all right.

As long as he didn't let her take over his life, as long as she meant nothing more to him than physical relief at the end of a hard day, a pleasure he looked forward to at night, as long as he didn't let her disrupt his duties ever again... *Thee mou*, he'd made so many promises to Theos just to keep her.

I chose survival.

Like a bone-deep bruise, those words lingered.

Was he prepared to face what he'd done to make his bright, cheerful, eighteen-year-old wife flee the moment his back had been turned, to learn that he was the one responsible for putting those shadows in Ari's eyes?

Suddenly, he questioned the sanity of everything he'd been doing since he'd found she was alive.

CHAPTER FIVE

MILES OF NEATLY manicured land greeted Ariana as the jet taxied into the private airstrip and they disembarked. The same airstrip where King Theos's staff had seen her into a jet that left Drakon ten years ago.

It wasn't as bitterly cold as it had been in Colorado. But the air was just as crisp and fresh. In the distance, the outline of the mountain range made the perfect horizon. Tall palm trees dotted a neat perimeter around the airstrip.

As Ari stood there, a strange thread of homecoming rang through her. She hadn't thought she'd missed Drakon but she had. Or maybe it was the sense of purpose that she'd found in herself that changed her view.

She wasn't swinging from guilt over her mother's death to the sudden, terrifying taste of freedom. Not running away from the fear that maybe her father had been right and she was good for nothing.

Suddenly, she was glad she was here. If only she could throw every derogatory word her father had called her about being a failure in his face, if only her mother were here to see that Ari had made something of herself, that Ari was utterly happy...

But you've not been utterly happy. Focused, dedicated, busy to the point of exhaustion and restless. But not happy, never happy.

That girl who'd laughed recklessly, who'd loved so generously, she'd just stifled her, desperate to avoid that heartbreak again. As if to punish herself for losing her baby boy.

But had it been anything more than a half-life?

Had it been anything but penance?

Three bulletproof cars arrived on the curb, the black-

and-gold flags whipping in the wind. Three separate teams waited for Andreas's attention, their curiosity evident in their scrutiny of her.

Her every action was going to be scrutinized and sanitized, her every word dissected to ensure it measured up against Andreas's image. But no one was going to intimidate her this time.

Andreas stood before her, his eyes holding hers captive.

She shivered and was immediately covered in a warm, long coat that fell past her knees.

Sandalwood and his body heat combined to make a potent drug emanating from the thick wool. The familiarly comforting scent curled through her.

His hand around her shoulders caught them up in their own little world. So close, she could see the tiny golden flecks in his eyes. Feel the wiry strength of his lean body.

She stood mutely as he settled the coat around her shoulders and buttoned up the first couple buttons so that her chest was adequately protected.

Her heart thudded when he lifted the ring finger of her left hand. The tiny point-one-carat diamond struggled to throw off even a spark. With gentle movements that suggested he loathed putting her through any discomfort, a startling contrast as he ripped the fabric of her very life apart, he pulled the ring off her finger.

His jet-black gaze held hers in a possessive dare as he threw the ring into the acreage behind them.

Ariana jerked but his hand around her nape arrested her. Even for her five-nine height, he had to bend down. "Welcome home, Ariana," he said, in a silky voice at her ear, before touching his mouth to the corner of hers.

His lips were warm against her skin, sending pockets of heat through her. Her entire body trembled at the searing contact, her hands rising to his chest automatically. T hold him close, to soak in his warmth.

She let her hands fall to her sides, heat swamping her face.

Andreas would always have this power over her, this... ability to turn her inside out. Accepting that was strangely calming.

She needed closure just as much as Andreas did.

She needed to figure out if it would always be a half-life without him. And if it was, would the little Andreas was offering be enough this time?

Because there was one thing she knew.

Andreas Drakos could never love.

The drive back to the palace was long but thankfully not intimate. Three of his staff, including Petra, joined them in the expansive limo, leaving Ariana to sit opposite him.

His cuffs rolled back to reveal strong forearms. Ariana followed the column of his throat, his chest tapering to a lean waist and then to his legs stretched out. His trousers cleanly molded the length of his muscular thighs.

Needing a reprieve from that overwhelming masculinity, Ariana leaned back and closed her eyes.

His words, assertive and rapid-fire, assaulted her senses.

Andreas answered questions and asked his own. Matters that would have been over her head and, quite honestly, boring, made more sense to Ariana this time.

Now, instead of being told by everyone how rapier-sharp Andreas's mind was, she saw it in play. His memory was astounding, his attention to detail when he was mired in so many matters awe-inspiring. She listened in fascination as he took the first draft of a speech written by one of his press team and shredded it to pieces by calling out clichéd phrases and for not addressing any of the scare rhetoric that the media had been doling out about him following Theos's madness in the last few years.

For the first time in decades, the populace was questioning what the royal house was doing for the people.

It was his coronation speech, Ariana realized, with unwise curiosity.

Absolute conviction rocked in his every gesture. "Drakon enters a new era with me at the helm. We shall not rest on the past laurels of the House of Drakos anymore. The royal house will begin the process of decoupling from the cabinet in coming years."

Ariana scoffed. The sound was like an elephant blaring in the quiet interior.

"Do you have something to say, Ariana?"

"Nothing you would want said in company, Your Highness," she replied sweetly.

"We do not want my staff to believe you're afraid of me, do we?"

That put her spine up like nothing could. Even as she'd been utterly overwhelmed by him back then, she'd never let him intimidate her. There was a distinction, an important one they both knew.

She sat forward, looking him in the eye. "Decoupling the House of Drakos and the Drakon cabinet? Andreas Drakos walking away from power to rule the lives of millions? That's like a lion giving up its ability to hunt.

"That power is in your blood, your bones, your very skin. You will never do it."

"I'm not giving up power so much as I'm redistributing it into the right hands," he said surprisingly receptive to her criticism. "I want more checks and balances. The Crown Council was supposed to do that, but Theos controlled them with his power and wealth. Until there was no one to question his executive command of the cabinet.

"Nikandros already has the economy of Drakon in his hand. He's always been the financial genius.

"Eleni, if Gabriel lets her accept my proposal, will become the formal liaison between the palace and the hundreds of charities we support."

"Your brother and sister? That's your power distribution—other members of the House of Drakos? You think they will go against your wishes?"

"You would understand if you had…" He bit his accusation off, aware of the staff watching them with a hungry fascination. "My father hoarded power, until it drove him to madness. Until he began to think of even me as his enemy.

"I don't intend to let that happen to me.

"After all, I have a personal life now and I intend to enjoy it."

As much as she wanted to fight it, the truth of it shone in his eyes. "Control is everything to you."

In the intimacy of the dark night, even as he had shocked her with his demands and his carnality, he'd not once let her lead. Even as he'd lost himself in the pleasures of sex, it had still been very much calculated.

The very devil glinted in his eyes. "Is that another challenge then, *agapita*?"

She felt a collective hiss of exhale from the two women in the car. Not that she could blame them.

He's mine, she wanted to say, that wildness she'd tried to bury surfacing with a vengeance. Maybe it was the air of her homeland, maybe it was facing Andreas as the woman she was now, but restlessness slithered under her skin.

"Don't make promises—" she raised a brow, and almost pulled it off "—that you cannot keep, Your Highness."

His eyes shone with unholy mirth, deep grooves dug into his cheeks. His brows went all off-kilter. "Worried that you might not be able to resist me after all?"

A reluctant smile curved her lips and she looked out the window.

The outline of the mountain range became vague as the car entered the city, the white stone structure of the King's Palace sitting atop the small hill emerging ahead.

Was he serious about all these changes? What had brought it on?

The more she spent time with him, the more she was realizing that something had changed in him. But the very idea of revealing the last bit of truth she had hidden, the condemnation in his eyes if he learned of what she had lost... Fear skated over her spine.

They arrived at the King's Palace with very little fanfare.

The lack of his family's presence was conspicuous and Ariana was caught between relief and a bit of disappointment, if she were honest.

She had obsessively followed every bit of palace gossip over the last few years. The changes it seemed Andreas was determined to bring to Drakon. Even the rising sentiment against the once-beloved Crown Prince.

She knew that the Daredevil Prince, Nikandros, had returned to Drakon after a years-long rift between him and Andreas. That Nikandros had married the ex-soccer player Mia Rodriguez and had two infant children.

That Eleni Drakos, dubbed with the cheap moniker the Plain Princess of Drakon for years, had recently married Gabriel Marquez—Isabella Marquez's brother, the same woman Andreas had been engaged to after Ariana fled.

Were these changes Andreas had brought out too?

Two security guards accompanied her through the miles of corridors.

Barely a staff of five, Andreas's personal retinue greeted them. She was shown into a set of rooms done in elegant creams and mauves. A lounge, a bathroom that spanned the square footage of her legal aid agency, and a massive bed that was the pride of place in the bedroom.

"Do not even think of running, Ari," Andreas suddenly whispered at her ear and Ariana jerked.

Her hand fluttered to his chest and she kept it there now, loving the solid feel of him under it. Needing suddenly the reassurance of his presence before he was lost to her in the maze of the palace.

"Do not give me reason to, Your Highness," she quipped back, trying to hide her elation that he hadn't forgotten about her as soon as they had set foot in the palace. That, this time, he had actually brought her to the palace and not hidden her away.

God, but she was pathetic that even the smallest crumbs from him made her heart dance.

He didn't smile. But covered her hand with his, the long fingers tangling with hers. "Rest up for a couple of hours." His gaze caressed her face, as if looking for proof that she wouldn't faint again. "My family wishes to meet you."

"More people who hate me, yay," she said, a sudden panic seizing her chest. "Andreas, couldn't we—"

"No, Ariana. I have defied every tenet I had for my personal life and pushed every Crown Council member that hates me to the edge by bringing you here." A dark smile touched his eyes. "You're ten years late, *pethi mou*. Drakon wants its queen and I want my wife."

Ariana watched him leave, but instead of fear, a fierce determination filled her.

She had gone from a train wreck to something hopefully akin to a woman who knew her own mind.

Was it possible for the Crown Prince of Drakon to change, too?

CHAPTER SIX

"WELL, IS SHE HERE? What does she do? Where did she go after she left you?" Eleni demanded the moment Andreas walked into the Green Room at King's Palace.

His head was pounding after the quick report he'd had from his aides.

Nikandros had been right. The situation with his popularity ratings was much worse than even he'd anticipated.

Soon, he had to find a way to turn the sentiment that was rising against him. "Calm down, Eleni," Gabriel muttered. Andreas felt a flash of sympathy for his brother-in-law. It had to be hard to see Eleni continue like the little dynamo she was when she was pregnant.

"She's a lawyer," Andreas answered while accepting the drink Nik had poured him. "She set up a legal aid agency with the money she took from Father."

Gabriel whistled, a devilish light in his green eyes. "The controlling bastard that you are, I always thought you needed a woman with steel balls. A woman who could perhaps be your saving grace. She sounds like it."

"I didn't realize I needed saving."

The insufferable smile slid from Gabriel's mouth. "You do. Before you end up like your father."

Nothing fractured his self-control these days more than being compared to Theos. "I interfered in Eleni's life because I wanted her to be happy. Because I knew what Theos did to her and I wanted to do right by her."

"Leave it, Gabriel. It is his life," said Nik.

"Being a member of the illustrious House of Drakos doesn't mean you're above the law," Mia added, glaring at Nik.

"She gave him little choice when she decided to marry another man, Mia." Eleni's loyalty for her brothers had always been absolute. The scowl on Gabriel's face made Andreas grin despite the open bashing of his morals. "If it came out later that the King of Drakon's secret first wife had committed bigamy, it would—"

"It would have made the scandal of the century for the populace of Drakon," said that husky voice Andreas would know in the darkest of nights.

Ariana walked into the evening lounge where they had all gathered for predinner drinks with the aplomb of a queen. Every cell in him came to attention, his skin tight over his muscles. There was a bright glitter in her eyes.

"A headline that could rival even the stories about that first band of warriors conquering the dragon. And believe me, your people need new material. That dragon lore..." Ariana rolled her eyes when Eleni, a staunch believer in all myths, dragons and the superiority of the House of Drakos, gasped. "It gets boring as hell after a while. Not to mention, it isn't something to crow about to the world."

Stunned silence met her prosaic announcement.

Disbelief etched on his family's faces. Andreas flexed his fingers trying to forget the feel of her silky skin.

"Andreas," she said, "introduce your family. After all, I did answer your royal summons." She turned to the rest of them and smiled. "Apparently, ten years has only made Andreas's penchant for control worse."

Nikandros broke the ice. "We didn't give him a choice, Ms. Sakis." He took her hand in his and shook it. "Welcome to Drakon, I'm—"

"The Daredevil Prince," she said with that wide smile of hers. Andreas scowled. She leaned into Nik, her voice lowered to a whisper that wasn't quite one. "Come, Nikandros," she said with that easy familiarity that was second nature to her, that made Andreas want to pull her to his side, "you really don't expect me to believe that Andreas bowed to pressure from someone else, do you?"

Eleni bristled. "Is it hard to believe that we would want to meet our brother's wife?"

"As far as I remember, Andreas did not share a close relationship with you or Nikandros. I have mostly found that he is incapable of nurturing relationships."

Andreas stared into his drink, knowing that she was right. It was only in the last few years that he'd begun undoing the damage he'd done to his brother and sister.

He had still made mistakes, as Gabriel had pointed out.

"Maybe you do not," Eleni replied, sending Ariana a cool look, "know our brother as well as you think you do."

Her nostrils flared, her chin set in stubborn lines, Ariana looked like she wanted to argue. In the end, she shrugged.

"Point to the House of Drakos," she added, with a wink at Gabriel.

Gabriel took her outstretched hand into his while Mia walked over to Ariana's side and introduced herself.

Within minutes, Ariana had Mia and Gabriel roaring with laughter. Brows raised, Nik conveyed his own surprise about her with a twitching mouth.

Irate at his brother's humor, Andreas turned to watch her. Acknowledged the fact that physical possession of Ariana was never going to be enough.

The cap-sleeved floral knee-length dress in white and pink with a string of pearls jarred with the elegant ambience of the palace as he accompanied Ariana to dinner. Her hair was in a riotous knot at the back of her head, wavy tendrils already falling away from it and framing her gamine face. Bright red lipstick made her full-lipped mouth stand out even more than usual amidst her stark features.

Even for a man who rarely understood fashion, Andreas was immediately aware that the whole outfit and makeup and what he knew of Ariana just didn't gel.

When she moved to the other end, he forced her to sit on his right. Forced her to brush her body against his as she sat down. Still, she wouldn't spare him a look.

Nothing however could leave Ariana daunted for too long. The moment the first course was served, she said, "I know what you must all be thinking. Not only is she an almost bigamist, but she has the most atrocious sense of style, *ne*?"

Mia just stared back with a rueful glint in her eye while Eleni flushed.

"You see, Andreas's secretary—who very efficiently arranged these clothes for me because your brother kidnapped me in my torn wedding dress—and I have this cold war thing going on. From years back.

"Petra is making a point that everyone loyal to Andreas is dying to make right now. That I'm not fit to polish your brother's handmade Italian boots much less to be his wife. A fact that was drilled into me with a sledgehammer in Version One of our marriage."

"By our father," Nik finished for her.

She shrugged. "In your father's defense, King Theos already knew from my father what a failure I was. I got thrown out of three finishing schools, ran away from home three times, embarrassed and humiliated my father in a hundred different ways.

"For a military general whose sparkling reputation and pride were most important, I was a huge letdown. I had neither academic smarts, nor did I fit well with his friends' high-achieving children.

"I was an utter failure, a fact he constantly reminded me of."

Andreas stilled with his glass of water halfway to his mouth. The thought of Ariana running away sat like a boulder on his chest. *Christos*, he'd never known. He'd never even asked her about her life with her parents. "Why did you run away?"

"Whenever I… I defied him, my father locked me in my room." A vacant expression emanated in her eyes. "Probably not a huge thing. But he would cut me off completely for days. I would be given food and water. But nothing else. He thought it character-building.

"I found the silence…unbearable. All it did was make me resolute that I'd never be caught again.

"Anyway, when King Theos inherited my guardianship, I don't think he knew what to do with me.

"He sent me off to a corner of Drakon until I turned eighteen. Only a few months later, there I was, his worst nightmare.

"To find out what his dear heir had done…to see me stand at his doorstep as the future Queen…" A shiver went through her.

"Theos went ballistic," Nikandros finished for her.

Eleni asked, "What did Father do?"

For the first time since she had blown into the room like a summer storm, Ariana met his gaze. "I was installed in an apartment, away from the gilded walls of the palace, a stain to be hidden away. Theos's team put me on a diet of history lessons, etiquette lessons, posture training. I was cut off from the few friends I had. Petra and her team had nothing but contempt for me. I was not allowed to leave the apartment. I was not allowed to contact anyone for fear of leaking who I was to Andreas.

"I was in a cage again. And my jailer was the man I loved, the man I had trusted."

The clatter of his fork against the plate sounded like an explosion in the room.

Her chin tilted up boldly, taut lines carved around her mouth, she stared at him.

Nik's expression became haunted. "I'm aware of our father's routine to mold people, Ms. Sakis. His penchant to strip one of every good thing. Only Andreas could ever bear his rigorous requirements and stay standing." He turned an accusing look toward Andreas. "Where were you when this was happening?"

"If your father thought to mold me," Ariana answered with a glittering anger in her eyes, "it was only with Andreas's encouragement. Andreas visited me when he needed—" their eyes met, and he saw the dirty truth there "—a *diversion* from his busy life," she finished and looked away.

Why the hell hadn't she told him any of this back then?

Because he hadn't been available. Because he had never even asked.

Because from the moment Andreas had realized the magnitude of his mistake in marrying her, he'd tried to limit the damage. To the crown or to himself, he didn't know to this day.

"It was for your own good," he said, trying to fight the guilt that settled on him. For the first time in his life, trying to offer justification. "You had neither the education nor the background to survive in my world. You would have been shredded to pieces.

"I had to salvage the situation. I had to make you worthy of—"

Her chin reared down, her body tense. "Worthy of you, Andreas? I never pretended to be anything but what I am."

No, she hadn't. She hadn't even wanted to marry him. Only he had seduced her into it.

This was what he had done—clipped her wings, caged her, and for Ariana, for the girl who had defied her father's abusive edicts, for the girl who had loved so freely, freedom was everything. She had loved him and he had choked the life out of her.

His father had been right. Andreas only knew destruction.

He'd wanted answers and here they were. The rest of the dinner proceeded in a strained manner, Andreas unable to contribute anything more. Unable to see past the haunted look in Ariana's eyes.

Grappling with the magnitude of the mistake he'd made in marrying her and refusing to give her up, he'd retreated from her. He had given her over to his father to be molded into whatever the hell Theos thought she should be.

All he'd wanted was to get his life back to normal. Before he'd lost sight of what and who he was, and what he was not capable of.

He had delegated her to a small part in his life. The relief from the loneliness, a respite from the increasing demands of his father, an escape from the fact that Theos's dementia had begun to manifest even back then, making him feel the burden of Drakon on his shoulders.

"The dragon lore, Ms. Sakis?" Eleni piped up just as Ariana excused herself. "A band of warriors defeated the dragon and made its treasure their own. They provided land and riches to their community. What is there to not crow about?"

Ariana's gaze pinned him. "You never told anyone what we found in that old library?"

Andreas shook his head, a savage clamor inside him at how easily she had used *we*. At the light that came on in her eyes when she spoke of those months. At the connection that seemed to have survived between them despite the destruction wrought.

She moved toward him, unconscious of her own movements, he was sure. The weight of her brown gaze, the concern in them, pinned him. "You never finished your book?"

"No," he replied, shying away from the shock in her eyes.

"What book is this?" Nikandros asked, his gaze shifting between them.

Her fingers pulled his wrist. "You never shared it with anyone?"

Feeling as if his entire insides were being pulled up for display, Andreas stepped away from her. From the emotion ringing in her eyes. "No." When he had returned and thought her dead, the last thing on his mind had been his research. And after a few years, everything relating to that time had become far too private and precious. A part of his life—*their life*—that he wasn't willing to share with anyone.

"But it was your dream, Andreas," she whispered. The loss of it shone in her eyes, in the tremble of her lips.

Had his dream meant that much to her then? *Thee mou*, he couldn't tolerate this turmoil within. Couldn't stand the weight of his guilt bearing down upon him. Anger had been so much better.

"Andreas came to that village," she said turning toward his family, her voice pitched carefully, "because he'd found a trail to the warriors' first settlement leading back hundreds of years there. We..." She colored under his gaze. "He found a manuscript that was written in one of the old Hellenic languages. He spent weeks trying to translate it.

"You know that Andreas can read and write in eight languages, right?"

Everybody in the room looked stunned. But she had eyes for no one else. Nor he for anyone but her. "There was a price to pay for defeating the dragon so easily. In fact, that manuscript suggested the leader of that band hadn't so much defeated it as made a deal with it."

"A deal?" Eleni asked.

"The dragon demanded a price. The warrior was to sacrifice his wife to its fiery jaws and it would relinquish the treasure." Her brown eyes shone with a wet brilliance.

And suddenly Andreas realized why she was so emotional about the story. Why she looked as if she was about to break like a piece of glass.

She saw him as the head of that fierce band of warriors. The man who had so ruthlessly sacrificed his wife for duty and glory, a woman who had loved him completely.

"The warrior accepted," she finished. "And became the first King.

"He was given the name Drakos and when he married again, his family became the House of Drakos."

A long sigh left her, her body almost weaving at the spot. Finally, she lifted her gaze away from him. But the recriminations he had seen there had already latched on to him.

"There you are, Mrs. Marquez. That is why I don't think it is something to celebrate. But of course Drakonites must have their tales.

"And House of Drakos its fairy-tale reputation to live up to."

Her head held high, she left the room without looking back, leaving Andreas standing stunned.

He *had* sacrificed her, hadn't he? He had treated her as a possession to be used when he needed it, a toy he could wind up when he wanted to play.

He'd given no thought, ever, to her dreams, her fears. Even to her needs. *Christos*, he hadn't treated her any better than a staff member. Or a mistress, hired for his pleasure.

It had all been about what she could give him. About his desires and wants.

Gabriel was right. He had been, he still was, just like his father. Using people for his own means, hurting the ones closest to him. It had always been hard for him to see beyond his own needs, his privilege. To see anything that he didn't control as a weakness.

It had never been about Ariana. It had always been about what she made him feel. What she brought to his life.

Now he saw the distinction between what he had done

to her versus how Nikandros had been ready to sacrifice his own happiness for Mia's. Now he understood why Gabriel had been willing to love Eleni even knowing that she might not love him.

The thought of being that vulnerable felt like needles under his skin.

Had Theos destroyed his ability to care for anyone but himself?

Was he willing to do the same to Ariana again?

Ariana left the dining salon and stumbled into another vast room. She needed to catch her breath. She needed a reprieve from everything Andreas made her feel, despite her every effort to stay rational.

Pink Carrera marble as far as she could see, claw-toothed arm chairs, velvet-upholstered chaise longues, the luxury was unprecedented, understated.

Gilded portraits looked down from the walls, witness to every event. It seemed the walls themselves were seeped with the history of the House of Drakos. And yet, she knew that Andreas had had a quiet happiness in that small village that he had not found here.

Something reverberated in her at being inside the palace. She'd been denied this the last time. Because she had been deemed unfit for its hallowed halls. Denied her rightful place by his side.

Did she want it this time? Did she want to carve a place for herself in Drakon by his side?

Turning around, she saw Andreas, leaning against the high arch, his gaze studying her intently. Hands tucked into his pockets, dark shadow outlining his jawline, he was heartbreakingly gorgeous.

And determined to keep her in his life. The little fact weaved its own web around her.

"You look… I don't know what that look is, to be precise," she heard him say as she walked around the room, checking where the myriad doors led.

She stilled, stunned that he had recognized her...confusion.

Slowly, she turned around, ready to face him. "I thought you would be furious with me."

He didn't move, just raised a brow.

"I didn't mean to...wash our dirty linen in front of everyone."

"Then why did you?"

She ran a fingertip against the arm of a huge wingback chair. "Being here...unsettled me. Seeing your family look at me with accusing eyes...disconcerted me. I was ashamed of what I did and it just came pouring out.

"I... I've never been part of a big family and if they're going to be mine, I need them to understand that what I did was cowardly but not malicious."

"I'm not angry, Ariana. At least not with you."

Her head jerked up, their gazes colliding across the vast room. Was it that simple to give his forgiveness?

He shrugged, sensing her disbelief. "My family knows what Theos made me into. You've already turned them."

Only Andreas could ever bear his rigorous requirements and stay standing.

Nikandros's flyaway remark hit her hard.

"Nik? What did he mean by it? What did your father do to you?"

"It's irrelevant, Ari."

"It is not, Andreas. Our pasts have made us this. We hurt each other...because of what was done to us. Please...let me understand, too."

His face tightened, his gaze far away. "He isolated me from everyone else. I had no friends, no playmates. I was not even allowed a pet, because my father thought it would weaken me.

"He put me through rigorous physical routines, harsh enough to chill a grown man, much less a boy of ten, because he thought I was becoming a bookworm. He thought the Crown Prince could not be all brains and no brawn.

"He made me join a military unit at fifteen because he thought it would toughen me up.

"He sought to make me invincible."

And he had, in a way.

Ariana sat in the chair, stunned, the implications whirling through her head. That's why there had always been such a wall around him. In the beginning, she had thought it was his station in life, his privilege that made him oblivious to the world.

"No wonder you thrived on the isolation in that cabin." The words fell from her mouth without conscious thought.

"I do not thrive on solitude, as much as it is all I've ever known," he offered. "For years, I had no one for company except books and tutors and my father. I had no other role in life except being the Crown Prince. Not even a son to Theos. Not a brother, not a friend.

"I rarely even heard anyone call me by my name. It was always Your Highness.

"I learned to keep myself happy with my books or go crazy.

"I was not allowed to see Nik unless they were supervised visits. Anything that was assumed could be a weakness, anything that I could depend on, I was forced to get over it.

"Then slowly as I grew older, I began to chafe at Theos's restrictions. Drakon was still everything to me but Camille, Nik's mom, made me see that I could have a life outside it, too. Then Eleni, who was always there, who never asked for anything. I began to realize how different life could have been. But it was too late by then.

"Being alone became second nature.

"It became who I was."

She felt like crying. "How did you survive it?"

"How did you survive being locked up?"

Even having known the best part of him, she had so easily stereotyped Andreas into that uncaring role. In her naive stupidity, she had barely even tried to understand the pressure he must have faced from Theos, the duress of having to fix the gaping hole of Drakon's economy.

She had always blamed Andreas for knowing her so little. Had she been any better? But suddenly, it was as if she was seeing the true Andreas for the first time.

The man at the village, and the Crown Prince—it had always seemed like two polarizing opposites that she could never understand. She had struggled to fathom how she'd misjudged him so terribly.

He had wronged her, yes. But she had done just the same.

Suddenly, she wanted the past cleared between them. She wanted a fresh start. She walked back to him, purpose in every step. "Do you believe me? That it was never my intention to deceive you?"

His jet-black gaze held hers for what felt like an eternity. Something had changed in his perception of her, she realized now. The truth of their marriage? "Does it matter to you that I believe you?"

Frustration flared and she forgot to temper her response. "Of course it does."

Only when he smiled, a soft light in his eyes, did she realize that she had betrayed herself in the now.

What he thought of her had always mattered to her.

Still mattered, it seemed.

He traced her cheek with his knuckles. As if that small fracture in her resistance of him was a prize. As if he would give her the world if only she became that Ari again.

I got used to being loved by you.

What did that truly mean? she wondered now. For a man

who'd had everything, had her love meant something? Did he want that again?

His gaze searched hers, as if he wanted to see through to her soul. "Because it alleviates your guilt?"

Her hands rose to his chest. His heart thundered under her palm. She wanted to pull away the layers of clothes, feel the silk of warm skin tightly stretched over muscle. Emotions battered at her from all sides, and only this awareness of him was constant, this heat and hardness of his body the only real thing. "No, because I...never wanted to hurt you. Because I need you to know, even after all these years."

He didn't say she hadn't hurt him, and in his silence, in the things he said without saying anything, Ariana found a world of hope. The moment stretched between them, wanting and morphing, his heart thundering away under her palm, her own beating a thousand a minute.

A moment between the past and the future.

His fingers crawled to her nape, not pressing, not moving. Just touching. His other hand moved to her hip, the tips of those long fingers reaching the jut of her hip bones.

Her entire being wanted to melt in his arms. To curl up in his heat. God, this was it. This was exactly what had been missing from her life.

What her heart and soul had desperately needed.

She had needed him to understand the truth of what she had done. But given up all hope that he would look at her like this...like she still mattered.

"Andreas? Please, you have to—"

Gently, he pushed her back until he could see into her eyes. "Yes, *pethi mou*. I believe that all you did was run away the moment I turned my back," he replied, twisting her words.

She sensed his confusion and something more in that. A loss that she hadn't stood and fought for them? She waited for him to say more, to call her a coward even.

After all, she'd declared again and again that she loved him, hadn't she?

But no more came from him.

"Your father went through an elaborate scheme to make me unforgivable in your eyes. He couldn't have been worried that you would chase me. You'd have hated me too much."

Something glittered in his gaze. "Are you asking me or telling me?"

It was one of those moments that defined life. A door opening. Years of tightly suppressed hope unfurling. "I'm asking you," she whispered, hiding her face in his chest.

God, she was so tired of staying strong. Of...denying, even now, that he meant something to her, after all these years.

"I would have come after you, yes." A long sigh fell from his lips. "There's no moving forward without facing the past, is there?"

A rush of tenderness filled her. "No."

He did care. He cared that he had hurt her. He cared that he had driven her away. Too little, too late, but God, she hadn't been without culpability. She hadn't made it easy with her flights of rage and her sulks and that fear that she had fallen in love with a man so horribly wrong for her. So much a despot like her father.

"I'm sorry for what I let him do to you."

But what about what you did? she wanted to ask. *What about your incapability to love me? To see me as anything other than an obsession or a weakness. Incapable of giving me a tiny, tiny piece of your heart.*

But she wouldn't be, she *wasn't* that needy girl anymore.

She didn't need to be loved by him to know her worth. Maybe she'd even lost her own ability to love, to trust someone else with her happiness, the ability to share fully of herself.

Seeing her son's small, unmoving body had done something to her.

She had lost her ability to love and he'd given up his dream.

Sanitized and sterile, weren't they perfect for each other now? "You could have any woman in the world. Why me?"

He grinned, suddenly looking incredibly boyish. "Is this one of the reasons then? That I didn't compliment you enough?"

"Compliment me enough? Andreas, our entire dialogue was comprised of you usually warning me off something or the other. What we excelled in truly…" she raised her brows "…was nonverbal communication."

His chest rumbled with his quiet laughter while his fingers dipped into her hair. Prickling warmth spread down from that touch.

"I hate to diminish the impression you have of my power and influence," he added, and she snorted, which in turn made him grin, "but Drakonite law prevents me from divorcing you for at least eighteen months."

She didn't even panic anymore. "So I have eighteen months to bring you to heel then?" She traced the flat of his brow with the tip of her finger. "I'd better start taking inventory of the weapons I can use against you."

"You've become bolder, *pethi mou*." His fingers dug into her flesh, feral hunger blazing in his eyes. "I didn't think it possible."

Her skin prickled with answering need. How could she forget that the harsher his control, the deeper his need for her?

"You and I will celebrate a jubilee even as the only King and Queen of Drakon together in two hundred years because I intend to prove that Theos was wrong."

"You said he didn't control you anymore. And what do you mean jubilee?"

"For two hundred years, there hasn't been a jubilee celebration. And no, Theos does not control me," he said cryptically. She hated the harshness that came into his eyes every time they talked of his father. The patrician features tightened, the easy humor fell. "Giving you up, giving up on this marriage will mean he wins, *agapita*. And I could not let Theos win. I could not let him be right…"

"Revenge against your dead father is no more a better foundation for marriage than an inexplicable obsession is. It will never work."

"It will work because I refuse to give in.

"If you truly are dedicated to making a difference in the world, if you really care so much about the work you did at that legal aid agency, you could do it from here.

"You could have the prestige and power of the King's Palace behind you. Or lead the pampered life of a queen.

"Find your place in my world, Ariana. I do not care what it is. But stop running away from me and from yourself."

Ariana stared, tremors running through her.

Every time she thought she finally understood him, he went and did something like this. And yet, she was beginning to understand him, beginning to see how his mind worked.

Andreas didn't know how to handle guilt any more than he knew how to handle the little something he had felt for her back then. So this opening to her. Not because he thought it was important to her or because her happiness mattered to him.

Yet, here was the perfect way to know whether they could ever work, the chance to pit the Ariana she was now against the future King's personality. The chance to see if that connection that had brought them together years ago could mean anything.

The chance, as he said, to prove the great King Theos wrong when he had called her a curse upon his heir's life.

"You're on, Your Highness," she whispered.

Hands crawling up his chest, rising to her toes, she touched her mouth to his.

For a few seconds, he was stiff, shock tensing his entire body against her. But Ari didn't care. She needed a taste of him, she needed courage to see this thing between them through.

His mouth was hard and unyielding but this time, she knew. She knew what simmered beneath that stoic, unaffected exterior. She knew the raw passion that dwelled under the academic's soul.

Hands perched on his shoulders, she licked the seam of those sculpted lips. When he growled, when he roused out of that momentary freeze, she swiped her tongue inside his mouth. Nibbled at his lower lip.

Heat poured through her in liquid rivulets, pooling in her lower belly.

And just when his hands descended to her hips, just as he slammed her chest against his, Ari somehow managed to slip away from his hold.

Breaths harsh, dark pupils wide, he scowled at her. "Come back here, Ari." The tension that poured out of his lean frame was a balm to her soul.

Holding his gaze, she made a show of wiping her mouth with the back of her hand. As if it was that simple to erase the taste and feel of him from her being. "No."

"No?"

She smiled, feeling a freedom, a joy she hadn't known in years. "That was just a small test for myself, Your Highness."

A vein fluttered at his temple. "A test?"

She nodded, loving his frustration in that moment. "A test to see if I still had it in me to bring you to your knees."

"And?"

Andreas Drakos reduced to blank questions…was there

a sweeter victory? "Are you ready to fall to your knees, Your Highness?"

He said nothing. And yet the gleam in his eyes told her all she needed to know.

She still had it in her and this time, she was going to use it to design the life she wanted.

CHAPTER SEVEN

ARIANA SPENT THE first two weeks as Andreas's wife being swept up in the storm that was the King's Palace and the Crown Prince's life.

True to Andreas's warning, there had been no time to center herself before the news had been leaked that the Crown Prince had married in secret.

Had, against every popular opinion and to the shock of the populace of Drakon, fallen irrevocably in love.

A strategic leak by his own PR team, she'd learned later. A way to massage the truth.

All of Andreas's overseas trips now had a perfect explanation. Having accidentally met Ariana, a young beautiful lawyer, General Theseus Sakis's daughter, in the States, he had fallen violently in love with her and, due to some obscure legal obligations, had to marry immediately.

It was as if Drakon and its people had been hungry for some explanation like this about their Prince. The tale of their stoic Prince falling in love and marrying in secret seemed to fill a much-needed hole in the country's perception of him. Overnight, Andreas turned into a romantic figure, vulnerable as any of them.

The moment the formal press statement from him had hit the news cycle, Ariana was lost.

Invitations to balls, charity galas and state dinners began pouring in. Dress fittings, appearances by Andreas's side, private dinners with powerful members of the cabinet and Crown Council, Ariana held her own through it all.

Even as she realized that she was mostly ornamental on Andreas's arm, even as most of the times, the men—powerful traditionalists—talked as if she couldn't understand a word of import, even as she realized that the Queen's role was mostly titular, Ariana behaved with the perfect decorum.

And the shift in the perception about him, the picture his PR team painted of the Crown Prince's marriage enabled Andreas to make his own headway in the political zone.

Tax reforms that had been introduced temporarily passed through the cabinet. A host of new members were appointed to the Crown Council—most of them direct appointees handpicked by Andreas and Nikandros—small business owners, professors from universities, had been met with resistance but finally passed.

That he was serious about the changes he had spouted gave Ariana much to think about. She saw the power that rested in Andreas's hands, the duty of serving his country that he thought was inviolable. Saw the magic of it in Nikandros's round-the-clock efforts to make Drakon's economy sustainable, the pride and tears in Eleni's eyes as Andreas, against Gabriel's threats to kidnap her away from Drakon if she accepted, appointed her the executive chairwoman for the House of Drakos charities that involved millions of dollars.

More than once, she'd caught surprise, humor, even curiosity in Andreas's eyes as she acted the perfect hostess, the adoring spouse to the serious Prince. Almost as if he didn't believe the meek image she'd presented to the world.

Thanks to Eleni, she'd chosen a stylist that understood her personal style. Petra ran her life as smoothly as she did Andreas's and for now, Ariana relented control. Her first few public appearances with Andreas would define her future as the Queen and she toed the line. She might be a lawyer but she didn't know the intricacies of a political system like Drakon's so she listened and learned.

No one could find fault with her, not even the staunchest royal critics. Thanks to Eleni's constant advice and unrelenting support—once she'd learned that Ariana meant to stay—she'd sailed through those first two weeks. Even King Theos would have been surprised.

Everything went great except one thing.

All the time she'd spent with Andreas could be counted down to minutes. Their exchanges limited to discussing the weather, which had turned dismally cold.

Nothing personal touched their words. At the end of the day, they retired to separate chambers, even as tension seeped through the very air between them.

Ariana saw his desperate need for her in his restrained touches, in the hot, hungry look he leveled her way even in the midst of a crowd. Felt the answering shudder of her own body.

He wanted her, and yet he'd barely said two words to her since that evening. Barely shared the pressures of his life, the constant stress that he must be under. What he wanted, again, was relief and she was damned if she was going to be it. Damned if she was going to let him slot her again.

It suited her just fine, she told herself. She didn't need him to hold her hand through her new life. She definitely didn't feel deserted when he left on a trip to Asia without so much as a goodbye.

It was her own naïveté in not realizing how busy his life was. In not understanding that Andreas could never truly belong to anyone. After the storm of the first couple of weeks, she finally had a moment to breathe. And her own plans to make, so she shut up that internal voice that said nothing had changed and threw herself into her work.

Only it wasn't that simple. Going up against Andreas and his will, she should've known, would never be simple. She wanted to learn more of Drakon, she needed to be more than an accessorized, haute-couture figurehead.

The first wake-up call came in the third week, when she'd decided to visit a woman's shelter in the capital city.

Petra had relayed the answer. *His Highness feels that such a visit would not be wise in the current time.*

Somehow, Ariana had kept her cool.

Then, she had decided to scout for premises near the palace where she could set up her legal offices. Before she could set a foot out of the palace, security had waylaid her.

His Highness has ordered an apartment to be cleared for Mrs. Drakos's use in the South Wing of the palace.

A mansion of a wing, attached to a team of lawyers who would do the grunt work while bearing the stamp of her name.

Somehow, she had kept her temper.

Next, she'd been drafted, without her agreement, to an afternoon tea with a host of powerful patronesses of charities from Drakon. Ariana had managed to not choke on the tea.

Next, the interview she'd given to a press member about her background in law dealing with domestic disputes and her aspirations to start a legal aid agency in Drakon had been sanitized until Ariana had sounded like a mouthpiece for the palace and a colorful accessory that belonged on Andreas's arm.

The last straw came when she'd learned, through a slip by Petra, that all the calls she'd been receiving from her friend Rhonda, whose divorce case had been pulled up on the calendar, had been rerouted without a word to her.

Ariana had had enough.

It had taken him mere weeks to revert back to type. To relegate her to a small part of his life. To turn her into nothing but a figurehead. *Thee mou*, if all he'd wanted was a placeholder, why had he gone to the lengths of kidnapping her? Why make her those promises?

God, she was a fool to have ever believed him, a fool to hope that they could make this work, even without love complicating matters.

But this time, she would not run away, she told herself walking the perimeter back into the royal wing. If he wasn't going to come to her, she would go to him. She knew he'd returned from his trip almost a day ago. And she was done waiting.

She pushed her way through the small corridor off her lounge and barged into the other master suite that was connected to hers through it.

She snarled at a sleekly dressed bodyguard when he blocked her in front of the massive double doors. "His Highness does not let anyone enter his private suite." When she raised a brow, the guard shrugged. "Not even his brother or sister."

"Did the Crown Prince have a wife before?" Ariana demanded in a soft, utterly privileged voice that would have surprised even her father.

After what seemed an eternity, the guard nodded, threw open the massive doors and moved aside.

Ariana stepped inside, blinked and came to a still. A faint thread of sandalwood and something so intrinsically Andreas curled through her muscles.

From the wide French doors on the side to the huge high windows, everything was covered with light-blocking blinds. She rubbed her arms. The room was cool.

Dark mahogany wood, almost black furniture dotted around the vast semi-circular room. A wide desk sat next to the French doors, which would open to a view of the mountain range in the distance, she knew. Not a single pen or paper was out of place on the gleaming wood yet there were reams of paperwork on it.

In the center, the room retreated farther back. Darker and quieter than the rest. Did it lead to his bedroom?

Pulse zigzagging, Ariana forced herself to look away.

One whole wall behind her was floor-to-ceiling bookshelves. She didn't need to go close to see they would be books mostly on the history of Drakon, and the history of the world, neatly filed in alphabetical order.

Moving on feet that felt no reticence, she went to the bookshelf. Her fingers, she noted, were trembling as she ran them over the spines of some familiar titles. Warmth filled her limbs, the books greeting her like old friends.

They were, in a way. All the months he'd spent at the fishing village, these books had been in the library of the Drakos estate. She'd gotten so used to seeing him carry them around, she had one day asked him to talk about them.

A whole new side of the Crown Prince had been revealed to her when he spoke of history with passion, wonder, a love in his voice that she'd never thought him capable of.

She moved along the shelves, sometimes smiling at a familiar title, sometimes frowning. Until a title hit her like an invisible punch.

Dragon Captured: A New Look at the Ancient Lore of Drakon, by Andreas Titus Drakos.

Ariana plucked it from the shelf, heart thumping hard against her rib cage. The book he'd been writing when he'd taken the sabbatical.

Why had he lied?

The gilded spine, the crisply expensive paper told its own story. It was a customized collector's edition. It had been his dream to share his love for the history of his country with the world.

That rich, new-book scent stole into Ari's blood as she slowly flicked the thick jacket open. She traced the title and his name on the inside with shaking fingers. Turned another page and her heart jumped into her throat.

For the girl who loved me.

The book fell from Ari's hands and landed on the thick carpet with a muffled thump. She fell to her knees, tears making big splotches on the thick paper. A silent sob falling from her mouth, she picked up the picture that had fallen out of the book when it landed.

It was her. She didn't even remember when it was taken. Her body was turned away from the camera, her hands full with a tray of dark coffee and a slice of oozing baklava.

The same thing that Andreas had ordered every day for months in the café.

But her face was turned toward the camera, that big, goofy, wide grin curving her mouth. Her hip jutting out at a cocky angle, her entire body screamed a sultry invitation, and her eyes were warm and sparkling.

Thee mou, she'd been audacious, teasing and taunting the Crown Prince like that. She'd been bold and brave, grabbing what she wanted from life. Something she'd forgotten. She folded her legs under her and sat on the thick carpet, the picture in her hands, the book sprawled open in her lap.

She read a few pages here and there and smiled, hearing his passion in his words. She traced the lines of her own face in the picture, worn-out and fading, a startling contrast among the crisp, new pages of the book.

Had Andreas looked at that picture again and again? Her mind raced, aided by her heart, raring to jump to all sorts of conclusions.

Like a leaf in a storm, she sat there. Guilt and hope vied. There it was, the proof that maybe Andreas had cared. A little. At least after he'd thought she'd died, said a bitter voice, the voice that wanted to keep her safe.

No, this was proof that his heart had not been carved from the same rock on which his palace sat. Something that had hardened in her chest loosened. The guilt that she had carried along for so long…it thawed at the sight of that rumpled picture.

She replaced the picture in the book and the book on

the shelf. On legs that felt like jelly, she ventured deeper into the suite.

The room was cavernous, with soaring ceilings that seemed like they could touch the sky. The huge skylight had dark shades.

The king-sized bed with a cream upholstered headboard and pristine white sheets beckoned to her. Andreas slept on his stomach on one side of the bed, the sheets up to his waist. Leanly muscled, his bare back was strikingly dark against the white sheets.

A smile broke through her at the sight of his large feet peeping out of the sheets. No couch or bed or sheets were ever tall enough for Andreas. Her sheets had looked like a child's blankets on him.

Ariana moved to the head of the bed, pulled by an urge she couldn't understand, much less fight. He had left her to fume and he was sleeping?

Then it came to her. He was used to not sleeping for days, went into that intense focus mode when an important matter came up and then he would crash, sleep through the day and night.

His face was to the side on the pillow, his arms under it. Even in the dark, she could make out those distinctive features. Impossibly long lashes fanned toward the slope of his cheekbones. His mouth, a rigid, stiff line, was relaxed into a soft curve. She ran a finger over the impossibly sharp bridge of his nose, traced the wing of his eyebrows, the defined line of his jaw.

Something fluid and desperate, a twisted longing rose through her. For weeks now, she'd been racking her mind as to why she'd run away like that, why she'd had to take her guardian's help, whom she had never liked, to flee Andreas.

Why hadn't she just stayed and made him understand what he'd been doing to her?

Now she knew. A part of her was always going to b

weak when it came to him. A part of her was always going
to be that eighteen-year-old who'd fallen in love with him.
A part of her was always going to hope that maybe, just
maybe, he would love her a little.

She needed to walk out of here and think, she—

Long fingers wrapped around her wrist, arresting her,
half prostrate over him and the bed. She slapped a hand over
her mouth, but it was too late. Black eyes, that shouldn't
have been shining in the dark, stared at her, sleep diluting
the usual forbidding expression.

"Ari? What's wrong?" His voice was husky and sleep-
mussed. Like he had sounded after sex.

"Nothing...is wrong." The sheets slithered around him
as he blinked and moved to his side, his eyes still adjust-
ing to the darkness. "I...didn't mean to disturb you. Go
back to sleep."

Desperate to escape, Ariana wiggled in his grip, but it
tightened. She gasped when his arms went under her shoulders and tugged her onto the bed.

His dark face hovered over hers, his sleek, taut body
propped on his elbows, his breath hitting her nose in soft
strokes. Not even out of breath as he watched her like that,
his body a heated canopy over hers.

"It is hard enough to sleep knowing you are in the next
suite, *finally*, after all these months. You should know better than to taunt me in my own bed."

Her hands rose to his shoulders to push him off. Hard
and tense, he was like velvet-covered rock under her questing fingers. Heat swirled and pooled in her lower belly and
she shook from head to toe. Standing on the edge of the
abyss. Waiting to fall.

That faded picture of her, hidden away in a book he
hadn't showed to the world, beckoned like a beacon.

Their eyes met and held in the dense dark, that connection, always so strong between them, tangible again.

Oh, but with his legendary self-control in play, he did not kiss her. He would not break his promise. Would not give in until she asked. She could see the desire in his glowing eyes, in the flaring of his patrician nose.

"Ask me to kiss you." Clipped and serrated. On edge. Only the Crown Prince of Drakon could make a request sound like an arrogant command. His body was tense, his breath, because she knew him so well, a little shy of normal. "*Diavole*. Ask me to kiss you, Ari."

CHAPTER EIGHT

ARIANA LICKED HER LIPS, longing cleaving her in half.

This, him. This fire that he invoked with a single look. It was all she'd been missing in her life.

"Kiss me," she said simply, throwing herself off the cliff.

His arms on either side of her head, his fingers digging into her hair tight, he slanted his mouth over hers. Tiny, numerous frissons shook through her body at that first contact. Firm and supremely male, his lips touched her in a soft, silken, barely there caress that was nowhere near enough.

A taste of whiskey and him. Fingers tracing his collarbone, Ariana shook all over.

Another butterfly-soft brush, there and gone again.

A sweep of his tongue over the seam, and then nothing.

Slow kisses. Soft kisses. Testing the suppleness of her lips. Tempting to steal her breath. Again and again. Over and over.

Her body bucked off the bed, seeking more, needing more. "*Please*, Andreas," she whispered half sobbing, every nerve ending taut with hunger.

A taunting smile breaking out on his mouth, Andreas moved to his side, and threw a muscled leg over hers. Rock-hard thigh pressed hers into the bed, a languorous weight that her body craved. "I've forgotten how much it pleases me when you say please."

"I have forgotten how much I hated you in bed."

"I have had two years to imagine this, Ariana. You've had days." Pure devil glinted in his wide smile. "Now that you're here, I intend to take my time."

His arms sidled under her as if she were a featherweight, tugging her onto her side. A long finger traced a lazy trail along the neckline of her loose T-shirt. Her breasts were thrust up, the upper curves visible through the hanging neckline. Up and down, until the pulse at her neck throbbed violently.

Anticipation was fire in every muscle every time his finger skated the edge of one curve. *Thee mou*, he'd adored her breasts. Worshipped them. So much so that she had once orgasmed just with his mouth on them.

The memory slid over skin like a silky caress. Fired nerve endings.

His finger hovered over the upper curve of one breast, his breath a harsh whisper. "Your body has changed."

A profound ache twisted through her. All she could do was nod.. Even as fear whispered over her spine, she needed this intimacy. Craved it for so long. Here, in the dark, the world shut away, maybe she'd find the man she'd fallen in love with.

Jet-black eyes held hers, possessive and powerful. "It turns me on even more." She saw the edge of that hunger in his eyes, the deep grooves of need around his mouth. "Although, nothing could turn me on faster than seeing how eager you always were."

She lifted her hands to his face. With the pad of her thumb, she traced the long curve of his lower lip. A stern, stiff line until he smiled. Or kissed. "And you were never desperate enough."

He frowned, but Ariana had had enough of the power play. She needed to know if it was as magical as it had been back then. She needed to know if this heat between them was worth burning herself all over again.

Sending her seeking fingers into his hair, she tugged his arrogant head down. Breath rushing in and out, she licked that sensual lower lip with the tip of her tongue. His growl reverberated from his hard chest. Without waiting, she opened her mouth over his and dragged it from one end to the other. Another growl, a warning. She didn't heed it. She kissed him again and again, until heat sparked where their lips touched, until she was out of breath. Until her lips stung.

Until the need to shatter that control was a scream in her blood. She dragged that lower lip between her teeth and then flicked her tongue over it. The curse he spewed was a balm over her heated skin. In a fraction of a second, she was pushed onto her back and his mouth crushed hers.

Her upper lip banged against her teeth. Her scalp prickled at how tightly he gripped her with one hand, while the other clasped her jaw, holding her still for his assault.

Spotlights filled her vision as the taste of him exploded through her body. There were no more games, no more teasing. Angling his head, he deepened the pressure until the heat of their fused mouths was enough to scald them both.

With a stark groan, she opened her mouth. He swooped in. The slide of his tongue as it chased hers was so erotic that her toes dug into the sheets. Again and again, he devoured her mouth, his wicked tongue dipping in and out with a frenetic rhythm that her body recognized. Craved.

His hands gripped her hair tight, his mouth opening and closing over hers, sucking and nipping, until she was trembling with a fever beneath him.

Until the taste of him was forever embedded in her.

She had no control over herself, no will of her own. She was begging with her body, her hips thrusting into empty air. His hands moved down to her shoulders, between her heavy breasts and then down to her abdomen. Again and again, up and down, touching, marking, staking a claim, while he ravished her mouth. Stroking her body higher and higher, promising her that cataclysm, enslaving her will.

"Tell me you need more, little wife." His tongue traced the rim of her ear in a silken stroke that had her clutching her thighs tight. The tip of it moved behind her ear, before his teeth caught her lobe. "Tell me where you want my hands and my mouth." A wicked, wild promise in a deep, husky voice she barely recognized as his.

His hand lay palm down on her chest, the tips of his long fingers touching her neck. Her heart thundered against this palm. Her breasts swelled, begging to be cupped in those powerful hands. Her nipples ached to be sucked into that mouth.

And he missed nothing.

His gaze flicked down toward the tight tips of her breasts visible through the thin fabric of her top, the trembling of her body, the tight clutch of her thighs. Naked satisfaction lined the angles of his gorgeous face. "Ask me to be inside you, Ari. *Dio*, my mouth, my hands, whatever you want, wherever you want."

Her entire body was screaming her need for him, her desire evident in her shallow breaths. And yet, for the devil in him, it was not enough.

He moved his hand down her stomach, down her pelvis until it rested over her mound. Her hips jerked against his fingers resting against the covered lips of her sex. Wetness drenched her panties, a fact he knew. For a dark strip of color scoured his sharp cheekbones.

"Ask me, Ariana." His voice fell to a whisper. His lashes fell and rose slowly. His breath a soft hiss in the dark. "I will do it with pleasure."

How was it that he gave her the power and yet it was Ari that was falling?

His body next to her was a fortress of need, yet controlled with that ironclad will. Ariana pushed her hip into him. He jerked back, his fingers digging into her hips. Arresting her movements. But too late.

She had felt the evidence of his desire. Her breath slowed, the faint tremor in his powerful shoulders telling her how on edge he was.

Only his control was better. Over his body, over his mind, always. He would never let himself lose that will.

She hadn't seen that back then. She hadn't realized that it pervaded every part of his life. Hadn't understood that for the Crown Prince of Drakon losing control of himself in bed was akin to giving Ariana a real place in his life. That it would mean him needing Ariana and not just the other way around.

The more she'd asked him for his attention, his time, the more he'd distanced himself. As if he didn't know what to do with her. As if she didn't fit in the neat box he'd made for her.

Needing her meant giving her power over himself, over his emotions.

And he was doing it again. He was compartmentalizing her because she made him feel.

Why had King Theos been so worried about him? Andreas's heart was stone.

A laugh erupted from her mouth. Whereas she… Ten years hadn't made a dent on the wants of her foolish heart. Every inch of her body, every beat of her heart wanted to grab this chance with him again. Wanted to find that happiness, that sense of completeness she had had with him in that village.

But not on his terms. Not at the cost of losing herself.

"*Oxhi,* Andreas," she managed, her lips stinging from the heat of his lips. The sound of her denial, somehow given voice, filled up her lagging will.

His hand didn't move from her sex. For a few seconds, Ari wondered if he'd even heard her. He looked up. A flash of consternation in his eyes before he exhaled roughly and buried his face in the valley between her breasts.

The damp warmth of his mouth made her nipples poke through her T-shirt. Ariana shivered, unraveling over the strength it took to resist him.

"I said no, Andreas." Steady and almost assertive. "Possible you don't understand the word because you've never heard it. Especially from me."

His laughter, muffled against her body, sent tremors through her. Eyes glinting with humor, he stared at her. But the curiosity was there. He was taken aback by her refusal, she was sure. "You and I both know why you walked into my suite, Ariana." A sultry dare. "I have never held your desire for me against you."

So sure of her always. So sure of her devotion, of her hunger for him. Once he'd given in to their desire, she hadn't challenged him in any way. Wherever he had led with that arrogant confidence, she had blindly followed. When he'd decided they would marry, decided not asked, she'd happily forgotten all her dreams.

Because, of course, this worldly, powerful, sophisticated Crown Prince of Drakon, a man women lost their hearts to, had chosen her.

Her.

No wonder he'd thought she was another part in his privileged life. She jerked away from under him, his supreme arrogance lighting a fire in her. "You're an arrogant bastard, did I ever tell you that, Your Highness?"

"No." He pushed his hand through his hair roughly. Harsh and accented. She could have laughed at the irate expression on his face if her mind wasn't jumping from thought to thought. "You're right. For a minute there, I forgot that you hate me now.

"You'd never have ventured into my room without a reason. Not unless you were desperate."

"You're doing it again." She cringed at the anger in her voice.

"I don't understand."

"You ripped me from my life, brought me to this palace,

and you go on your merry way. *Again*." For the life of her, she couldn't stop the last word from tumbling out.

His stillness betrayed his shock. "Ari, help me understand."

He'd never used that tone with her. He had ordered her around, he'd dared her. He'd condescended to her. But never had he asked her in that tender voice. As if it really mattered to him.

"Ari, so help me God, if you don't explain yourself, I will—"

"What? You will lock me up?" she said on a laugh. "I can at least count on you to buck me back up." She sighed. "If all you wanted was a placeholder, why go to the trouble of kidnapping me? Why make promises to me?"

He truly looked so disconcerted that Ariana didn't know whether to laugh or cry. He pushed up on the bed. The sheet slithered to his waist, baring his torso. Lean, ropey muscle stretched tight over his abdomen when he sighed. "If this is about me not breaking down the door to your suite and ravishing you in your bed—"

"I'm not talking about sex. Is that all the use you see for me?"

"By your own admission, I needn't declare you Queen in front of the whole world if all I wanted was to screw you." The words were like tremors on the ground. So softly spoken but powerful enough to pull the ground from under her. He pushed a hand through his hair roughly.

Already trying to patch the little rip in his self-control. Already putting the veneer of civility over the confusion she saw in his eyes. The strain his desire for her put in his face.

Ari slowly got off the bed, every inch of her balking at walking away from sure pleasure. But she wouldn't be able to deny him or herself another time. And sleeping with Andreas when he saw no other use for her was like signing away her soul. Again.

And she couldn't do that.

Every cell in her wanted to grab this chance fate had given them both.

No, not fate. Andreas had done this. She didn't care that he called it payback for what she'd done to him.

He'd come for her. From what Nikandros had said, Andreas had scoured the world for her for two years, while Theos had clammed up. At the cost of risking his duties to the crown.

Of course, the man didn't know what it was to love. But to the best of his ability, Andreas had kept that commitment he had made to her. Was it his fault she wanted what he couldn't give?

"You promised me I could carve whatever role I want in your life, in this life, and yet you...you deny me every step of the way.

"I don't think you quite know what to do with me."

"What the hell does that mean?"

"You denied my visit to the women's shelter."

"It is not safe for you." His jaw tightened. "And damn it, Ari, you made the trip anyway. You drove the security staff nuts with your little stunt."

She tilted her chin up, raring to go at him. "You forced me to it. Just as you created office space for me in the palace. In a bloody wing of the palace, Andreas. My career is not a joke."

"As my wife and Queen, you will be far too busy to take up a full practice. This way—"

She pushed her face into his, her blood running hot now. "Did I let you down in any way? Did I not act as the perfect ornamental wife?"

His mouth twitched. Finally, he was catching on. "I couldn't believe my own eyes that it was you. So biddable and meek." He took a step forward. The predatory glint in his eyes sent sparks up her spine and she took a step backward. "All I could think of was whether I wanted you like that in bed."

"Andreas, I… I will do everything you need as your wife. But it doesn't mean I'll give up a single part of my life. It doesn't mean I'll let you or your staff decide how I live my life. I…can't…*we can't* make the same mistakes all over again."

"Kala," he said, almost conciliatory in his tone. "Tell me what you want from me to achieve that."

She straightened her spine. "For starters, I want my laptop, my personal belongings and my case files. I need to speak to Magnus. I want someone allotted to me, someone other than Petra, to see to my needs."

Every spark of humor disappeared. "No."

"What do you think I'll do over Skype, Andreas? Disappear like they do on spaceships? Have Skype sex with the man I lied to for ten years?"

"I do not like another man's name and the word *sex* together on your mouth, *agapi mou*. If you want to negotiate with me, you should know better than to provoke my ire."

"There are things I can do to help Magnus, until he finds a replacement. A couple of the cases, those two women are my friends. The law does very little to protect them from their powerful, abusive husbands. Too many people have already let them down. I refuse to be one.

"I can't just disappear off the face of earth and let them believe the worst.

"You have your commitments and I have mine."

The lines around his mouth deepened. His dark eyes became flat, all that emotion wiped away. But Ariana was beginning to learn his cues again. The harder something hit him, the more shuttered he became. As if he could only implode. As if showing that emotion meant actually feeling it.

As if it were handing a weapon to Theos to use against him.

He pressed his fingers to his temple, his jaw clenched

so tight that it might break. "Is that what I did to you, what motivated you to study law? Were you afraid of me, Ari?"

"What? No, of course not." The truth that she had left unsaid glimmered like a phantom around the room, sending a cold whisper through her. When his expression didn't budge, she hurried on. "For years, I was directionless. I hated my father for forcing things on me, so I never even discovered what I would enjoy, what I would be good at. I joined Magnus's legal aid agency as a clerk. Literally my job was to keep the filing in order.

"The more I saw the women that came through the agency's doors, the more I thought of my mother. My father never beat her, as some of those women were, but he... abused her just the same and I was powerless then.

"But I realized I could change that. I worked hard to get my law degree.

"I can still provide help to Magnus with the paperwork. And I want a couple of my friends to be flown here. Rhonda is going through a rough patch and Julia has no place to stay since her husband froze all their assets until the divorce proceedings finish."

Something like shock filled his eyes and Ariana felt a surge of satisfaction. Clearly, until this moment, he hadn't taken her seriously. "Here where?"

"To Drakon. To the King's Palace."

"You want me to provide sanctuary for two women who are running away from their husbands, and maybe even the law? To turn the palace into...some sort of pseudo-shelter?"

"I want to invite a couple of my good friends so that they can reassure themselves that the husband I have been hiding from for ten years is not a complete monster. And yes, they get a vacation.

"There have to be some perks to being the Crown Prince's precious wife, *ne*?"

"Kala," he said after a long gap. In a sudden move-

ment that sent her heart lurching to her throat, he caged her against the wall. He took her mouth in a furious kiss that was all tongue and teeth and left her clinging to him. A sob burst out of her when he buried his mouth in her neck.

"Any more demands?"

Oh, his mouth was such a sensuous trap. So harsh when he dealt out commands and yet so soft when he kissed. She licked her lips and he leaned in closer, until his breath was a whisper across her heated skin. "I want Giannis back."

"*Oxhi.* Next?"

She placed her hands on his chest and pushed, determined to win this battle. "I want *my* people around me. People who care about *me*, people who don't think I'm your downfall. People who will stop me from feeling as if I live in a vacuum.

"I'm not a toy you play with, dress up and then put back on the shelf. That was me stopping before I fell into old, harmful patterns. I came—"

"Harmful patterns?" A vein pulsed dangerously at his temple. "Toy I played with? After every lie you've told, after everything you've done, I am still prepared to give you a place as my wife. A position coveted and sought out by the most beautiful, most accomplished women in the world today."

She flinched but refused to back down. "But you chose me. Whatever it is that sits in the place of your heart, wanted me, Andreas. In my own naive way, I didn't appreciate the magnitude of how uncharacteristic your choice was. How far off the mark you had gone."

She pushed against his hold on her wrists until her upper body grazed his. The hiss of his breath drowned her own. Jaw set, fingers taut over her wrists, he searched her face. As if he was seeing her for the first time.

"You still want me. You wish you didn't. And not just for a quick screw, or you would have taken me on the flight and dumped me. You could never be that ruthless with me then, and you won't now.

"Andreas Drakos has a weakness and it is me."

He pressed into her, a feral curve to his mouth. Bare chest crushed her breasts, and Ari threw her head back. Mouth drifting over her neck to the pulse, he smiled against her skin. "Point to Ariana Drakos. So why the hell are you not letting me give us both what we desperately need?"

"Because I'm not that train wreck reeling from her parents' deaths anymore. My primary function in life is not to provide you with sex and relief from your duties. I'm not awed that you noticed me, much less chose me." If her breath caught at the lies she was spouting, she hoped he didn't notice.

She twisted her hands in his grip and he let go, as if she'd burned him. But Ariana was not through. A fire ran in her veins, a sense of rightness that she belonged with him. A new hope that she could live with Andreas without losing herself.

She clasped his face in her hands, determined to make him see her.

"I'm not that girl who thought the sun and moon rose out of your eyes, Andreas. I will not be another cog in the machine of your life like Petra or Thomas or your chauffeur.

"Unless you're prepared to meet me as an equal, unless you're prepared to share your life with me, I'll run away again.

"And believe me, if I know one thing, it is how to escape from situations. This time, when you catch me—" his eyes gleamed at her acknowledgment "—I will come with a scandal that will rock your precious House of Drakos.

"So decide, Your Highness, if you want me in your life or not."

CHAPTER NINE

ANDREAS FORCED HIMSELF to let Ariana go, stripped off his drawstring pants and walked into the cold shower. The mosaic tiles were startlingly cold against his overheated skin. He turned the jets to biting cold and still it took a few minutes for his arousal to abate, for his rational mind to grasp hold of the situation.

By the time he was out of the shower, he was shivering. He wrapped a towel around his waist and stood in front of the mirror.

His hair was overlong, falling past his ears. His eyes still had those dark shadows but had lost that bruised look he'd been walking around with for God knew how long. Gone too was that black void he'd carried inside of him for months.

And the black, biting, cold rage after Theos, in one of his mad rages, had spilled that Ariana was alive. It was as if his world was beginning to tilt back to normal again. He was beginning to understand that he had known nothing about her back then. Nothing of substance at least.

Even now, he knew there were things he still could not grasp. Things he knew he saw in her eyes when she had lain in bed next to him.

Things he struggled to put into words.

If you want me in your life, Your Highness…

Laughter, shocking even him, burst out of him at the audacity of the woman.

She had always been reckless and defiant, and yet there was something new to her. A self-possession that was as intoxicating as it forced him to pay attention.

She clearly thought he'd miss that adoration, and a part

of him did. But this woman, who challenged him even as she trembled with her desire for him, she couldn't hold a candle to that girl.

He had no doubt she meant every word of her threat. No doubt that she would bring scandal, if not ruin, to his feet if he didn't give her whatever it was she wanted.

The challenge, instead of riling him, made anticipation flow in his veins.

He wanted to argue and negotiate with her. He wanted to dominate that defiance until it turned into desire. He wanted her under him, writhing and screaming.

Once he dressed, he could not however give her chase, as desperately as he wanted to.

The moment he had stepped out of his suite, Petra and his three aides had been desperate for his time. A contract he was signing with the House of Tharius came up and his thoughts veered.

His life would be so much better if he divorced her and took Maria Tharius for his wife. A doyenne of charities, Maria had been groomed since birth for a role like that. She would be amenable to his every wish, would know her place, be a proper mother for any children they had.

Maria would be the perfect Queen of Drakon. Maria would not demand that he give sanctuary to women fleeing their lives. Maria would not demand that he locate a security guard who worked in the palace ten years ago, who clearly had broken protocol and befriended the Crown Prince's young wife. Much less order that he not only be reinstated but join her personal team, knowing that it made her husband...uncomfortable that his wife was...chummy with that man.

Face it, Andreas. You're insanely jealous.

A growl rose through his throat and his team froze around him.

Dio, was this what she reduced him to?

In his heart of hearts, he knew Ariana wouldn't have cheated on him. And yet he'd been insanely jealous of her friendship with that young guard.

And he still was, given that Ariana clearly still had affection for Giannis.

He, the future King, jealous of a small-time guard.

Yet the thought of sitting down to dinner with Maria for the next thirty years, the thought of seeing Maria's placid smile across a crowded ballroom, a woman who would always remain a stranger because he just knew she'd stick to her place, the thought of taking her to bed... Distaste filled his mouth.

Thee mou, now that he had found her again, only Ariana would do.

Ariana, who had already won over his family with her effervescent personality.

Ariana, who would not give a damn about protocol and etiquette when it came to their own children. No, she would be the first one to slide down the side of a snow-covered hill. The one who would encourage them to break as many rules as possible. The one who would...love them unconditionally, whether they were an academic like him or a sick child like Nik had been. Or a little girl craving acceptance, like Eleni had been.

The one who would give a new definition to the future reputation of the House of Drakos.

"I want a Giannis Petrakis located as soon as possible," he said to one of his aides. "He used to be a security guard with the palace. Have him report to Mrs. Drakos."

"Mrs. Drakos?"

His aide paled when Andreas pinned him with a look. "Yes, Mrs. Drakos, my wife."

In the following week, he chose to avoid her, chose to immerse himself in the most pressing state matters. Tried to lose himself in the riot almost brewing among the members of the Crown Council after he had passed the latest edict, relinquishing them of their powerful positions.

His opening their real estate to Gabriel's company, and Nikandros's risky financial ventures, had already caused waves.

The people didn't understand investment when their national debt was already in millions of dollars. But Andreas had persisted.

It had taken everything he'd had to trust Nikandros, but he had. And it was the best decision he had made, for Gabriel's company had already boosted the employment rates in the remote areas of Drakon.

There were a hundred matters for him to see to.

Yet all he felt was this raw, fierce need to possess her. To shatter the defiance he saw in her eyes, to own the fiercely strong woman she'd become.

To fix whatever she thought they had to fix between them so that he could drag her to bed and drive himself inside her.

She would be unlike any Queen Drakon had seen, yes. But at least she would not let him descend into that kind of megalomania that Theos had fallen into over the last few years. She would not let Andreas complete the transformation into becoming that hard man who, despite having all the riches and power in his hands, would forever remain alone in the end.

The man his father had forced him to become.

A man who would always be feared but never liked. Never loved.

He'd give her everything she asked for, this time. Everything that was in his power to give.

It was late evening almost a week later when Andreas was finally free. He'd had Petra invite Ariana to dine with him in his private suite. He was determined to be civil tonight, and not slide down the slippery path to their disturbing past.

They needed a fresh start and for that, he needed to believe Ariana. He needed to understand, as much as it burned him, that Ariana had left him because he'd made living with him unbearable.

He had barely time to shower after his long day and put on fresh clothes when Ariana walked into his suite.

A panorama of expressions crossed her face as her gaze fell on the intimate table set out on the veranda, overlooking the courtyard, with a spectacular view of the horizon. He tried to see it from her point of view. Crystalware twinkled in the orange glow of the setting sun. A bottle of champagne sat in an ice bucket. Their food was already sitting on the table since he'd dismissed the staff already.

"*Kalispera*, Ariana."

He saw her head come up but she didn't turn.

So easily she snagged at his temper. Until he saw the tense line of her shoulders. Until he remembered that this was Ariana and emotional control didn't come to her easily.

In fact, it was the opposite of her nature. Which had been what had attracted him to her in the first place.

His amazement that anyone could live with such free rein given to their emotions.

Knowing what he did now about her background, it amazed him even more how fearlessly she had lived then. How generously she had given of herself to anyone who had come into the sphere of her life.

She slowly turned toward him, as if she needed the extra minute to compose herself. Something caught in his chest, a twinge of regret maybe, for how things had been once. The wariness in her eyes...he was determined to push through it.

He wanted the old Ariana back. The Ariana who had

worshipped him. The Ariana who would have never filtered anything that had come to her mouth, especially with him.

The Ariana that had made him feel that he was, finally, not alone. That he need not be alone.

"*Kalispera*, Andreas," she replied back softly. The wariness didn't abate but neither could she stop her gaze from devouring his face nor from sweeping down his body and back up. As if she had been starving for the sight of him.

Just as he'd been for her.

He felt no such compunction about showing his own interest, however. He had had a week from hell and all that had kept him going was that he would come back to this.

To her.

That tension that had become second skin flickered over his muscles as he swept his gaze over her.

She was dressed differently today, like the Ariana he remembered.

Sexy, confident, yet with a thread of vulnerability beneath.

A simple beige sheath dress that barely touched her knees, that made her golden skin glow with a burnished sheen. It showed off her toned arms and lithe figure with its simplicity. Black pumps made the most of her long, long legs, bringing her face almost to his chin.

Thee mou, he'd always loved how well she had fit against him. But now, that angular look was replaced by soft curves. Curves he wanted to feel beneath his body, softness he wanted to surround himself in.

She left her hair to fall softly around her shoulders. It softened that stubborn jaw of hers.

When their gazes met, he smiled and raised a brow. "You look gorgeous."

She flushed but held his gaze. "*Efharisto*. You look—" her mouth twitched, and so did his entire body in response "—very…dashing."

"Can I assume that the cold war between you and Petra reached its conclusion?"

"Let's just say we reached a mutually satisfactory agreement."

"What is that?"

"To stay out of each other's way. And now that I have my own people, her attitude doesn't bother me at all."

He frowned, remembering all the small tidbits she'd thrown out during the dinner with his family. The near panic he'd seen in her eyes as she'd stood by his bed.

"I have appointed Giannis as my aide and I've been interviewing candidates for an administrative assistant and a PR person. Eleni's miffed, I think, that I chose someone Mia recommended."

He half nodded, his mind still on the previous issue.

Knowing Petra's loyalty, and even her bit of possessiveness when it came to him, he didn't doubt the veracity of Ari's words. Regret, piling up as high as his guilt, made his voice harsh. "Petra is invaluable to me, *ne*. But not indispensable, Ariana.

"I will have her moved to another department instantly."

"Oxhi," she replied instantly but with such shock in her eyes that Andreas momentarily stilled. "Not necessary."

Christos, did she really think he would put a staff member before her, even now? After everything she'd told him about how isolated she'd felt then? About how Petra and her team had taken their lead from Theos's treatment of her, even from Andreas's own retreat as he'd struggled with his own emotions?

He reached her, refusing to let her shy away from him. "Why not?"

"Because it would mean that I'm still that insecure girl. It sends a message that I'm helpless and I hide behind your power." She lifted her chin. "I mean to hold my own, against you and against everyone in your world this time, Andreas."

He nodded, pride filling his very veins. She had come a long way from that girl and he needed to see that. "I think you've already proved that."

"I could not believe it when Petra told me you wanted to dine with me. Now I'm astonished that you went to this much trouble."

"Why?"

"For one thing, I know how busy you are. And for another, I didn't think you would take my ultimatum seriously. But I guess that's the one chink in your armor, *ne*? That I might somehow go to the media. In the current sentiment the people have with you, a woman crying kidnapping is the last thing you need."

He poured them both a glass of the champagne and handed it to her. "So let me get this straight." A thread of chill filled his tone and her head jerked up. "The only reason I'd want to spend time with you is for damage control."

Her white knuckles around the champagne flute were the only sign that she wasn't as breezy as she sounded. "Is it not?"

"No, Ariana." He put his glass on the table with not quite a steady hand, and then took hers. Then he went and stood in front of her. He plucked the small velvet box he'd had his aide retrieve from the royal treasury and held it out.

She didn't look up but her chest fell and rose with her shallow breaths. He waited, knowing in that moment how much he had crushed her tender heart ten years ago.

How he'd done exactly what he'd feared he would do.

"Ari, look at me." When she didn't, his patience finally unraveled its last thread. Clasping her chin with both his hands, he tilted it up.

Whatever he meant to say fluttered away at the sight of

her lush lips. Angling his head, he took her mouth with a hunger that punched through him.

Thee mou, he'd forgotten how sweet, how perfect she tasted. Lust surged through him as she swept her tongue over his lower lip.

No reluctance, no hesitation.

No lies, no dares.

Pure Ariana, pouring every inch of her emotion into the kiss, right down to the hoarse chuckle when their teeth banged in their hurry to get at each other.

But Andreas was not in a laughing mood today.

He was in a devouring mood. *Dios*, he'd waited so long for the taste of her. So long to feel like he would combust if he didn't slide inside her wet warmth.

Her hands moved to his chest, her body arching like a bow toward him.

The more he took of her mouth, the more he needed. Wrapping his hand around her neck, holding her still, he licked and stroked with his tongue, bit and suckled with his teeth, until she was whimpering against him. Trembling with need.

The kiss flared higher and hotter. The dinner was forgotten. Promises he'd made misting in the heat of their passion.

The press of her breasts against his chest, her long thighs straddled by his own, that scent of her skin…it was like striking a match to hot cinders.

He moved his hands to her hips and then to the curve of her buttocks. Roughly, he pulled her until she was plastered to his lower body.

His erection lengthened.

She moaned and arched into his touch, always so responsive. Always pushing Andreas toward a bit more madness.

He lifted her on the next breath and arranged her on the table. The ice bucket clattered to the ground with an almighty thud, the slide of ice cubes on the concrete a hiss in the silence.

She was breathing hard, her eyes heavy lidded, a protest on her lips, he knew. She meant to talk, throw up another one of her demands. Or dares.

He didn't let her get the words out. Instead, he stole them from her lips in another kiss that had them both growling against each other.

Thee mou, he wanted her like this—spread out on the table on a veranda of the King's Palace where sky and the stars would know that she was his. Her dress had already bunched up her thighs, giving him easy access to soft, silky skin. One hand sliding up her thighs, he buried the other in her hair and tugged her up.

Eyes glossed over, mouth trembling, she was utterly beautiful.

"I'm going to touch you, *glykia mou*," he whispered at her ear. "I'm going to see if you're wet for me already or not."

He held her against his chest while his fingers found the dampness through the thin fabric of her panties. Fire spewed in his muscles, his erection pressing persistently against his trousers. *Christos*, she was so ready, so wet for him. Burying his mouth in her temple, he pushed a finger into her sex and she jerked against him.

"Andreas, *parakalo*…" Head thrown back, she pushed her hips against his hand when he pressed his thumb against her swollen clit. A sob fell from her lips. The setting sun made her flushed skin shimmer like pure gold. His fingers had made a mess of her hair. Beads of sweat dotted above her lip. He licked that lush lip. The scent of her arousal spread through his blood like a drug.

He tugged the neckline of the forgiving sheath and growled at the sight of her bare breast. He gave the brown puckered tip a lick and her spine arched hungrily.

Her fingers moved to his hair and he complied. He rubbed his jaw against the wet tip before he closed his mouth and sucked.

She was close now. He could feel her body swelling around his fingers. The muscles in her pelvis tightening against the very pleasure she craved.

"You did not wear a bra," he whispered against her skin before he laved the plump nipple again. "Tell me, Ariana, that it was for me. Tell me that was because you knew how mindless I go at the sight of your breasts."

Her eyes flew open, unfocused, sluggish, before they settled on him. Desire made them glitter like the finest gems. An impish smile curved her mouth. "The material... it shows straps. Not for you."

Even now, she denied him that satisfaction.

He hooked his finger inside her tight entrance and waited, breath punching through him like bellows. She shuddered against him, and let out a slew of curses that had laughter thunder through him.

Her hands clutched his wrists, and her lithe body pushed against him. "Yes, okay. I went without a bra for you, *kala. Parakalo*, Andreas. More."

Fierce satisfaction raging through him, he pumped his fingers into that fast rhythm her body loved. He intended to dismantle all the defenses she had built. He intended to have that Ari of old again.

Her body tensed and bucked, like a boat flung against the waves. Sounds ripped from her throat, needy and raw. Bending his mouth, he nuzzled at her breast and like Independence Day fireworks, she fell apart around him with a keening moan.

Her thighs trapped his hand between them, her breath still harsh for several seconds.

She fell into his chest like someone had removed the bones from her body. Andreas pulled the dress up to cover her breasts, his own body screaming for release. And yet, utterly satisfied on another level. He swept his gaze over her, that possessive instinct she always brought out in him in full riot.

Long, quivering limbs, golden skin flushed, a smile hovering about her lips, her sensual repose was just as arousing as her uninhibited response.

On a deep level he didn't even try to understand, he felt as if his world was finally being righted.

From the moment he'd seen her standing in front of the city hall, her face pale, a stricken look in her eyes, he'd needed this.

He had needed to see her splinter with pleasure, pleasure he gave.

He had needed to know that Ariana was still his.

She opened her mouth and pressed a kiss to his chest, creating a damp patch. "I…" Her sigh whispered over his skin, his shirt no barrier to sensations. Another open-mouthed kiss against his abdomen. Which clenched like a steel wall. Her hands moved over him, stroking, touching, questing with a possessive flair that was more revelatory of Ariana than anything else. "What was that about?"

He tilted her chin up. "If you're asking me questions, clearly it was not that good."

Ripples of her laughter shook her slender frame. "Oh, believe me, it was an earthquake. But I still want to know… what—"

"That was about the present."

She looked up, and frowned. "What?"

He couldn't help himself. He dipped his head and kissed her swollen lips again. "Neither the past, nor the future. It was about now." He tucked a defiant curl behind her ear and stared into her eyes. The words came so easily to his lips. So clearly. "I wanted to kiss you, Ari. I wanted to see you shatter in my arms and I followed that urge."

The most beautiful smile spread over her face, something almost incandescent flickering in her eyes. That quality that defined Ariana. That quality that he wanted pervading his own life.

She nodded, clasped his jaw and kissed him softly. Slowly. As if she never wanted the moment to end.

A feeling he was coming to recognize within himself.

"Going with that urge was good. Andreas Drakos giving in to urges is *very* good. Provoking you to that urge—man, I feel on top of the world." She ran a finger over his lips, tracing them over and over. "I…have an urge, too." He held his breath as her hands traveled down his chest, past his trousers and slowly came to rest on his groin. He became still, arousal spiking through him as she traced his shape. "We can't go to bed yet, but your wife has other means to satisfy you."

How he managed to hold her fingers from wreaking havoc on him, he had no idea. Even he was impressed by his willpower. His erection throbbed in rhythm with his heart, his breath serrated. "Why can't we go to bed, exactly?" he asked softly. He hadn't planned any of this. He hadn't even meant to touch her until things between them had reached a new stage. But, of course, in his relationship with Ariana, passion had been one of the things that had always been right.

But now that she denied him, he wanted to know why.

A shadow passed across her face, though she tried to cover it up. "I started my pills again just the other day. So we won't be protected."

"Protected against what? I'm clean."

"Against pregnancy," she answered in a soft voice.

The moment stretched through awkwardness and fell directly into something altogether painful.

When he waited with a raised brow, she moved back

from him. An edge to her movements, she straightened her dress, careful not to meet his gaze.

A shiver snaked up his spine. "There is something called a condom."

She shrugged and ran a hand through her hair. Straightened her already perfect dress a little more. Buying time. "You hate condoms. More importantly, condoms are not foolproof. Nothing, actually, is foolproof."

Déjà vu hit him like a strike to his solar plexus. "Ariana..." he said but arrested anything that wanted to come out.

He ran a hand over his face, tension corkscrewing through him.

They had been through this once before. Their biggest, dirtiest fight when he'd asked her to get off the birth control pills.

The closest he'd ever come to losing his self-control because of course, she had absolutely refused to do so. And then his threat that he would not sleep with her unless she did.

Dios, he had been like a wounded beast.

Of course, Ariana could never take a dare lying down. They had ended up in a heap in front of the fireplace, clinging to each other after the stormy sex and having realized that something had been broken irrevocably between them.

The only time, the single time, sex had been something other than a source of joy between them.

He had left for the oil summit three days after that without a word to her. And when he'd returned, she'd disappeared from his life.

He had used sex against her, corrupted the only pure thing between them.

Desperation, he realized now, had clouded reason, good judgment. And *Thee mou*, he recognized only now how desperate he'd been back then to stop her retreating from him. His desperation to keep the one good thing in his life amidst the mounting pressure from Theos and the crown. And his own inability to fix the situation between him and Ari. His own inability to handle what she did to him.

He cursed at the color leaching from her face. In a second, the moment turned from sensual languor to a minefield.

Frustration made his voice rise. "Ariana, you need to share what you're thinking with me."

She nodded, but the wariness was in full force. Her hands around her midriff signaling untouchability. Barriers that he wanted to break but didn't know how. "I just don't want us to chance it. We're not ready."

"Not ready for what?"

"For children, Andreas."

The more she denied him something, the more he wanted to dig in. Andreas wanted to break that harmful pattern of their relationship. Yet something didn't feel right. Something goaded him to provoke her into a reaction. Into an answer. "Sooner or later, we will come to this point."

"It will be later then." Her spine straightened, a combative look in her eyes. "Andreas, we've barely made it through one evening, one, without going at each other's throats.

"I just don't want to bring children into this. At least not yet."

"Why not?"

"Because…between us I don't trust us to get this right."

"You mean, you don't trust me." Frustration coiled up inside him. After everything he had granted her, she still wouldn't give him everything.

Would she ever?

She came to stand in front of him. Lacing her fingers through his, willing him to listen. "It's not that I don't trust you, as much as I…am afraid.

"Please do not force this issue, Andreas."

Again.

The unsaid word hung in the air, morphing and growing like an impenetrable, invisible wall. A thread of disquiet ran through him. A feeling that if he didn't do something, anything, it would always stand between them.

"I want a family. I have always wanted children, you know that."

"You wanted heirs. There's a distinction." Her reply was instant, her eyes saying so much she didn't give voice to.

Feeling as if he was walking through a dark maze blind-folded, an experience his father had forced him through when he'd been eight and confided that he was scared of the dark, he formed and discarded several answers. "The requirement for an heir to the crown is always going to be there, Ariana. Our first child, a boy or a girl, will inherit everything.

"When the Crown Council and Theos put pressure on me to marry these last few years, I considered never doing so. I kept postponing coming to an agreement with Maria's father."

Listening to the other woman's name on his lips sent a shiver through Ariana. "Because of me?"

He shrugged. "I just was not eager to repeat the experience when I thought you were dead. After I found out you were alive…" Ariana had never wished more that she could understand what was going on in his mind. "Nikandros and his children were more than good enough for continuing the House of Drakos.

"So, yes, the heir to the House of Drakos is always going to be a question that will be raised.

"But what I want is…to be a father to my children. To give them the…" She saw him swallow. "The kind of life that I never had."

"What is that?"

"A normal, happy, carefree childhood."

Ariana stood transfixed as emotions buffeted her from all directions.

Guilt and grief choked her breath. Here was the proof that he had truly changed. Just as she had.

Could they make it work this time?

Could she trust that gut instinct of hers that said he cared at least?

She took his hands when he would have moved away. When the small distance she was insisting on could become a chasm neither of them could cross. "I need time. I need it to be just us first. That is, just you and me and Drakon at least."

His gaze probed hers, as if he wanted to know all of her secrets. He lifted their joined hands and kissed her knuckles. The tenderness of the gesture melted her from within.

Lifting his gaze, he held hers. "You've changed," he said finally, his thoughts running parallel to hers.

"I have stopped throwing myself headlong into everything, yes."

He nodded, a set to his jaw. "But I want that old Ariana back. The Ariana that was quick to laugh. The Ariana that loved so generously. The Ariana that lived life to the fullest.

"I assure you, *pethi mou*, I will have that old Ariana back."

CHAPTER TEN

OVER THE NEXT couple of weeks, Ariana found herself more and more captivated by her husband. It was as if he had mounted a campaign to conquer her—mind, body and soul.

And he was winning.

One evening had been a leisurely two hours where they had discussed the red tape she was having to muddle through for her legal agency; one dinner had lasted only an hour and had to be shared with two of his political aides who'd discussed his agenda on his upcoming trip to Asia; once with his PR team and hers, coordinating their schedules and events over the next few months, which had, of course, resulted in a fierce argument between her and Andreas, concerning her duties as the Queen and her increasing devotion to establishing her own career.

Neither of them packed their punches. Neither of them had won.

Ariana had loved every minute of it.

She loved pitting herself against his considerable will. While she never came out the victor, neither did she let him run roughshod over her.

If dinner could not be possible and there had been days when all she caught was a passing glance of him at a party they were both attending, she found him drifting into the small sitting lounge at precisely ten thirty every night, where she watched an American political satire show, a longstanding favorite of hers.

He would settle down next to her, his hard thigh pressed up against her. Sometimes they laughed at the comedy, sometimes they hotly debated the politics. Sometimes, when they were both far too exhausted, they just fell into a comfortable silence.

But whatever the scenario, a persistent thread of awareness flared between them over the most innocent of contact. Contact, she realized with heat flushing her as she waited for him, she seemed to initiate.

It was she who couldn't keep her hands to herself, who had undone his tie knot one evening when he'd looked utterly flattened after another meeting with the Crown Council, she who had quickly buttoned his shirt, covering that defined chest, when he hadn't quite finished dressing when she and Petra had arrived at the same time one evening, she who had pressed her mouth to his when he had given her his mother's ring.

All he did was watch her from those eyes, the epitome of patience and inscrutability. But Ari knew him as well as she knew herself. Knew that he was waiting for her to make the first move. Knew that it was his kind of foreplay.

He thrived on waiting her out, thrived on pushing them to the edge until every single touch was a fire that could sear.

She didn't know what she was waiting for. She didn't know why she couldn't take that last step in their new relationship. The last time she had jumped into a physical relationship with him, not knowing what was at stake. This time…this time, she knew the value of it.

She knew that when she took Andreas inside her, she would irrevocably lose a part of herself again.

Was it losing her will to his that terrified her?

Or was it the last bit of truth she still held on to?

She wanted nothing between them when he made love to her this time, nothing but want and need.

Except telling Andreas about their son that she had lost terrified her to her core.

They were finally getting to know each other. Finally

coming to understand what had gone so terribly wrong the last time. Finally realizing that something akin to magic existed between them. Even out of bed.

"You look utterly serious."

Andreas stood at the entrance to her bedroom. His suit jacket was gone and his white shirt was unbuttoned. The dark shadow of his chest held her attention, her lower body instantly tightening.

She blinked and tried to rearrange her face. "I'm just tired tonight," she replied, realizing it was true. All week, she'd been on conference calls with Magnus and Rhonda and her new lawyer.

He reached the sofa she was sitting on and took a seat without touching her. The tension in his frame radiated out in waves, dismissing her concerns. "Then you need to dial back on the amount of work you're taking on. Petra couldn't find a spare moment from you all of last week."

"Petra needs to stop spying for you," she countered with a smile. Even as his overbearing attitude toward her well-being grated, it also warmed a part of her. For years, she had looked after herself, with no complaints.

But now, she liked that Andreas worried about her. Now she could see his concern for her beneath his arrogant commands.

"Also, will you do the same with your work?" she asked and he grunted. "Very macho, Andreas. Your attitude is beginning to match your communication style."

A long exhale left his lips and he looked at her, a glimmer of a smile around his lips. "You keep up your duties as the Crown Prince's wife, you work all hours setting up your office and dealing with your friends' problems. And yet…"

That he was trying to put this into words rather than railroad her made joy bloom in her chest. "But I'm not being a real wife, am I?" she answered, covering the distance between them.

Dark desire made his eyes glitter. He fingered a wayward curl of her hair and tugged, his mouth a languid curve. "No. One of these days, *agapita*, my patience is going to run out and I'll be inside you and you cannot claim I seduced you.

"I have given you time, Ari." Gravelly and low, his voice pinged over her skin.

Suddenly, she was ready. Just like that.

Before he could blink, she straddled his legs and kissed him.

A long growl erupted from his mouth as he took over the kiss in an instant. Hands on her hips kept her pelvis ground against his, spiking her temperature.

His tongue caressed her with a silky slide, his fingers curling tightly around the nape of her neck.

Ariana moaned loudly when he took her lower lip between his teeth. Threw her head back in a wanton invitation when his hand covered her breast. Drifting her hands down his chest, she covered his groin.

Felt the jolt of his arousal against her palm.

She would have let him take her on the couch right there, if not for the loud peal of her cell phone.

"Ignore it," he growled against her breast.

And it was the command in his voice that made her realize the significance of that ringtone. She slid off him and picked up her phone. And her heart sank.

Andreas somehow managed to dig his senses out of the haze of arousal. Or maybe it was the fast leaching of color from Ari's face that did it.

Ignoring the distress that emanated from her, he wrapped his arms around her while she was still on the call. The lush roundness of her bottom incensed his deprived body a little more. But he liked holding her like that. Even if it was torture.

Somehow, urging his body to calm down, he kneaded the tense jut of her shoulders just as she ended the call.

He knew he wasn't going to like it the second she faced him.

"I have to go," she whispered.

The words sank like stones through his gut. He frowned. Tried to keep his voice even. "Go where?"

"To the States. To Colorado," she said absently, walking circles around the vast room.

"You're not going anywhere," he burst out.

Her awareness jerked back into the room. "Rhonda's divorce came through." Anguish painted her face deathly pale. "Her husband was so pissed off that he hit her. She needs me, Andreas."

Andreas reached for his own phone and called Petra. "I'll have Petra arrange for round-the-clock care for her. And security. That husband of hers won't touch her again."

She was still pale, her body tense. "I should have been there. She was...there for me when I had no one. When it mattered, Andreas," Ariana whispered, as if she hadn't heard a word he'd said.

The very idea made goose bumps rise on his skin. "If you had been there, then you'd have been hurt. *Christos*, Ariana, how could you not share how dangerous your cases are? What if you had been there and he had hit you instead?" Panic made his voice rise, made it harsh. He'd never felt panic like this. He didn't know how to handle it.

Thee mou, was this what came of caring about her?

He never wanted to imagine Ari hurt or worse. "If you want, we'll fly her here as soon as she's able to travel. And first thing tomorrow morning, you'll give over all your case files to Giannis.

"I want a security team vetting every case you take on in the future. You'll be a target as it is without taking on unnecessary—"

Ariana covered his mouth with her hand, her arm going around his body. He stiffened, rejecting her caress, wishing he could reject the answering thrum of his heart as she looked into his eyes.

When had she gained this power over him?

"If you curtail my career, if you do anything to change even the course of it, you'll lose me." Her words were a whisper, an entreaty. As if she understood what she did to him. As if she was willing him to trust this thing between them. Willing him to trust this strange coiling of his own emotions that he was feeling for the first time in his life.

When, suddenly, all he wanted to do was to fight the choke hold of it.

When all he wanted was to have his sterile, uncaring self back.

"It's the same as asking you to walk away from Drakon. Could you do it, Andreas? Could you do it for anything in the world?"

He pulled her hand away from his mouth, his pulse violently ringing in his entire body. "No."

She clasped his cheeks, forcing him to look into her eyes. Forcing him, again, to face what he didn't want to. "Then please trust me. Trust me to do what I need to do. Trust me to keep myself safe. Trust me to come back to you."

Pressing his mouth to the inside of her wrist, he took a deep breath. Letting her go was akin to tearing out a part of him.

But he needed to do it. For both their sakes. To keep a modicum of control over his own emotions.

Whatever madness had consumed his father and whatever manipulations he had run through his children's lives, Theos had been right in one thing.

Emotion was dangerous to men like them, men who held the fates of thousands in the palms of their hands. Men who could abuse that power so easily to rearrange the lives of people closest to them.

Even now, the urge to do something, to ruin her career, her case files, her associations, so that he could keep her safe, so that he could keep her to himself, was so rampant.

My jailer, this time, was the man I loved.

Never again. *Thee mou*, he couldn't do that to her again. He couldn't be the one who killed the spirit inside her.

He let her hand go, and turned away. "Fine, go. I'll give you a week before I'll drag you back here, by your hair if that's what it takes."

He felt her at his back, her arms vined around him, her laughter sending tremors through his frame. "I can't decide if I like you as an academic or a warrior." A wet kiss fluttered near his spine. "I think I like both." Her hands circled to his chest, moved sinuously lower until she was palming his arousal. "I want both."

A deep shudder went through him. Need shook him to the core. "You're a witch." He turned and took her mouth in a punishing kiss. He had to do it. He had to let her go, yet he hated the weakness in his gut. Hated the sweat that gathered at the thought of her not returning.

He poured everything he couldn't say into his kiss. Lifting her off the floor, he plastered her body to his, until even air couldn't separate them. Until she could have little doubt that she was his.

Longing rushed through Ariana, sending little tremors through her body. A haze descended on her and Ari struggled to keep her breathing even.

"Ari? What is it? Ari, are you having an attack?"

"No…" Ari whispered. She could hardly tell him that she was having one of those moments where you realized there was no hope for you.

That something in her was programmed to forever do

what was not good for her. It was like trying to straighten a dog's tail.

"Shh…*agapi mou*. Tell me what I can do, Ari. In this moment, just tell me what you want of me."

"Just…"

Just tell me you love me, please. Tell me so that I can say it back. Tell me so that I can scream it to the world. Tell me so that this time I can truly love you, knowing who you are and knowing who I am.

"You're mine, Ariana. I won't let you go. Anything except that."

Her laughter burst through the tears in her eyes. She had to give him points for constancy. "Just…hold me."

Silently, he tightened his arms around her. His skin was so warm around her, his body lean and yet somehow hard. His heart thundered under her ear as she placed her cheek against his chest. Nothing could equal being held by Andreas. Being dwarfed in his arms, being hit with that sensation of the world righting itself.

At the back of her mind, she was aware everything was changing. She was sinking, falling, and yet she could not stop. She could not be in his life and fight it. She could not be near him and resist what he meant to her. What he'd always meant to her.

She hid her face in his chest, afraid he would see everything in her eyes. "Never let me go," she whispered, shivering.

Three weeks later, coronation day dawned bright and sunny.

Her stomach twisting into a painful knot, her nerves stretched taut, Ariana stared at her reflection in the floor-length mirror in her suite.

The silence was startling after hours of hubbub with designers, hair stylists, her assistants running all over the palace and the palace jeweler, for God's sake.

Only a few minutes before she walked down those curving stairs to a waiting Andreas.

Only a few minutes before the world saw Ariana Drakos.

Only a few minutes before the ceremony that crowned Andreas as King and her Queen.

The gold-edged, oval, floor-length mirror made her dress shimmer as if it had been spun from pure gold.

The bright bulbs overhead made the diamonds in her combs—she'd had to draw the line at the tiara, which had looked more like a crown, and an old, tacky design at that— glitter. The tiny combs, nestled in the complicated up-do she'd twisted her hair into, winked as if there were stars in her hair.

Only now in the first minutes of what seemed like privacy, after hours and hours of makeup artists and stylists and her own secretary hovering over her, did Ariana admit the existence of the football-stadium-sized butterflies in her tummy. Admit to herself that this mattered to her. Far too much.

Of course it did.

It was the moment she had partly run away from. Andreas had given her a reason, yes, but he had also been right.

All Ariana had known then was to run away from difficult situations.

Her father, King Theos, Andreas—they had all been so sure that she'd amount to nothing. Until a few months ago, Ariana had thought she'd never measure up, either.

Had never believed in herself. Had never believed herself worthy of Andreas and everything he had thrust on her in that little fishing village.

Tonight was the culmination of years of sticking to her chosen path, the culmination of the heartache she had suffered, the doubts that had filled her in the darkest moments that her father may have been right, that she was bound to be a train wreck her entire life.

The added layer was that tonight the outer surface matched what she finally believed herself to be inside.

She looked bold, fearless, stylish, a woman who had seduced the ruthless Crown Prince into love. Even she, who had never been into clothes much, had to admit that there was something to be said for the confidence the right designer duds gave.

Her gold ball gown had been a bold choice. Her choice, since Petra and her own secretary likewise thought it unnecessarily defiant. Far too radical.

Ariana didn't give a hoot.

The gold silk was so soft that the soft corset naturally clung to her torso, drawing attention to the meager curves of her breasts. Baring her shoulders, it had a straight neckline and sleeves that fell off her shoulders. At her waist, it flared into a wide skirt.

As she ran a hand over her tummy to calm the butterflies fluttering there, she stilled, stunned by something she hadn't realized until now.

For weeks now, she had tried to shrug off the sinking tentacles of Drakon and all its centuries of glory. Had pretended to scorn the import of today, of her reception by the population of Drakon, to anyone who'd tried to lecture her on the importance of it.

Which meant Eleni, Petra, Andreas's PR team, her own PR team, Nikandros, who thought it hilarious and particularly revelatory when she'd asked him to honestly tell her about the women who'd been running contestants for the coveted role of the future Queen and how she compared against them.

Only Andreas hadn't put that pressure on her since she'd returned—later than the week he'd allotted but in time for the madness that was coronation day.

Only Andreas hadn't filled her head with well-intentioned advice, or warnings, or phrases to be memorized.

Only Andreas had just let her be.

He had not once told her what he expected of her. No questions about if she'd familiarized herself with the Who's Who of the guest list for the ball after, no questions about if she had memorized her statement on her husband's policies about his new directive for the Crown Council.

No comments about sanitizing the reality of the cases she'd dealt with in her everyday life. Cases like Julia's and Rhonda's, cases that rattled some of the most powerful men in the world.

Not even a teasing question about her dress.

Only now, away from the breath-stealing intensity of his gaze, away from that sizzling awareness between them, did she realize that Andreas had showed trust in her abilities, her judgment.

Had he kept his doubts quiet because of their history, or because he actually trusted her to see this through?

Whichever it was, Ariana found she didn't actually care. Did he know what a gift it was that he did not think her unequal to tonight's celebration and fanfare?

Dare she take the risk and tell him the last piece of the past that shimmered between them like a ghost?

The longer she waited to tell him, the harder it was getting. She saw the question in his eyes sometimes. Knew that he didn't like her answer about starting a family. That her lack of trust in him, in them, bothered him.

She did trust him, didn't she? She trusted that he'd changed just as much as she had. That they were both different people now. That any child they might have would be loved by him. In his own way.

Tonight she would tell him. After the coronation, when the frenzy of these few months came to an end. When they could just be Andreas and Ariana again in the intimacy of their bedroom.

She would tell him about the boy they had lost. She would tell him how much she loved him. She had never wanted to so desperately believe her gut instinct. And yet had never been so terrified.

Trembling from head to toe, she turned when she heard someone behind her.

Giannis stood there, his eyes taking her in with a wide smile. "It is time, Your Highness," he said with a nod that acknowledged everything he saw in her eyes.

Head high, Ariana walked to him. On an impulse she couldn't deny, threw herself at him. The good man that he was, Giannis not only caught her but ran a hand over her back comfortingly.

Ariana straightened and nodded, more than grateful for a friend who saw and understood everything.

She was ready for Drakon and its King.

Ariana realized something was wrong the moment she came down the huge, curving staircase and looked into Andreas's dark eyes.

She faltered on the last step and he caught her. His grip was so tight that she was sure she'd have bruises on her hips from his fingers. A fact he wasn't even aware of, she knew, as his gaze swept over her from head to toe.

Her body rang like a pulse at his slow perusal, at the stark possession in his eyes.

A cold hand fisted her spine.

He knew.

Somehow, he knew what she'd hidden.

"Andreas, I…"

"Did you know that I have been prepared all my life for this moment?" The catch in his throat stunned her, scared her. "To be the King of Drakon, I'd been taught, was my only duty in life. My only purpose.

"And now that the day is here...you have destroyed everything, Ari. Even my belief in myself."

"Andreas...wait, please. How did you know?"

"One of my aides thought it would be a good idea to make sure you had no surprises in your past. The media has a way of getting to those skeletons. And my team always tries to stay two steps ahead of them.

"Imagine the poor man's shock and his nerves when he had to bring that hospital report to me... Can you imagine what you have done to me?"

The next few hours were the most torturous of Ariana's life. Not one of her father's passive-aggressive punishments, not even the pain of premature labor and not knowing if she and the baby would come through, nothing could equal the agony of smiling at people she neither knew nor cared about, when Andreas wouldn't even look at her, nothing could trump the fear that she had, once again, ruined her happiness with her own hands.

But where she normally would have shattered and screamed at the unfairness of it all, she stood ramrod straight by Andreas's side on the ramparts of the King's Palace and waved at thousands of people lining up the streets of the city.

She never let her smile slip as she accompanied him in an armored car through the streets, never let the tension tying her belly into knots show as they posed for pictures outside the palace.

When she saw Maria Tharius, who seemed to be the very embodiment of poise and patience and every other virtue Ariana didn't possess, and Andreas speaking to each other, his body language utterly relaxed with her, she didn't rant and rave like a lunatic.

The one time she thought she would humiliate herself

and the House of Drakos was when they had returned to the ballroom for the first ball given in their honor. When the string quartet began playing and Andreas and she were supposed to open the dancing.

For a few knee-buckling seconds, she thought he would not ask her. Five hundred distinguished guests watching their every interaction like vultures waiting to pick at her flesh. If he didn't ask to dance with her… Nausea rose up.

A harsh exhale left her when he finally uncoupled himself from Maria Tharius and came to stand before her. The perfectly nice smile he had been wearing didn't slip one bit. Only the cold chips of his eyes betrayed his emotions.

The string quartet started a sonata and with a fluid grace she should have expected, he pulled her onto the dance floor. Her heart dipped to her knees and stayed there when he held her as if she were the most precious thing on earth.

Their bodies, which had always fit each other like two puzzle pieces slotting into one, moved in perfect sync. Ariana didn't have to look around to know that they had captured everyone's attention. She wouldn't have to look at the media reports tomorrow to know that the King and Queen of Drakon, unprecedented in the history of Drakon, were madly in love with each other.

When the dance ended and there was a thunderous applause, he pulled her to him and kissed her in complete contrast to the propriety that protocol demanded.

Her heart lurching painfully in her chest, her mouth clinging to his, only Ariana realized what it truly was.

There was no softness, no passion. He punished her with that kiss. Fingers crawling into her sophisticated up-do, he ravished her on the dance floor there. His tongue pushed into her mouth, enslaving her.

Even knowing what he intended, Ariana still clung to him. Her breath hung on a serrated edge, her body teased into painful arousal. Made even more cheap by his poisonous remark against her ear. "Welcome to our future life, my Queen." Color slashed his high cheekbones. "It never fails to amaze me how sweet you taste even when you are filled with the bitterest lies, *agapi mou*. Good thing, too. Because all we have left between us is lies and lust.

"At least conceiving our children should not be as odious a task."

Like jagged thorns, his words pricked Ariana. "What are you talking about?"

A feral gleam erupted in his yes. "I do not give a damn about your timeline, Ari. We will have children and we will have them whenever the mood strikes me.

"Smile, Ariana. You have won over all of Drakon with your perfect act. Someone should benefit from the sordid game you play with our lives."

Swallowing back the tears and the ache from his words, Ariana turned to the guests and smiled. Until her jaw hurt. Until the knot in her throat seemed to cut off the very breath from her lungs.

Andreas was a consummate politician. It was a kiss that generations of Drakonites would talk about.

The romance of a century for their future King and Queen.

The twist that Andreas had wanted to start his reign with had paid off perfectly.

The whole world believed in their love story. And it was in ashes at Ariana's feet.

CHAPTER ELEVEN

IT WAS PAST midnight by the time Andreas, along with Ariana and his brother and sister, had been able to see off the last guest.

As he'd told Ariana, the evening had been a tremendous success on one measure.

Drakon and the crème de la crème of its society had bought the story of his romance, hook, line and sinker.

They had seen what they had wanted to see—their stoic, emotionless King, made too much in his father's mold, and his beautiful wife with whom he'd irrevocably fallen in love.

It was the stuff of fairy tales, and Drakonites loved their tales more than air.

He had done his duty toward Drakon. More than that, he had given Drakonites something to look forward to after decades of his father's cold, impersonal rule.

Somehow, he'd kept a lid on his exploding temper through it all. No, not somehow. He'd been programmed to behave like this, to put duty to the crown and Drakon above everything else. He'd been programmed until it became a second skin to bury his own emotions, to pretend as if nothing had happened even when he stared at a clinical, cold summary of what his eighteen-year-old wife had suffered.

To find out that she had not only been pregnant when she had left him but that she had almost died delivering his son—his stillborn son—in some godforsaken little village at the foot of the Rocky Mountains with no one around her, it was a picture Andreas could not wipe from his eyes.

And yet, he had carried on like the automaton that he sometimes felt like.

Even Nik and Eleni hadn't suspected anything as he conversed with cabinet ministers and Crown Council members alike.

But now, in the deafening silence of the cavernous palace that had been a prison in so many ways, another chain around his ankles, a sense of utter unreality descended on him. As if something inside him was disconnecting from everything that had always shackled him.

He took the stairs three or four at a time. But there was no running from the very thing that was fracturing inside of him. Propelled by a whirlwind of emotion he had never felt, much less understood, Andreas strode into his suite and came to a standstill.

The massive doors flew back and crashed together at the force with which he had burst them open.

In the gold dress that rippled over every high and dip of that sensuous body, Ariana stood leaning against his vast bed, his downfall and his salvation together in those stricken brown eyes.

As if she belonged in here.

For a minute, all he could do, even now, was stare at her. Drink her in so that maybe it would keep other ghastly images of her at bay.

She had never looked so breathtakingly beautiful, so poised and perfect as she did tonight.

It was no wonder the media and his very discriminating guests had lapped up the story they had been fed. With that mystifying combination of confidence and innocence, strength and vulnerability, Ariana made it very easy to buy that any man, even he whose heart was made of stone, would tumble recklessly into love with her.

That any man would defy conventions and propriety to own her. And it was not just how she had looked today. It was how she had engaged people. No amount of coaching or being prepped by his team of aides would have made her look more like the genuine article.

Would have made her speak up with more passion about serving the people. About joining her husband in seeing to it that Drakon emerged victorious again after the last decade in a funk.

Against all odds, it was clear that Ariana had finally accepted Drakon. That she had finally come into her own for the role he'd always wanted her in.

She had become everything Theos had wanted in the future Queen.

She'd almost died, something inside him screamed again. It was as if the loss that had nearly destroyed him when he'd returned from the oil summit, he'd have to live through it again.

His brain provided vivid images of her pale and unconscious lying in some wretched hospital, surrounded by strangers.

Afraid and alone, yet determined to not return to him at any cost. Consigning him to a life of loneliness, destroying the little joy she had brought him.

"Get out of my suite."

"I'm not going anywhere." Defiance and something else screamed from every angle of her body. "Never again. I…" She looked away and then back at up him again. "I was going to tell you today. It's been killing me to hold it inside. Please, believe me that I was going to tell you today."

"Your words mean nothing to me anymore."

The intensity of the fury building inside him, the jagged edge of betrayal, threatened to take him out at his knees.

Was this what he had dreaded ten years ago? Had he always known that she would reduce him to this—the lowest denominator of himself—that his father had worked hard to beat out of him? Had Theos known that Ariana would have the power to bring him to his knees like this?

Her hands went around her midriff, her body faintly swaying from side to side. "No. I want to discuss this."

Ignoring her, he walked toward his closet and she blocked him. Like a drug addict, he pulled the scent of her skin deep into his lungs.

"Get out of my way, Ariana."

She stood in front of him, tension radiating out of every pore.

"If you don't move out of my way, I will not be responsible for what I do."

"I'm not afraid of you, Andreas. I was afraid of what... I became around you, of what our lives would become if I stayed. I was immature, reckless."

"Nothing you say or do today is going to change the way I feel."

A jagged laugh fell from her mouth, far too close to the sound a cornered animal would make in its last bid for freedom. "If only I had known that this last piece of bitter truth was what I needed to spill to get you to talk about your feelings, then I would have done so a long time ago."

Rage clawing through him like a tsunami, Andreas backed her into the wall until she was caged by his body against it. "What the hell is wrong with you that you would joke about such a thing? How dare you mock me about hiding the fact that you had my son and nearly—" his throat felt like there were pieces of glass in there "—died in the process?"

Finally, she must have seen something of what he was feeling in his eyes for her brown eyes widened. And even that lasted only a few seconds before she tilted her chin up and looked him square in the eye. "I lived through that, Andreas. I know what I suffered." Tears filled her eyes and ran down her cheeks. "The guilt that something in me made that happen, the grief that drowned me for months... they will not leave me in this lifetime."

She ran the back of her hands over her cheeks roughly and swallowed. "I'm not defending my decision making at that time. I was—"

"A pathological liar? A woman incapable of thinking maturely?"

"By the time I found out that I was pregnant, you were already engaged to another woman. Think this through, I had already signed papers agreeing to dissolve our marriage.

"If I had come back, if I had told you back then that I was pregnant, you would have made my life miserable as hell. Loving you with nothing in return was already half killing me.

"The fact that I even got pregnant when it was the last thing we needed in our lives is not my fault. The fact that you thought bringing a child into a…rocky relationship would fix everything…that was your fault."

Every word out of her mouth was truth that raked its claws through him. "I asked you to get off the pill because it was the only other way I could convince Theos to accept you. I knew, in the back of my mind, what he was doing to you. I saw the stricken look in your eyes, I saw how subdued you were becoming. I thought I was losing you.

"If you became pregnant, then I could convince him. Then we could give each other a chance…"

Shock made her lips flatten. Hard. "So my choice was to lose myself or to become your broodmare?"

"At the time, you were good for nothing else, so yes. If I wanted to keep you in my life, those were your choices."

She flinched at his words but he didn't care. God, nothing mattered except that he hurt her back as she had hurt him. Nothing mattered except to assuage the pain ripping him open inside.

Even caged against him, she was not feeble. Not fragile. Something glowed in her face, as if there was a light in her again. As if she was that girl who could conquer any-thing with her very will to live. With her laughter. "How about the simple reason that you loved me just as I was? That you needed me in your life, just as I was? How about standing up to the mighty King Theos and telling him that you were so desperately in love with me that you couldn't go on without me?

"That despite his every cruel treatment, despite his every effort to make you into stone, you still felt so much for me. That you…you loved me and it made you so off balance, so disconcerted that you immediately tried to push me away when we returned?

"That you're, after all, human, Andreas."

Bitterness was a rock in her throat. A jagged-edged one. She was truly lost if she thought he had loved her. "*Christos*, I ruined your life, Ari. Isn't that what you've been try-ing to tell me for weeks now?

"If you want to call it love, then you're as screwed up as I'm, *glykia mou*. Do you not see that?"

"I loved you so much and your incapability to handle what you felt for me…your inability to accept it for what it was, that's what drove me away. That's what terrified me about coming back.

"The fate of becoming my own mother again…dying inside a little every day."

Andreas turned away from her, just the act of breath-ing hurting his lungs.

Did it drill down to that as he'd always known, always feared? Did it come down to the fact that even now, he could not process or admit to his own feelings?

She pressed against his back, her body trembling. "I was afraid of what you and your father would do to our child. I was afraid that if I came back to you, you would…"

He turned with a vicious snarl. *Dios*, he just couldn't take anymore. But she was determined to rip him up, she was determined to prove that there was something in him worth loving. "We would do what?"

"I was terrified that King Theos and you would repeat history. That it would be another person your father would control. I was terrified that you would turn our son into... another you. That like my own mother, I would have no say in the bringing up of our child. I stayed away for the baby, Andreas."

The bare truth of her words fragmented the last thread of his self-possession.

He crushed his mouth to hers, for he couldn't stave off that fear spreading through him. Couldn't find a way to hold off the anger, the desperation and worst of all that hurt that seemed to saw through him.

She was right. Theos had made him into this and there was nothing he could do. He could not love her. He still had nothing to offer her.

All the rage he felt at himself, his father and Ariana mutated into this raw, overwhelming need to possess her, the only time in his entire life when he felt something.

The only thing in his life he still had, the only thing that was real and constant in his tilting world.

He poured everything he had ever felt into that one kiss, dragging his mouth over hers desperately. As if she was air and he would expire if he let go of her.

Her mouth was sweet and soft, a cavern of welcoming heat. A place where he'd always found something he didn't know he was missing.

"Andreas, please—"

A sob burst out of her mouth when he buried his hands in her hair and tugged roughly. He had no control anymore and he didn't give a damn. He tangled his tongue with hers, licking in and out of her mouth. The more he kissed her, the more he wanted.

In some portion of his mind, he was aware that she was

trying to talk. That she had more to say. But he didn't want to hear any more. He didn't want excuses. He didn't want more accusations even though he knew most of what she said was true. He wanted nothing but to drown himself in sensation.

So he took her mouth again and again, rough and hard.

He bit her lip when she tried to argue.

He licked at that nip when she sobbed.

He thrust his tongue into her mouth when she moaned.

He molded her body with his hands when she thrashed against him.

At some point, she had stopped trying to get him to listen and began giving as good as she got. Slim hands were clutching him, pushing back his suit jacket. Nails digging into his nape. Fingertips gripping his buttocks.

He laughed against her mouth, a bitter, twisted sound. He'd forgotten how much she loved his body. How many hours she'd spent kissing and licking him. Testing and teasing. Theos's excruciatingly rigorous physical regimen had come in handy in this.

Desire banishing any sense, he picked her up and ate up the few strides to his enormous bed. The French doors were open, he could hear the whisper of the staff walking back and forth across the courtyard. But he didn't care.

All he needed was to be inside her.

He devoured her and she devoured him, their focus so completely on each other that the outside world melted.

"Andreas...you didn't let me finish. Please, let me—"

His questing hands found the zipper of her dress and half pulled, half tore it away from her pliant body. Bra undone, her breasts spilled against his hands. The tips engorged when he ran his knuckles over the nipples. He pushed her onto the bed and her hair billowed on his pristine white sheets like burnished copper.

A string of silk was the only thing that separated him

from the warmth he needed. From the moment Theos had let it slip that she was alive, he'd needed this. Only with her had he ever been like this. An animal that let instinct rather than reason drive him. Years' worth of need burst through him like water through a dam.

He saw so many things in her body. So many things she'd given him with her generosity and all he'd done...

Only staring at her gorgeous body held off the pain. The ache of how much they'd lost. The fear...the stabbing fear that he was still that same man.

That he would only destroy her again.

With his palm splayed on her lower back, he pushed her onto the bed.

He ripped off the flimsy piece of silk from her body. Dizzying need. Glorious freedom.

The taut curves of her buttocks. The neat little indentation of her waist. The fluid arc of her spine. The long, trembling muscles of her thighs. The toned arms that she had spread under her. The fingers digging into the silky sheets for purchase.

He let his gaze rove up and down her body like a starved man staring at a feast. Goose bumps were rising on her skin, exposed suddenly to the cold air.

There was no mercy in him tonight.

She laid her head on one cheek, her shallow breaths making the air near her head fly in a mesmerizing rhythm. Their eyes met and held. There were tears in her eyes, unspilled, making them huge in that gamine face. Her already pouty lips were swollen and a voluptuous pink.

He might as well have been a predator holding down prey for the continual shudders that coursed through her body.

Exposed to him like this, she should have looked feeble. At least fragile. Yet there was a fire in her eyes that dared him to take her like that. To continue on the explosive path he seemed to have pushed them to, even as she quivered like a finely tuned string under the softest of his touches.

"*S'agapo*, Andreas. So much. Always." *I love you, Andreas.*

The words seared him like lashes against bare skin. Like lightning striking things to ground. Like hot spewing lava burning up everything in sight.

The true meaning of those words terrified him, bound him when all he'd wanted was to walk away.

Just once, he promised himself. He would take her for this one night. He would let himself revel in those words this one time.

Holding her gaze like that, he unzipped his trousers and pushed them and his boxers down. His erection sprang free and he saw the tiniest flicker of something—hunger, fear, he didn't care what the hell it was—in her eyes. Heard her breath quicken.

His arousal lengthened at the greed in her eyes. With a growl he couldn't contain, he shed his shirt and undershirt. "Spread your legs, *agapi mou*," he whispered and she complied like a nice, docile wife.

Legs straddling hers, he bent his body over hers. The skin-to-skin contact sent heat ripping between them. She was like spun silk against his rough chest. Her buttocks an inviting cradle for his rock-hard flesh. When she tried to move against him, he locked her movements with his hands on her wrists, using a bit of his own superior strength against hers.

Sounds ripped out of their mouths in unison, a hoarse symphony of need and desire. Sensations they had both long forgotten shimmered close. Fluttered in and out in their harsh breaths as their bodies recognized things their minds hadn't.

God, he loved her like this. He needed this submission from the woman who constantly defied him, who again and again set his world upside down. He needed her willing and wanton beneath him because it was the only place where there was complete honesty between them.

Where she couldn't hide anything more from him.

Where she couldn't retreat behind lies.

Where he was enough for her.

He dug his teeth into her upper shoulder. She bucked under him, thrusting into his hardness with a sob. "More, Andreas. Everything you can give."

The sheets whispered and slithered around them as he grazed a few more spots on her lovely back. He licked the tender spots, already bruising. Sensual and all woman, her taste licked through his veins, incinerating.

His erection caught between their bodies was like velvet-encased steel.

She was moaning and clawing at the sheets when he slipped his hand between her legs. Her slick warmth was like molten fire over his fingers. He felt her writhe under him, trying to arch her pelvis into his hand, searching mindlessly for the rhythm that would bring relief.

He stroked her long and leisurely, opened her up and sank his fingers into her, never giving her the pace she wanted. Stringing her along until she was one long pulse of sensation underneath him.

In a flash of movement, she turned under him, until she was facing him. "Don't retreat from me, please. Andreas. Don't treat me as if I'm nothing but a body to you."

"But you're just that, Ariana. I can give you nothing but this. I have never given you anything but this, *agapi mou*. When will you learn?"

"No, no, no," she said, thrashing against him. Bringing her body flush against his, she brought her mouth to his in a crushing kiss. Her breasts were crushed against his arm, her legs tangled with his. She kissed as if she meant to hold him to her with it.

"I was wrong," she whispered against his mouth, pressing kisses all over his face. "We are both different now, Andreas. We have a chance and I will not—"

He slammed his mouth against hers. Kicking her legs apart, holding her with his hands on her hips, he entered her welcoming warmth with one deep stroke. No warning, no waiting.

A groan ripped from his throat. Her snug sheath closed around his hardness like a glove.

Like they'd never been apart. As if in this moment, in this place, they were not two but one.

Anchoring her with one arm, he palmed her breast with another. The tip was an erotic contrast surrounded by the lush softness. Pleasure coiled and corkscrewed in his groin, and shivered down his spine. Lost to the demands of his own body, he pulled out and thrust back in slow, hard thrusts that had her silky body sliding up against the sheets.

Sensation spiraled through him, erasing the grief and guilt and betrayal, the only thing that could wash away the powerlessness he felt.

Mouth buried in her neck, he slammed in and out, branding her, making her his in every way. She was perfect under him, around him, the one woman who had always made him feel that he was not alone. That made him dream that he did not have to be alone.

S'agapo, *Andreas. So much. Always.*

The words mocked him, taunted him. Charged the moment with so much more than the pure carnality of it all.

He wrapped his hand around her neck, and pulled her up, until on each thrust in, her sex felt him. All of him. He increased the pace just as her body was tensing up around him. Her muscles clenched and released around his hardness, her body bucking and throwing. She orgasmed with a soft moan, her eyes open and holding his, daring him—

oh, how they dared him—always to make nothing of this moment.

It was the fire in her eyes that pushed Andreas over the edge. Lost to desire, he plunged into her with hard, rough, desperate strokes.

His climax was violent, explosive, moving through him like a storm he would never survive. This connection between them had always made everything worth it. Had somehow made sense of everything else.

Heart pounding inside his chest, he stilled. Loath to give up her warmth, he stayed inside, swallowing away the aftershocks of her orgasm still rocking through her.

Sweat-dampened, her skin glistened and invited. Her mouth looked like it had been stung by bees. Faint bruises on her hips showed where he had held her down while he had thrust into her.

Long lashes flickered up slowly. The musky scent of their sweat and sex filled his nostrils.

He couldn't walk away, even though it was exactly what he'd intended to do. Still intended to do.

CHAPTER TWELVE

WHEN ARIANA WOKE up the first time, morning had come. Even through the light-blocking blinds, she could see the world outside had started on its day. Every inch of her body was sore in the most glorious way. A muscular, hair-dusted leg lay possessively over hers, hindering her movement. The oversize T-shirt she wore bunched up to her midriff thanks to the arm curled around her waist holding her caged against the hard muscles behind.

She tried to shift to a more comfortable position and gasped at the unfamiliar sting between her thighs.

The night before came back in a rush. Instinctively, her gaze fell on the darkly handsome face sharing the pillow. His other arm was under her head, his biceps muscles curling tight. Faint shadows under his eyes, even in sleep, Andreas looked like he had the weight of the world on his shoulders.

Or was it the weight of her lies?

Had she lost him forever this time?

Only now, when it was too late, did she realize the destruction she had caused with her secrets and her cowardice.

But the stinging throb between her legs, the faint bruises on her body said something else. She had been terrified that he would throw her out. Or walk away.

Last night, she knew, was the first time Andreas Drakos had ever lost complete control of himself. There had been no finesse to his lovemaking. *Thee mou*, it hadn't even been lovemaking. It had been sex in its most primitive form. It had been pure possession, as if he meant to steal something away from her.

It had been his incapability to walk away from her even at the worst moment of their lives.

The rough graze of his teeth over the most tender spots of her body, the flash of emotions, too fast for her to even notice, in his eyes. The frantic, animalistic thrusts, uncaring of whether he hurt her. Ariana reveled in every ache and pain that her body sang this morning.

She had wanted, desperately needed, every sensation he'd evoked in her.

She had loved every minute of it.

For it meant that she could still hold on to a thread of hope. That meant that despite what he thought was the biggest betrayal, Andreas still couldn't help himself.

He had carried her to the shower, she remembered faintly. While she had stood there numb, her body sore, he had washed her, wrapped her in a towel and brought her back to bed. Dressed her in his T-shirt.

When she had thought he would leave her, she had clung to him, she remembered now, even her subconscious mind knowing that to let him walk away then was to lose him. She had begged him to stay with her, at least until she had fallen asleep. She had begged him to give her one night.

His dark hair fell onto his forehead. He needed a shave and sleep and rest in that order. God, Andreas needed to be loved. Needed to be showed that he could love, too.

She ran her fingers over the defined line of his jaw, the sharp bridge of his nose. Her fingers shook at the soft give of his mouth. The scent of sex and him lingered in the air, an anchor Ariana needed in the chaos she had created.

Anxiety curling through her, she ran her hands over warm, olive skin stretched taut over lean muscles. Every inch of him was precious to her. Every inch of him was a map to her own happiness, to her joy.

She pressed her mouth to his chest, listening to the quiet thunder of his heart. She began to whisper words and phrases that made no sense yet meant everything to her. Things she should have told him before about her life in Colorado. Times when she had missed him so terribly that it had been a physical ache.

Nights when she'd craved his arms, even in the last few weeks.

Moments during the past week when all she'd wanted was to walk into his bedroom and climb into his bed. When all she'd needed was to be held in his arms.

At some point, the words had begun to tumble out without any conscious plan. His body lost that languid sleepy warmth. Tension filled the very air, the quiet hitch in his breath the only sign that her words had begun to register. Without meeting his eyes, for Ari was terrified he would walk away the moment she acknowledged him, she kept talking. The dark helped. The physical intimacy aided. Running her hands again and again over him kept her sane, as if touch were her only tether to keep him there.

She was on her side, and he on his, facing her. She spoke the words into his chest, words she should have uttered the moment she'd seen him standing in front of the church.

The moment she'd realized that without Andreas, she would always be incomplete.

She didn't know if he was listening. She just kept talking, her throat hoarse, her body sore. "By the time I realized my period was far too late, even worse than usual, I was three months pregnant. I... I took four different tests, and they all came back positive." He was so tense around her, suddenly so cold. As if someone had injected him with ice. She rubbed his arms and his chest with her palms, her tummy a tight knot. Expecting him to any moment push her away. "I...should have been terrified and yet I was not. I know you will call it another sign that I was immature and juvenile, but I wasn't. I felt an instant connection to the baby. I...felt like finally I had a part of you with me.

Just for me. Something no one could take away from me. Not even you.

"I…had already found an apartment. Until then, I'd proudly refused to use the money Theos gave me. But that night, I went into the bank, checked my account.

"For months all I did was eat, sleep, wait. I was determined to take good care of myself. I…put on so much weight," she said, her throat catching at the memory.

"Everything was perfect until one afternoon it wasn't.

"Rhonda drove me to the hospital because pains had started and showed no signs of relenting.

"I was knocked out by the drugs and when I finally woke up…" her tears soaked Andreas's chest. Her throat burned. Her lungs felt as if they were being crushed. "I screamed at the doctor, demanding to know who had decided that my life was more precious than his.

"I was hysterical.

"They told me he'd never had a chance. I insisted on seeing him and fell apart at the sight of that tiny bundle."

Soft sobs began to shake through her body and Ariana could no more stop them than she could stop breathing. Andreas's arm came over her and crushed her to his chest. He held her hard and tight, in an almost bruising grip. The heat from his body was a blanket over her, warm and comforting.

It was exactly what she'd needed for so long. This grief, it was his, too. And she had cheated him out of it, because she had been so…afraid of never being loved in return.

"Shh…*agapi mou*," he finally said. Shaken and hoarse, as if he had damaged his throat, too. She felt his fingers move through her hair, his mouth breathing the words into her temple. "I would have made the same choice if it had come to that, Ari. I would have chosen your life…"

"I did everything right, Andreas," she said, needing to tell him this. Needing his forgiveness in this above everything else. "I was careful. I ate well. I took walks. I slept well. I went in to see the doctor for every twinge and ache. I... But I still failed at protecting him. I...never wanted to—"

His fingers were now digging into her arms, but holding her together, too. "Ariana, listen to me. He was...he was not meant to be. But it is not your fault, do you understand? All the things I said about you being reckless... I can comprehend how much you must have loved...that baby. I know how you love, *agapi mou.*"

Ariana lifted her gaze, her heart beating rapidly in her chest. Grief made the planes of his face harsher, even more stark. He ran the pad of his finger against her cheek, hesitant. Naked emotion fluttered in his eyes, for the first time since she had known him. "You... How long were you out for?"

He had been so afraid for her last night, she realized now. She saw the nightmare of it in his frenzied movements, in his shattered self-control. The words in that clinical report had been enough for him to imagine what she had been through. "Two days. They said I had lost too much blood."

He nodded, a far-off look in his eyes. A look she knew very well. His detachment look. His "burying away emotion because he didn't know what to do with it" look.

His retreat look.

"After they discharged me, after I came back to my apartment, one evening I sat with the phone in my hand, my fingers hovering over the numbers. I...had never felt so alone in the world. Not even when they came to our house and told me that my parents' car had crashed.

"I...desperately wanted to see you, wanted to be held by you. To just give myself over. To let you mold me into whatever you needed me to be. Anything felt better than what I had done with my life."

"Why didn't you? *Thee mou*, Ariana, why did you not call me? Had you no trust in me at all?"

"There was nothing good left by then. Everything was in ashes and I... I realized I had to move on. I had to make sense of my life. I had to change how I lived it.

"I always used my father's rejection of me as motivation to ruin my life. To do as I pleased. I realized... I was just proving him right. I decided that night that I wouldn't let him be right.

"The next morning, Rhonda got me a job at the agency. And I never looked back."

"I saw it in your eyes the first moment I laid eyes on you. I knew immediately you had changed."

Ariana nodded, dismay coiling up at how...unangry he sounded. So much like the normal Andreas. As if he had gone through the entire range of emotion from fury to grief and was now back to his default state of feeling nothing. "I think a part of me died with our son. I...never wanted to love like that again. I didn't want that pain again. I thought..."

She cupped his face in her hands, desperate to make him understand. "Andreas, when you found me standing at the church, I... I was about to call Magnus. I was about to call it off."

His dark eyes held hers. Wariness and something else she couldn't even identify. "Call what off?"

"The wedding. I realized I just couldn't go through with it. After everything I thought needed to change in me, it seemed nothing had changed where it mattered. I knew you were going to announce your alliance with... You were going to announce your choice for a wife.

"You...would be King and have a new Queen.

"Whether you knew it or not, whether you were in my life or not, it didn't matter. You still had a part of me. You still had possession of my heart after all those years." She felt the tension that rippled through his hard body. Every inch of him screamed rejection. Every inch of him wanted to walk away.

The very instinctual gesture sent deep shivers of fear through her.

He had always wanted her love. Thrived on it. Even a week ago, he'd challenged that he would win it back.

All she was now was an emptiness in his eyes. A resignation that was clawing through her. "I...realized the happy, safe, grown-up life I thought I had with a nice man... I just didn't want it, after all. That you had ruined me for any other man."

"Ariana..." A warning.

She pressed her finger against his lips, desperate for the right words. "I was not ready to admit it to you when you showed up. I wasn't ready to admit it to myself, but I... I never stopped loving you.

"I love you, Andreas.

"I have always loved you. I just... I needed to be worthy of you. Worthy of standing by your side, to rule Drakon. I needed to be more than the train wreck my father thought I was before I could truly understand the meaning of loving you."

The moment stretched, his silence deafeningly heavy in the wake of her words. It was as if she was trying to hold on to this moment between them, trying to freeze time, and it insisted on getting away from her.

"Andreas...please say something. Curse me. Rage at me."

Turning away from her, he pulled up on the bed. Face buried in his hands, he exhaled roughly. "What we have, this, is never going to be enough, Ariana. We might as well accept it.

"The choice is yours."

Fear was a bitter taste on her tongue. "What choice?"

"Whether you want to stay with me or not." Black eyes became opaque pools, reflecting nothing. As if there was nothing. He took her hand in his, traced the veins on the inside of her wrist. As if he was asking her out to dinner while in reality, he was shredding her to pieces.

Rising to her knees, Ari pleaded with him. "Punish me all you want, Andreas, but please give me a chance. Give me a chance to prove that you can forgive me."

"Punish you? Forgive you?" He shook his head. The bleakness in his eyes made nausea rise up in her throat. "Do you still not see, Ari? Do you not see how much we've lost, how much we… Every time I close my eyes, *I see you*. Lying on some stretcher, pale, out of it. Alone. I drove you to that.

"Even if I forgive you, I cannot forgive myself.

"Even if I trust you, I can't trust myself. To not destroy you all over again."

The shudder that went through his powerful frame sent Ariana through a spiral of desperation. "You've changed," she whispered, her voice husky and rough from all the screaming. "I've changed. We have walked through fire, Andreas. And we have both come out strong."

She traced the angles of his face with shaking fingers. Wet, warm, open-mouthed kisses, she spread them over his torso as if she were sprinkling her own brand of fairy dust.

As if she could somehow make him believe that he could love her, too.

Hands fisted by his sides, he closed his eyes. His breath became harsh, falling on her like soft strokes. She pulled away the duvet that was tangled around their legs and strad-dled him.

Sinking her hands into his hair, she kissed his temple, his eyes and finally his mouth. He didn't move, he didn't react.

A sob rising through her, Ariana dug her teeth into his lip. Moved her mouth down his throat, licked the velvet rough skin of his shoulder. "You love me, Andreas. I will believe it enough for both of us, until you do. You love me, you love me, God, I was such a fool to not see it then. I was such a fool to not stand and fight for you." She whispered into his skin, the love she felt for him overflowing out of her.

Pushing onto her knees, she pulled off the oversized T-shirt he'd put on her. Arms wrapped around his back, she vined herself around him. His chest crushed her breasts, the angular ridge of his hips digging roughly into her inner thighs.

And then she kissed him. Softly, slowly, stroking and tracing every inch of his sculpted mouth. Pouring everything she felt for him into that kiss.

Only then did he open his eyes. Dark color slashed his cheekbones, his breath out of rhythm. His hands descended to her hips and spread her open, wicked desire glinting in his eyes.

Her breath hitched. Every particle in her stilled as he delved his fingers into her slick flesh. "This proves nothing, Ari. You were right. You have always been my weakness." One finger and then two penetrated her sensitive flesh. He licked circles around her nipple, never touching the tip.

Making her crazy for more. "You want to be a part of my life? *Kala.* You want me to continue—" his mouth closed over her nipple and he suckled so deeply that Ariana rocked her pelvis into his washboard stomach "—giving you this mindless pleasure that is the only real thing between us, *kala.* I'm more than happy to, but that's all it is, Ari.

"Your destruction, *agapita*, will not be at my hands this time."

Sensations spiraled through her. Her spine arched, and Ariana tried to hold on to her thoughts. To not give in to the riot of pleasure that forked through her lower belly. Breathing hard, she stilled his fingers wreaking havoc inside her sex. Just the way he knew would drive her over the edge. "You came for me. After everything I did, you still came for me. You searched for me for two years. That counts—"

His thumb pressed at her clit in erotic circles. Daring her to continue. Drowning her in delirious sensation. Sweat beaded on her skin. All rationality was lost again.

The second he rubbed the thick head of his erection against her swollen flesh, Ariana screamed. Tears gathered in her eyes but there was no turning off the kaleidoscope of sensations arrowing down her lower belly.

"This is all I can give you. This and the status and the respect that I would give any woman I'd have married. I would not cheat on you, but I would not love you, either.

"I will not care what you do with your life, you could learn cabaret for all I care, but I would not love you."

Ariana bit her lip hard, wondering if actual physical pain could arrest the climax building through her.

"But—"

Holding her gaze, he wrapped his fingers over her buttocks, lifted her and then sank her down onto his rock-hard flesh. So fully and completely. It stung first and then fire spread through her muscles. He pushed up into a sitting position, his thighs pressing hers inward, one hand locking her wrists.

His mouth buried between her breasts, his voice ragged. "Move, Ari. Move as your body wants you to, *pethi mou*." His eyes closed as her body did its own instinctual, age-old thing to relieve the ache there. "This I will give you, Ariana." With that promise, he took her nipple in his mouth, wrapped his tongue around it.

There was no way to control her body's response. Ariana moved up and down sending guttural groans out of their mouths. His hips surged up, cleaving through her, his eyes glittering in the dark. Stark possession shone in them. "We should not have ever come together, Ari. I…should have never married you."

Tears streaming down her cheeks, her body racing toward the peak, Ari bent down and kissed him softly. "I will choose to believe it was love that brought you to me.

"I will believe for the rest of our lives if that's what it takes. I will be here day and night. Waiting for you. And wanting you."

She repeated the words again and again as pleasure skewered through her body and he covered it with his own, chasing his own climax. He filled her completely, utterly.

And yet Ariana had never known such loss.

When she woke up again, among cool sheets, sticky and sore between her legs, he was gone. The huge room was dappled in afternoon light, bright and pricking her eyes. She didn't have to get up and ask his secretary to confirm what she already knew.

He would have already left the King's Palace.

CHAPTER THIRTEEN

ARIANA HAD FORGOTTEN. Or had she given up counting the number of days since Andreas had left the King's Palace? After the third day, nights and days began to merge.

There were no tears this time. She hadn't ranted and raged after he had walked out.

She lost herself in studying for the bar exam. In developing the contacts she'd made at the ball that would aid in her starting her own legal agency. Under Petra and Giannis's expert guidance, she gave an interview about the work she was going to take up once she was licensed to practice law in Drakon.

She visited two different organizations in the city, who provided relief and shelter to abused women, and came up with action items to tackle the poorly funded shelters. Eleni, she was slowly realizing, was a veritable mine of information on the topic of fund-raisers and charity auctions.

Taking her advice on board, Ariana threw herself into organizing her fund-raiser.

She worked from sunup to sundown, trying to exhaust herself. But when her head hit the pillow in that big king bed of Andreas's, sleep still eluded her frantic mind.

If Ariana had thought him unapproachable before, he was nothing short of the arctic freeze now.

He was utterly polite to her. He constantly checked with her to make sure she had everything she needed to realize her own dream. He respected her opinion, he even let her accompany him on a short trip to some of the key rural areas where Gabriel's firm was investing in the economy by building world-class resorts.

He treated her like he would have treated any other

woman he could have married. With the utmost civility. As if she were a complete stranger he was sharing his life with. As if there was no more to him than the perfect ruler, or the polite husband.

The worst part was that Ariana had no idea if he was doing it to distance himself from her, or if he truly felt nothing. The probability that she had lost him this time…had robbed her of a single night's peaceful sleep.

After the first three weeks of being simply stonewalled, she'd lost her patience one night. Clearly, giving him space and time wasn't working.

Nothing, it seemed, was working.

In an attempt to talk to him, to confront him, she had crawled into his bed one night, knowing that he'd returned at midnight from another trip. After waiting for hours, she had finally fallen into a restless sleep. She had woken up to realize it was his mouth on her neck, his hands on her legs that had hurtled her out of sleep.

He'd hardly even greeted her before he covered her mouth with his. He gave her hardly a chance to breathe when he pushed her legs apart, rid her of her panties and pressed his mouth to her sex.

Ariana didn't remember how many times he'd made her climax that night before he had pushed her face down, spread her legs and taken her from behind. He had exhausted her so deeply that her bones had been jelly, her entire body so sensitive and sore that finally she had fallen into a deep sleep.

When she'd awoken, showered and dressed on buckling knees, he had been gone again.

The pattern continued for two months. Every time he went on a trip, he stayed away for longer. He sent her the most exotic, expensive gifts. He barely even met her eyes anymore. If he found her in his bed, he made love to her. If she wasn't there, he didn't seek her out.

Sometimes they barely got their clothes off, he was that desperate and rough. Sometimes, he made love to her with soft, soothing words. So tenderly, as if she was the most precious thing he had ever beheld. As if he couldn't help himself.

Nikandros and Mia, Eleni and Gabriel had even stopped inquiring about what was wrong. Said only that she looked like a wraith and that Andreas was...well, more unapproachable than ever. She heard the staff, even Petra, who was as loyal as they came, say that he was even more unforgiving than before. That anyone who made one mistake, one misstep with him, got their head chewed off. While to the outside world, they couldn't be happier and more in love. More perfect for each other.

And slowly Ari began to lose hope.

The whole palace was in a mad rush because Eleni had gone into labor all of a sudden.

Ariana had wrapped the little booties and sweater she had knitted in soft tissue paper, eager to visit the little infant, when she heard two aides talking.

Andreas was returning tomorrow, was cutting his trip short to see Eleni's little girl. Eleni had already told Ariana that she wanted Ariana and Andreas to be their little one's godparents.

When Ariana had argued they were the last couple who knew anything about babies, Eleni had shook her head and said she trusted her little girl with the both of them.

As always, Ari's heart thundered at the thought of his return. Longing twisted through her, entangled with hope that, this time, things would be different. That this, the distance, would have been enough for him to see she was here. And that she had no thought of leaving him.

Slowly, as if someone was siphoning away life from her, she lost steam. Coming to rest against a dark mahogany door, she tried to catch her breath past the glass in her throat.

Was she just deluding herself?

He would smile and nod at her with those dark eyes. Tell Eleni that she would make the perfect godmother. Then walk away, especially because this was about a child.

A matter that would always be raw and guilt-ridden between them. A matter it seemed he could not get over.

Then, if she was fortunate, he might come to bed. And if he did, and Ariana tried to talk, he would make love to her until she forgot her own name.

Come morning, all she'd have was a sore body and a crushed heart.

Maybe he was right. Maybe things between them were so broken that they could not be fixed again. But *Thee mou*, she could not live like this.

She couldn't be near him and love him and live day after day knowing that he might never accept his love for her. This was even worse than what she'd run away from. She couldn't bear this…any longer.

Tired and beaten down, all she wanted was to run away. To escape.

But she couldn't. Andreas hadn't given up on her in ten years and she hugged the fact to herself.

She wiped her palms over her mouth, instructed one of the staff to give her present to Eleni and then went back to her suite. Dismissing everybody else, she took Giannis into confidence, told him how to reach her in an emergency.

Like Andreas raising a palace-wide search for her. But no, she was sure he would hardly even notice for a month or two.

She packed a small bag personally, throwing in just enough necessities. Had a car brought round to her, got into the driver's seat and drove away.

She was not running away, she told herself. She was playing the only card she had left to win him over.

Andreas walked away from Eleni's suite, his gut a hard coil of twisting emotions. His new niece, Maria Drakos Marquez, had fit into half his forearm.

She had smelled like baby powder, and new life, and utter joy.

Her eyes glittering like Gabriel's, her mouth stubborn like her mother's, she had been the most absolutely precious thing Andreas had ever beheld.

The infant's little smile felt as if it had clawed into his chest and thumped his heart into a thunderous roar.

His vision had shimmered so dangerously for a second that he had quickly given her over to Nikandros, who was a proud and wonderful dad to his twins.

All he'd been able to see for a few seconds had been another child. With dark hair, and dark eyes like his, as Ariana had told him.

A boy, his son.

His heart thumped painfully in his chest and he couldn't even breathe.

Seeing Eleni and Gabriel ecstatic over their little girl, seeing Nik and Mia offering them advice, he had felt a cold chill pass through him.

As if a ghost had passed through him, his father's ghost. Clearly the pace he had been setting for himself was driving him mad. Finally, he would be like Theos in this, too.

But the laughter he imagined, the mocking *I win* smile that his father would have worn, knowing that he had won in the end—that he had made Andreas as hard and ruthless as him, as he'd always wanted to…it was the thing that broke through his self-imposed punishment.

God, he felt so tired in his heart. So alone and utterly miserable.

He'd tried his hardest to keep away from Ariana, used every tenet he'd used in life to stay strong enough for his father, but nothing worked.

He loved her so much. He missed her so much. Even when she'd hated him, his life had felt more alive than like this. Being near her, sleeping wrapped up around her, smelling the scent of her on his sheets—it had been hellish.

Walking away every time was like losing a limb.

A torture treatment designed just for him.

He wanted to protect her. He wanted to give her a chance to walk away. To find life away from him. To find her happiness without him.

But *Thee mou*, the stubborn woman didn't go. She was in his skin, in his blood, in his soul. With her, he felt complete. He felt joy unlike anything he'd ever known.

He had snubbed her, avoided her, stonewalled her for two months, ripping away his own heart in the process. But she was nowhere near gone from his mind or body or soul.

He had tried to live without her. And it was slowly, but surely, unraveling him. Heart pounding in his chest, Andreas walked toward their private suite. His long strides were just not long enough today.

He went through her suite and then returned to his own. The silence screamed over his nerves. There were no staff members, nor her, nor any of her friends.

Determined to find her, he turned. Giannis, her aide, stood at the door, his chin lifted high. "Looking for something, Your Highness?"

Andreas felt his knees buckling under him. Had she left him again? Had he finally driven her away?

Giannis knew. Of course, her little friend knew. And whose fault was that when he wouldn't even give her the time of the day? When he had used her for pleasure but wouldn't even meet her eyes?

Ariana needed so much, deserved so much in life and once again, all he'd done was starve her.

"Where is she?" Panic made getting the words out so hard.

"She left," Giannis said with something like sympathy in his eyes.

Andreas nodded and gritted his teeth. "She left me then."

"No, she…she said she needed a break. That she needed time to think. She…said she would go back to the only place in the world where she'd been happy.

"Delirious with joy," he said, imitating Ariana's fondness for superlatives.

Ariana and he had both been happy, delirious with joy, in only one place.

Only one place where the world had been at bay. Where it had been just them. Made for each other.

Andreas stilled against the door, his heartbeat slowly returning to normal. At least she hadn't run away. She hadn't left him. He extended his hand to the other man, who looked on it with complete disbelief in his eyes. Finally, when he shook his hand, Andreas smiled. "Thank you for always being her friend, Giannis."

Giannis gave him a completely unnecessary bow of his head. "I would give my life for my Queen, Your Highness. She is worth it, even when she had been just a friend who asked about my *ya-ya*."

"She is," Andreas whispered.

New life breathed in his veins. He knew where she was. He would find her and he would tell her how much he loved her. He was a weaver of words, a teller of past tales, a world-class orator.

How could words be hard to come by in the most important thing of his life?

Within minutes, he asked for a chopper. Since no pilot was available in the last minute, Nikandros volunteered to give him a quick "lift." Andreas had a feeling Nik was only coming along to see Andreas suffer.

"Thank God, Andreas. Eleni and Mia were planning another intervention for you, and only Eleni's labor put a stop to that. Gabriel thought we should simply knock you over the head with a club. Repeatedly, until you came to your senses."

A long time ago, Andreas would have been extremely uncomfortable with the conversation. He wouldn't have seen the point in it, even. What point was there in discussing and pouring out one's feelings to a brother or a friend when those feelings had to be suppressed anyway?

He laid his head back against the seat rest and smiled. "I would not have minded that, Nikandros. I would even go so far as to say I probably needed that. But you tell Marquez that and I will deny it."

Laughter boomed in his ears. "Only loyalty to my King forbids me to tell him that, Andreas. Gabriel would love nothing better, believe me.

"You deserve happiness. Did I ever tell you that?"

His eyes flew open, he stared at Nik. "No. But Camille has. A lot of times. Whether I paid attention to her or not, she repeated it again and again. That it was okay for me to feel anger, want, affection, jealousy, even inadequacy. I don't think I ever told you this, Nik, but I thank you for sharing your mother with me. I would not have known any kindness if not for Camille."

His blue eyes glittering, Nikandros looked away. "Among all three of us, you deserve it the most."

"I'm sure Mia would not agree with that."

"I think she would. You walked the hardest path with Theos. You could have become like him. I worried it was already too late for you. I was terrified you would never know the happiness I know with Mia.

"All because of him."

"I almost didn't. But Camille and you and Eleni…and Ariana…" He swallowed the emotion that sat in his throat like a boulder. Gabriel, the smug bastard, had been right. "Ariana saved me." She had done it even then.

He just hadn't been able to see it. Or understand it.

With one smile, and an outrageous question, she had melted the ice around his heart.

She was right. He was ready. He was a different man. A man who could love the extraordinary woman his wife had become.

Soon, they were up in the sky. Andreas clutched the book in his hands, his book. It was the only thing he had to give her, other than his heart, the only thing that would be valuable to her. The only thing she would truly appreciate.

Ariana had spent most of her first day trying to locate the owner of the old log cabin. The sleepy fishing village had no registration office to speak of. So she had just haunted the old café where she had worked.

But before she could ask a single question, she had been recognized. As the King's wife, Ariana Drakos. The Queen. Thankfully also as the girl who had worked there for one summer a long time ago. She had instantly been mobbed by the friendly crowd, for whom her appearance was a once-in-a-lifetime thing.

In the end, she had eaten dinner there, made a reservation at a nearby hotel, but had no more knowledge about the owner.

The second day had gone with more useless searching and then sleeping away the rest of the day because she had been exhausted.

Tears filled her eyes. Damn it, all she wanted was to have a quick look inside. To bolster her faltering faith in Andreas and her.

She dashed away the tears as she dressed on the third morning. She cried over every small thing these days.

Dressed in jeans and a thick sweater, oversized and falling to her knees, she had stolen from Andreas's closet, she pulled on knee-high boots. She thought she was hungry until she stopped at a coffee shop. Instead the smell of it sent her hurrying away from the cute café. She wasn't able to get much dinner into herself, either.

She grabbed a map instead. She knew the trail through the forested woods pretty well, but it had been ten years.

Pulling a knit cap tight on her head so that a bit of her hair was covered too, as she had totally forgotten about being recognized, she made her way past the first sign.

The air was redolent with scents of pine. She slid her hands under her armpits. She had also forgotten how cold it got here during winter, so close to the mountains. Her spirits lifted as she realized she could make out the path without referring to the map at all.

Fifteen minutes later, she was breathing hard—something else she *had* forgotten about was the steep climb at the end—but standing in front of the log cabin.

The red exterior was gleaming as well as it had been back then. The area in front of it was as always neatly cleared. A huge pile of freshly chopped wood sat on one side. Smoke came out of the chimney.

Her eyes filled up again. But she was extremely glad that someone had lived here all these years. Had taken such good care of it.

Now that she was here, she couldn't return without a look inside. Heart beating with a renewed energy, she walked up the small steps to the porch and knocked on the door.

"Kalimera..." She began her practiced speech before the door swung open completely. "I'm so sorry to bother..."

Andreas was standing inside the cabin, his arm on the

top side of the door, his eyes devouring her with a tangible hunger.

"*Kalimera*, Ariana. Will you not come in?"

Stunned, lost for words, Ariana nodded and stepped inside. Suddenly, she didn't at all feel brave. She felt vulnerable and lonely. And juvenile, if the look in Andreas's eyes was anything to go by.

She caught the groan that rose. Why hadn't she realized he would just see it as another ploy for his attention?

Did she really care if he did?

Taking in his long legs and taut behind, clad in tight jeans and the sheer breadth of his masculinity, she also felt deprived. As if the most delicious dessert was placed in front of her but she was not allowed to touch it.

His hair was curling over the collar of his shirt, over which he had worn a thick sweater like her. The scent of sandalwood soap that he used left a thread in the air and she hungrily followed it into the lounge.

Her eyes wide, she looked around the cozy hall. Everything was gleaming and polished. Everything was exactly as they had left it. There was even a reference book of Andreas's and a magazine of hers. Not collecting dust. But neatly arranged.

She frowned. Wait—what was Andreas doing here? So soon after she had left, too?

"You look beautiful," he said in that deep voice behind her and she turned.

Far too fast apparently, because she was suddenly dizzy and would have knocked herself into the pillar if he hadn't caught her.

She shook her head trying to find her balance again while he watched her from under those thick lashes. Scowling. "I don't know what happened." She cleared her throat, and stepped back from his grasp of her hands.

Which didn't go unnoticed.

"I... I just came by to see this place." A lump lodged in her throat as she spotted the shiny silver frame on the mantel. It was still here? She had bought it in a junk shop in this very same village.

She plucked it off the shelf and once again, breath left her. Another picture of her. This one in her wedding dress—or rather the pink, frilly dress that she had worn that morning.

She looked absolutely, utterly in love. And full of happiness.

Hands shaking, she put away the frame and turned. To find him leaning against the pillar, staring at her. "What are all these things, our things, doing here? I tried to find out who had bought the place but no one really knew. I... I thought it would have become a relic. Like us," she said, and looked away.

She was not going to cry. She was not going to beg.

"I own it," he finally said, and her head whipped up. "I should say, we own it."

"When? When did you buy it?"

"The moment we left here." He looked around at the high ceilings just like she had done. Rubbed the smoothly polished wood with affection. "It took a while to convince the old guy who lived here...but finally he caved."

"Of course—the Crown Prince want something and not get it?"

In two quick strides, he reached her, crowding her along the wall. "What is that supposed to mean?"

She licked her lips, suddenly nervous. She had never seen him like this, so blatantly aggressive. "I... It's not like you're used to being denied what you want, Andreas."

He frowned. "True, but I never used the weight of the crown to persuade this guy. I just told him it was the place where I spent a week trapped with my future wife, the one

woman I was going to spend my life with, and that persuaded him.

"It turned out he was an utter romantic."

She nodded, working hard to keep her gaze on his face
when the column of his throat beckoned. "You never told
me."

A sigh fell from his lips. "I meant for it to be a surprise.
I thought we could come back here regularly, but…"

"But everything fell apart when we returned to the city,"
she finished. God, she had had enough of these games.
"Well, I'm sure it would have been a nice gesture." She
slipped away from his grasp and faced him. "It works out
for me, at least."

"What works out for you?"

"I… I'm not returning to the Palace with you, assuming
that's why you're here, *ne*?"

"For what?"

"Stop answering questions with questions."

He put up his hands, as if she was the one being unreasonable. She was totally not prepared for dealing with him
here. Any more of this and she'd dissolve into a puddle of
tears. "You're here because you think I'm throwing one of
my fits and you need to chase me back to the palace for
some weighty matter that requires your wife.

"There's four days before the next state dinner and I'll
be by your side that morning."

He shrugged. "*Kala*. I will inform Petra we will both
return that morning."

"You're crazy. There must be a hundred details to see
to."

"As you've pointed out in the past, I have three teams to
do my bidding and to arrange my life and one of them will
see to the hundred details. I was going to write the speech
myself anyway and I can focus better here."

Tears filled her eyes. "Why are you playing with me,

Andreas? What is it you want of me?" Her heart felt like it was shattering anew.

He pulled her into his arms instantly. "I didn't mean to make you cry. *Thee mou*, do not cry, *agapita*. I just… You looked so beautiful, so painfully lovely standing there that I forgot what I meant to say.

"I have not come to take you back. In fact, to hell with the dinner if you just want to hole up here for a couple of months. I have enough wood and food to see us through the winter." Now Ariana was alternately laughing and crying into his sweater.

"Why are you here?"

"I…came to give you something." He plucked a book, his book, from the coffee table and handed it to her.

Smiling, Ariana opened the jacket, read the dedication. Again. "I saw it in your bedroom months ago. I… I've been even reading it when you're…" She looked up and flushed. "When you're not there.

"It made me feel like you were still there with me. Especially, the part of you that I fell in love with."

He nodded and swallowed. "Ariana, will you ever forgive me?"

Words did not come, choked by the tears. She shook her head, then nodded, a deluge of emotions drowning her. "If you forgive me."

His mouth came down on hers. Frantic words fell from his mouth as he kissed her, and tasted her. Ariana didn't know whether she was crying or laughing.

Her heart jumped into her throat when he went to his knees in front of her and looked up at her.

He was so tall that his head still reached her abdomen. She buried her hands in his hair, her heart bursting to full.

"I love you so much. My life is empty of joy, of laughter, of everything without you, *glykia mou*.

"Will you come back to me, Ari? Will you come back because I love you and I can't live without you?"

Ari nodded and fell to her knees. He caught her in his arms and she burst into sobs. Pitiful, wrenching sobs that she could not stop no matter what she did.

Andreas felt as if his heart would shatter all over again. God, he couldn't bear her tears. He couldn't stand the wretched sound of her grief. How heartless he had been to bring her to this?

He pulled her into his lap as he'd done once, a long time ago. Fingers stealing into her hair, he pulled her face up, until she was forced to look at him. "I promised myself I would never again hurt you, Ari. Not at any cost.

"Rage at me. Punch me. But forgive me, *pethi mou*. Forgive me for taking this long to understand this thing between us.

"I adore you. I love you so much that I'm still terrified of all the tumult I feel."

He kissed her mouth and she sighed against him. "I would like to answer one of your questions."

She frowned. "Which one?"

"About why I hadn't publicized that manuscript."

"I know why," she said wiping her eyes. "You didn't want to take away the faith and fantasy it gave the people. I even understand how hard it must have been because it was your life's work, your real passion."

He shook his head. "No. I...think I didn't like it myself. I didn't like that he so easily sacrificed the woman he loved. Even when I didn't understand why, it didn't sit well with me.

"It almost felt like if I revealed it, it would become true. Almost a sentence, a fate for all the rulers of Drakon.

"Even when I thought you were gone, I needed the happy

ending. I needed to believe that I'd had my chance of happiness. That I had grabbed it with both hands while I could.

"But since I learned what price you paid for my—"

It was her turn to shut him up. She did it by kissing him softly, slowly, her entire being soaring with that kiss. By pouring all the love she felt for him into the slide of her mouth. "No, no past, Andreas. Only future."

He nodded and wrapped his arms around her. His big palms came to rest on her tummy and suddenly Ariana knew. The dizziness, the nausea at the smell of coffee when she usually needed an IV of it, the lack of hunger...

She shivered violently and he was instantly in front of her. Concern etched in his face. "Ari? What is it?"

"I'm not sure. But I think..." She pulled his hand to her tummy and held it there. "I think we're pregnant."

The silence, which lasted maybe only ten seconds truthfully, stretched her nerves taut. "I don't know how it happened. It's not something I planned without telling you, I mean—"

With a soft growl that made her laugh, he plucked her off the ground as if she were a featherweight. "No more disappearing without telling anyone. No more eating at strange times. And definitely no more sudden twisting and twirling."

He wasn't even out of breath when he put her on the bed and came on top of her. His lower body flush against hers, he propped himself on his elbow. "Is this okay?" he asked, signaling to his body over hers.

Ariana nodded, determined to hold back the tears. Deep grooves etched around his mouth, a wary concern in his eyes. It was clear that the King of Drakon was absolutely terrified. Thankfully, with him by her side, she was not. She stretched like a cat under him and arched into the arousal she could feel against her leg. "You can do whatever you want to me."

A gleam in his eyes, he kissed her tenderly for a long time. Torturously slow when all Ariana wanted was to feel him inside her.

When he let her come up for air, Ari pushed him back on the bed and laid her head on his chest. She didn't know how long they lay like that, staring at each other, smiling sometimes, nibbling at each other's lips other times. Not needing words.

"Do you want a boy or a girl?" she finally asked.

He placed his palm on her tummy, and lifted his eyes to hers. "I do not care. I just want you both safe. I just... I can't imagine my life if something were to happen to you, Ari."

She kissed his temple, his brows, the tip of his arrogant nose, trying to soothe the raw fear in his voice. "Nothing will happen. Not as long as we're together."

He nodded and swallowed. Looked away. Another silence followed, his fingers tight against hers.

She knew he was processing all this. Knew that the emotion he felt for her, the depth of his love for her...it was not an easy thing for him. So she waited, her heart full of tenderness and love. She would wait an eternity for the privilege of being loved by Andreas.

He looked down at her, a fierce light in his dark eyes. "All I know is that you will be a fierce, wonderful mother and I... This child will be so lucky to have you.

"I am so lucky to have found you, Ariana."

Ariana nodded, and reached for his kiss again. "And I'm honored you chose me, Andreas, of all the countless gorgeous, accomplished, beautiful women that have the hots for you all over the world."

He laughed, and she laughed because she loved his laugh. Covering her body, still smiling, he pulled her sweater off. A devilish gleam in his eyes as he realized the sweater was his.

"You have to stop filching my clothes," he said, with his wicked mouth buried against her neck.

"Never," she replied arching into the sensuous warmth of his body.

"*Kala*. You can have my sweaters, my shirts. And my heart."

She loved him so much that her heart felt like it would never settle down. "And you have mine," she managed to whisper somehow just as he licked the puckered crest of her nipple.

Sinking her hands into his hair, she held him tight.

He was the people's man. He had duties to so many. So many responsibilities. Even his time was not his own.

But his kisses and his laughter had always been hers and only hers.

She didn't need anything more than that.

EPILOGUE

Seven months later

THE KING OF DRAKON jumped out of the chopper mere seconds after it hit the tiled terrace of the King's Palace, heart thundering in his chest.

He was late. Damn it, he'd promised her he'd be by her side and he was late. He'd gone half-crazy being stuck in a cabin on the other side of the world, locked in by a hurricane while she had needed him. Even their communication had been cut off and once her labor had started, Andreas could not distract her just to reassure himself.

At least she was not alone, he consoled himself. Nikandros and Mia, Gabriel and Eleni and even Nik's mother, Camille, had been with her. They would have seen to her every need.

The knowledge that she had delivered and both she and the baby were fine was the only thing that had kept him from going utterly mad.

She and the baby had even been transported back to the palace. When Nik would have spilled the beans to the public, Andreas had forbidden him.

He wanted to see her first. He wanted to see for himself whether his wife had given him a boy or a girl. He needed, desperately, to be a husband and a father, at least for a few minutes, before he had to think like a King. Before he had to make an announcement that Drakon had its heir.

Without breaking his stride, he handed off his laptop case, his long jacket and gloves to his waiting teams. He checked his phone and let another curse fly.

A day, he was late by a whole day.

Long strides took the stairs three and four at a time and by the time he reached his wife's suite, his heart had crawled up into his throat.

The silence hit him hard, ratcheting up his pulse, forming all kinds of scenarios in his head. Uncaring of the sounds he made, he rushed to the huge bed in the center of the room.

Only when he saw her did his breath return to normal.

She lay in the center of the huge bed, a little pale, dark shadows under her eyes, far too thin in his mind. And absolutely beautiful in that glowing, tired kind of way. He was about to reach for her when he heard the soft cry.

A gurgle to be exact.

Like a man possessed, he followed the sound to the tiny crib sitting in the corner of the room. Breath punched through his throat as he looked at the tall infant staring up at him with jet-black eyes.

Long lashes. A thin blade of a nose. Thick hair the color of a raven's wing.

It was like looking at his own reflection—except pudgy, toothless and utterly adorable.

Another gurgle. Almost a command.

His knees buckling, Andreas had to hold on to the wall beside him. This was a part of him—his own flesh and blood. And the emotion that filled his body threatened to take him out at the knees.

"Pick him up," said a husky voice behind him. "He wants you to pick him up."

Andreas jerked around, tears blurring his vision. "Him?" he whispered, past the lump in his throat. "It's a boy?"

Her own eyes luminous with tears, Ariana nodded. Hauling her into his arms, he pressed a rough kiss to her mouth. The taste of her exploded through his body, an anchor, a siren's call. Home.

He tried to swallow her grief—the memory of the son

they'd lost—into him when she trembled. When tears leaked out the corners of her beautiful eyes. "We'll always have his memory," he whispered against her temple and felt her answering shudder.

He crushed her to him, uncaring of how feeble she was. God, he needed the warmth of her body. Needed to hear the hitch of her breath as he peppered kisses all over her face. "Have I told you how much I love you?" he said, his throat gruff and scratchy. "I'm so sorry, *agapita*. I'm sorry I wasn't here when you needed me."

Sinking her fingers into his hair, she brought his face up. "No apologies needed. Not if you promise to be here for the next three."

Laughter burst out of him at the running joke between them. He'd said one, terrified of losing her, and Ariana had said they would have four. Flushed and breathtakingly beautiful, she made it look so easy that for the first time, four seemed like a splendid idea.

"It's a deal," he said against her mouth, wild with love. Crazy with a soul-deep longing that he knew would never abate.

That he knew was his strength in all things.

A loud growl came again from the crib and Ariana dissolved into giggles against his mouth. "Your son demands your attention, Your Highness."

"Does he?" Andreas asked, stalling for time.

And she knew. Somehow, his wife knew how terrified he was. By how much he wanted to do right by his tiny son. By how much he already loved that little infant. By how inadequate he felt for the task.

Leaning her forehead against his, she met his gaze. "If you love him half as much as you love me, Andreas, he will know it. He will know it and he will love you back just as much," she said with a confidence that unmanned him. Another quick kiss over his lips. A tug in his hair. "Go hold your son, before his numerous cousins descend upon us."

Nodding, Andreas stood up and walked toward the crib. *His son.* It was as if the entire world had tilted on its axis and refused to return to normal.

Hands shaking, he lifted the chubby body that was only as big as his forearm. Heart in his throat, he walked to the bed and climbed into it. His son wailed as Andreas settled him snugly against Ariana, his forehead all scrunched up.

"He's a little high-maintenance, isn't he?" Andreas whispered, awed by the tiny fingers that had latched onto his mother's breast.

"Like someone I know," Ariana said with a glorious smile. A blush climbed up her chest and her neck as Andreas unabashedly watched his son suckle at her breast. He had thought he couldn't be any happier these past months. But now his family was complete.

Theos had had all this with him, Eleni and Nikandros. But he had ruined it all with his own hands.

Andreas would never let that happen to him. His life, his fate had delineated from the moment he had seen Ariana in that café and he was thankful for that moment a million times over.

Sliding down on the bed, he buried his nose in her neck, the ever-present desire a thrum under his skin.

"How long is he going to do that?" he asked, a wicked growl in his voice.

She frowned. "A few months at the least. Why?"

Andreas licked the pulse at her throat, tasted the salt and scent of her. His body's tiredness melted away, his world tilting on its axis again. "I just don't like sharing what's mine. Even with him," he whispered, and laughed when his wife blushed.

She was his Queen, a lawyer with a fierce reputation and now a mother. But when she looked at him like that, she was only the woman he loved with all his heart. The woman who'd made his life worth living.

"I'll always be yours first, Your Highness," she whispered against his mouth, and Andreas fell all over in love again.

* * * * *

If you enjoyed HIS DRAKON RUNAWAY BRIDE
don't forget to read the first two parts of
THE DRAKON ROYALS *trilogy*

CROWNED FOR THE DRAKON LEGACY
THE DRAKON BABY BARGAIN

And also by Tara Pammi...

MARRIED FOR THE SHEIKH'S DUTY
THE SURPRISE CONTI CHILD
THE UNWANTED CONTI BRIDE

All available now!

MILLS & BOON®
MODERN™

POWER, PASSION AND IRRESISTIBLE TEMPTATION

MILLS & BOON®

EXCLUSIVE EXTRACT

Charlotte Adair has spent her life locked away – but once freed, she finds the one man she's ever loved, billionaire Rafe Costa, is now blind, believes she betrayed him, and is bent on a vengeful seduction! Weeks after their scorching encounter he learns she's pregnant—with twins! Rafe steals Charlotte away, but she is a far from biddable prisoner. She is irresistible, defiant—and Rafe must seduce her into compliance!

Read on for a sneak preview of Maisey Yates's book
THE ITALIAN'S PREGNANT PRISONER
The final part of her Once Upon a Seduction... trilogy

Charlotte hadn't touched a man since Rafe. She'd had no interest.

She needed to find some interest. Because she was going to have a normal life. Whatever she did, it would be her choice. And that was the point.

She didn't know what answers she had expected to find here. Right now, the only clear answer seemed to be that her body, her heart, was still affected by him.

He excused himself from the group, and suddenly, he was walking her way. And she froze. Like a deer caught in the headlights. Or rather, like a woman staring at Rafe Costa.

She certainly wasn't the only woman staring. He moved with fluid grace, and if she didn't know better, she would never have known his sight was impaired at all.

He was coming closer, and as he did her heart tripped over itself, her hands beginning to shake. She wished she could touch him.

Oh, she wanted it more than anything. In that moment, she wanted it more than her next breath. To put her hands on Rafe Costa's face one more time. To kiss those lips again. To place her hand over his chest and see if she could still make his heart race.

It was easy to forget that her stepmother had told her how Rafe had left, taking an incentive offered by her father to end his tenure there earlier. It was easy to forget that and remember instead the way it had felt when he had kissed her. Touched her. The way she had pleaded with him to take her virginity, to make her his in every way.

Really, he had never wanted her. He had simply been toying with her.

She should remember that. Her treacherous, traitorous body should remember that well. But it didn't. Instead, it was fluttering. As if a host butterflies had been set loose inside her.

Suddenly, he was there. So close that if she wanted to she could reach out and touch the edge of his sleeve with her fingertips.

Could bump into him accidentally, just to make contact. He wouldn't know it was her. He couldn't.

Suddenly, he turned. He was looking past her, his dark eyes unseeing, unfocused. But then, he reached out and unerringly grabbed hold of her wrist, dragging her toward his muscular body.

"Charlotte."

Don't miss
THE ITALIAN'S PREGNANT PRISONER
By Maisey Yates

Available October 2017

www.millsandboon.co.uk

MILLS & BOON®

Why shop at millsandboon.co.uk?

Each year, thousands of romance readers
find their perfect read at millsandboon.co.uk.
That's because we're passionate about
bringing you the very best romantic fiction.
Here are some of the advantages of
shopping at www.millsandboon.co.uk:

* **Get new books first**—you'll be able to buy
  your favourite books one month before they
  hit the shops

* **Get exclusive discounts**—you'll also be
  able to buy our specially created monthly
  collections, with up to 50% off the RRP

* **Find your favourite authors**—latest news,
  interviews and new releases for all your
  favourite authors and series on our website,
  plus ideas for what to try next

* **Join in**—once you've bought your favourite
  books, don't forget to register with us to rate,
  review and join in the discussions

Visit **www.millsandboon.co.uk**
for all this and more today!

Join Britain's BIGGEST Romance Book Club

- **EXCLUSIVE offers every month**

- **FREE delivery direct to your door**

- **NEVER MISS a title**

- **EARN Bonus Book points**

Call Customer Services
0844 844 1358*

or visit
illsandboon.co.uk/subscriptions

* This call will cost you 7 pence per minute plus your
phone company's price per minute access charge.